D1505318

SLIVER OF TRUTH

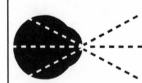

This Large Print Book carries the
Seal of Approval of N.A.V.H.

SLIVER OF TRUTH

LISA UNGER

THORNDIKE PRESS

An imprint of Thomson Gale, a part of The Thomson Corporation

3 1336 07618 7187

THOMSON

TM

GALE

Detroit • New York • San Francisco • New Haven, Conn. • Waterville, Maine • London

LIBRARY OF CONGRESS CATALOGING-IN-PUBLICATION DATA

Unger, Lisa, 1970–
  Sliver of truth / by Lisa Unger.
    p. cm. — (Thorndike Press large print basic)
    ISBN-13: 978-0-7862-9492-3 (lg. print : alk. paper)
    ISBN-10: 0-7862-9492-2 (lg. print : alk. paper)
    1. East Village (New York, N.Y.) — Fiction. 2. Women journalists — Fiction. 3. Large type books. I. Title.
PS3621.N486S65 2007b
813'.6—dc22   2007002530

Published in 2007 by arrangement with Crown Publishers,
a division of Random House, Inc.

Printed in the United States of America on permanent paper
10 9 8 7 6 5 4 3 2 1

FOR OCEAN RAE

Who, even before her arrival, changed
me in ways I never could
have imagined . . .
Who has brought more love and joy to
Jeffrey and me than we knew existed.
Just the anticipation of her was the
most magnificent gift . . . even when
she was just the glow of sunshine
on the water.
We are blessed by her presence
in our lives.

DECEMBER 25, 2005

■ ■ ■ ■

PART ONE:
DADDY'S GIRL

■ ■ ■ ■

Prologue

She wondered, Is it possible, maybe even normal, to spend twenty years of your life with someone, to love that person more than you love yourself sometimes and then sometimes to truly hate him, so much that you think about taking your new cast-iron grill pan and bringing it down on the top of his head? Or maybe these thoughts were just a result of one of her random yet tempestuous perimenopausal moments. Or the fact that the piece-of-crap air conditioner she'd been begging him to replace for two summers was no competition for a kitchen where there were three pans on the stove and a pork roast in the oven.

The heat didn't seem to bother him as he sat directly in front of the unit with a copy of the *Times* in his hands, his feet on the hassock, a glass of merlot on the table beside him. He'd offered to help; it was true. But in that kind of non-offer way he had: "Do you need some help?" (without looking up from the sports section), not "What can I do?" (as he rolled up his sleeves) or "You sit down a minute; let me mince the garlic" (as he poured her a glass of wine). Those were what she considered true offers of help. She wanted him to *insist*. Especially since she knew that she could never sit reading with a glass of wine while he slaved away at some annoying task like cooking for friends (friends of *his,* by the way), regardless of whether he'd rebuffed her offers of help or not.

She glanced at the clock and felt her stress level rise. Just an hour before their guests arrived and she hadn't even showered. She released a sigh and banged a pot down in the sink, which caused her husband to look up from his paper.

"Everything all right?" Allen asked, rising.

"No," she said sullenly. "It's hot in here and I need to take a shower."

"Okay," he said, coming over to her and taking the slotted spoon from her hand. He wrapped his arms around her waist and smiled that devilish smile he had, the one that always made her smile, too, no matter how angry she was.

"Take it easy," he said, kissing her neck. She leaned back from him a second, playing mad and hard to get, but soon enough she melted.

"If you need help, why don't you ask for it?"

he whispered in her ear, raising erogenous goose bumps on her neck.

"You should just *know*," she said, still pouting.

"You're right," he said into the space between her throat and her collarbone. "I'm sorry. What can I do?"

"Well," she said, suddenly feeling silly, "I guess it's mostly done."

He pulled away from her, took a glass from the cabinet, and poured her some wine. "How about this, then? You go take a shower and I'll get a head start on the cleaning, take care of some of these pans."

She took the glass from his hand, gave him a kiss on the mouth. After twenty years, she still loved the taste of him (when she wasn't imagining clocking him with a grill pan). She looked around their West Village apartment, most of which could be seen from the space over the bar that separated the kitchen from the dining and living area. It was small and cramped but filled with the chic clutter of objects and books and photographs they'd collected over their life together. The couch and matching love seat were old and worn, but good quality and as comfortable as an embrace. The cocktail table was an old door from an antique shop in New Hope, Pennsylvania. Their television, like the window air-conditioning unit, was a dinosaur that badly needed replacing. Their bedroom was so small that there was barely room for their queen-size bed and two bedside tables piled high with books. They could afford something better, something much bigger . . . maybe in Brooklyn or out in Hoboken. But they were Manhattanites to the bone and couldn't bear to be separated from the city by a bridge or a tunnel. Maybe it was silly, but between that and the fact that the rent was just six hundred dollars a month (as it had been since 1970), because the apartment had been grandfathered to Allen by his brother when his brother had moved to a lovely carriage house in Park Slope, they'd just stayed on there. The children they'd hoped for had never come; they'd never had a reason to expand. Only recently had things become uncomfortable for them.

The new landlord knew he could be getting about two or three thousand dollars a month for their apartment, so he was very slow to fix things that broke, hoping to force them out. And in an old apartment in an old building something was always broken, a fuse was always blown, something was always leaking.

They'd talked more about moving recently, but prices in the city were so outrageous. They'd lived a life where experience and travel had always mattered more to them than a status apartment or a flat-screen television. And though they'd done well, she as a crime reporter for various city newspapers and finally, now, at the *Times,* and he as a commercial photographer, choices had to be made along the way. Live well, travel well, and save for retirement, while doing without where the apartment was concerned. It had never been a difficult trade. They'd seen the world and were still explorers at heart. In their early fifties they were in good shape to retire in the next ten years, though they'd never owned any property.

She thought about these things in the shower, felt good about them. Blessedly, the hot-water heater was working today. Ella and Rick, Allen's friends from college, would arrive carrying a hundred-dollar bottle of wine; Ella would be wearing something outrageously chic and expensive, Rick would talk about his new toy, whatever that happened to be. They weren't snobs; they were unpretentious and kind. But they were very wealthy and it came off them in waves, demanded noticing, begged comparisons. And when she wasn't feeling good about herself, it bothered her in a way it shouldn't. Allen wouldn't have understood; his mind didn't work that way. He enjoyed his friends' successes, their toys, their vacation homes, as much as he would if they'd been his own. He didn't believe in comparisons.

She thought about this as she rinsed the conditioner from her hair. Somewhere in the apartment or maybe above or below them, there was a loud knocking, loud enough to startle her. It could have been the hot-water heater, or something on another floor. She just prayed, prayed that it wasn't their guests arriving early. Or the landlord, wanting to finish the fight they'd had with him earlier about the terrible leak in the bathroom when the people above showered. Today they'd threatened to start putting their rent into escrow until he fixed it once and for all. The conversation had devolved into him reverting to his native tongue, something harsh and Eastern European, and screaming at them unintelligibly. They'd shut the door in his face and he'd stormed off, yelling all the way down the stairs.

"Those Eastern Europeans are a hot-blooded lot, aren't they?" Allen had remarked, unperturbed.

"Maybe it's time. Interest rates are low. We have the money for a sizable down payment. Jack has been telling us we have to invest in real assets to be truly comfortable in retirement," she said, referring to their accountant.

"But the maintenance costs . . . And who's to say prices don't plummet in the next ten years." He paused and shook his head. "We couldn't afford to buy in the city."

She shrugged. It was an old conversation that neither of them felt very passionate about. She'd let it go and headed off to the farmers' market in Union Square for dinner ingredients. On the way back, she passed her landlord in the street and tried to smile. He marched right past her, yelling into his cellular phone in that guttural language.

She stepped out of the shower now and covered herself in a towel, wrapped her long red hair in another, and brushed her teeth. She could hear the stereo in the living room and thought it was louder than her husband usually liked it. But she didn't hear voices and she was grateful for that — no early dinner guests, no screaming landlords. She felt better from the shower and smiled at herself in the mirror. She thought that she was still pretty, with her big green eyes and lightly freckled skin, which was still relatively young looking if you didn't count the laugh lines around her mouth and eyes.

She hummed along with the radio, a catchy tune by one of those *American Idol* kids, and thought it was strange that Allen had chosen that on the radio and not popped in a Mozart or Chopin CD, which was more his taste. But he did try to be "hip" sometimes, especially when Rick was coming over. Because Rick was hip — or so he claimed. She didn't want to tell either of them that anyone who used the word *hip* probably wasn't. She and Ella always shared a secret smile when Rick and Allen tried to pretend they were up on recent trends.

There it was again, a knocking. This time, though, it was more of a heavy thud, and it seemed to come from the living room. She opened the bathroom door and called her husband's name. There was no answer, and the music seemed very loud now that the door was open and she was heading past the bedroom and toward the kitchen. Her heart started to flutter as she called his name again.

She saw something on the floor ahead of her. A glove? No, a hand. Her husband's hand on the floor. Everything seemed to slow down then. Her first thought was, Heart attack! as she came around the corner and found him lying there. She knelt down to him and he fluttered his eyes at her, tried to talk.

"Allen, it's okay, honey," she said, amazed at her own inner calm. Her voice sounded solid and sure. "I'll call an ambulance. Hang in there, baby. Don't worry."

It would be all right, she told herself with an odd stillness. Heart attacks were so survivable these days. He'd been taking his aspirin. She'd get him to sit up and take a dose while they waited for the ambulance.

But then she saw the blood pooling out from beneath him and the terror in his eyes. And then she saw the men standing by the door.

They were fully dressed in black. One of them held a gun, the other a terrible serrated blade red with blood. Both of them wore ski masks. They blocked her passage to the phone.

"What do you want?" she asked, her calm starting to retreat. "You can have anything you want." She looked around her apartment and realized they had nothing of any real value. Even her wedding ring was just a simple band of gold. She had twenty dollars in her wallet; Allen probably had less than that. She felt a wet warmth against her feet and realized the blood pooling out from beneath her husband had reached her. His face was pale; his eyes were closed now.

"Don't make a move," one of the men said, she couldn't tell which. The whole situation had taken on a foggy non-reality. Her mind struggled to keep up with what was happening. "Don't say a word."

One of the men came at her quickly, and before she could even put up a fight, he'd grabbed her wrist and spun her around, placing a black shroud over her head and tightening it around her neck. In her deepest heart, she knew what this was about. She just couldn't bring herself to believe it. Then there was a stunning pain at the base of her neck and a star shower before her eyes. Then there was nothing.

1

I'm running but I can't run much farther. The pain in my side already has me limping; there's fire in my lungs. I can't hear his footfalls. But I know he's not far away. I know now that he's been right beside me all my life in one way or another. I'm the light; he's the shadow. We've coexisted without ever meeting. If I'd been a good girl, the girl I was raised to be, I never would have known him. But it's too late for regrets.

I'm on Hart Island in the Bronx, a place known as Potter's Field. It's the city cemetery for the unknown and indigent — a grim and frightening place. How we've all wound up here is a long story, but I know the story will end here — maybe just for some, maybe for all of us. A tall abandoned building that seems to sag upon itself looms ahead of me. It's a darker night than I have ever known, in more ways than one. The sliver of moon is hidden behind a thick cloud cover. It's hard to see but I watch as he disappears through a door that hangs crooked on its hinges. I follow.

"Ridley!" The call comes from behind me. But I don't answer. I just keep moving until I am standing at the entrance to the building. I hesitate there, looking at the crooked, sighing structure and wondering if it's not too late to turn around.

Then I see him, up ahead of me. I call out but he doesn't answer me, just turns and slowly starts to move away. I follow. If I valued my life and my sanity, I'd let him get away and hope he did the same for me. We could go back to the way things have been. He dwelling in a world I never even knew existed, me going about my very ordinary life, writing magazine articles, seeing movies, having drinks with friends.

Fear and rage duke it out in my chest. Hatred has a taste and a texture; it burns like bile in my throat. For a moment, I hear the voice of someone I loved: *Ridley, you can release the hatred and walk away. It's nothing more than a single choice. We can both do it. We don't need all the answers to live our lives. It doesn't have to be like this.* A few minutes later, he was gone.

I know now that those words were lies. Hatred doesn't release. Walking away is not one of my choices. Maybe it never was. Maybe I've been in the path of this freight train all my life, lashed to the tracks, too weak, too foolish, too stubborn to even try to save myself.

As I enter the building, I think I might hear the rumble of boat engines. I feel a distant flutter of hope and wonder if help is coming. I hear my name again and look behind me to see a man who has become my only friend moving unsteadily toward me. He is injured and I know it will take him a while to reach me. I think for a second that I should go to him, help him. But inside I hear movement and the groaning of an unstable structure. My breathing comes shallow and quick. I step deeper inside.

"Stop running, you coward!" I yell into the huge darkness. My voice resonates in the deserted space. "Let me see your face."

My voice bounces off the surfaces around me again. I don't sound scared and heartbroken, but I am. I sound strong and sure. I take the gun from the waist of my jeans. The metal is warm from my skin. In my hand, it feels solid and righteous. This is the second time in my life I've held a gun with the intent to use it. I don't like it any better than the first time, but I'm more confident now, know that I can fire if pressed.

He steps out from the shadows, seems to move silently, to glide like the ghost that he is. I take a step toward him and then stop, raise my gun. I still can't see his face. A milky light has started to shine through the gaping holes in the ceiling as the moon moves through a break in the cloud cover. Shapes emerge in the darkness. He starts moving toward me slowly. I stand my ground but the gun starts shaking in my hand.

"Ridley, don't do it. You'll never be able to live with it."

The voice comes from behind me and I spin around to see someone I didn't expect to see again.

"This is none of your business," I yell, and turn back to the man I've been chasing.

"Ridley, don't be stupid. Put that gun down." This voice behind me sounds desperate, cracks with emotion. "You know I can't let you kill him."

My heart rate responds to the fear in his voice. *What am I doing?* Adrenaline is making my mouth dry, the back of my neck tingle. I can't fire but I can't lower the gun, either. I have the urge to scream in my fear and anger, my frustration and confusion, but it all lodges in my throat.

When he's finally close enough to see, I gaze upon his face. And he's someone I don't recognize at all. I draw in a gasp as a wide, cruel smile spreads across his face. And then I get it. He is the man they say he is.

"Oh, God," I say, lowering my gun. "Oh, no."

2

I bet you thought you'd heard the end of me. You might have at least hoped that I'd had my fill of drama for one lifetime and that the road ahead of me would not hold any more surprises, that things would go pretty smoothly from now on. Believe me, I thought so, too. We were both wrong.

About a year ago, a series of mundane events and ordinary decisions led my life to connect with the life of a toddler by the name of Justin Wheeler. I happened to be standing across the street from him on a cool autumn morning as he wandered into the path of an oncoming van. In an unthinking moment, I leapt out into the street, grabbed him, and dove us both out of the way of the vehicle that certainly would have killed him . . . and maybe me if I'd been thirty seconds earlier or later arriving on the scene. Still, that might have been the end of it, a heroic deed remembered only by Justin Wheeler, his family, and me, except for the fact that a *Post* photographer standing on the corner got the whole thing on film. That photograph (a pretty amazing action shot, if I do say so myself) led to another series of events that would force me to question virtually everything about my former perfect life and ultimately cause it to unravel in the most horrible ways.

The funny thing was, even after my life had dissolved around me, even after everything I thought defined me had turned out to be a lie, I found that I was still *me*. I still had the strength to move forward into the unknown. And that was a pretty cool thing to learn about myself.

My life may have looked as if it had been on the business end of a wrecking ball, but Ridley Jones still emerged from the remains. And though there were times when I didn't think it was possible, my life settled back into a somewhat normal rhythm. For a while, anyway.

If you don't know what happened to me and how it all turned out, you *could* go back now and find out before you move ahead. I'm not saying the things that follow won't make any sense to you or that you won't get anything out of the experience of joining me on this next chapter of my *vida loca*.

What I'm saying is that it's kind of like sleeping with someone before you know her name. But maybe you like it like that. Maybe you want to come along and figure things out as we go, like any new relationship, I guess. Either way, the choice is yours. The choice is *always* yours.

Well, I'll get to it, then.

I'm the last person in the world without a digital camera. I don't like them; they seem too fragile. As if getting caught in the rain or clumsily pushing the wrong button could erase some of your memories. I have a 35-millimeter Minolta that I've been using since college. I take my rolls of film and then drop them off at the same photo lab on Second Avenue I've been using for years.

I had a friend who thought that there was something inherently wrong with picture taking. Memory, he said, was magical for its subjectivity. Photographs were crude and the direct result of a desire to control, to hold on to moments that should be released like each breath that we take. Maybe he was right. We're not friends anymore and I have no pictures of him, just this memory that resurfaces every time I go to pick up photographs. And then I think about how he liked to sing and play the guitar after we made love (and how he was really terrible at it —

the guitar playing, the singing, and the love-making, for that matter) but that the sight of Washington Square Park outside his windows always seemed so romantic that I put up with the rest for longer than I might have otherwise. My memories of him are organic and three-dimensional, pictures that exist only for me; there's something nice about that after all.

So I was thinking about this as I pushed through the door of the F-Stop to pick up some photos that were waiting for me. A desk clerk I'd never seen before looked at me with practiced indifference from beneath a chaos of dyed black hair and twin swaths of eyeliner.

"Help you?" he said sullenly, placing a paperback binding up on the surface in front of him. I saw the flash of a tongue piercing when he spoke.

"I'm picking up photographs. Last name Jones."

He gave me a kind of weird look, as if he thought it was a name I'd made up. (A note about New York City: Here, if you leave a plain or common name, people treat you with suspicion. Meanwhile, if your name would sound bizarre or made up anywhere else in the world — for example, Ruby De-cal X or Geronimo — it wouldn't even raise an eyebrow in the East Village.)

The clerk disappeared behind a dividing wall and I thought I heard voices as I glanced around at some black-and-white art shots on the wall. After a short time, he returned with three fat envelopes and lay them on the desk between us. He didn't say anything as he rang up the sale. I paid him in cash, and he slid the envelopes into a plastic bag.

"Thank you," I said, taking the bag from his hand.

He sat down without another word and returned to his book. For some reason, I turned around at the door and caught him staring at me strangely just before he averted his eyes.

I paused on the street corner at Second Avenue and Eighth Street. My intent had been to stop by the studio and bring the photos to Jake. They were some shots we had taken over the last few months: a long weekend in Paris where we'd tried and failed to reconnect; an afternoon spent in Central Park, where we fooled around on the Great Lawn and things seemed hopeful; a miserable day with my parents at the Botanical Gardens in Brooklyn, character- ized by heavy awkward silences, mini- outbursts, and barely concealed dislike.

Faced now with the reality of dropping in on Jake, I balked, loitered on the corner staring at the sidewalk.

I don't want to tell you that my world has gone dark or that the color has drained from my life. That sounds too dramatic, too self-pitying. But I guess that's not too far off. When last you heard from me, I was picking up the pieces of my shattered life. I think we ended on a hopeful note, but the work has been hard. And like any protracted convalescence, there have been more lows than highs.

As of last month, Jake moved out of the apartment we shared on Park Avenue South and is living semi-permanently in his studio on Avenue A. Far from finding peace with his past and coming to terms with what he has learned, Jake has become obsessed with Project Rescue and Max's role in it.

By Max, I mean Maxwell Allen Smiley, my uncle who was not really my uncle but my father's best friend. We shared a special connection all my life. And last year I learned that he was really my biological father. I am currently struggling to recast him in my life as my failed father instead of my beloved uncle.

Project Rescue is an organization developed by Max, an abused child himself, to help pass the Safe Haven Law in New York State years ago. This law allows frightened mothers to abandon their babies at specified Safe Haven sites, no questions asked, no fear of prosecution. I discovered last year that there was a shadow side to this organization. Cooperating nurses and doctors were secretly flagging children they thought were potential victims of abuse and unsafe in their homes. Through a collusion with organized crime, some of these children were abducted and sold to wealthy parents. In a sense, I was a Project Rescue baby, though my story is more complicated. Jake is a Project Rescue baby for whom things went horribly wrong.

Lately, Jake has abandoned his art. And while he and I have not formally broken up, I have become a ghost in our relationship, behaving like a poltergeist, tossing things about, making noise just to get myself noticed.

I am reminded of something my mother, Grace, once said about Max: *A man like that, so broken and hollow inside, can't really love well. At least he was smart enough to know it.* They say we all fall in love with our fathers over and over in a sad attempt to resolve that relationship. Is it possible I was doing that before I even knew who my father really was?

"Ms. Jones. Ridley Jones." I heard a voice behind me and went cold inside. Over the past year, I had developed quite a fan club, in spite of my best efforts to keep myself out of everything other than my legal obligations involving Christian Luna's murder and the investigation surrounding Project Rescue.

Christian Luna was the man who started all of this. After seeing a clip on CNN about my heroic deed, he recognized me as Jessie Stone, Teresa Stone's daughter, a little girl he believed to be his daughter, as well. He'd been hiding for more than thirty years, since the night of Teresa Stone's murder and Jessie's abduction, certain that he'd be accused because of their history of domestic violence. I watched him die from a gunshot wound to the head as he sat just inches away from me on a park bench in the Bronx. He turned out not to be my father, after all.

Anyway, thanks to the myriad articles and newsmagazine specials featuring the famous *Post* photograph as the point where it all started, I have become the poster child for an organization that has altered thousands of lives, not necessarily for the better. They call. They write, the other Project Rescue babies. They stop me on the street. I've been lauded, embraced, assaulted, and spit upon. They are grateful. They are enraged. They come to me in the various stages of grief and horror, disbelief and anger. In each of them I see a sad mirror of my own journey toward healing.

I ignored the person behind me. I didn't answer or turn around. I have found that if I don't answer to my name when it's called on the street, sometimes people go away, unsure of themselves. Once upon a time, I'd heard my name called only in love or in query and I answered happily with a smile on my face. Those days are gone.

"Ms. Jones."

The voice had a kind of authority to it that almost caused me to turn. I've always been a good girl and have responded appropriately to commands. Instead I started to walk away toward Jake's studio. I heard a quickening of steps, which caused me to pick up my own pace. Then I felt a strong hand on my shoulder. I spun around, angry and ready to fight. Standing there were two men in smart business suits.

"Ms. Jones, we need a word."

His face was stern, not angry, not emotional in any way. And that calmed me. He had strange storm-cloud gray eyes, a tousle of ink black hair. He was tall, nearly a head taller than I am, and big around the chest and shoulders. There was a cold distance to him but a sort of kindness, too. The man at his side said nothing.

"What do you want?"

He pulled a thin leather wallet from his lapel pocket, flipped it open, and handed it to me.

Special Agent Dylan Grace, Federal Bureau of Investigation.

All of my trepidation drained and was replaced by annoyance. I handed the ID back to him.

"Agent Grace, I don't have anything else to say to the FBI. I've told you everything I know about Project Rescue. There's literally nothing left to say."

He must have heard the catch in my voice or seen something in my face because the cool mettle of his demeanor seemed to warm a bit.

"This isn't about Project Rescue, Ms. Jones."

His partner walked over to a black sedan and pulled open the back passenger-side door. The air was cool and the sky was a moody gunmetal. People turned to look at us but kept walking. Some thugs rode by in a tricked-out Mustang, bass booming like a heartbeat.

"What's it about, then?"

"It's about Maxwell Allen Smiley."

My heart thumped. "There's nothing left to say about him, either. He's dead."

"Can I have the photographs in your bag, Ms. Jones?"

"What?" How did he know about the photos, and what could he possibly want with shots of my almost ex-boyfriend and my very nearly estranged family?

He withdrew a piece of paper from his lapel pocket. I found myself wondering what else he had in there — a deck of cards, a white bunny, a ridiculously long strand of multicolored handkerchiefs?

"I have a warrant, Ms. Jones."

I didn't look at the paper. I just reached into my bag and handed him the F-Stop package. He took it and motioned to the car. I moved toward the sedan and slid inside without another word. By then I'd had enough experience with the FBI to know that they get what they want eventually. Whether it's the easy way or the hard way is up to you.

They took me to a building near FBI headquarters, and after taking my bag, left me sitting in a barren room with only a faux wood table on metal legs and two amazingly uncomfortable chairs. The walls were painted a miserable gray and the fluorescent lighting flickered unpleasantly.

They did this for a reason, I knew, left you sitting in an unwelcoming room with only your thoughts, no clock on the wall, nothing to distract you. They want you to think. Think about why you're there, about what you know or what you have done. They want you to wonder about what *they* might know. They want you to work yourself into a state of worry and anxiety so that by the time they return to you, you're looking for a confessor.

But of course, this works only if you're guilty or hiding something. I honestly had no idea why they wanted to talk to me, so I just became progressively more bored and annoyed. And exhausted. This encounter, and maybe my life in general, was exhausting me. I got off the chair and walked a restless circle around the room. Finally I placed my back against the wall and slid into a sitting position on the floor.

These days I tried not to think about Max, though sometimes it seemed as if the more I tried to be rid of his memory, the more he haunted me. I pulled up my knees and folded my arms over them, rested my head in the crook of my elbow to escape the harsh white light of the room. I used to do this when I was a kid when I was upset or tired, retreat into this cocoon of myself. When that didn't work, I'd hide.

I'm not sure how it all started, the hiding thing. But I remember liking to crawl into dark places and lie quietly, listening to the chaos of everyone trying to find me. My parents didn't think it amusing but I found it positively thrilling, the excitement of them running around, looking under beds and in closets. It was a game I always won, just by virtue of the reaction I created. It didn't occur to me that I might be angering or frightening anyone. I was too young to care about things like that. I just got better and better at finding places to hide. Eventually I had to reveal myself or never be found. There was something great about that, too.

At some point I got the idea that there was nowhere else in the house to hide. All my secret places had been discovered by my parents, or by my brother, Ace — or by my uncle Max. He was the big gun, called in when no one else could find me. He'd say, "Check inside that wardrobe in the guest room." Or "Try that crawl space to the attic in her closet." Somehow he'd always know where to find me. Once my parents realized that Max had this gift for finding me, the game started to get too easy, their reactions were not as much fun and the whole thing lost its charge. I had to raise the stakes.

I don't know how old I was, seven, maybe six — too young to go into the woods behind my house without Ace. I knew that much. It was just a shallow swath of trees about two miles long, that edged our neighbors' properties and separated our acreage from the yard behind us. A little creek ran beneath a stone bridge. The space was narrow enough that neighborhood parents felt safe letting us play back there without too much supervision. If you went too far, you just wound up in someone's backyard. But I wasn't supposed to go back there by myself. So naturally it was the perfect place to hide.

It was a hot summer afternoon when I left through the back-door of my house and entered the woods. We'd built a small fort back in the thick and I climbed inside the rickety thing. It was dim and warm. I felt pleased with myself. After a while of lying there, looking out the crooked window at the leaves sighing in the light wind, I fell asleep. When I woke up later, the sky was a deep purple. It was close to dark. It was the first time in my life I was truly frightened. I looked out the fort "window," and the woods I usually loved seemed full of monsters and witches, the trees smirked with their malice. I started to cry, curled up in a tight ball.

I don't think I was like that for long before I heard someone moving through the overgrowth.

"Ridley? Are you out here, honey?"

I was old enough to hear the worry in his voice. But my heart flooded with relief; I cried even harder until I saw Max's face in the makeshift doorway. He was too big to get inside.

"Ridley, there you are," he said, sitting down heavily on the ground. I could see that he was sweating, maybe from the humidity, maybe from fear. Maybe both. He put his head in his hands. "Kid," he said through his fingers, "you have *got* to stop doing this. You are going to give your uncle Max a heart attack. Your mom and dad are about to call the police."

He lifted his head to the night and yelled, "I found her!"

I crawled out of the fort and into his lap, let him enfold me in his big arms against his soft belly. He was damp with perspiration but I didn't care. Through the trees, I could see the glow from the lights of my own house, could hear my parents' voices drawing closer.

"How did you find me?" I asked him.

He sighed and took my face in his hands. "Ridley, there's a golden chain from my heart to yours." He tapped his chest lightly, then mine. "Trust me. I'll *always* find you." I never doubted he was right. And I never hid from my poor parents again.

I lifted my head from the crook of my arm and squinted against the harsh white lights of the interrogation room. I closed my eyes again and leaned my head against the cold wall, tried and failed to clear my mind and relax.

Agent Grace walked in shortly thereafter and offered me his hand, pulled me up from the floor with impressive strength.

"Starting to feel at home here?" he asked. There was something odd in his voice. Was it compassion? For someone who was completely innocent of wrongdoing, I'd spent more time with the FBI than Jeffrey Dahmer had. Or so I imagined, in my self-aggrandizing way. I gave him a short, tight smile, then kept my eyes on the eight-by-ten envelope he had in his other hand. We sat across from each other. He straddled his chair as if he was mounting a horse. Without a word, he opened the envelope and took out three eight-by-ten photographs and spread them out before me.

The first was a photo of me in front of Notre-Dame in Paris. I was eating a crepe filled with Nutella and bananas, gazing up at the cathedral. I wore my leather coat and a beret I had bought on the street just to be a dork. Hazelnut chocolate dripped down my chin. Jake had taken the candid. I think to the casual observer I would have looked silly and happy. But I wasn't. I remember waking up next to Jake that morning in our posh hotel room with the yellow morning sun beaming in. I looked at him as he slept and thought, I've been with this man for a year. He seems more like a stranger to me now than when I was first falling in love with him, when there were so many secrets and lies between us. How is it possible to know someone less intimately the more time you spend with him? The thought had filled me with sadness. He woke up as I stared at him and we made a slow, desperate kind of love to each other, both wanting so badly the connection we'd once shared. I carried the sadness of that lovemaking with me all day.

The next photo was a shot of me and Jake on the Great Lawn in Central Park. The grass looked a bright and artificial green

40

and the skyscape rose up over the tall trees painted gold, orange, and red in the changing season. We'd asked a young woman strolling by to take a picture of us on our blue picnic blanket and cuddled in close. She got only our heads near the bottom of the frame and everything irrelevant behind and above us. It had been a good day. In the photo I noticed that our smiles looked forced and fake. But they weren't. At least mine wasn't. I felt hopeful for us, I remember, like a terminally ill patient who thinks a brief cessation of symptoms heralds a miraculous recovery.

The final photograph before me was a snapshot from the miserable Sunday we'd spent with my parents. We went to the River Café in Brooklyn for lunch and then on to the Botanic Garden. This used to be one of my favorites dates with my father when I was younger. Arranging this get-together was my pathetic and desperate attempt to pretend we could act like a family. Well, we *did* act like a family, a hateful and unhappy one. Ace, who was also invited, didn't show and didn't call. My mother took an attitude of stoic endurance, issuing the occasional passive-aggressive comment under her breath. My father and I chattered on like idiots, mirroring each other in our efforts to

41

keep the faltering conversation flowing. Jake was silent and sullen. We shared an awkward meal. Then, unable to admit defeat, we proceeded to the Botanic Garden. My father used my camera to take a photo of me, my mother, and Jake. I put my arm around my mother's shoulders and smiled. She turned up the corners of her mouth reluctantly, but I swear she shrunk from me. Jake stood near us but just slightly apart. He looked distracted, seemed to have gazed off in the last second before the picture was snapped. We looked like a group of strangers, uncomfortable and forced together.

A powerful sadness and embarrassment washed over me. I looked up at Agent Grace with what I hoped was barely concealed hostility.

"It's not a crime to have a shitty relationship with your family, is it? Or to document your sad attempts to save your failing love affair?"

I leaned away, looked at the wall over his head. I didn't want to look at his face.

"No, Ms. Jones, it isn't," he said softly. "Can I call you Ridley?"

"No," I said nastily. "You can't."

I thought I saw a smile tug at the corners of his mouth, as if he found me amusing. I wondered how much trouble you could get in for slapping a federal agent.

"Ms. Jones," he said, "what interests us about these photographs is not the subjects, it's the background. Take another look."

I glanced at each picture and saw nothing unusual. I shrugged at him and shook my head. He kept his eyes on me, nodded again toward the photos. "Look closely."

I looked again. Still nothing.

"Why don't you just cut the crap," I suggested, "and tell me what you see."

He took a black Sharpie from his lapel pocket and circled the figure of a man behind us at the Botanic Garden. He was more like the specter of a man, tall and thin. His face was paper white, little more than a ghostly blur. He wore a long black coat, a dark hat. He leaned on a cane. He seemed to be looking in my direction.

Agent Grace circled another figure behind us in Central Park. Same coat, same cane; this time the man in the picture wore sunglasses. The figure in the photograph was so far away it could have been anyone.

He took the Sharpie again and marked another man in the doorway of Notre-Dame. This time he was caught in profile, more clearly, closer. Something about the shape of his brow, the ridge of his nose caused me to lean in. Something about the slope of his shoulder made my heart flutter.

"No," I said, shaking my head.

"What?" he asked, raising his eyebrows. Those eyes of his were weird, at once sleepy and searing.

"I see what you're trying to do," I said.

"What?" he repeated, leaning back. I expected to see smug satisfaction on his face but I didn't.

"It's impossible."

"Is it?"

"Yes."

I looked again. They say it's a person's carriage that allows you to recognize him across the room or across the street. But I think it's a person's aura, the energy that radiates from within. The man in the photograph was greatly dissimilar in physical appearance, perhaps as much as a hundred pounds thinner than the man I remembered. He looked twenty years older. He seemed a damaged, hollowed-out person lacking any of the radiant warmth I'd basked in most of my life. But still there was something familiar about this man. If I had not personally seen his dead body moments before cremation, had I not with my own hands scattered his ashes from the Brooklyn Bridge, you might have been able to convince me that I was looking at the man I'd once known as my uncle Max, who was my biological father. But the fact was I had done all those things. And dead was dead.

"I'll admit there's a resemblance," I said finally, after a brief but intense staring contest.

"We think there's more than a resemblance."

I sighed here and leaned back in my chair. "Okay, say you're right. That would mean that you think Max staged his own death for whatever reason. Why would anyone go to all that trouble just to risk being discovered a couple of years later?"

Agent Grace regarded me for a minute.

"Do you know the number one reason why people in the witness protection program get found by their enemies and wind up dead?"

"Why?" I asked, though I could probably guess.

"Love."

"Love," I repeated. That wouldn't have been my guess.

"They can't stay away. They can't help but make that call or show up incognito at a wedding or a funeral."

I didn't say anything, and Agent Grace went on. "I've seen his apartment. It's practically a shrine to you. Max Smiley did some terrible things in his life, hurt a lot of people. But if he loved anyone, it was you."

His words put a crush on my heart and I found I couldn't meet his eyes.

"I don't get it. Were you following me? How did you know about these photos? Do you have some kind of relationship with my photo lab?"

He didn't answer me and I hadn't really expected him to. I took a last glance at the pictures. That man could have been anyone; could even have been three different men, I decided.

"I don't know who this is," I told him. "If it is who you want it to be, then it's news to me. If you want to talk more, it'll have to be in the presence of my attorney."

I clamped my mouth shut then. I knew he could make life hard for me. Since the Patriot Act, federal authorities have more latitude than ever. If they wanted to, they could hold me indefinitely without counsel if they claimed it had something to do with national security. (Which in my case would have been a stretch. But I promise you, stranger things have happened.) I think, though, Agent Grace sensed the truth: I had no idea who the man in those photos might be.

He looked at me hard with those eyes of his. I found myself inspecting the cut of his suit. Not cheap, exactly, but not Armani, either. I saw he had a bit of a five o'clock shadow coming in on his jaw. I noticed that the knuckles on his right hand were broken, not bleeding but raw. He rose suddenly, gave me a look he might have meant to be intimidating, and left without another word.

Shortly afterward, his partner came and told me he'd escort me from the building. He slid the photos on the table into the envelope Agent Grace had left behind. He handed them to me with a cordial smile. "Thank you and come again," I expected him to say.

"Agent Grace wants you to have these . . . to look over more carefully."

I took the envelope from him, briefly fantasized about ripping it into pieces and throwing the shreds in his face, then tucked it under my arm instead.

"What about my other photos and my bag?" I asked as we walked down a long white hallway.

"You'll get your bag at the door. And your photos will be returned to you by mail once they've been analyzed."

The whole thing suddenly seemed ridiculous and I found I didn't much care whether

I got the pictures back or not. In fact, I didn't care if I ever took another photo again as long as I lived. My friend with the guitar had been right, they were inherently wrong, taken in an impulse to control something we couldn't control. And, frankly, they'd never brought me anything but trouble.

3

I wish I could tell you where things went bad with Jake. I wish I could say he cheated or that I did. Or that he became abusive suddenly or that I stopped loving him. But none of those things have happened. It was more like he just slowly disappeared, one molecule at a time. There wasn't a lot of fighting, never any unkindness. Just a slow fade to black.

There was the fact that he hated my family. Not that I could blame him, really. They hated Jake first. But even though a thorough federal investigation found my father innocent of wrongdoing concerning Project Rescue, Jake never believed that my father was completely innocent. (Note: When I refer to my father, I always mean Ben, even though Max is my biological father. Ben is and always has been my father in every way that counts. And even though a woman I don't remember by the name of Teresa

Stone is my biological mother, I'll speak only of Grace as my mother.)

Anyway, none of them have behaved particularly well, leaving me fractured and torn between them. I was trying to heal my relationship with my parents, find a common ground where we could move forward together, but in doing so I was hurting Jake. And by loving and having a life with Jake, I was hurting my parents. (P.S. Ace, my brother, hates Jake, too. But he also hates our parents. The only one he doesn't hate is me, or so he says.)

Maybe it was this tug-of-war where I got to play the rope that frayed the fabric of my relationship with Jake. Or maybe it was Jake's various obsessions regarding his own past, Max, and Project Rescue, all the things I was trying so hard to move beyond. When I was with Jake I felt as if I was trying to walk up a down escalator.

He was in the apartment when I came home. I heard him move toward the door as I turned the key in the lock.

"Rid," he said as I stepped into the apartment and into his arms. "Where have you been?"

I lingered there a minute, taking in his scent, feeling his body. The only thing that hadn't changed between us was this ravenous physical appetite we had for each other. No matter how far apart we were mentally and emotionally, we could always connect physically. It was something about our chemistry, the way our bodies fit together. These days, there was rarely an encounter between us that didn't end in sex.

"I was detained," I said, feeling exhaustion weigh down my limbs. He pulled back from me, held on to my shoulders, and looked into my eyes.

"Detained," he said. "Ridley, you should have called. I know things aren't great between us, but I was worried about you. I expected you this afternoon."

I looked at the clock; it was nearly eleven.

"No. I mean *literally* detained, by the federal authorities," I said with a mirthless laugh.

"What?" he said sharply, looking at me in surprise. "Why?"

I handed him the envelope and moved over toward the couch, where I flung myself down like a bag of laundry. I told him about my encounter with Agent Grace and the FBI. I should have just kept my mouth shut, given the intensity of Jake's obsessions. But I told him, probably because he was literally the only person in my life I could talk to about any of this. Any conversation relating to Max, or to the events that so changed all of our lives, was strictly forbidden in my family. Even Ace had suggested that I "move on" the last time I tried to talk to him about some things that haunt me still. Isn't it funny how the people least impacted by tragedy are the most eager to move on? I was eager to move toward healing, believe me. But I was caught in this space between my parents, who wanted to pretend none of it had ever happened, and Jake, who seemed to think nothing else would ever happen again.

I finished talking and closed my eyes, heard Jake flipping through the photographs. When he didn't say anything, I looked over at him as he sank into the chair across from me. I tried not to notice how hot he was in his black T-shirt and faded denims, or to watch the tattoos on his arm, the way they snaked around his muscles and disappeared into his sleeve. My body responded to him even without his touch.

"Well?" he said, raising his eyes from the photos to look at me.

"Well, what?" I said. "They weren't able to make a case against my father. The prosecution's case against Esme Gray was so weak they couldn't hold her for more than twenty-four hours. They can't really get Zack for things that started long before he was ever born." I took a deep breath. "They're looking for someone to prosecute and they're willing to resurrect the dead to do it."

I hated to even think about Esme, the nurse who had worked at my father's practice and assisted him in his clinic since long before I was born. She's also the mother of my ex-boyfriend Zack Gray. At one time, Esme and I were closer than I was to my own mother, but she was intimately involved in the shadow side of Project Rescue, as was Zack. I can no longer be close with either of them for more reasons than I can recount here.

Jake didn't respond, just stared at the photos, one after another. There was something so strange on his face. He wore a half-smile but his eyes were dark. I saw him give a small shake of his head. An ambulance raced by, siren blaring, filling the apartment briefly with light and sound.

"What?" I asked him. "What are you thinking?"

"Nothing," he said, putting the photos on the table. "I'm not thinking anything."

He was lying. He put his head in his hands, rested his elbows on his knees, and released a deep sigh. I sat up and crossed my legs beneath me, watching him.

"What is it?"

He looked at me. "Is this him, Ridley? Is this Max?" There was something desperate in his voice. And something else. Was it fear?

"No," I said. "Of course not. Max is dead. I saw his dead body in the casket. I scattered his ashes. He's dead."

"His face was unrecognizable, shredded by glass when he went through the windshield. The face you saw was reconstructed from a photograph."

"It was him." What Jake said was true. But I remembered Max's hands, his rings, the small scar on his neck. There wasn't an open-casket viewing for him, but we were able to see the body once it had been prepared for cremation. My father had arranged for postmortem reconstruction of his ruined face so that we could all say good-bye to something we recognized. I guess in retrospect it was pretty macabre (not to mention a huge waste of money), but at the time it felt right.

"Because if this is Max . . ." He let his voice trail off and kept his eyes on me.

"It's not," I said firmly.

"Ridley," he said, rubbing his eyes. "There's a lot you don't know about this man."

Sometimes Jake frightened me. That was the other thing that had started to eat away at our relationship. Not that I was physically afraid of him, but the intensity of his obsessions seemed like a natural disaster, something that could shift the ground beneath our feet, open a chasm in the earth. I always wondered when it would swallow him whole — and me along with it.

"You know what?" I said, rising. "I can't do this with you right now."

"Ridley."

"Jake, I want you to go." I walked over to the door and opened it.

"Listen to me —" he started but I stopped him with a raised hand.

"No, Jake, *you* listen to *me*. I can't do this. You need to leave." I didn't want to hear what he had to say. Not at all.

He looked at me for a second. Then he nodded, stood up, and walked over to the bar that separated the kitchen from the living area. He took his leather jacket off one of the stools. I felt bad; I could see that I'd hurt him. But the fatigue I'd felt earlier had burrowed into my soul. I only wanted to close my eyes and disappear into blissful black.

"We do need to talk," he said, leaning in and kissing me on the cheek at the doorway.

"Okay," I said. "Tomorrow."

He left then and I closed the door behind him. I walked across the loft and went into the bedroom we used to share. I kicked off my shoes and lay on the bed, sinking into the down comforter, and sobbed for I don't know how long from sheer exhaustion and the crushing sadness that had settled into my heart and threatened never to leave.

I guess I fell asleep because it was hours later that the phone woke me. I looked at the clock to see that it was 3:33 a.m. I reached over to the bedside table and picked up the receiver, thinking it was Ace. He called at all hours — typical of his recovering addict's personality, totally self-centered. I, the recovering enabler, never hesitated to pick up.

"Hello," I said.

There was a heavy static on the line, the sound of distant voices, a tinny strain of music. I glanced at the caller ID, which told me the number was unavailable.

"Hello?" I repeated.

I heard the sound of breathing on the line, then it went dead. I put down the receiver and waited for it to ring again but it didn't. After a while I got up and brushed my teeth, stripped off my clothes, and got under the covers. I drifted back into an uneasy sleep.

4

You may remember that I am a writer. Up until recently, I wrote articles for major magazines and newspapers — features, profiles of celebrities and politicians, some travel pieces. I've done well and I've always loved my work. But like so many things, that has changed over the last year. (Not that I don't still love my work, although I'm not sure *love* is the right word for it. It's more that I'm indivisible from the work that I do, simply couldn't be or do anything else.) Lately I've been attracted to more serious subjects, wanting to explore things that have real meaning. I've found myself interested in survivors, people who have faced extraordinary circumstances and not just lived to tell it, but gone on to create greater purpose in their lives. I am fascinated by human endurance, by the capacity some people seem to have to turn tragedy into victory. Imagine that. Personally, I felt as if I had the whole tragedy thing down. It was the other part that remained elusive.

The next morning, bright light flooded the loft as I made a pot of coffee. I turned the television on to watch the *Today* show as I got ready to head out, but muted it finally because I couldn't stand the chatter, the incessant commercials. I zoned out on the screen for a minute as I sipped the strong coffee. There was a picture of a smiling man and woman in the corner of the screen. The words *Missing Couple* were emblazoned above them. I think they'd been missing awhile, no clue to what might have happened to them. I got the horrible unsettled feeling I get about this type of thing when I considered the possibility that no one might ever know their fate. I don't like unanswered questions, unsolved mysteries. They give me angst. I turned away from the screen. I had my own problems to worry about, not the least of which was a looming deadline for *O Magazine.*

I peered out the window and saw that the people moving along Park Avenue South were in coats and hats. It was sunny but cold, my favorite kind of New York City day. I lingered for a while and found myself searching the street for the man I'd seen in the photographs. I looked for the tall, thin form, the sunken face. But, of course, he wasn't there. And Max was dead. I wasn't sure of much in my life. But I was sure of that.

I took a shower and got dressed. As I bundled myself up in my black wool pea-coat and light-blue cashmere scarf, I pushed aside the events of yesterday and headed out the door.

Elena Jansen was a tiny bird of a woman, a former dancer with the New York City Ballet. She had a grace and strength to her carriage, a steel to her posture that made her seem powerful in spite of the fact that she just barely cleared five feet. Her eyes, a deep cocoa brown, were warm and liquid, her handshake firm and sure. I expected to find a shattered woman, to see some evidence of her tragedy in her physical bearing. But what I saw was defiance, a dare to the Universe to try to take her down again. I'd seen this before. In fact, I'd say it was the defining feature I'd found in the survivors I'd interviewed lately. A refusal to cower, to surrender, even when the world has revealed all its ugliness and horror. I imagined that sometimes I'd seen it in my own reflection, though that might have just been wishful thinking.

60

I followed her into a warm parlor over-looking Central Park. The room was decorated in deep reds with cream and gold accents. The walls were a gallery of photos of her years as a dancer and of her children. She was beautiful now in her early fifties, but as a younger woman, she had been truly stunning. I'd seen many of these photos in my preliminary research for this article I was writing for *O Magazine.*

"Well, then," she said, sitting elegantly in an overstuffed brocade chair by the window. She motioned toward the matching sofa across from her. I took off my coat and extracted my notebook and pen from my bag and sat. "Shall we begin?"

She seemed not to want to waste any time, launched right into her story. "People say 'stormy,' and there's a kind of romance to it, you know?" she said, looking straight into my eyes. "But I don't think many people understood how dark, how dangerous those storms could be. At first even *I* thought his temper, his jealousy were signs of how much he loved me. But I was a stupid girl. What did I know?"

She told me how she met her husband. He was a wealthy surgeon who fell in love with her as she danced across the stage at the Met, was bold enough to send her a dozen white roses every day until she consented to dinner. Their engagement was brief, their wedding one of the social events of the year. She constantly heard how lucky she was to have found a man so in love, so devoted. She believed it, too, so it took her longer to notice the signs — or maybe she just ignored them — that there was something wrong with him, something frightening about him.

Slowly, the things she'd found so charming became oppressive. Things that were once romantic — the way he planned all their evenings, showed up unexpectedly in cities where she was performing — started to feel controlling. After a year, she began to wonder if they'd married too quickly. She felt trapped, oppressed, and her performance suffered.

"Maybe *trapped* wasn't the right word," she said, looking at me. "Because I could have left, really. I guess I liked the illusion as much as everyone else. And there were plenty of good times. I don't know . . ." She let her voice trail like a woman who'd spent a lot of time contemplating the past and still came up short on answers.

Then the children came, first Emiline, then Michael. By the time Alex, their third, was born, she had stopped dancing. Gene seemed more relaxed now that Elena was settled into her roles of wife and mother, with most of her independence and her life without him a memory. Not that the marriage was ever what she hoped it would be. Gene was an emotional and physical abuser, an angry controller demanding perfection from Elena at all times.

"But it just became normal," she said with a shrug. "He never touched the children. And I developed techniques for avoiding his rage — he was predictable in the things that set him off. I just *managed*."

"You never thought of leaving him?" I asked. It was hard for me to understand how a woman of such obvious strength would endure a marriage like that, but I knew enough to understand the psychology of an abused woman. There's a systematic erosion of self-esteem, a slow fading of personal power.

She laughed. "I thought about it every day. But the consequences of leaving just seemed too monolithic. In a weird way, I didn't have the energy — he robbed me of that."

Emiline was eight, Michael six, and Alex just three when she finally realized she was unable to *manage* anymore and decided to leave her husband.

"There was no event I could point to, exactly. It was more like I looked at myself in the mirror one day and I saw a woman I didn't recognize. I looked . . . haggard. My hair was brittle and going gray. There were black circles beneath my eyes. The corners of my mouth had started to turn down, as if I hadn't smiled in years. I couldn't remember the last time I'd laughed. I saw someone shelled out . . . empty. It wasn't so much that I was afraid for myself — I'd abandoned myself a long time ago. I was afraid of what kind of role model I had become for my children."

The divorce and custody battle that followed was textbook in its viciousness. But Elena attained full custody; Gene was allowed to have the children every third weekend. Elena had lobbied for supervised visitation only, but she lost that fight.

The weekend after their divorce was final and the uneasy custody arrangement had been settled, Gene picked up the kids for some time in the country. Elena would remember that he seemed relaxed and cordial, even regretful on their last encounter. He was taking the children to a rented cabin on the grounds of a resort in the Adirondack Mountains. Emiline loved birds and Michael was learning to horseback ride.

Alex just adored his father and couldn't wait for the canoe trip Gene had promised.

She never imagined that Emiline wouldn't see any birds or that Michael would not ride a horse, that Alex wouldn't get his canoe trip. She couldn't have conceived that Gene would take their children that weekend and kill each of them, suffocating them as they slept, then shoot himself in the head.

Elena's face had changed subtly as she recounted her story for me. The color drained and her eyes had grown distant. She suddenly looked gaunt, haunted. How could she ever be anything else? How could she ever have a moment of peace or joy again? I wondered. We were interrupted then by a small voice.

"Mommy?"

A little girl toddled in, unsteady on her white sneakers. Her mother leaned down and outstretched her arms; the little girl ran happily to her.

"Sorry, Elena," said a young woman, probably the nanny, as she came in behind the toddler.

"That's all right," Elena said, smiling, pulling her little girl into her lap and giving her a squeeze and a kiss before letting her go back to her nanny.

"I never would have believed that life

could continue," she said to me when the two had left the room. "In those dark, dark years that followed, I often wished that death would come for me, too. But it didn't. And I was too cowardly to chase after it. Then *life* came for me instead."

She told me how she met another man and fell in love again, how they married and had a daughter. She told me how she turned her life into a crusade to help women trapped in abusive marriages, offering counseling and, if necessary, a means of escape through an organization she founded called Follow the Signs.

After all of it I asked her, "Were there signs that you missed? Did you know on some level what your husband might be capable of doing?"

She looked at me and gave me a slow, thoughtful nod as if this were a question she'd asked herself a million times. "Because what he did was so unimaginable, I can't really say at the time that I did. But knowing what I know now . . . yes, there were signs."

She sighed. I didn't push her to go on. Then: "I think we can cast people in our lives, almost assign them roles and then stop seeing them as they truly are. And when we sense something truly dark, something monstrous, we can pull a veil over our eyes . . . because to acknowledge it is to take responsibility. Once you know, you have to do something about it. And that can be the most frightening thing of all."

Her words were ice water on my face. I felt every nerve ending in my body come alive. I knew all about pulling the veil away from my eyes. I just didn't want to believe that there might be more to see.

After the interview I took the train back downtown and walked from the Astor Place station to Jake's studio on Avenue A. I found him in the office, a small windowless room that stood to the side of his workspace (where I knew he hadn't done any sculpting in six months). The last thing he worked on, a huge Impressionist figure of a man, hulking and mysterious, brooding and strange, stood half-finished and accusatory beneath a bright light.

He heard me come in, got up from his computer, and walked over to me.

"What's up?" he asked, looking into my face in that way that he had, concerned and knowing.

"I want to know," I said.

"What?"

"I want to know what you've learned

about m— Max." I had almost said *my father,* but I caught it at the last second. He put his hands on my shoulders and looked hard into my eyes.

"Ridley, are you sure?"

"I'm sure," I said. I might have even meant it.

5

The Detroit Metro Airport was absolutely grisly. The walk from my gate past dirty walls and over worn, hideous carpet was endless; I swear it was at least a mile before I made it outside. Standing out in the bitter cold, I waited for what seemed like an eternity for the rental car shuttle as the wind whipped at my thin leather jacket, snaked up my sleeves, and chilled me to the bone. I felt nervous on top of it. I was shaken by the things Jake had told me yesterday and had a strange feeling of being watched. I hoped I was just being paranoid.

The area surrounding the airport was equally grim. I stared out the filthy shuttle-bus window at miles of flat gray landscape, black dead trees, and ground already dusted with snow though it was only early November. Because of the thick cloud cover, it was hard to imagine the sun ever shining down on this place.

I'd been here before as a child, though I barely remembered those infrequent visits to my grandparents when they were still alive. My father hated the place where he'd grown up with Max. They both hated it, remembered it as a rough industrial town grinded by poverty, crime, and bitter cold. He and Max spoke of their leaving as if it had been a prison break.

"Places like that breed a low expectation of what your life can be. That grayness leaks concrete into your skin. So many people never leave, never even think of leaving. Once you do, you can hardly stand to go back even to visit."

My father had told me that more than once, and driving out of the rental car lot, I could see it. The landscape alone was exhausting in its ugliness. As I pulled onto the highway, I thought about Max and Ben, how they never talked much about their childhoods.

"Not much to tell," my father would say. "I worked hard at school. I obeyed my parents. Then I left for Rutgers and never went back for more than a weekend at a time."

But really, there was a lot to tell. My father and Max grew up together, met each other while riding Big Wheels up and down the

70

block. Ben was shy, the good boy, loved and cherished by strict parents, an only child. Max was the wild one, always unkempt, always in trouble. My father told me he'd look out his window late at night sometimes, after eleven, and see Max riding his bike up and down the road beneath the yellow glow of the street lamps. At the time he was envious of Max's freedom, felt like a baby in his Howdy Doody pajamas, his homework done and packed in his bag for the next day, his clothes cleaned and pressed and laid out for him.

"I worshiped him," my father had said of Max. Max echoed the sentiment more times than I can remember.

If you've been with me from the beginning, you know what happened to Max. His father, an abuser and an alcoholic, beat Max's mother into a coma where she languished for weeks and finally died. Max's father was found guilty of murder, largely due to Max's testimony, was sentenced to life in prison, and died there years later. Rather than let Max become a ward of the state, my grandparents took him in. Max, who'd always been in trouble, who'd always done poorly in school, calmed down and excelled in my grandparents' care. They raised him as their own and somehow managed to help both boys through college on my grandfather's autoworker's salary.

This is a story I've known all my life. I've known that my wonderful and loving grandparents took Max in and saved him from God knows what fate. That Max was the wild boy, the rebel child. That my father was the good boy, the honor student. But that wasn't the truth. My truth was that *my* father was the abused child, that *my* grandfather murdered my grandmother and then later died in prison. That was my legacy, that's what I came from. When I think about it, I feel as if someone hit me in the head with a two-by-four.

I have always been the good girl with my pajamas on and my homework done . . . just like Ben. Except lately I've begun to wonder, what if I'm not like Ben at all? What if at the core of who I am, in the strands of my DNA, I'm more like Max? Even before I knew we were kin, I knew we were kindred spirits. What if nature wins out over nurture? Who am I then?

I thought about the conversation with Jake that had precipitated this unscheduled trip to Detroit. He'd had a lot to say about Max. None of it made much sense and I was seriously starting to doubt Jake's stability. The conversation ended with us screaming at each other like trailer trash and my storming out. I did a lot of storming out where Jake was concerned. Always had, even from the beginning. He had this way of being his most calm when I was at my most furious. And it never failed to throw me over the edge. Okay, so it was me who ended up screaming like an idiot last night in Jake's studio, while he sat in a state of patient empathy. He's lucky I didn't punch him, I hated him so much in that moment. But he was used to this. Jake's karma was to be the truth sayer, to seek out and bring to light the things that everyone else wanted to bury. It seemed to me that that was his cosmic role, in my life especially.

"I'm just not sure you're going to want to hear what I have to say," he'd predicted.

"I do," I'd said. "I really do."

Elena Jansen's denial had cost her the most precious things in her life — her children. There's always a cost for denial. How *high* a cost depends largely on the importance of the truth being ignored. You deny that you're unhappy in your chosen profession and the cost might be, say, migraine headaches. You deny signs that your abusive husband has a psychotic need to control you and he kills your children.

Not that I'm blaming Elena, of course. Of course *not.* What I'm saying is that our actions, our choices have consequences that are sometimes impossible to predict. But when our actions and choices are based on fear and denial . . . well, nothing good can come of that. Ever. I had learned this the hard way. Was still learning. That was why I had decided that if there was something to know about Max, I wanted to know it. Not that I believed that he'd come back from the dead.

"Okay, Ridley," Jake said with a sigh. "As you know, after the feds cleared your father and found Esme Gray to have too small and ambiguous a role to prosecute for Project Rescue on anything but possible conspiracy charges, they decided to close the case," Jake began. "All the major players — Max, Alexander Harriman namely — were dead. Everyone else who might have been involved in the shadow side of the organization was a ghost. There were no records. Project Rescue was a labyrinth of dark connections, impossible to navigate."

"I know all this," I told him, sitting on one of Jake's work chairs.

He nodded. "Those were hard days for me, Ridley."

"I know," I said softly, remembering. I

thought maybe I hadn't been there for him like I could have been, but the truth was that I didn't have a whole lot to give on the subject; I wasn't exactly standing on solid ground myself.

"I just couldn't get past it," he said. "I just couldn't accept that there were things about my past that I'd never know. That the people responsible for fucking with so many lives would never face any consequences. It ate at me."

This was the point where Jake disappeared from the relationship, mentally and emotionally. It was like being in love with an addict. He could never be present because he was always jonesing, always fidgeting and preoccupied with his next fix.

"So I went to see Esme Gray."

I felt a lump in my throat. I used to love Esme like a mother; now the thought of her made my stomach clench.

"What? When?"

Esme had been briefly taken into custody around the same time Zack — her son, my ex-boyfriend — had been. The conditions of her release were still unknown to me. She never stood trial for anything involving Project Rescue, I knew that much. I also knew that she'd retired from nursing. (Zack, though he was never prosecuted for his role in Project Rescue, stood trial, was found guilty, and is serving ten years in a state penitentiary for attempted murder — the attempted murder of me and Jake, by the way. But that's another story. Even after all that he has done to us, it's still hard to think of him in prison, of what has become of his young and promising life. He blames me, of course, and has told me so in numerous disturbing letters that I can't keep myself from opening.)

"I looked in your address book and found out where she lived. I followed her around for a couple of days. I broke into her house and was waiting for her when she came home. I wanted her afraid and off guard when I approached her," he said. "But she wasn't. It was like she'd been expecting me."

A year ago we'd talked about Esme as being the last remaining person who might know what had happened to Jake when he was a child, other than my father (who denied all knowledge). I knew someday he'd pursue that.

"Why didn't you tell me this before?"

"I know you've been trying to forget. I can't blame you for that."

I nodded, waited for him to go on.

"I was rough with her — not violent, but loud. I wanted her to think I'd come unhinged. But she stayed calm, sat down on the sofa and said, 'After the kind of men I've been associated with, you think I'm afraid of a punk like you? You might as well cut the shit and sit down if you want to talk.' "

I had to smile to myself. On the outside, Esme looked like everybody's mom: pretty and roundish with a honey-colored bob and glittering blue eyes. She was pink like a peach. But at her core, she was metal. When we were all kids — Ace, Zack, and me — she, along with my mother, never had to yell or threaten; just a look and all bad behavior ceased.

"She told me if I cared about you, I'd give up on finding out what happened to me. She told me I should start my own family and move forward. She said, 'If you continue to insist on dredging up the past, you might find things you can't put back to rest.' "

It was an echo of something she'd said to me once and it made me go cold inside. I didn't say anything, just listened as he recounted his conversation with Esme.

"She said to me, 'Nobody knows what happened to you, Jake. Nobody knows who took you after you were abducted by Project Rescue and why you wound up abandoned by the system. Why do *you* need to know so badly? Do you want to cast someone as the villain in your life? Do you want to prove to someone that you were a good boy who didn't deserve the awful things that happened to you? Do you want *revenge?*' "

He paused here a second and looked above my head. She'd gotten to him, I could see that — hit him dead center. She'd always been an uncanny diviner of motives.

He went on: "She sounded tough, sure of herself. But I started to realize something while she was talking to me. Her hands were shaking and there was sweat on her forehead. She was afraid. She was afraid of something or someone, and it definitely wasn't me. She knew I wasn't capable of hurting her."

I leaned forward on my seat. "Did you ask her what was frightening her?"

"Of course. She said, 'I've made a deal with the devil, Mr. Jacobsen. And he'll be waiting for me when I die. I'm afraid all the time. Afraid I'll get hit by a car, have a heart attack and have to face him before I've atoned for my sins. The things I've done . . . you couldn't have convinced me they were wrong at the time. But now I see the damage we caused.' "

Jake shook his head here, stood up. "But

that wasn't it," he told me. "It wasn't a spiritual fear. She was afraid of some clear and present danger. I told her I thought as much. I told her she could start atoning for her sins right now by telling me what I wanted to know.

"I kept at her, asked her, 'What still scares you? What are you still hiding? Everyone associated with Project Rescue is dead and buried, Esme.' "

When she didn't answer him, Jake explained, that's when an idea struck him.

" 'He's alive, isn't he?' I asked her, not even believing it as I said it. 'Max Smiley. He's still alive.'

"She looked at me like I'd slapped her. Her face went paper white. She screamed at me to get out, told me I was crazy, that she'd call the police. She wasn't just scared; she was *terrified.* I tried to calm her down but she was freaking. 'You idiot,' she screamed at me. 'If you know what's good for you, you'll take Ridley and get as far away from here as you can. Change your names and disappear. And don't come near me again.' "

"Jesus," I said.

"That's when I started to suspect that Max was still alive."

"Jake," I said with a light laugh. "Esme's

79

obviously come unglued. She's sick with guilt."

"No. Well, maybe. But not only that. You didn't see her. She was panicked when I talked about Max."

"Okay. But telling you to take me away, to change our names and disappear? Those don't sound like the words of a well woman."

"They're the words of a frightened woman. And with the things I've learned since then, Ridley, I think she had good reason for saying what she did."

He sat next to me and I leaned away from him. There was something bright in his eyes, a tension to his bearing. I felt my heart start to thump. I didn't know if I was afraid of what he was saying, or afraid of him. It sounded to me as if Esme had lost it. And if he believed her, did that mean he'd lost it, too?

"Max is dead," I said again.

"Then how are you explaining those pictures to yourself?" He said this in a tone of smug condescension. In the past, he'd accused me of being more comfortable in a state of denial than I was in reality (which never failed to throw me off the deep end, since it was my favorite criticism of my mother). I heard the echo of that judgment in his voice.

"There's nothing to explain," I said, raising my voice a little. "Those pictures were out of focus. That man — he could have been *anyone.*"

He looked at me hard but I couldn't read his expression. It could have been disappointment, disbelief.

"Come. *On,*" I said to him, yelling now. I stood up and started moving toward the door. "I thought you had something real to tell me, Jake. This is just more insane speculation on your part. More craziness. *What* are you trying to do to me?"

He looked at me sadly, stood, and followed me out into the loft space. "I'm sorry, Ridley."

"You're *not* sorry!" I screamed. I took a deep breath and lowered my voice. "You just want me to be as miserable and obsessed as you are. You want me trapped with you in a past that neither one of us can ever change no matter how badly we want to. It's not fair. I don't want to be here with you anymore."

He didn't react, though I could see the pain in his eyes. He walked back into his office for a second, returned with a file folder.

"Just read this stuff, Ridley. I'm not going to say another word about any of this to you . . . ever again. Just read my research and come to your own conclusions. Call me when you're ready."

I wanted to throw the file at him. I wanted to throw myself at him and punch him as hard as I could a thousand times. I wanted to take him in my arms, comfort him and be comforted by him. Instead of any of these options, I exited the loft in silence. I could have left him and the file behind and never looked back. But, of course, you know me better than that by now. Once we've started on the road toward the truth, there's no turning back. The Universe doesn't like secrets.

Following the directions I'd printed out from MapQuest, I pulled off the highway and onto a smaller main drag that led past strip malls and office buildings. This suburb of Detroit seemed like a parade of prefab buildings, indistinguishable from every other American 'burb: Chick-Fil-A and Wal-Mart, Taco Bell and Home Depot, the mandatory Starbucks. Peppered among the chains, small run-down independent stores — a butcher, a mechanic's garage, a consignment shop — stood like rebel soldiers protesting the encroachment of the corporate giants. They seemed dilapidated and near defeat. I noticed that there were no sidewalks, though I could see houses on the back streets. I drove for miles and didn't see one person walking. And people think New York City is scary.

The area seemed to improve after a while and started to look familiar as I neared my grandparents' old neighborhood. I knew that their one-story ranch house, where my father and later Max had been raised, had been purchased by a young professional couple and torn down, replaced by a much larger, brand-new home. I turned onto their old street, narrowly avoiding a side-impact collision that would have been completely my fault. (I'm the world's worst driver, partially from inexperience and partially from my mind's tendency to wander. Many New Yorkers, most maybe, don't drive — we walk or we *ride.* We take the subways or — too often in my case — hail cabs. These are activities where mind-wandering is perfectly acceptable, even preferable. Driving, I've noticed, requires more focused attention.)

I looked for my grandparents' lot on the street, but it seemed that most of the homes had recently been erected. I couldn't remember the street number nor could I pick it out based on any of the nebulous memories I had. The old ranch houses that had once characterized the neighborhood were now mostly gone, except for a few that looked dwarfed and gray among the gleaming new two-stories. At the end of the street, I found the address I was looking for: 314 Wildwood Lane. It was easily the oldest and most run-down house on the street, with an old Chevy up on blocks in the driveway. I pulled along the side of the lawn and came to a stop, felt my heart start to hammer.

You're probably wondering, What the hell is she doing in a Detroit suburb? It was a question I asked myself as I sat in the rented Land Rover, heat blasting. I was starting to wonder if I was as nuts as Jake, in my own way.

I'd left Jake's loft filled with fury, but on the train ride home, I felt the black fingers of depression tugging at me. I'd been fighting them off for a year, but the blackness always loomed, threatening to take me over. I knew if I stopped moving and turned around to see its face, it would eat me alive. My anger faded, leaving a killer headache in its wake.

I didn't even take my coat off after I entered my apartment. I just sat at the dining-room table (a mammoth metal thing Jake had made and which I hated more with each passing day for its cold and utterly unwelcoming aura) and flipped open the file, which was crammed with newspaper articles, documents, and pages of handwritten notes in what I recognized as Jake's nearly illegible scrawl.

At first glance it seemed like a jumble of unconnected pieces of information, most of which was already known to me. I noticed a copy of the medical examiner's report from the night Max died; I flipped through the stapled pages, but nothing seemed out of the ordinary to me (not that I'd ever seen an actual medical examiner's report). Jake had circled the estimated time of death, but it seemed consistent with what I knew about that night. I saw that Esme Gray had identified the body. This gave me pause. I had always believed that my father had been the one to ID the body. Max's face was ruined, I remember him telling me; he wasn't wearing a seat belt and had gone through the windshield. Jake had circled Esme's name but I couldn't determine why.

There were a few articles from the days following Max's death reporting the incident, as well as some larger features about Max and his philanthropy, about his foundation being established to fund programs that aided battered women and abused children, about his incredibly successful career as a real-estate developer. I flipped through these without really reading Jake's notes in the margins — the ones I glanced at seemed vague and somewhat weird, paranoid. For example, next to a sentence that lauded Max's charity work, Jake had written: *Lies!*

The next grouping of articles seemed to have no relationship to Max at all; they were various crime stories about the tristate area and from around the world. The London *Times* reported on a frightening trend of young women in Eastern Europe disappearing from nightclubs and raves, never to be heard from again. The *Guardian* reported on the investigation of the murder of a young black woman whose torso was found floating in a canal. Police were making tentative connections between the young woman, who was of African Caribbean descent, and the ritual killings of a young boy and a prostitute earlier in the year, whose dismembered bodies were found in close proximity. A printout from the BBC website reported on the trafficking of women and children out of Albania and their subsequent torture and sexual slavery. The whole enterprise was nearly impossible to prevent or prosecute because of the Albanian and Italian police forces' collusion with organized crime and the unwillingness of the women who had been rescued to identify their captors. There were pictures of an Albanian Mafia speedboat being intercepted by police in the Adriatic Sea, some photos of pretty, sad-faced women standing before a judge, some blurry images of known mobsters at a table in a café.

There were several articles from the *New York Times* related to organized crime, to body parts found in the East River, a murder on the Upper West Side, some missing young women. At the time, I didn't see anything that connected them. Ugly news about an ugly world — what else was new? I realize now that I came to that file wanting it to prove that Jake had grown unstable, that he was grasping at straws. And I saw what I wanted to see: nothing. I released a sigh and realized that I was sweating. I shifted off my coat and closed my eyes. When I opened them again the room swam with my fatigue; I decided to close the file and go to bed. As I flipped the folder closed, a single article floated out. I picked it up off the floor, registered the date and region.

I opened the file again and saw that it came from a grouping of *Detroit Register* articles obviously printed from microfiche. They were the articles written about Max's mother's murder and the trial of his father. There were some grisly crime-scene photos that I would have rather not seen; I couldn't believe that they'd actually been published in a newspaper.

I looked at the article in my hand. The headline read VICTIM'S NEPHEW PROTESTS GUILTY VERDICT.

I sat in the rental car for a few minutes until I saw a light snow start to fall. I turned off the engine and stepped out into the bitter cold. I watched my breath cloud and I pulled my coat close around me. Then I walked up the short drive toward the stout brown house, listening to the gravel crunch beneath my feet. No interior lights burned that I could see. I glanced at my watch and realized that anyone who might live there was probably still at work.

According to the *Register,* Max's cousin had come forward after Race Smiley's conviction to say that he'd seen another man there the night of Lana's murder. He claimed not to have come forward earlier because he thought he'd been spotted and he was afraid for himself and his family. The police disbelieved the boy and found no evidence to corroborate the story. They said he might just be trying to help his uncle. The article had fired me up for a couple of reasons. First of all, no one had ever mentioned this cousin of Max's, though he'd apparently grown up on the same street as Max and Ben. I found that odd and intriguing. And the idea that maybe my grandfather wasn't a murderer after all, that he had been wrongly accused and convicted, gave me some weird kind of hope. Maybe the place from which I'd come wasn't as dark and joyless as a tar pit.

I'd used the Internet to search for Nick Smiley and found that he was still living in his childhood home. The phone number was listed but I couldn't bring myself to call. What would I say? *Hi, I'm Ridley, your second cousin. How's it going? So, about the night my grandmother was beaten into a coma . . .*

My father always says that people get into trouble when they have too much money and too much time on their hands. If I had a nine-to-five job where I was accountable to someone for my days or if I struggled to make ends meet, I might not have been able to do what I did. But maybe it was more than just opportunity, a lack of anything better to do. There was and always had been a drive within me to know the truth of things. That's what had caused all the trouble in my recent life. I thought about that as I booked myself on the next flight to Detroit.

"What do you want?"

A bulky, bearded man had appeared from the side of the house. One word summed him up: menacing. He had a heavy brow and deep-set dark eyes. His thin line of a mouth seemed as though it had never smiled or spoken a kind word. Clad in a thickly lined flannel shirt and brown corduroy pants, he looked squared-off, ready for a fight.

"I'm looking for Nicholas Smiley," I said, fighting an urge I had to run back to the Land Rover and drive away as fast as possible, tires screeching up the street.

"What do you want?" he repeated.

What did I want? A good question.

I figured there was no use softening the blow with a guy like this; he looked as if he could take a punch and might even like it. "I want to talk about the night Lana Smiley died."

He jerked and stepped back as if I'd thrown a stone at him.

"Get off my property," he said. He didn't advance or retreat farther, so I held my ground. We stared at each other while I tried to think of something to say that might convince him to talk to me. I didn't come up with anything.

"I can't," I said finally. "I need to know what you saw that night. And I'm not leaving until you tell me." I pulled back my shoulders and stuck out my chin. It was a sad display of bravado since I think we both knew that if he'd advanced toward me, I would have run screaming for my car. Maybe that's why he seemed to soften up just a bit, his shoulders sagging, his eyes on the driveway.

"Ancient history," he said. "They're all dead now."

"Yes," I said. "Lana, Race, and Max . . . they're all gone. But I'm still here and *I* need to know what you saw that night."

He let out a short, unpleasant laugh. "Well, who the fuck are *you?*"

"I'm Max's daughter." I almost choked on those words; they tasted so much like a lie on my tongue. He didn't say anything, just turned his dark, suspicious eyes on me. I couldn't tell if he didn't believe me or if he just didn't care. I felt him examining me, looking for signs of Max in my face. A blizzard of snowflakes had collected in his hair and the beard that covered most of his face.

"Let the dead lie, girl," he said, and

turned away from me.

I raised my voice and called after him. "You said you saw someone else kill Lana. You said Race wasn't even home when she died. If that was true, why did you wait until after he was convicted to say anything?"

He stopped in his tracks but he didn't turn around.

"Please," I said more quietly. "I need to know what happened that night. They're all dead now, Mr. Smiley. What harm could it do to tell me the truth?"

He turned around to look at me, then glanced uneasily up and down the street. There was no one about, no one standing in a window watching. I was really feeling the cold work its way into my center; I started to shiver. Then something in his face went from angry to sad. I wasn't sure what changed his mind about talking to me; to this day, I still don't know. Maybe I looked as pathetic and desperate as I felt. Maybe he didn't want me to make a scene in his driveway. But he began walking toward the house and motioned for me to follow. Then it was my turn to change my mind. Maybe he was just luring me into his house to kill me, or tie me up in his basement, or something equally terrifying. I hesitated as he disappeared around the side of the house.

Finally, curiosity got the better of me. I hurried after him.

"People know I'm here," I said as I caught up to him. Unfortunately, this was a complete lie. The truth was no one even knew I was in Detroit. If I were to go missing, how long would it take people to notice I was gone, to track me here?

Tall hedges separated his property from his neighbor's; round concrete blocks acted as a path. He walked through a side door that led into a neat kitchen that looked as if it hadn't been updated in decades. I followed him over the threshold and shut the door behind me, but kept my hand on the knob. He walked over to the sink and filled a kettle with water, placed it on the stove, and turned on the burner.

"You gonna sit?" he asked me.

"No," I said. "I'd rather stand." I was nervous.

"I never knew Max had a daughter," he said, his back to me as he stared out a window over the sink.

"I didn't know until last year, after he died. It's a long story. I was raised by other people. In fact, you probably know the man who raised me, Benjamin Jones."

He nodded slowly, seemed to take in the information. "Bennie Jones. We came up together right on this street. He was a good kid. Haven't seen him in years. Decades."

We were silent a minute. I could hear the water in the kettle, little clinks in the metal pot as it changed temperature. I realized it wasn't much warmer in the house than it had been outside. I looked around at the old wallpaper patterned with little cornices overflowing with fruit, the yellowed Formica countertops, the green tiled floor.

"Tea?" he asked. I was surprised by the civility of his offer.

"Sure," I said. "Thanks."

He moved to get some cups out of the cupboard. He tossed a look behind him as he took teabags out from a white ceramic canister. "I'm not gonna hurt you. You might as well sit."

I nodded and felt silly. I moved toward the kitchen's round wood table, pulled out a chair, and sat down. It was wobbly and uncomfortable but I stayed seated just to be polite. He came to the table and sat across from me, bringing the tea with him. I took the cup he offered gratefully and warmed my hands on it.

"This is a bad idea," he said, shaking his head. My heart sank; it looked as if he might be clamming up on me. His face had gone still. He'd pressed his mouth back into a thin line. I gave him an understanding smile. I wasn't sure what to say to convince him to talk, so I said nothing.

"You seem like a nice girl," he said, holding my eyes briefly. "I don't want . . ." He let his voice trail off and didn't pick up the sentence again. I closed my eyes for a second, drew in a breath, and said the only thing I could think of.

"Please."

He looked at me sadly. Gave me a quick nod.

"I haven't thought about that night in a long time," he told me, but for some reason I didn't believe him. I suspected he'd thought about that night a lot, and maybe this was the first time in years he'd been able to talk about it. Maybe he *needed* to talk about it. Maybe that's why he changed his mind.

" 'Course, it's not the kind of thing you forget, either. It stays with you, even when it's not on your mind directly. I busted an arm at work about five years ago, been on disability ever since. The arm healed but it's never been the same. Some things are like that. After they happen, nothing's right again." I could definitely relate to that.

He didn't seem quite as menacing as he had on first glance. He seemed softer and kinder now, more beaten down than angry. He didn't say anything else for a minute, just stared into his cup. I listened to the clock ticking above the sink and waited. Finally:

"We'd been over there, at Race and Lana's, for supper. We always spent the holidays together," he said, looking at the tabletop. His voice seemed hoarse, as if it had been a while since he'd used it so much. I wondered if he'd feel unburdened by the telling of this. Or if it would be like exhuming a body, an unholy dredging of something better left to rest.

It struck me again, as it had when I first read the article, that I had never heard of Nicholas Smiley or his family. Neither Max, my father, nor my grandparents had ever mentioned this cousin who'd apparently grown up with Max and Ben, living just down the street. I wondered if there was any end to the layers of secrets and lies.

"It hadn't been a very good night," he said, looking at me shyly. "Race didn't show up for dinner and Lana was drunk and mad as hell. Ranting about her shit life."

He looked down at his teacup again and I could see that his hand was shaking just slightly. For some reason, the sight of that made my heart rate rise.

"Race was a bastard. Beat the crap out of Lana and Max, ran around on her. Everyone knew it." He spoke in short, quick-fire sentences, as if he had to get the words out before a timer went off. But there was something rhythmic, almost metered, about the way he spoke. I felt hypnotized.

He must have seen something on my face. Any good interviewer knows to keep judgment out of her voice, and I'd always been okay at that. It was keeping it off my face that gave me trouble.

"I don't know why no one ever did anything," he said, as though I'd asked the question I'd been thinking. "Been plenty of years to regret that. I guess in those days you just didn't interfere between a man and his family."

I nodded my understanding and he went on.

"Anyway, we left early. Lana had, like I said, been ranting and Max had barely said a word the whole night. He got that way sometimes, like he was trying to be invisible. Not that I blamed him; it was like living in the valley between two active volcanoes. You never knew which one of them was gonna blow."

"Lana was abusive to Max as well?"

"Oh, yeah," he said. "She got her licks in."

Max had always spoken of his mother as if she were the Madonna and Mother Teresa wrapped into one. I'd heard him talk only of her beauty, of her kindness, of her strength.

"You look a lot like her. Did you know that?" Nicholas said to me.

"No," I said. "I didn't." I hadn't wanted that information, didn't even know what to do with it. Suddenly I regretted coming.

He shrugged. "Compared to Race, she wasn't so bad. But that kid never knew where it was coming from. Never knew if he was going to get stroked or slapped."

I didn't know what to say, thinking about this abused little boy who was not my uncle but my father. I waited for emotion to bloom in my chest, but instead it felt as if it was filled with lead, heavy and numb. I looked into my teacup and saw that the milk had curdled slightly.

"Max and I got walkie-talkies that year. But in my parents' rush to get out of there, we'd left mine under the tree by mistake. I wanted it, couldn't think or talk about anything else, drove my parents crazy. Tomorrow, they promised. But to a kid tomorrow seems like forever. I waited for them to go to bed, then I pulled on my coat and boots and snuck out of the house."

I could picture it. The block dark, but illuminated by Christmas lights on the houses and from the trees glimmering inside, snow on the ground. I could see him trundling up the street in his coat and pajamas. I could smell the cold winter air, hear the cars on the busy road that ran perpendicular to their block.

"If Max was sixteen that year, I was fourteen. But Max was huge for his age. Not quite as big as Uncle Race but getting there. I figured Race wouldn't be pushing Max around much longer. Still I looked for Race's car in the driveway. He been home, I'd have gone right back to my house."

I could tell he was back there on that night; his eyes had taken on a kind of shine and he looked right through me. I kept quiet.

"I remember that the air seemed different, like the night already knew something bad had happened. I didn't go to the door. I went to Max's bedroom window, but he wasn't in there. I could hear the television up loud, so I went around to the living-room window."

He stopped and released a sigh, as if the memory still frightened him all these years later. He put his head in his hands, then lifted it again. "That's where I saw Aunt

Lana," he said. "I only recognized her by the outfit she'd had on at dinner. Her face was a pulp; her clothes were soaked with blood."

"But Race wasn't there?" I asked.

He looked up at me. "I told you, his car wasn't in the drive."

"He could have come home, killed her, and left again," I said. "He could have been parked on the street."

"No," he answered.

"How can you be sure?"

He looked at me with something like pity in his eyes. I guess I sounded as desperate as I was feeling at that moment.

"I saw him standing over her. There was blood on his fists, on his shirt, and on his face. His eyes were glazed over and he was smiling, breathing hard like a prizefighter."

"Who?" I asked him, horrified.

He shook his head at me and tears fell down his cheeks and into his beard. He shook his head again and opened his mouth but no words came out.

"Who?" I asked again, leaning forward in my chair.

"Max," he whispered.

I couldn't have been more shocked or devastated if he'd hit me in the head with a crowbar. I wished he had; I wished I could just pass out and get amnesia, forget I ever heard anything he'd told me. I hated myself for being so stubborn and curious and for being there at all. I was having trouble getting a full breath of air.

"No," I said. "You were so young. It was dark and you were terrified by seeing your aunt like that."

He stared at me. "I know what I saw," he said softly. "Won't ever forget."

"Then why didn't you say anything? You let an innocent man die in jail," I said.

"He turned around and saw me in the window. He wasn't the Max I knew. He was . . . a monster. Those dead, empty eyes on me — I knew if I ever breathed a word, he'd rip me in two. I ran and waited all night for that devil to come and turn *my* face into hamburger. But he didn't. The next day Race was arrested; Lana died a few weeks later in her coma. Max went to live with Bennie's parents."

"Why didn't he come live with you? You were his only family."

"My parents were barely making it. With me and my three sisters, they couldn't afford another kid. As it is, they died in debt, a debt *I'm* still paying." He looked around him. "I'm barely holding on to this house."

He cast his eyes to the floor.

"I've never even heard of you," I said angrily. I hated him for what he'd told me and was looking for reasons he could be lying or wrong or just crazy. "Neither Max or Ben has ever spoken of you or your family."

"They judged us for not taking Max in. Nothing was ever said, but from that point on, we didn't have much to do with Max."

I looked hard at his face. I could see, at least, that he believed what he was telling me. The fear and sadness, the ugliness of his memories made a home in his face.

"But it wasn't the money, not really," I said. "That wasn't why they didn't take him in, was it?"

Nicholas shook his head.

"You told your parents what you saw that night. And they believed you."

"Yes," he said. "That's right."

"But no one said anything as Race was arrested and stood trial. You were all so terrified of a sixteen-year-old boy?"

"We waited," he said, clearing his throat. "Hoped that Race would be found innocent. That we'd never have to come forward with what we knew. Even when Race was convicted, my parents still didn't want me to go forward."

"Because they were afraid of Max?"

Nicholas released another sigh. "No, it wasn't that. I think they just didn't want Max to go to prison. Maybe guilt that they hadn't stepped in earlier to stop some of the violence in that house. And, well, Race might have been innocent of that murder, but in a lot of ways he was guiltier than Max. That kid was raised with violence; he didn't even know another way. My parents thought that maybe he just didn't know his own strength that night. That a lifetime of suffering and regret was punishment enough."

"But you didn't think so?"

"He wasn't sorry," said Nicholas, holding my eyes. "I could tell by the way he looked at me. He was so sad-faced for everyone else. But when we were alone, he turned those eyes on me and I knew. He killed his mother, accused and then testified against his father. Effectively, he killed them both. And I don't think he lost a night's sleep over it."

I tried to reconcile this version of Max with the man I knew. The child Nick Smiley described was psychotic — a murderer and a liar, a scheming manipulator. I had never seen *anything* in Max that hinted of that. Never.

"That's why you came forward finally?

Because you didn't think he was sorry?"

"I don't know that you'd call what I did coming forward. It was a half-assed attempt to undo one of many wrongs that had been done that night and all the nights leading up to it. I was racked with guilt, couldn't sleep and couldn't eat. Finally my parents took me to the police station and I told the cops that I saw someone else there that night. I told them about the walkie-talkies, that I hadn't seen Race's car, and that there was another man there, a man I'd never seen before. I never told them about Max."

He took a sip of his tea, which I knew from my own cup was stone-cold by now.

"I told them I hadn't come forward because I was afraid this stranger I made up would come and kill me and my family, too."

"They didn't believe you?"

He shook his head. "There was nothing to show that anyone else but Race had been there. No one else saw a strange car or saw anyone come or go other than Race later that night. They told me I'd just had a nightmare. I mean, they weren't going to reopen a case that was long closed, the accused tried and convicted, because of the ramblings of a kid. But someone in the station leaked the story and an article ran in the paper the next day.

"That night I woke up to rocks being thrown at my window. I looked out on the street and saw Max standing there. He had a crowbar in his hand. He just stood there under the streetlight and I could see those eyes. He knew I was a chicken — hell, he'd been pushing me around since we were in diapers. I never said another word."

I sat in silence. He seemed like an honest man, simple and down-to-earth. The kitchen was neat and clean, like any working-class suburban kitchen — nothing fancy but everything in decent shape. His story had just enough detail but not too much flourish. It had the ring of truth — I could see that he believed the things he'd said, that it still haunted him. I didn't know what to say. I must have just stared at him with my horror and disbelief because he shifted uncomfortably beneath my gaze.

"I told you to let the dead lie," he said. "You should have listened."

Nobody likes a know-it-all.

6

My uncle Max (of course, he'll always be that in my mind) was a great bear of a man — big in stature with a heart and a personality to match. He was an amusement park, a toy store, an ice-cream parlor. Occasionally, my parents would travel and have Ace and me stay with him (and a nanny, of course, because Max was not one for tying shoes and making grilled-cheese sandwiches). Those memories are among the happiest of my childhood. I never saw him without a smile on his face. His arms were always filled with gifts, his pockets full of money or candy or small surprises.

At least these are my memories of him. These days, though, I distrust my recollection of the past — not the actual events, necessarily, but the layers and nuances that clearly had eluded me. So much of my life was built on a foundation of lies that my past seems like a dark fairy tale — pretty on the surface but with a terrible black under-current. There were monsters under my bed and I was too naive to even fear the dark.

On the plane back to New York, I searched my memories for fissures, for the spaces through which the "real" Max might show himself, this psychotic and abused young man who killed his mother and framed his father and terrorized his young cousin into silence. The "real" Max, my father.

I thought about the last conversation I had with him.

It was nearing the end of my parents' annual Christmas Eve party. My father had led a group out for the inevitable neighborhood candlelight stroll, and my mother was furiously scrubbing pots in the kitchen, rebuffing all of my attempts to help her with the usual implication that no one could do it the way she could. Whatever. I wandered into the front room in search of more cookies and found my uncle Max sitting by himself in the dim light of the room before our gigantic Christmas tree. That's one of my favorite things in the world, the sight of a lit Christmas tree in a darkened room. I plopped myself down next to him on the couch and he threw an arm around my shoulder, balancing a glass of bourbon on his knee with his free hand.

"What's up, Uncle Max?"

"Not much, kid. Nice party."

"Yeah."

We sat like that in a companionable silence for a while until something made me look up at him. He was crying, not making a sound, thin lines of tears streaming down his face. His expression was almost blank in its hopeless sadness. I think I just stared at him in shock. I grabbed his big bear-claw hand in both of mine.

"What is it, Uncle Max?" I whispered, as if afraid that someone would find him like this, his true face exposed to the world. I wanted to protect him.

"It's all coming back on me, Ridley."

"What is?"

"All the good I tried to do. I fucked it up. Man, I fucked it up so bad." There was a shake in his voice.

I shook my head. I was thinking, He's drunk. He's just drunk. But he grabbed me then by both of my shoulders, not hard but passionately. His eyes were bright and clear in his desperation.

"You're happy, right, Ridley? You grew up loved, safe. Right?"

"Yes, Uncle Max. Of course," I said, wanting so badly to reassure him, though I was uncertain why my happiness meant so much to him at that moment. He nodded and loosened his grip on me but still looked at me dead in the eye. "Ridley," he said, "you might be the only good I've ever done."

"What's going on? Max?" We both turned to see my father standing in the doorway. He was just a black form surrounded by light and his voice sounded odd. Something foreign had crept into him. Max's whole body seemed to stiffen, and he released me as if I'd burned his hands.

"Max, let's talk," said my father, and Max rose. I followed him through the doorway and my father placed a hand on my shoulder. Max continued and walked through the French doors that led to my father's study. His shoulders sagged and his head was down, but he turned to give me a smile before he disappeared behind the closing doors.

"What's wrong with him?" I asked my father.

"Don't worry, lullaby," he said with a forced lightness. "Uncle Max has had a bit too much to drink. He's got a lot of demons; sometimes the bourbon lets them loose."

"But what was he talking about?" I asked stubbornly, having the sense that I was being shut out of something important.

"Ridley," said my father, too sternly. He

caught himself and softened his tone. "Really, honey, don't worry about Max. It's the bourbon talking."

He walked away from me and disappeared behind his study doors. I hovered there a minute, heard the rumbling of their voices behind the oak. I knew the impossibility of listening at those thick doors; I'd tried it many times as a kid. Plus, I ran into my favorite aunt in the hallway. You remember her, Auntie Denial. She wrapped her arms around me and whispered comforting sentiments: *Just the bourbon. Just Max's demons talking. You know Max. Tomorrow he'll be fine.* As fragile as she is, she's powerful when you cooperate with her, when you let her spin her web around you. Yes, as long as you don't look her in the face, she'll wrap you in a cocoon. It's safe and warm in there. So much nicer than the alternative.

That's the last time I saw my uncle Max. His face still wet with tears and flushed with bourbon, his sad smile, his final words to me. *Ridley, you might be the only good I've ever done.*

Those words had taken on different meanings for me with every new thing I'd learned about Max. They meant one thing when I thought he was just my sad uncle whom I had loved and who had died later that night.

They meant another when I found out he was my father, a man who'd made so many awful mistakes, who'd failed me in so many ways. I wondered what they'd mean to me at the end of the road I found myself on now. I flashed on the articles in Jake's files — those grisly crimes, those missing women, children and girls abducted from nightclubs and sold into prostitution. Why had he saved those articles? What did it have to do with Max? And why was the FBI still interested in him?

The man next to me snored softly, his head leaning at an awkward angle against the airplane window. The girl across the aisle read a Lee Child novel. Normal people leading normal lives. Maybe. They probably thought the same of me.

I found the harder I reached for my memories of Max, the more vague and nebulous they became. One thing was certain, though: If Nick Smiley was right, if Max was who Nick believed him to be, then I had never met that man. He'd been so well-hidden behind a mask that I'd never even caught a glance. I'd seen only a sliver of the man, the part of himself he'd allowed me to see.

In the cab on the way home from La Guardia, I pulled the cell phone from my bag. Yes, I'd kept my cell phone in spite of my repeated threats to get rid of it. You might remember my disdain for the things (I hate them even more than I do digital cameras). Cell phones are just another excuse for people to not be present, another reason for them to be even ruder and more unthinking than they normally are. But what can I say? I got hooked on the convenience.

There were three calls from Jake, according to the log, but no messages. I was aching to call someone. Not Jake; I didn't want to fan the flame of his obsession. I couldn't call Ace or my father; neither of them would want to hear the questions I had to ask (though my father was the most logical person to go to). I hadn't had a real conversation with my mother in over a year. I leaned my head back against the vinyl seat and watched the glow of red taillights and white headlamps blur in the darkness.

Then the phone, still in my hand, started to ring. I didn't recognize the number on the caller ID, but the 917 exchange told me it was a wireless phone. I picked up out of sheer loneliness.

"Detroit's nice this time of year," said a low male voice when I answered. "If you like shitholes."

"Who is this?" I said, my stomach clenching. Nobody knew I'd been to Detroit. I'd told no one, took off that morning, paid a ridiculous sum for a round-trip same-day ticket.

"Let me guess. The pictures got to you, right? Then I suppose you talked to your boyfriend. Has anyone ever told you that you have an investigative mind? You might have missed your calling."

"Agent Grace?" I said, annoyance replacing trepidation, a feeling that was beginning to characterize our encounters.

"So what did Nick Smiley tell you?"

"That Max was a psychopath," I answered, figuring he probably already knew that much. "A killer."

"Do you believe him?"

"I don't know what to believe anymore," I said.

"An interesting fact about Nick Smiley: Did he tell you that he is a diagnosed paranoid schizophrenic who has been doped up on lithium for the last twenty years on and off?"

"No," I said. "He failed to mention that." Something like relief made the muscles in my shoulders relax a bit.

"Doesn't make him a liar. Just makes his version of the truth questionable."

Isn't that what the truth comes down to? An agreement of variations? Think about your last family drama or the last fight you had with your spouse. What really happened? Who said what and when? Who was the instigator and who was the reactor? Is there an absolute truth, one that exists separately from the personal variations? Maybe. But maybe not. Quantum physics tells us that life is a series of possibilities existing side by side in any given moment; it is our choices that create our version of reality. Nick Smiley has chosen his memory of Max. I have chosen mine. Who's right? But maybe the truth is that Max was a shape shifter, becoming what he needed to be to control whatever situation he was in. He controlled Nick with terror, me with adoration, and kept his true form hidden from both of us.

"So what are you trying to tell me?" I asked him. "And why are you following me?"

"I don't have to answer your questions," he said calmly.

I thought on it for a second. First they snatch me on the street and take my photographs, then they let me go after showing me blowups of a man they obviously believe is Max even though I know him to be dead.

Then Agent Grace makes this call, clearly toying with me, clearly letting me know that they're on my every move. I couldn't figure out his agenda, what he was trying to accomplish. Maybe he was just lonely, alone with his obsession, like me, like Jake. Maybe he needed someone to talk to.

"You still there, Ridley?"

"I told you not to call me that."

"You still there, Ms. Jones?"

"No," I answered, and hung up.

Of course, he was waiting for me on the street in his sedan when the cab dropped me off. His partner stayed in the car as he climbed out the passenger side. I ignored him as I put my key in the lock.

"I figured you for a driver, not a passenger," I said, nodding toward the sedan.

"I'm not allowed to drive the government cars for a while," he said with a smile that told me he thought a lot of himself. "I've totaled three cars in seven months. I've got to pass an evasive driving course. Till then, shotgun."

For some reason, I found myself comparing him to Jake. There was a kind of arrogance (or maybe it was just confidence) to him that contrasted with Jake's kind humility. He lacked Jake's essential sweetness but also the rage Jake held at his center. Jake was physically *exquisite,* not just handsome or sexy but truly beautiful to behold. Agent Grace . . . well, there was a hardness to him, a lack of artistry. If Jake was marble, he was granite. But in the curve of his lips, the lids of his eyes, there was an animal sexuality that made me nervous, like you would feel in the cage of a tiger that you'd been assured was as gentle as a lamb. Agent Grace made me miss Jake, the safety I felt in his arms.

I decided I didn't like Agent Dylan Grace at all. I might have even hated him a little.

"Good night, Detective," I said, just to be annoying.

"I'm a federal agent, Ms. Jones."

"Oh, right. Sorry."

I was shutting (slamming) the door on him when he stopped it (hard) with his hand.

"Can I come in? We need to talk."

"In my experience, federal agents are like vampires: Once you've invited them in, they're very hard to get rid of. Next thing you know, they've got their teeth in your neck."

He smiled at this and I saw a flash of boyishness there. It softened him a bit. Then he ruined it by saying, "I don't want to take you in again, Ms. Jones. It's late. But I will."

I didn't want him to take me in again, either. I was way too tired. I considered my options, then stood aside and let him walk through the door. He let me pass and then followed me into the elevator. We rode to the fifth floor in silence, eyes on the glowing green buttons above as they marked our passage upward. It was so quiet I could hear him breathing. We were so close I could smell his aftershave.

"Nice building," he said as we stepped into the hallway. "Prewar?"

I nodded as we came to a stop at my door. I unlocked it and we stepped inside.

"Your boyfriend home?"

I turned to look at him as I shifted off my jacket and dropped my bag on the floor.

"What do you want, Agent Grace?" I asked, anger in my chest, tears gathering in my eyes. I felt invaded and helpless against it. He was trampling on every boundary I had, and it was infuriating me. When I'm mad, I cry. I hate that about myself, but I don't seem to be able to change it no matter how hard I try. "I mean, seriously," I said, my voice breaking. "You're playing with me, right? What do you want?"

He got that horrified look on his face that a certain type of man gets when he thinks a woman is going to cry. He lifted his palms.

"Okay," he said. "Take it easy." He spoke carefully, as if he were talking a jumper in off a ledge. He glanced around the room; I'm not sure what he was looking for.

"Don't you get it?" I asked him. "I don't know *anything.*"

"Okay," he said again, pulling out a chair at the table and motioning me to sit. I sat and put my head in my hands, noticing that Jake's file was still on the table where I'd left it. I'm not sure why, but I had expected it to be gone when I came home. Agent Grace sat across from me and I slid the file toward him. Mercifully, my tears retreated soon after and I was spared the humiliation of weeping in front of this stranger who'd forced his way into my life and my home.

"What's this?" he asked.

"Jake gave it to me," I said, looking up to show him I wasn't crying. "The article on top — that's how I knew about Nick Smiley, why I went to Detroit. I couldn't make any sense out of the rest of it."

He was quiet for a minute as he shuffled through the pages, then he closed the file with a little laugh.

"Your boy has got an ax to grind, huh?"

I nodded.

"You think he wants a job with the FBI?"

I glared at him. "Something in there has meaning to you?"

He took out the New York Times clippings and turned them toward me. "What do these articles all have in common?"

I glanced through them again and nothing popped. I shrugged and looked up at him. He had been watching me as I looked through them and didn't take his eyes away. There was a strange expression on his face. He reached across and pointed to the byline. I couldn't believe I hadn't noticed it. What writer reads an article but doesn't look at the byline? They were all written by the same person: Myra Lyall. The name rang a bell but I couldn't quite say why.

"Who is she?"

"She's a career crime writer, short-listed for the Pulitzer twice. Most recently she wrote for the Times."

" 'Wrote,' past tense?"

"She and her husband, a photographer, went missing about two weeks ago."

I flashed on the news story I kept seeing on television and in the papers. Still, I had the feeling I'd heard the name somewhere else.

He went on. "Friends showed up for dinner; Myra and her husband, Allen, weren't there. After a day of trying to reach them, the police were called. There was a pool of blood on the floor in the apartment, no sign of the couple. The table was set for dinner, a roast in the oven, pots on the stove."

I started to hear that noise I get in my right ear when I'm really stressed out. "What was she working on?" I asked.

"We don't know. Both her laptop and her box at work had been wiped clean. Even the *Times* server had been cleared of all her e-mail exchanges."

I thought about this. I wasn't sure what to make of it.

Finally I asked, "So this is your case? This missing couple?"

He nodded.

"What does it have to do with me?"

"The last story Myra Lyall published was about three Project Rescue babies, how each had been affected by what happened to them. It was a feature for the *Magazine,* something softer than her usual investigative pieces."

I remembered now where I'd last heard her name.

"What does this have to do with me?" I asked again, though it was clearer now.

"She had your name and number in a notebook. According to what she'd written there, she'd tried to call you three times for comment but you never returned her calls."

"The only people I enjoy speaking to less than FBI agents are reporters."

He gave a little laugh. "Aren't *you* a reporter?"

I bristled at this. "I'm a writer," I said haughtily. "A feature writer. It's not the same thing."

"Whatever you say," he answered.

It wasn't the same thing. Not at all. But I wasn't going to get into it with this bozo. Subtleties and nuances were lost on people like Agent Grace.

"So you said they've been missing two weeks?" I asked.

He looked at his watch. "Two weeks, three days, and approximately ten hours, according to the time line we created."

"But those pictures — my pictures — some of them were taken months ago."

He nodded, looked down at the table. I got it then.

"The FBI has been watching me?"

"For over a year, yes."

"Why?"

He took the ME's report out of the file. "There are inconsistencies in this report. Time of death is about ten hours off, according to our experts." He pointed to something Jake had circled. "This body weighed a hundred and eighty-six pounds. But you know Max was a much bigger man than that — must have been over two-fifty."

I looked at the document in front of me. "Okay. So this was a small-town medical examiner. He made some mistakes. It happens all the time. What did he say when you interviewed him?"

"He's dead," Agent Grace said. "He had a fatal car *accident* just a few days after he filed the report, right around the time this body was cremated."

I noticed how he kept saying "this body."

"What do you mean *accident?*" I asked, mimicking his inflection.

"I mean someone *accidentally* cut his brake lines."

I scanned the report, feeling desperate and afraid. "Esme Gray identified the body," I said weakly. "They were lovers once. She would have known it wasn't Max if it wasn't."

Agent Grace looked at me with something like pity on his face. "Esme Gray is not exactly unimpeachable."

I thought about that last night with Max, how he'd started to cry, how my father had appeared, a dark form in the entryway, how he'd taken Max into his office and shut the doors on me. *It's the bourbon talking,* my father said, before closing the door.

"So the FBI has been watching me since then, thinking *if* he was alive, *if* he would contact anyone, it would be me? Love, right?"

He nodded. "Has he tried to reach you, Ms. Jones?"

"Who?" I asked obtusely.

"Max Smiley," he said impatiently. "Your uncle, your father, whoever the hell he is to you."

"No," I said, almost yelling.

"There was an overseas call to your number the night before last at around three-thirty a.m.," he said sternly, leaning into me.

I remembered the call. Had forgotten about it until then.

"There was no one on the line," I said more softly. "I mean, whoever it was, they didn't say anything. I thought it was Ace."

He looked at me hard, as if he were trying to see a lie in my eyes.

"If you're monitoring my calls, then you know I'm telling the truth."

"We're not monitoring your calls," he said, though I'm not sure why he'd think I'd believe him. "I subpoenaed your phone records this morning, trying to figure out why you went to Detroit."

123

"Can you do that?" I asked, indignant. "I haven't broken any laws."

"If I thought you were aiding and abetting a wanted man, certainly, I could listen to your calls, have someone on you twenty-four seven."

"That's a lot of time and money for someone like Max. Meanwhile, I still don't get what this has to do with your missing couple."

Like the last time we'd met, he had a dark shadow of stubble on his jaw. I wondered if it was a look he was cultivating, something to make him look older, possibly unruly. He wasn't like any of the other FBI agents I'd ever met. All of them had been stiff and clean-shaven, good boys with spotless records — or maybe that was just their shtick. Dylan Grace seemed lawless.

"I mean I *really* don't get it," I said when he remained silent. "You see my name in a notebook belonging to this missing writer, right? So instead of calling me and interviewing me, you make some arrangement with my photo lab to steal my pictures, then you accost me on the street and haul me in? It seems like you overreacted a little. I was a perfectly logical person for her to call — I'm practically the poster child for Project Rescue."

He didn't say anything, just kept those eyes on me.

"Okay, so there's more to it," I said after a moment of the two of us staring at each other. I thought about it a few seconds longer. "You plugged my name into whatever computers you have over there and you found out I was already under surveillance."

He still didn't say anything. It was pretty annoying.

"That's right," I said as he stood up and moved toward the door. "You get to ask all the questions. What is it you want from me?" I asked.

He opened the door. "Good night, Ms. Jones," he said. "Sorry to have bothered you. I'll be in touch."

"Just tell me one thing," I said, getting up and following him out into the hallway. "That overseas call? Where did it come from?"

"Why do you want to know?" he said, turning around.

"Just curious," I said. "Maybe it was someone I know. You know, someone innocent."

He considered it for a minute. Then: "London," he said. "The call came from London. Know anybody there?"

I shrugged. "I guess not."

After he left I tried to figure out what he'd gained by our conversation, and I couldn't come up with anything. I'd received quite a bit of information, however. For the rest of the evening, I felt as if I'd gotten one over on Agent Grace. I wouldn't figure out until later that he'd been the one to get over on me. He'd pressed all my buttons. Wind her up and watch her go.

About an hour later as I lay on the couch watching a rerun of *Gilligan's Island,* trying and failing to block out for a while everything that had happened and everything I had learned, I heard the key in the lock and Jake walked in. He wore a black wool coat over a gray V-neck cashmere sweater I had given him and a pair of Levi's I think he's had for ten years. He spotted me on the couch and moved toward me. I sat up and then went to him, let him take me into his arms. He held me hard, put his mouth to my hair. I pulled off his coat and he let it drop to the floor as he pressed his mouth to mine. The only feeling I had in my heart was desperation, this desperate need to connect to someone, to know someone well. I let him back me into the bedroom, let him lift my sweater over my head and watched as he lifted his off as well. I put my face to his chest and felt the silky hardness of his abs and chest.

"Are you okay?" he asked as he crawled on top of me on the bed, the frame creaking lightly beneath us. I could hear the television in the other room, see its blue flicker. I felt the heat of his body, watched his muscles flex and relax as he moved. I could smell the scent of his skin.

"Yes," I breathed, putting my hands to his face. I felt the smoothness of his clean-shaven jaw, the ridges of his cheekbones. Everything about his face was so beautiful to me; when I looked into his green eyes, I could see his goodness, his strength. I loved him so much. It didn't change all the reasons we couldn't be together, but it kept me returning to his body, kept my skin seeking his skin over and over again in the sad dance we did.

The light coming from the doorway cast our shadows huge on the far wall, as the rest of the clothing that separated our flesh found its way to the floor. I let him take me hard, felt the need of his body and the greater need within him rocket through me, recognized the same need within myself. The song says that love is not enough (and we all know how true that is), but in that moment, in the electric pleasure of our lovemaking, in the sating of that awful need, I could almost believe it was enough and more.

"I went to detroit," I said to him as he lay beside me, hand on my belly. "I talked to Nick Smiley."

He didn't seem surprised. Nothing I ever did seemed to surprise him. It was as if he'd already read the script of my life and was just waiting for events to unfold.

"Did he talk to you?" he asked, pushing himself up on his elbow. He seemed to be looking at a spot behind me somewhere.

"He did," I answered.

"He's crazy, you know," Jake said after a minute. "Like clinically. Been in and out of psychiatric hospitals, has taken lithium for most of his adult life."

I kept looking at his face; it seemed very still. "What are you saying?"

"I'm saying forget about all of this," he said with a sigh, finally meeting my eyes. "You said last night that you wanted to move on. Why don't you? I'm going to try to move on, too."

"But the medical examiner's report and Myra Lyall's disappearance . . ." I said, incredulous, thinking of all the meticulous and obsessive notes in that file.

He nodded. "That ME was incompetent; made numerous mistakes throughout his career. Myra Lyall . . . no one has ever found anything to link her disappearance to any of the stories she was working on. Her landlord has strong connections to the Albanian mob. He's going to get four times what they were paying for that apartment — these days that's as good a motive as any."

I didn't say anything, just watched his face. There was something strained and fatigued about his expression, something about the corners of his mouth, the lids of his eyes. "The NYPD is looking at the landlord now," he said. "They've moved away from the stories she was working on."

"This is an FBI case," I said, sitting up and pulling the sheet with me. "This is why they yanked me in."

"Well, the FBI stuck their nose in when the NYPD found the Project Rescue connection, and maybe they're working their own angles, still looking for someone to hang, like you said. But I know the cop that's working the case, and he says they're looking hard at the landlord."

"The ME who processed Max's body was murdered," I said. He didn't meet my eyes; a muscle worked in his jaw.

"He had a car accident."

"The brake lines were cut."

Jake issued a little laugh. "That's not a very effective way to kill someone. Besides, a very cold brake line could snap cleanly enough to look like a cut."

I didn't say anything. I didn't even know if that was true or not.

"I mean, it leaves a lot up to chance," he went on in the silence. "There's no guarantee that a car accident would be fatal."

I shrugged. This was such a one-eighty, such a complete role reversal from his usual stance about this topic, that I was caught off guard, didn't know what to say.

"If you really want someone dead, you shoot him," he said. "Even if you want it to look like an accident, you throw him off a building or push him in front of a train. Brake lines? If they're cut, the fluid leaks out and eventually they stop working, but you'd never know exactly when. It's unreliable."

"You seem to have given this a lot of thought."

He sighed again and lay down on his back, put his hands behind his head.

"And those articles from the London *Times* and the BBC online," I said. "What does any of that have to do with Max?"

"Nothing," he said. "I don't know. I was

just searching the Web for information on missing children, looking for leads, possible connections to Project Rescue. I was casting, Ridley. Looking to see if what we know is just a small piece in a bigger puzzle."

"And?"

"And you know what? It isn't. And you know what else? When I thought about those articles, it gave me some perspective. The things that happened to me, okay, they were bad. But not as bad as what happened to the girls and the kids in those articles. I'm still here. We're still here."

I shook my head. I couldn't believe my ears.

"You were really upset last night," he said to the ceiling. "After you left, I realized for the first time how much I'd been hurting you, how I was keeping you locked in this thing. Instead of looking for reasons to keep digging, I tried to look for reasons not to. And these are the things I came up with. Max is dead — you're sure of this. No one is going to pay for Project Rescue. It's unfair, it's unjust, but it's not for me to bring justice. I'm going to ruin what's left of my life with this." He turned to look at me. "And I'm going to lose you, if I haven't already."

It sounded so good, exactly what I had

wanted to hear from Jake for so long. I could almost sink into it and believe we would be okay after all.

Whether he was trying to protect me from something that he had learned, or trying to find a way to let me off the hook once and for all, or trying to fix our broken relationship, I didn't know. But I knew with a stone-cold certainty that he was lying. I knew then, too, that he'd *never* give up looking for what he thought was justice until he found it or until it killed him. I wasn't sure he cared which.

"Have I?" he said, sitting up and pulling me to him. "Have I lost you?"

I wrapped my arms around him and let him hold me tight. "I don't know, Jake. I really don't." I was a liar, too. Liars in love.

When I woke up in the morning, Jake was gone. There was a note on his pillow: *Had to go. I truly love you, Ridley. We'll talk later.* Something about the note and his scrawl on the piece of paper that he'd taken from my desk chilled me.

When I walked into the kitchen, I saw without surprise that his file was gone.

7

You've probably noticed that I don't have any friends. It wasn't always that way. I had many friends in high school. In college I knew lots of people, got along well with my roommates, had a few boyfriends. I had a handful of close female friends — you know, the kind of people you spend all night talking to, eating tubs of frozen yogurt with, reading one another's tarot cards. But I'm not sure I ever spilled my guts the way they did. I didn't have a whole lot of angst when it came to boys. To be honest, I think I caused more heartbreak than I endured. At that time, I didn't really have any pain relating to my family, except for Ace, and that was a secret I guarded carefully. Maybe I held back, didn't give as much of myself as I could have. Maybe that's why those relationships fell away over the years.

I did keep in touch with a few people I knew after college as we all moved from our bohemian academic existence into the workforce. There was Julia, a tough-talking, martial-arts-studying graphic artist; Will, my guitar-playing friend and sometimes lover; Amy, a perky, sunny person who went into publishing. But one by one, these relationships started to fall away. Julia and I seemed to be in some kind of competition that neither of us could ever win. Will always wanted more from me than I wanted to give. And Amy disappeared into a relationship with an overbearing Italian guy and seemed to just stop showing up.

There were other reasons, too, why I seem not to have any enduring friendships. Of course, Ace has always taken a lot of my energy. I've always been unusually close to my father, precluding the need for a confidant. Then there were my years with Zack, who wasn't a very social person; we stayed in a lot. Then there was the whole Project Rescue thing, then Jake. Don't get me wrong; I have plenty of acquaintances, colleagues. I get invited to lots of parties — professional parties, that is. But as for real friends, friends of my heart? I guess there's no one but Jake and my father, and obviously those relationships were seriously challenged.

But maybe it isn't any of these things,

these external reasons. Maybe it's me, the writer in me who always stands just apart, observing. In enough to belong, out enough to really *see.* Maybe people sense that about me, sense the distance I unconsciously keep. I don't know. Whatever the reason, I find myself alone a lot of the time these days.

I was thinking about this because I had to ask myself why I did what I did next. My guess: I had no place else to turn, no one with whom to talk all this out, no one to advise me against my next action.

It was cold as I sat on the porch. I pushed myself back and forth on the wooden swing that hung from the roof and watched some kids play kickball on the street. They were all pink-faced and yelling, mostly boys with a couple of girls hanging tough. It was a pretty rough game — some pushing, a couple of trips to the concrete, some tears, but nothing too awful. I remembered those street games when I was a kid. There was something about that combination of excitement and physical exertion, some kind of electric charge that you don't get much as an adult. Now everything that feels that good comes with some sort of baggage to weigh it down.

I could see my breath cloud and my feet were numb. I'd waited a couple of hours, was prepared to wait longer if necessary. As the sun started to set, I saw her get off a bus on the corner and walk toward me. She looked thin and hunched over in a plain wool coat and a blue woolen hat. She carried grocery bags, her eyes on the sidewalk as she approached her house. At the gate, she paused, looked up at me. She shook her head.

"I can't talk to you," she said. "You know that."

"The investigation's over. You can talk if you want to."

She put down her groceries and unlatched the gate, walked up the path. I didn't get up to help her. It wasn't like that anymore.

"Okay," she said. "Then I don't want to. I have nothing to say to you, little girl."

She looked drawn and pale as she unlatched the door. Black smudges under her eyes told me she wasn't sleeping well at night, and something within me took a cold, dark victory in that. I didn't get up as she unlocked the door and pulled her groceries inside. She closed the door; I heard it lock. I walked over and looked at her through the glass.

"I know he's alive," I told her loudly. I didn't really know that. I was, in fact, convinced that he was dead. But I wanted to see what her reaction would be.

She brought her face close to the glass. I expected to see fear; instead I saw some combination of anger and pity.

"Have you lost your mind?" she asked me.

"You identified the body that night," I said. "Why didn't my father do it?"

"Because he couldn't bear it, Ridley. What do you think? He couldn't stand to see his best friend's face shredded by glass, unrecognizable, see him dead upon a gurney. He called me. I came and I spared him that."

"Why you? Why not my mother?"

"How the hell should I know?" she snapped. Her eyes looked wild.

"You're sure it was him? Or did you lie about that, too?"

She closed her eyes and shook her head. "You should think about getting professional help," she said unkindly.

I let a beat pass. I looked for the person I used to love, but she was gone in a way more total than if she had died.

"What are you afraid of, Esme?" I asked finally. I was surprised to hear my voice infused with sadness.

Her face went pale, I think more out of rage than anything else. And hatred. She hated me and I could see it, could feel it coming off of her in waves. "I'm afraid of *you,* Ridley," she said finally. "You've destroyed us all and you're *still* coming around with a sledgehammer. You should be ashamed for what you've done."

I laughed, fogging the glass between us. It sounded loud and unpleasant even to my own ears. I knew she believed all of what had happened was my fault. I knew my parents felt that way a little, too. It was amazing how this had become about what *I* had done to *them.* It was a staggering show of narcissism, but I guess it's the same narcissism that allowed them to do what they did to all those children, to me. They would have needed to be utterly convinced of their own self-righteousness. It made me a little sick sometimes; I tried not to think about it. I think it was the single reason that Jake disbelieved my father's claims of innocence, that he couldn't forgive.

Once upon a time, it would have hurt to know that Esme hated me. Now it just made me angry.

"I'll keep swinging until I know all the answers," I said with a smile.

"You do and you'll wind up like that *New York Times* reporter," she said with such venom that I took a step back. Her words set off bottle rockets in my chest.

"What?" I asked her. "What did you say?

138

Are you talking about Myra Lyall?"

She gave me a dark look and I swear I saw the corners of her mouth turn up in a sick smile. She closed the curtain on me then, and I heard her walk down the hall away from me. Behind the gauzy material I saw her shadow disappear through a bright doorway. I called after her a few times, pounding on the door, but she never answered. I noticed the kids on the street had stopped playing their game. Some of them were staring at me and some of them were walking off.

Finally I gave up and walked toward the train, my heart pounding, head swimming. I was so shocked by what she had said that I couldn't even come up with any questions to ask myself. I just felt this belly full of fear, this weird sense that I was about to walk off the edge of my life . . . again. Everyone around me seemed full of malice; the sky had taken on a gray cast and threatened snow.

My parents lived only one train stop from Esme's, so I headed that way. I knew they were gone, having left last week for a month-long Mediterranean cruise. My father had been pushed into semiretirement, so now they were "finally doing some of the traveling we'd always wanted to do," as my mother said with a kind of forced brightness. I was happy for them (not really), but something about it galled me, too. I felt wrecked inside and they seemed to be so blithely moving on. It hurt somehow that they could move on while I couldn't. I know that's childish.

I walked from the train station through the precious town center, zoned to look like a picture postcard, with clapboard restaurants and shops, a general store that sold ice cream, original gas lamps still in working order. I followed the street that wound uphill, past beautifully restored Victorian homes nestled on perfectly manicured lawns. Every season had its character here; it was always lovely. But today with most of the trees shedding their autumn color, and the hour still too bright for the streetlights to come on but dark enough to be gloomy, it didn't seem as pretty. I didn't take much comfort in coming home these days, and especially not today.

I let myself in the front door and went directly to my father's study. I stood in the doorway, my hand resting on the scroll handle. When Ace and I were kids, this room was strictly forbidden unless there was adult supervision, so naturally, I had always been fascinated by it. I was forever trying to finagle an invitation in, as if spending time in there with my father would signal that I had become a grown-up. But the invitation never came.

I didn't want to sneak in like Ace did; I didn't see the point in that then. But Ace always wanted to go where he shouldn't. And, in fact, he was hiding behind my father's desk the night he overheard Max and Ben discussing Project Rescue and the night Max brought me home to Ben and Grace. But I didn't know about that for a long time.

As I got older, I started to see this room as my father's haven, a place where he could be alone, away from the needs of his children, the criticisms of his wife; where he could smoke a cigar out the window or have a bourbon in peace. Now I just saw it as a symbol of all the secrets that had been kept from me, all the lies that had been told.

As I walked inside, the whole house seemed to hold its breath in the silence. The room seemed cluttered and dusty; it was the only place my mother left alone on her relentless cleaning regimen. It smelled lightly of stale cigar smoke. The couch and matching chair and ottoman were the same evergreen velvet pieces that had sat there since my childhood. A low, heavy coffee table of dark wood was covered with books and magazines. The fireplace contained some fresh wood and some kindling, awaiting its next lighting.

My father used to sit, transfixed by the fire, his eyes taking on a strange blankness as he looked into the flames. As a kid I always wondered what he thought about when he was alone in here. Now I wondered if he thought about the night Max brought me here, asking them to raise me as their child; about the other Project Rescue babies and what had become of them; about the night Max's mother died. Did he know what Nick Smiley thought had happened that night? Did he worry that there was another side to Max? If he did know, why had they remained so close?

Any affection I might have had for this forbidden place was gone. Now all I wanted to do was tear through it, open drawers, pull books off of shelves. I wanted to find anything this room was hiding. I hated it for all the secrets it had kept, including some of the last moments of Max's life. What had the two men said to each other that night after the doors closed on me?

You probably think that I am, as usual, in a state of denial about Max. You're thinking about the photographs, the inconsistencies in the medical examiner's report, Esme's bizarre behavior and her threats. You're probably already convinced that Max was still alive. But the fact of the matter was that Max, *my* Max, was dead. There would be no resurrections. The man I had adored was lost to me forever.

If it turned out that Max Smiley lived, by some bizarre chance or nefarious design, he would be a stranger — or worse — to me. The man I thought I knew was a fantasy, an archetype: the Good Uncle. The real man remained a mystery — a terrifying mystery I wasn't sure I wanted to solve. But if he was alive, I was going to find him and look him in the face. I would demand to know who he was, what had happened the night I was abducted and my biological mother was murdered. I would demand to know what had happened to Jake. I would force him to answer for Project Rescue. I would force him to answer for every ounce of rage and heartbreak he had caused. Sounds like a tall order, right? You have no idea.

I sat at my father's computer and booted it up. It was a dinosaur and took forever. In the meantime I rifled through drawers and found some pens, old rubber bands and paper clips, a bunch of files containing fascinating evidence like water, phone, and electric bills, the deed to a property they owned in New Mexico but had never built on, their marriage license and other legal documents. Finally the screen lit up and demanded a password. I didn't have to think for long. I entered *lullaby,* the nickname he'd always had for me. A strain of electronic music praised my excellent deductive powers.

"What are you looking for?" I asked myself out loud.

My father had just been through a federal investigation. Anything incriminating on this computer would have been found by the authorities or deleted. Probably. I shamelessly began searching through Word files, scanning his "Household," "Speeches," and correspondence folders. He wasn't a very computer-savvy guy, my father, so there weren't many documents. It took me only about twenty minutes to go through everything and to find nothing but the most innocuous stuff: a letter to a painter who'd taken their money and left his work unfinished in the kitchen, a speech he gave on the signs of child abuse to which physicians must be vigilant (I doubt anyone's been asking him to make that speech lately), a list including various organizing tasks around the house.

Next I scanned his e-mail. The usual slew of spam popped up when I opened his Outlook box. The cure for erectile dysfunction, hot nude girls, and an international lottery win vied for my attention. I searched through his sent mail, his recently received mail, and his recycle bin. Everything was empty, wiped clean, not one e-mail saved. I found this strange. I thought about my own e-mail box. I was compelled to save nearly everything I sent and everything I received, cataloged by person and purpose. It seemed odd that he'd save nothing; he was an even bigger pack rat than I was. Maybe that federal investigation had left him feeling skittish.

I started to feel as if I was wasting time, when I remembered something Jake had taught me. Your computer remembers every website you've visited. The websites you visit send a little message to your computer called a cookie and your computer saves that cookie to identify itself the next time you visit that site. There's also a log on your computer that shows all the websites you've visited in the last week or few days, depending on how your computer is set.

I visited the cookies file and saw a bunch of them from places like amazon.com and

Home Depot, some investment and news websites. Nothing unusual or interesting. I went to the log of visited sites and, at first, nothing caught my eye there, either. Then I ran across a site that seemed a little odd, just a collection of seemingly random numbers, letter, and symbols. As I scrolled down I noticed that he'd visited the site ten times in the last week and a half. The log was set to delete any listings more than two weeks old, so past that, I didn't know. But it seemed safe to assume he was visiting this site nearly every day.

I cut and pasted the address into the Web browser and waited for the site to pop up. When it did, it was just a blank page filling the screen with a bright red glare, so bright it actually hurt my eyes. I waited for some type of intro or log-in prompts to pop up. Nothing. Just that bright red screen with no images and no text. Something about it was unsettling. It was the color of danger.

I dragged the cursor over it and double-clicked in various places but nothing happened. After a few minutes of staring at the red blankness, I felt my chest constrict in my frustration. I knew I was looking at something important but I couldn't figure out what it meant. My impatience blossomed into a childish anger and I fought a sudden overwhelming urge to put my fist through the screen. I gripped the edge of the desk until my inner tantrum passed. I released a breath I hadn't even realized I was holding and wrote down the mysterious URL on a piece of scrap paper, which I shoved in my pocket. I deleted all the junk e-mails that had downloaded during my visit and turned off the computer. (I had the urge to go to the kitchen, get some Windex, and wipe down the desk, the keyboard, and anything else I had touched — but that was just me being weird.)

I took a quick walk through the house, through the empty rooms of my childhood. The family room where we'd gathered for television or games was much the same, though the furniture had been updated recently and my parents had replaced the old television with a new big-screen. My parents' bedroom on the ground floor looked out over my mother's garden. In the spring, she'd leave the French doors open and let the room fill with the smell of roses. I remembered watching her sit at her vanity, doing her hair and makeup, and thinking she was the most beautiful woman in the world. The room, decorated in a sort of Martha Stewart/Victorian theme with heavy brocades and floral prints, was typically tidy with stacks of books on each of the night-stands. Upstairs, I sat on my old bed for a minute, looked at my framed diplomas, my debate trophies, and the first article I'd had published in my school paper. My bed was still made with my old Laura Ashley sheets. A place that once had seemed the happiest and safest in all the world now seemed cold and dark; the heat was down and I pulled my jacket tight around myself. I felt those fingers of despair tugging at me again, but I brushed them off as I hurriedly left the room and moved down the stairs. I left my parents' house, locked the door behind me, and headed back into the city.

I have a tremendous ability to compartmentalize my emotions. Some people call it denial, but I think it's a skill to be able to put unpleasant things out of your head for a little while in order to accomplish something else. For the next few hours I didn't think about Agent Grace or Myra Lyall or about my truly devastating encounter with Esme Gray. I didn't think about Max or if those ashes I scattered off the Brooklyn Bridge were really his. I just wrote my article about Elena Jansen, proofread it carefully, and e-mailed it in to my editor at *O Magazine*. I had already had most of it written in my head — it was just a matter of getting it down on paper. For me the actual writing is only about ten percent of the process; ninety percent is the thinking about it. Much of that is unconscious. I guess for me all action is like that.

I felt better after writing the article. Elena Jansen's tragedy made the drama in my life seem silly and inconsequential . . . for a second or two, anyway. Maybe that was why I was writing these kinds of pieces, why I was drawn to these survivors. They reminded me that my own story wasn't so bad. That other people had endured less survivable events. They made me feel as if one day I'd find my way back to a normal, happy life. Is that selfish?

Once I'd sent in the article, though, all the other stuff started nagging at me. I took the strange website address from my pocket and plugged it into my own browser. The same red screen popped up; I stared at it, transfixed for a minute. I dragged the cursor over the whole page, clicking randomly, like I had done at my parents' house. Nothing. It started driving me a little crazy. I knew there was something there; if the website was down, the screen would show an error message. My father had been visiting this site every day. There must be a way in.

The phone rang then.

"Hey," said Jake when I answered. "What are you doing?"

"Just working on an article due tomorrow."

"Want me to come over?"

"Not tonight. I'm feeling pretty wrecked. And I don't want to blast this deadline."

"Anything wrong?" he asked after a pause.

"No," I lied. "Nothing."

"How are you feeling about everything? Max and all that."

"Honestly," I said, "I haven't even thought about it today."

The long silence on the other end told me he didn't believe me. "Okay," he said finally. "Talk to you in the morning?"

"Definitely."

"Well, good night, Ridley."

"Good night, Jake."

8

After a terrible night's sleep, I got up in the morning and made a few phone calls. Esme's words and the things Agent Grace had told me about Myra and Allen Lyall were smoldering in my center. I'd seen a poster of their faces on the way back into the city the night before. There was an update on the morning news, which basically consisted of a downcast detective saying that there were no new leads and asking anyone who might have seen anything to come forward.

I felt connected to Myra Lyall now. I started to wish I'd returned her phone calls when I'd had the chance. And there was something else. I wondered if she'd found something out — something about Project Rescue or about Max — that had gotten her killed. It was a terrible itch. Of course, I had to scratch it.

I knew a couple people over at the *Times*: an Arts & Leisure editor named Jenna Rich and a sportswriter I dated briefly, a guy named Dennis Leach (unfortunate name, I know). I didn't reach either of them, so I left messages. I made a few more visits to the mystery website, had the same experience I'd had the night before, and hopped in the shower. As I was finishing up and pulling on some clothes, my phone rang.

"Hey, it's Jenna," said a youthful voice when I answered. "How are you, stranger?"

"Hey, there. Thanks for getting back to me," I said. "Can't complain. You?"

Jenna was a talker, which is why I'd called her. She was a one-woman corporate rumor mill. She told me how she'd married last year, been promoted, and was pregnant with her first child. I knew we were about the same age, and though I was happy for her, it made me feel somehow *behind,* like she was clearing the hurdles with grace and skill and I was still hovering around the starting gate. As she chatted on, I spent a moment wondering how this conversation would have gone if I'd married Zack when he'd asked two years ago, if I'd be having this conversation at all. Would I be pregnant? Would I have taken one of the many staff writing positions that had been offered to me over the years? Would I be happy in the ignorance of my past, in marrying a man I knew I'd never love but with whom I was more or less compatible? I didn't dwell on it too long; not much point in that. We make our choices. We forge ahead. Or we curl up and wallow in regret. Both alternatives have their appeal. At the moment I was forging.

"So what's up?" she said after the niceties had been exchanged. "You have an idea for me?"

"Not exactly," I said. "I'm wondering what you know about Myra Lyall. I had some calls from her a few weeks ago. I suppose something to do with Project Rescue. I was thinking about returning her call but I wanted to see if you knew her first."

She was quiet for a minute. "You didn't hear?"

"What?" I said with concern and interest, playing dumb.

"God," she said with a sigh. "She and her husband disappeared a couple of weeks ago. Apparently someone accessed our servers — which, by the way, is supposed to be next to impossible — and wiped her hard drive and all her e-mail communications. People here are pretty spooked. It's just terrible, Ridley."

"Wow," I said, trying to sound suitably shocked. "That's *awful.* What are the police saying? Does anyone have any idea what happened?"

"There are all kinds of theories floating around," she said, her voice dropping to a whisper. "One has to do with her landlord. She and her husband were at war with him. They lived in this rent-controlled apartment they'd been in since the seventies. The new owner had recently bought the building and wanted them out so that he could get the market rate for the apartment. Suddenly they had terrible mice and roach problems, the heat never worked. Apparently, they'd decided to put their rent in escrow until he fixed things; that sent him over the edge. Word is he has ties to the Albanian mob."

"But that doesn't explain how the *Times* server got wiped clean . . . or why."

"No. It doesn't," she said softly.

"So . . . what else are people saying? I mean, what was she working on at the time?"

I thought Jenna might clam up. I could hear her breathing. She was a pretty woman with small, serious features and bright green eyes, peaches-and-cream skin. It had been a while since I'd had any face time with her, but I could imagine her frowning, tapping her pen on the desk.

"A lot of people around here think she stumbled onto something. It's just a rumor."

"Something to do with Project Rescue?"

"I don't think so. She put that story to bed over a month ago. And that was more of a human-interest piece than her usual investigative work. She kind of got pushed into it by this new editor — you know, put-some-faces-on-the-crime kind of a thing. Besides, as far as news stories go, there wasn't any new ground to cover."

"So . . . what, then?"

"I dated one of the IT guys for a while ages ago. Grant Webster. He's kind of 'into' his job — a little bit too into it, if you ask me. That's one of the major reasons we broke up. On top of his job, he has this whole website devoted to the history of hacking, all this conspiracy-theory tech stuff. Anyway, he said it wasn't the usual kind of hacking. It's one thing to get in and read e-mail, or to try to steal subscriber credit-card info, or to take over the site for a while. It's quite another to hack in to the level necessary to erase data from a server. He thinks it might have been someone in-house, someone who was paid to do it . . ." She let the sentence trail off.

"Or?" I said.

"Or it was one of the federal agencies."

I let the information sink in. "Like the CIA or the FBI?"

"Right."

"So the rumor is, she stumbled onto something she wasn't supposed to know about, possibly involving one of the federal agencies, so someone made her disappear and erased all her e-mail correspondence?"

She didn't pick up the skepticism in my voice.

"And her hard drive, containing anything she might have been working on now plus everything she'd ever worked on in the past, though of course most of that has been published. And her voice mail," added Jenna. "Which, according to Grant, is a lot easier than erasing e-mail."

"That's quite a theory," I said.

"It's just, you know, get a bunch of reporters and IT people together over a few beers and you can't believe the stuff we come up with," she said with a little laugh. "Those IT guys are all conspiracy theorists at heart."

She went on a bit about Grant and how she suspected he'd been writing code in his head while they were making love, how his idea of a good time was a box of Twinkies and a nineteen-inch flat-screen monitor. She mentioned his website again and I jotted it down: www.isanyonepayingattention-.com. I let her go on, giggled with her where appropriate, made the expected affirming noises, not wanting to seem overeager for more information on Myra Lyall.

I segued back to that topic awkwardly, but she didn't seem to notice. "Any other *wild* theories about Myra?"

"Hmm . . . I guess the only other thing I heard was that she got some kind of anonymous tip that she followed up on a few days before she disappeared."

"What kind of a tip?"

"I don't know. According to her assistant, she got some e-mail — or was it a phone call? — that sent her skating from the office. That's as much as anyone knows, I think. All her e-mail, even her notebooks —"

"Are gone," I finished for her.

We were both quiet for a second and I could hear her other line ringing in the background, the staccato of her fingers on a keyboard.

"Hey, you want me to keep you posted?" she said. "If I hear anything else?"

"That would be great, Jenna. Also, can I have Grant's contact info? I'm doing an article on computer crimes. I'd love to ask him a few questions."

She hesitated a second. "Sure," she said. "That doesn't sound like your usual beat."

"I'm branching out these days. Trying to broaden the scope of my writing, you know?"

She gave me his information. Before she hung up, she said, "Hey, don't tell him any of the things I said about him, okay?"

"Never," I assured her.

We hung up and I thought about our conversation as I poured myself another cup of coffee and walked over to my window. Then I returned to my computer and visited Grant's website. A flash intro read bold white on a black screen: *Is anyone paying attention?* Another screen followed: *The federal government is fucking with us.* A third screen: *And we sit around watching* Survivor, *eating pizza, just letting it all happen?* ***Wake up!*** The screen started flashing. ***It's time for a revolution.*** The flash intro ended and the home page opened. It was heavy on the blacks and reds, laid out to look like a newspaper page. The center headline read: **WHERE IS MYRA LYALL???**

The article recounted the known details of Myra and Allen Lyall's disappearance, things I had already been told and had read in the articles in Jake's file. It went on:

The NYPD and the news media would

like you to believe that the Lyalls' Albanian landlord is responsible for their disappearance, that the Albanian mob executed them for their "grandfathered" rent-controlled apartment. Isn't that just like America? Shove all our problems off on the third world? But the reality is: very few people have the resources and the technology required to hack into the *New York Times* servers and wipe data. Her voicemail? Okay, amateur-time. Just a log-in and a password and you're golden. But to access her e-mail and her database, not just on her box but the backups on the servers? Nearly impossible. Unless you're the CIA or the FBI, or some other nefarious government agency.

Some of us think Myra stumbled onto something she wasn't supposed to know. We know for sure that the last piece she published was about Project Rescue (talk about the ultimate government cover-up; did anyone ever get prosecuted for that? Hundreds, maybe thousands of underprivileged kids abducted from their homes and SOLD to wealthy families. And no one's even in prison??? Doesn't anyone think that's fucked up?)

I had to cringe here, wondering if he'd

mention my father or Max, but he didn't. It was weird to hear someone talk about Project Rescue like that. I'd never really thought of it as a conspiracy and a cover-up, but I guess I could see his point.

We know for sure that Myra received a phone call before she left on the Friday prior to her disappearance, that she left the office in a rush. Her assistant described her as "excited and a little nervous." And that's the last time anyone at the *Times* saw her.

If Myra had backed up her notes on a disk and hidden it somewhere (like I'm ALWAYS advising to do, people, when you're working on something sensitive), we might have more to go on. Anyone with more information on Myra or with insights and theories, get in touch with me. I want to help. But for crying out loud, be careful who you talk to, what you say, and how you say it. For secure communication, call me at the following number and we'll arrange a meeting.

I scanned through the rest of his pages. There were articles about the flu shot, Gulf War syndrome and depleted uranium, the dangers of website cookies, SARS, reality television, and a hackers hall of fame (using screen names only, of course). According to Grant, pretty much everything that is remotely disturbing about the world can be traced back to the "evil empire," the United States federal government. He had an infectious writing style, and by the time I'd finished scanning the site, I was starting to agree with him.

I got up from my computer and walked over to the window to think. Something was bothering me. I know: Take your pick, right? I headed back into my office and sifted through some papers on my desk until I found a small pink notebook where I log in telephone messages. I flipped through the pages and found where I'd written down Myra Lyall's name, number, date, and time of her calls. Jenna told me that Myra had put her article to bed over a month ago. The last call was just over two and a half weeks ago, a couple of days before she and her husband disappeared, according to Dylan Grace. If she hadn't called me about the article she was writing on Project Rescue victims, then what?

Even though Max had been dead for years, his apartment still sat untouched as he'd left it. My father refused to sell it, though the monthly maintenance was ridiculous. After Max's death we both used to visit it like some people visit a grave, to remember, to feel close.

I used to go to Max's place after he died to smell his clothes. I'd stand in his closet. It was a giant affair, bigger than my bedroom at home. With beautiful wood cabinets and a granite-topped island containing drawers for socks, underwear, and jewelry, it looked more like the designer men's department at Barneys than anyone's closet. I'd walk among the long rows of silk and wool gabardine, touch my fingers to the fabric, and breathe in the scent of those suits. I could smell him there — not just the trace remains of his cologne still clinging to the suit jackets, but something else. Something uniquely Max. It hurt me and comforted me simultaneously, the rainbow of silk ties, the neatly arranged boxes of shoes, the orderly parade of shirts in muted colors — white, gray, blue — one hundred percent cotton only, no starch. Anything else irritated the skin on his neck.

"It's just stuff," Zack, my ex-boyfriend and would-be murderer, used to say when I'd go up there. "It has no meaning now that he's gone." He couldn't understand why I'd fall asleep on the couch among the million pictures of our family, feel safe and connected to a happier past when everyone was together.

Of course, that was before, when the loss of him was a hollow through the middle of me that I thought would never fill again. That was before I knew he was my father.

As I walked through the doors that mid-morning, after my conversation with Jenna, it wasn't to comfort myself with memory. There was no comfort to be had there any longer. My sadness for Max had waxed and gone cold. Now in my heart there was only anger and so many unanswered questions. Sadness was a place I couldn't afford; it buckled the knees and weakened resolve. And I had a sense that I'd been a puddle of myself for too long. It was making me soft.

I suspected anything that might have offered some clue as to who Max had been — who he'd *really* been — was long gone. I'd discovered over a year ago that the lawyers had taken all his files and date books (which he kept like journals), and his computer. Valuables like watches and jewelry, and all other personal effects, had gone to my father and mother. So I didn't know what I was looking for exactly. I just started opening drawers and cupboards, sifting through old books, looking behind photographs.

But the drawers and file cabinets were empty. There were no secret safes in the floor or behind pictures. Everything was just as it had been when he was alive, in perfect order . . . except that it was all dead. Void of the energy of a life being lived, of vital paperwork and important files. Gone.

Something I'd always noticed about Max while he was alive was his fastidiousness. His sock drawer, with each pair precisely folded in careful rows, organized by color, made me think about how he was always straightening — the pictures on the wall, the silverware on the table, the arrangements of objects on his desk or dresser. It used to drive my mother crazy, probably because she was equally particular. She seemed to think it was some kind of competition when he came to the house and rearranged the table she had set, fussing with the centerpiece or aligning the silverware even more precisely.

Of course, Max always had a staff of people following him around, cleaning up after him, but he held those people to such exacting standards that turnover was always high. Personal assistants, maids, cooks, came and went, a parade of polite and distant strangers, always nervous around Max, always replaced in a matter of weeks or months. Only Clara, who acted as maid and part-time cook and sometimes babysitter for me and Ace, stayed through the years, never seemed rattled by Max or his demands. What did this say about Max? I didn't know. It was just something that came to mind as I sifted through the apartment. Maybe it didn't mean anything. Maybe nothing did.

After a while, frustrated and unsatisfied, I sat on Max's bed, a gigantic king swathed in 1,000-count Egyptian cotton sheets and a rich chocolate-brown raw silk comforter, piled high with coordinating shams and throw pillows. I leaned back against the plush surface and tried to think about what I was doing there, what I was looking for, and what I intended to do once I found it.

After a minute, I got up again and walked over to the recessed shelving in the opposite wall that held a large flat-screen television, another legion of photographs (mainly of me), objects he'd collected in his travels around the world — a jade elephant, a large Buddha, some tall giraffes carved delicately in a deep black wood. My eyes fell on a familiar object, a hideous pottery ashtray formed by a child's fingers — a pinch pot, I think we called them in kindergarten. It was painted in a medley of colors — purple, hot pink, evergreen, orange. In the center, I had painted, *I LOVE MY UNCEL MAX,* and my name was carved on the underside. I didn't remember making it but I did remember it always being on Max's desk in his study. I wondered how it had wound up in here. I lifted the piece of pottery and held it in my hand, felt a wave of intense sadness. As I was about to put it back down, I saw that it had sat on top of a small keyhole. I quickly searched the shelving for a drawer or some clue as to what might open if a key was inserted, but it seemed to be a keyhole to nothing. I resisted the urge to hurl the little piece of pottery against the wall.

I walked back over to the bed and flopped myself down on it.

That's when I smelled it. The lightest scent of male cologne. Not a sense memory of Max but an actual scent in the air, or possibly in the sheets. It made my heart thump. I got up quickly from the bed, my eyes scanning the room for something out of place. The small clock beside the bed suddenly seemed very loud, the street noise a distant thrum.

A haunting is a subtle thing. It's not flying dishes and bleeding walls. It's not a mournful moaning down a dark, stone hallway. It's odors and shades of light, a nebulously familiar form in a photograph, the glimpse of a face in a crowd. These nuances, these moments are no less horrifying. They strike the same blow to the solar plexus, trace the same cold finger down your spine.

As I stood there, my nose to the air, my limbs frozen, I took in the scent of him. Max. Whatever the alchemy of his skin and his cologne, it could be no one else. Like my father, rainwater and Old Spice, or my mother, Nivea cream and something like vinegar . . . unmistakable, unforgettable. I listened hard to the silence. A sound, soft and rhythmic, called me from where I stood. I walked over the carpet and into the master bath. Another huge space, embarrassingly opulent with granite floors and walls, brushed chrome fixtures, a Jacuzzi tub and steam-room shower. I paused in the doorway and noticed that the shower door and the mirrors were lightly misted. I walked over and opened the glass door to the shower. The giant waterfall showerhead that hung centered from the ceiling held tiny beads of water in each pore, coalescing in the center and forming one enormous tear that dripped into the drain below. My mind flipped through a catalog of reasons why this shower might have been recently used. This was a secure, doorman-guarded building. My parents, the only other people with access, were both away. I reached in and closed the tap; the dripping ceased.

My breathing was deep and there was a slight shake to my hands from adrenaline. Once a month, I knew, a service came in to clean. But I was sure they'd already been here this month, and I'd never known them to leave a faucet to run or surfaces wet.

I went to the cordless phone by Max's bed to dial the doorman.

"Yes, Ms. Jones," said Dutch, the eternal doorman, whom I'd passed on my way in.

"Has someone been in this apartment today?"

"Not on my watch. I've been here since five a.m.," he said. I heard him flipping through pages. "No visitors last night or all day yesterday. Not in the log."

"Okay," I said.

"Something wrong?"

"No. Nothing. Thanks, Dutch," I said. I pressed the button to end the call before he could ask me any more questions.

The phone rang while it was still in my hand. I answered without thinking.

"Hello?"

There was only static in my ear.

"Hello?" I said again.

The line went dead.

■ ■ ■ ■

Sometimes I think it's not the ghosts themselves but the dark spaces where they might reside that are the most frightening. I was filled with dread as I continued my search of the apartment. I approached each space with a kind of reluctance, a turning away, wanting to cover my eyes like I might if watching a horror movie by myself at night. Looking back, I guess it was more that I was searching to find *nothing* than looking for something in particular. I wanted to do my due diligence so that if the worst were true, I could leave self-blame off my list of emotions. I wanted to know I hadn't closed my eyes the way Elena had.

The sky outside had turned dark blue in the twilight, and I was starting to feel tired. The scent had deserted the apartment and the bathroom was now dry as a bone. I was already starting to wonder if I'd imagined the whole thing. I flipped on some lamps to chase back the gloom that was settling on me. As I did, something caught my eye.

In the light I saw a small corner of white peeking out from beneath the coffee table. I got down on my knees and retrieved a matchbook. I turned it in my hand. There was an opalescent symbol embossed on each side, which could be seen only when it was held at a certain angle to the light. Three interlocking circles within a larger circle. There was something familiar about it, but I couldn't place it. I felt my stomach start to knot; a light nausea crept up in my throat. I flipped the matchbook open. Inside a single note had been scrawled: *Show this at the door. Ask for Angel.*

In my dreams, I sit with him and ask him all my questions. He sits beside me like he did our last night together. The tears fall and he is talking, answering me with pleading eyes, his hands on my shoulders. His lips move but I can't hear what he's saying. He touches me but he is behind some invisible barrier. I can't reach out to him and I can't hear his voice. I try to read his lips but I can't until he says the words *I'm sorry, Ridley.* He reaches for me again and I back away. The anger and the hatred I feel in these dreams are more intense than anything I've felt in my waking life. I realize there's a gun in my hand.

That's when I wake up, feeling desperate and helpless. I never believed in recurring dreams before. But any shrink will tell you that it's your mind's way of resolving something you haven't been able to resolve in your waking life. Doesn't take much to figure that out. Too bad it didn't seem to be working for me.

9

In my mailbox at home there was a postcard from my father, sent apparently from their port of call in Positano. *Having a wonderful time!* it read in my father's sharp, scrawling hand. *Thinking of you as always.* The thought of them traipsing around Europe snapping photographs and mailing off postcards, frankly, made me sick. I threw the postcard in the trash, poured myself a glass of wine from the half-empty bottle on the counter, and played my messages. I had an uneasy feeling, found myself looking around my apartment, peering through the doorway into my dark bedroom.

"Hey, it's me." Jake. "Can we get together tonight? Come to the studio around eight if you feel like it. We'll go to Yaffa. Or wherever."

I looked at my watch. It was six-thirty. I was hungry and lonely and considered heading downtown to meet him.

Beep.

"It's me." A low male voice, smoky and depressive. Ace. "Haven't talked to you in a couple of days. I'd like to see you. I have some things on my mind."

Great. Another catalog of indictments his shrink was encouraging him to bring up against my parents — and me, I'm sure.

"Yeah," I said to my empty apartment. "Looking forward to it." I suddenly had the horrible thought that I'd liked my brother better when he was a junkie. Though he'd been equally depressive and blame-laying, he wasn't nearly as self-reflective.

Beep.

"Hey, there, it's Dennis. It was nice to hear your voice. Give me a call back when you can." That *Times* sportswriter I dated briefly. He sounded enthusiastic. I knew he worked late usually, so I took a chance, went into my office, looked up his number, and gave him a call. I forced myself to sound light and flirty when he answered, gave him the same spiel I gave Jenna about wanting to return Myra Lyall's call.

"A very weird, scary thing," he said when he'd finished telling me basically all the same stuff Jenna had revealed.

"That's terrible, Dennis," I said. I let a beat pass. "Do you know her assistant well?

173

I got a call from her as well — what's her name again?" Lie.

"Sarah Duvall."

"Right."

"Yeah, she comes out for drinks every once in a while with my crew. Nice girl. She's a bit adrift at the moment. No one knows if Myra is coming back, but no one wants to admit that she isn't, so Sarah's in a kind of professional limbo. It's been weird for her."

There was an awkward silence on the phone. I remembered how Dennis and I went out together one night and he got so drunk over dinner at Union Square Café that he halfway passed out against the wall at a club we visited later. I literally had to support him as we stumbled to the street and deposited him in a cab while he tried to lick my neck. It was a bit of a turnoff.

"So . . ." he said finally. "Feel like getting together?"

"Sure," I said. "Let me look at my schedule next week and I'll give you a call back."

"Great," he said. "I'll look forward to it."

We hung up, both of us knowing that I had no intention of doing any such thing.

I had a strange sense of unease as I hung up the phone, as if there were eyes peering at the back of my neck. I spun around in my chair and confronted the emptiness behind me. I walked through my apartment, but there was nothing I could point to, nothing I could say might have been moved. I wondered if I was being paranoid, but something just didn't feel right. The energy was off and I couldn't wait to get out of the apartment.

I headed downtown, deciding to walk. So I went south on Park Avenue South and cut through Madison Square Park at the point of the Flatiron Building, to Broadway. I went down Broadway, and then east on Eighth. I do all my best thinking in motion through the city. It energizes me, the noise and all the different personalities of each neighborhood. And as the self-conscious fanciness of Park Avenue South morphed into the bustle of Broadway and then into the familiar grit of the East Village, I thought about my time at Max's apartment today. I tried to put my head around things, like the red website and the book of matches, the ghostly scent of Max and the wet bathroom, the call from Myra Lyall and her disappearance, the wiping of the *Times* servers, the things Jenna had told me. It gave me a headache, ratcheted the tension in my shoulders. The more I thought about these things, the foggier my head got, the more nebulous and vaguely menacing it all seemed. And then there was Agent Dylan Grace, his strange and threatening appearances, his hasty retreats.

"What's happening?" I asked, saying it aloud without realizing. My own words startled me but no one on the street around me seemed to notice. The sky had gone dark and the air had grown colder. I wasn't dressed warmly enough, as usual. I felt my phone vibrate in my pocket and I withdrew it with a stiff, cold hand gone pink from exposure. There was an anonymous text message. It read: *The Cloisters. Tomorrow. 8PM. Trust no one.*

I was still shaking when I pushed through the studio door. I hadn't stopped to think why it might be open as I bolted up the dark, narrow staircase and stepped into the large loft space. I felt as if someone was pursuing me, though I'd seen no one suspicious on the street. I could barely control my breathing and had to stop a minute. The studio was dark, the only light coming from Jake's small office off to the left. I felt for the switch on the wall to my left and tried to turn on the lights but nothing happened. The space was an old warehouse, nearly windowless and bare; the electricity failed as often as it worked.

"Jake," I called when I had my wind back. No answer. I moved past the large covered forms of his sculptures; they were as familiar to me as a gathering of friends — the thinking man, the weeping woman, the couple making love — though tonight each of them seemed weird and angry. For a moment I imagined them coming to life beneath their white sheets.

I moved past them quickly, toward the light coming from Jake's office. I expected to see him hunched over his laptop, headphones blasting over his ears, oblivious to my arrival as usual. But the small room was empty. His laptop hummed. I walked over to the desk. A cup of coffee from the pizzeria downstairs was cold.

I sat down in the chair and rested my arms on the desk, my head on my arms. I could still feel my heart beating in my throat. But in the familiar space, I started to feel safer, calmer. After a few minutes, I sat up to take my phone from my pocket and look at the text message again. In doing this, I jolted Jake's laptop. The shooting-stars screen saver vanished and it took me a second to register what I was seeing. It took another second after that to believe it.

It was the same red screen I'd been staring at on and off at my own computer. The
same website. Except now there was a small
window open in the upper right-hand corner
of the page, some kind of streaming video
of a busy street corner bustling with chic
pedestrians. I leaned in closer. It only took
the flow of traffic for me to identify the city
— the fat black taxis, the towering red
buses. It was London. The low brown buildings, boutique shop windows, and street
cafés made me think it was SoHo, possibly
Covent Garden.

I watched. It was night, the street lit by
orange lamplight. People were dressed
warmly, walking quickly. If the webcast was
live, it would be after midnight. The people
looked young, were mostly in groups it
seemed, maybe heading home from the
pubs, from late-night drinks after the the-
ater. I moved my face close to the screen,
looking for I don't know what. I half-
expected to see the shadowy form I had
seen in the photographs that had started all
of this. But there was nothing to see, just
groups of jovial people, hurrying from one
place to another in the cold evening.

After a while, I leaned back in the chair
and rubbed my eyes, which had started to
sting and tear.

"What am I seeing here?" I asked myself aloud. "Why would Jake have this on his computer?

A soft sound from the loft space was my only answer. That's when it occurred to me that the door downstairs had been unlocked. In all the time I'd been coming here, that door had been unlocked only once. I felt my throat go dry as I got up slowly and walked toward the doorway that separated the loft and the office. I noticed that the high narrow window, the only window in the place, was open. The night had turned windy and the breeze blowing through the window rustled the white covers over Jake's sculptures. It took only a second for me to identify with relief that this was the sound I'd heard. In the movement of the air the covered forms looked like a population of restless spirits, rooted to the ground but dreaming of flight.

I scanned the room and my eyes fell on something else: a large black kidney-shaped stain on the floor near the standing artist's lamps that Jake turned on when he was working. Beside the stain was the hammer he used to bend and shape the metal. I walked slowly toward it, wary of the rustling shapes behind me, my right ear (my stress alarm) buzzing loudly. I reached up the thin metal rod that held the light, felt for a switch and found one. Though the ceiling lights hadn't come on, this one did. The glaring white from the bulb made me blink. It took my eyes a few seconds to adjust.

When they did, I could see that the stain wasn't black, of course, but deep red. Blood. Too much of it to be healthy for anyone. I stepped back. The room tilted unpleasantly.

There was thunder then, a distant and insistent pounding. I thought it might be coming from my own head, but eventually I recognized it for what it was: the sound of footfalls on the stairs. I was in a kind of shock, lost in a place of fearful imagining of the scene that might have left that stain on the floor, wondering whose blood it was, praying that it wasn't Jake's. I turned to see a man charging up the stairs, gun drawn. Every instinct told me to run, but there was only one way out of the loft.

And then I heard my name: "Ridley?" It was a voice I recognized.

When he stepped into the light, his face looked softer and kinder than I had known it; not arrogant, not full of some secret knowledge. Agent Dylan Grace.

"Ridley," he said, putting his hands on my

shoulders. "Are you okay?" His eyes moved to the bloodstain on the floor. "Are you hurt?"

"No," I said. "No."

"What's happening? Why are you here?" he asked. I wanted to break away from the intensity of his gaze. I started to struggle against the grip he had on my shoulders, but he held me fast, forced me to hold his eyes.

"Listen to me," he said. "Esme Gray is dead. Witnesses place Jake Jacobsen at the scene around the time of death. Where is he?"

I shook my head. "I don't know. There's blood on the floor."

I felt as if I was breathing through a straw. Esme was dead. There was a horrible amount of blood. Where was Jake? White spots bloomed before my eyes, a sickening fireworks display. I don't remember much that happened for a while after that.

I have to admit, I am prone to blacking out under extreme circumstances. It's something I have recently learned about myself. If you've been with me since the beginning, you might remember this about me. It's not a fainting or swooning. It's more like a short circuit. Too much awful imput, too many terrified and confused thoughts, and *poof!* — lights out. But it's *not* fainting. So stop thinking that.

My head was still reeling when I was aware of things again. I found myself slumped in the chair by Jake's desk. Agent Grace produced a bottle of water; he cracked the lid and handed it to me. He looked sad, had dark circles under his eyes.

"Did you say Esme Gray is dead?" I asked, wondering if maybe I'd dreamed it.

He nodded. "She's dead. Someone beat her to death with his fists."

I thought about this; it brought to mind the horrors Nick Smiley had revealed, as well as my last encounter with Esme, her image of me with a sledgehammer, swinging at everyone's life. That she was dead and that she had died so horribly were abstract concepts to me. It didn't seem real and I felt nothing but a kind of light nausea.

"Not Jake," I said.

He shrugged. "Jacobsen was last seen on her porch, pounding to be let in. About an hour later he was seen running from her residence."

"When?"

"Earlier today."

"Who called the police?"

"Anonymous caller."

"But you have a positive ID?"

"Esme's next-door neighbor recognized him from a prior visit. Apparently Esme had told her who he was, asked her to call the police if she ever saw him around when she wasn't home."

I shook my head. "If he was going to kill her, he'd have been more careful."

"Unless it wasn't premeditated."

I shook my head again. I knew the heart of exactly one person in the world. Yes, I knew the sadness and the rage that dwelled there, but I also knew the sheer goodness of him. I *knew* Jake. No way.

It still hadn't sunk in that Esme was dead. Later I would grieve her and everything she was to me once. Now all I could think about was Jake.

"Trust me," I said. "I know this man. There's no way he would ever kill Esme, especially not like that."

He seemed to consider saying something, then changed his mind. I could almost guess what he was thinking: that I'd been wrong about people before, that maybe I wasn't the best judge of character. He might have wanted to say that at one point nearly everyone I knew turned out to be someone different than I'd thought.

I stood and pointed toward the loft. "What

about the bloodstain on the floor? Something's happened here. Maybe the person who killed Esme hurt Jake, too."

I thought about the red computer screen (hidden for the moment behind the screen saver), the street scene in London, the matchbook with its odd symbol and note still in my pocket. It was all on the tip of my tongue. But I remembered the text message: *Trust no one.* It seemed like good advice. I kept my mouth shut.

"What?" asked Agent Grace. His eyes were trained on my face as though he could read my thoughts there. "What are you thinking right now?"

I could almost believe that I might trust him, turn all of this stuff over to him to investigate or to dismiss. It is so easy to turn over power, to shift off responsibility and walk away. Maybe if Jake wasn't missing (not that he was *missing* exactly, but we weren't sure where he was at the moment), a bloodstain marring his floor, I might have been more willing to enlist Agent Grace's help. Something deep told me to heed the advice of the text message, that Jake might be the one to pay if I didn't.

"I'm *thinking*," I said, sounding slightly hysterical to my own ears, "that something has happened to Jake. And I'm wondering what you're going to do about it."

He didn't say anything, just kept those gray eyes on me.

"If someone killed Esme and there's blood on the floor here" — I was yelling now — "doesn't that seem like a connection to you?"

"I'm *looking* at the connection, Ridley."

Now it was my turn to go silent.

"My missing couple, Myra and Allen Lyall. A dead woman, Esme Gray. A large bloodstain on the floor of Jacobsen's apartment, Jacobsen nowhere to be found, last seen leaving the scene of a homicide. What do these people have in common? What links all of them?"

You didn't have to be a genius to figure out where he was going.

"I'm not the only thing that links them," I said defensively.

"No," he said slowly. "There's Project Rescue. But you're intimately linked to that as well."

I sat back down in the chair. Agent Grace pulled the other chair close to me and tilted it back against the wall, balancing on its two rear legs. I wished he would fall backward, hit his head and look like an idiot.

"When's the last time you saw your boyfriend?" He leaned on the word *boyfriend* with some kind of sarcasm or even hostility, maybe both. I thought about telling him that Jake wasn't technically my boyfriend any longer, but I didn't want to be disloyal to Jake. Or answer the questions that would follow about the current nature of our relationship.

"The night before last."

"And the last time you heard from him?"

"He left a message earlier today. Asked me to meet him here for dinner around eight."

"What time did he leave the message?"

"I don't know. Around three or four, I guess."

"How did he sound?"

"Fine." The truth was I couldn't quite remember what he had sounded like.

"Did he call you from the landline here," he said, nodding toward the phone on Jake's desk, "or from his cellular phone?"

"I don't know. I think from this phone. I can't remember." He'd called me from his cell; I could tell by the background noise. At least I thought so; I would check my caller ID when I got home. In any case, I didn't want Agent Grace to know that he'd been on his cell; it seemed incriminating somehow. I was dying to call Jake now but didn't know if it was wise to do this in front of Agent Grace.

He continued with the questions, writing my answers in a little black notebook he'd extracted from his pocket. "Where were you today that you weren't available to take his call around that time?"

I hesitated, thought about lying, decided against it. "I went to Max's apartment."

He looked up at me. "Why?"

I explained to him the reasons I sometimes visited that place. I could tell by the look on his face that he didn't understand, thought my behavior was suspicious. Which, of course, it was.

"Can anyone confirm that you were there?"

"The doorman, Dutch." I watched him write. "Is that the time around when she died?" I asked, deducing as much from his questions. "This afternoon around three or four?"

He didn't say anything, just kept scribbling in his pad. I felt a tide of panic swell for Jake, a desperate worry aching in my chest.

"I have to be honest with you, Ridley," said Agent Grace after a moment. "I don't think you're telling me everything you should be. I'm having a hard time trusting you right now."

I tried for indignation but it didn't take. I shrugged instead. "I really don't give a shit what you think of me, Agent Grace," I said, keeping my voice mild. It was true; I couldn't care less. This was new for me; I used to be worried about what people thought, eager to please and play by the rules. But that was before. Before I knew I was Max's daughter. "I don't trust you, either."

I wondered how long it would be before he started sifting through Jake's office, before he looked at the computer and discovered the strange website. I wondered if he'd make the connection between the streaming video in London and the overseas call that had come into my apartment. Of course he would. He was all about making connections. I wondered how much he knew already. Probably a lot more than I did.

"I'm going to have someone take you home, and I want you to stay there, Ridley."

"I want to stay here in case Jake comes back," I said.

"If he comes back here, I guarantee he won't be available for dinner," he said coolly. "Give me your cell phone."

"What? Why?"

"I want to call Jacobsen from your phone.

We've been trying to reach him but he hasn't answered. I'm wondering if he'll answer a call from you."

I didn't know what my rights were here. I felt another wash of panic, folded my arms across my chest, and looked down at the floor. He held his hand out.

"Seriously?" he said. "Don't make me wrestle it from you or take you into custody and confiscate your belongings, search your apartment. I might have to do that eventually, but it doesn't have to be right now."

It seemed like he was always issuing threats of this kind. I looked at his face and saw that he meant it. After another second's hesitation, I handed my phone to him, watched him scroll through my address book and hit send. He put the phone on speaker and we both listened to it ring. I closed my eyes, praying silently for Jake to answer, until the voice mail picked up. My heart dipped into my stomach as Agent Grace ended the call. I held my breath, wondering if he was going to scroll through my call log, check my messages. But he didn't do that; he simply handed the phone back to me. I was surprised; it seemed like a logical thing for him to do, to check my incoming and outgoing communications. We locked eyes and I considered giving everything up to him. Later I would look back on this as the last moment I could have asked for help out of the hole I was climbing into . . . a moment I let pass.

A stone-faced young man with a blond crew cut and a scar from his neck to his ear drove me home in a white Crown Victoria. I recognized him as Agent Grace's partner. I didn't remember his name. In the passing streetlights, his head looked like a wire brush. I stared out the window and cried quietly, hoping he couldn't tell, until he handed me a tissue without a word. I was afraid for Jake, afraid for myself, unsure of what to do next.

The man at the wheel didn't say a word as I exited the vehicle. I almost thanked him (that's what a good girl I am), but I held it back and slammed the door instead. As I let myself into my building, I noticed that he turned off the engine and seemed to make himself comfortable, as if he were settling in for a while.

Memory is elusive for me these days. When I learned that most of the things I had taken for truth about my life were lies, I lost faith in memory. The past events of my life? I started to remember them differently; odd tones and nuances started to emerge. And I couldn't be sure any longer if my original memories or the new ones were truer to the things that had actually transpired.

Like the hours Max and my father spent in his study, for example. I had always imagined them in there laughing and relaxing, drinking cognac and smoking cigars. Now I wondered what they talked about in there. Me? Project Rescue? If Max had had this awful dark side, did my father know about it? Counsel him on how to deal with the "demons" he referred to that last night?

Or the harsh conversations between Max and my mother. She disapproved of the parade of anonymous women through Max's life, resented bitterly their presence in her home and social life. They argued about it, but only when they thought my father was out of earshot. I wondered now why she cared. In the anger of their tones, was there something more? Intimacy? Jealousy?

I thought about those women. Who were they? All I remember was that they all seemed to be blondes, all in high heels, beautiful and distant, with something cheap about them. Were they call girls? Maybe some of them were. I didn't really know. I never knew their names, never saw any of them more than once. What did that say about Max? I could have started making connections here: the picture Nick Smiley had painted of Max, the accusations of matricide, how Max had never had a serious relationship with a woman. But I didn't. Not yet.

Max was not a handsome man. His skin was sallow and pockmarked from the acne he'd suffered as a teenager. His dark hair was thinning. He was big, awkward with his size. But he had a magnetic charisma that drew people to him like metallic dust. And, of course, there was his outrageous wealth. This drew people as well. But even though he was always surrounded by people, he carried an aura of aloneness. In fact, he was the loneliest man I've ever known. Maybe because he had so many secrets to hide.

After being dropped off at my apartment, I lay on the couch in the dark and searched my memories again for Max, for moments when I might have glimpsed the man and not my creation of him. But I couldn't get past the myth, the one to which I had been clinging. When I was a kid, I used to bring my face up close to the television screen and try to look beyond its edges. I was sure there was more to see. But there was nothing, just the two-dimensional image. Now I tried to look beyond the borders of my memory. There was nothing there.

I tried not to think about Esme and how she'd died. I remembered what Jake had said, about how scared she'd been. I'd seen the fear, too. It seemed she'd had good reason to be afraid. Who had killed her and why, I couldn't begin to imagine. I recalled the last words we'd said to each other.

I'll keep swinging until I know all the answers, I told her.

You do and you'll wind up like that New York Times *reporter,* she'd answered.

The memory was ugly and I cringed inside thinking of it.

I periodically picked up the phone and dialed Jake's cell, got his voice mail, and left a message or hung up. I tried not to think about the blood on his floor or what kind of trouble he might be in, or if he was hurt . . . or worse. Otherwise, my panic and helplessness were like something alive in my chest.

I called Ace.

"Took you long enough to get back to me," he said by way of answering the phone, presumably having seen my number on his caller ID. Or maybe I was the only person who ever called him. He was living on the Upper West Side near Lincoln Center in a one-bedroom apartment looking out over the Hudson. It was pretty nice, though sparsely decorated with just a couch, desk, computer, and television in the living room, a bed and dresser in the bedroom. He claimed he was trying to write a novel, a claim that annoyed me to no end for reasons I can't explain.

"I've got things going on, Ace," I said, maybe more harshly than he deserved. "The whole world doesn't revolve around you."

"Christ," he said. "What's *your* problem?"

I unloaded. I told him everything that had happened over the last few days, everything I'd learned, everything I'd found, about my trip to Detroit, about Esme, about Jake missing. I even told him about the text message in spite of its ominous warning. When I was done I went silent, waited for him to make some sarcastic comment, tell me to move on, or claim that I was losing it completely. He didn't say anything right away. I listened to him breathing.

"Ace, are you even listening?"

Sometimes he'd channel-surf when he was talking to me, or I'd hear him tapping on his keyboard, engaged in an online chat during our conversation. But God forbid I'd get a call on the other line while he was talking, or if he got the sense I wasn't giving him my full attention. He'd flip out. I know; he's kind of an asshole.

"I'm listening," he said. He sounded strange and grave.

I paused. "Did you ever get the sense that Max was someone . . . else?" I asked. "Did you ever see anything in him that would make you think there was something wrong with him? Like *really* wrong with him?"

He let go of a sigh, or maybe he was exhaling smoke — even though he'd given up cigarettes as part of his detox after rehab.

"Well," he said softly, "I never saw him the way you saw him."

I didn't say anything; I could tell he was collecting his thoughts.

"He was always a hero to you," he said finally. "You didn't know he was your father, but maybe on some cellular level you did. You used to look at him with these wide eyes, this adoration on your face. I never understood your relationship. It confused me as a kid. I was never sure what you were seeing."

I was surprised by what he said, by its presence and wisdom.

"What did *you* see?"

"Honestly? I saw someone angry and very lonely, someone who glommed on to our family because he didn't have one of his own. He was always drunk, Ridley, with some prostitute on his arm." He paused a second and inhaled sharply, telling me definitely that he was smoking. "I'm not sure why Ben and Grace allowed him so much unsupervised time with us. I was never sure what *they* saw in him, either."

I took this all in.

"You know he hit me once, hard in the mouth," he said.

"When?" I asked, surprised.

"I was thirteen, maybe. I was arguing with Mom." I hadn't heard him call her that in so long. He always called our parents Ben and Grace, as a way to express the distance he felt from them, I guess. "We were screaming at each other — I can't remember about what. Seems like there was so much screaming between us. I can't remember a whole lot of peace in our house, can you?"

I couldn't answer him. We'd had such different childhoods, though we grew up in the same house with the same people. I've said before that the two of us extracted different people from our parents, saw different faces. From Max, too, I guess. Max had never so much as raised his voice to me, never mind his hand. He'd never even been stern with me.

Ace didn't wait for me to answer. "He

came at me quickly," he said. "Told me not to speak to my mother like that, and he clocked me in the jaw."

"With a closed fist?"

"Yeah. Probably not as hard as he could have, but hard enough."

"What did Mom do?"

"She freaked. She kicked him out. She comforted me, put ice on my jaw, but she made me promise never to tell Dad."

"Why not?"

He was quiet for a second. "I don't know."

I felt sorry for him, also angry with Max that he would hit my brother like that, and confused that my mother would want to keep the incident from my father.

Ace lied a lot; it's an element of the addictive personality. He exaggerated much of the discord in our house, or so *I* thought most of the time. I'd always believed that it was his way of excusing the bad choices he'd made over the years. But he wasn't lying about this. It lacked the usual self-conscious drama. It wasn't followed by a tirade about how it made him feel and what it led him to do to himself.

"Do you believe me?" he asked. He sounded almost sad. The curse of the liar: When you have a truth to tell, no one believes.

"Of course I do," I said. If we'd been beside each other, I would have wrapped my arms around him. "I'm sorry, Ace."

"For what?"

I thought about it for a second. It seemed lonely for him that he'd had these feelings about Max. Max was my father's best friend, my hero, my mother's . . . I don't even know what. It seemed so strange and sad that all along Ace was seeing Max as someone else completely, and that he might have been right.

"I don't know," I said finally.

I heard the metallic flick of a Zippo, the crackle of burning paper, and a sharp inhale.

"Ridley, is it even possible for you to keep yourself out of trouble?" he said with a long exhale. His usual arrogance and sarcasm were back. It was almost a relief.

"I didn't ask for this. Not for any of it."

"Are you sure about that?"

"What's that supposed to mean?"

"I mean, a year ago you could have chosen to turn away from all of this. You didn't. Now you have the chance to turn all of this over to that FBI guy, but you're not going to. You're the one who's always going on and on about choices, how they impact the course of our lives, blah, blah, blah. So what's it going to be?"

No one likes their own philosophies thrown back at them. Though I had to admit that he was right in certain respects. I *had* made some questionable choices. I *had* been guilty of putting myself in the path of harm when I could have easily crossed the street. But sometimes turning away just isn't an option.

"I don't know," I said. "I have to think."

"Well, I bet I know where to find you tomorrow night at eight."

I thought about the text message, about Jake. The fear in my chest made my breathing shallow.

"Ace?" I said, remembering suddenly what it felt like to be a kid, needing my big brother to chase nightmares away.

"Yeah?"

"Will you come with me?"

"Shit," he said, drawing out the word softly. I thought of how he never wanted me to crawl into bed with him when we were little, but that he always shifted over to the side to give me room.

"Will you?" I said, surprised at how scared my voice sounded.

I heard him sigh. "Okay."

I drifted off into a fitful sleep on the couch, the cell phone in my hand. I woke up a couple of times, sure I'd heard it ringing, expecting to see Jake's number blinking on the screen, only to find I'd imagined it. When it did finally ring, I answered it without even looking to see who it was.

"Jake?" I said.

"No. Not Jake." Agent Grace.

"What time is it?"

"Three a.m."

"What do you want?"

"Your boy is O negative, right?"

I thought of the pool of blood, how dark and thick it had been.

"Yeah," I said. I knew this only because the time we'd been in the hospital together, I'd peeked at his chart. He is what they call a universal donor — he can give his blood to anyone but can receive blood only from another type O negative. This seemed so unfair to me. And Jake is most definitely a giver; he never asks for anything in return.

"The blood in his studio is AB positive."

I felt something release its grip on my heart, let relief wash the tension from my muscles. Whatever had happened there, it hadn't been Jake bleeding out on the floor. That was something. Then I wondered: Was it Jake who sent the text message?

"I thought you'd want to know."

I didn't say anything. It was uncharacteristically nice of him to call. But I figured he had another agenda.

"Did you happen to look at his laptop while you were there?" he asked me.

I thought about lying but couldn't seem to force the words out.

"Don't bother answering," he said. "Your fingerprints are all over the keyboard."

I found it fascinating that he could carry on an entire conversation without my having to say a word. It was a real skill.

"That website with the streaming video of London — does it mean anything to you?"

"No," I said, just to feel as if I was part of the conversation. "I have no idea what it is."

"Have you ever seen it before?"

There was a knock at my door then; I heard it on the phone, too.

"Can I come in?" he said.

I walked over to the door and opened it for him. He looked tired. His hair was a mess, and there was some kind of grease stain on his shirt.

He ended the call and put the cell phone back in his pocket. "One of your neighbors let me in downstairs. Must have been coming in from a late night," he said, answering a question I hadn't asked.

"Where's your partner?" I said, shutting

the door. I was starting to get used to these little intrusions, found that tonight I didn't even mind. Now that I knew it wasn't Jake's blood on the floor, I was feeling less tense and had my sense of humor back. All the other things seemed far away, almost like a vanishing nightmare.

"He's in the car."

"Aren't you supposed to go everywhere together? How do you run the whole good cop, bad cop thing without him?"

"We don't get along very well."

"Imagine that."

He gave me a dark look. "Believe it or not, I'm not the bad guy here. I may be the only friend you have."

I thought again about how he didn't look or act like any FBI agent I'd ever seen. The agents I'd dealt with during the Project Rescue investigation had been all about rules and procedures; they'd been clean-cut and officious, bureaucratic and precise. In other words, the exact opposite of Dylan Grace.

"Where did you first see it?"

"What?"

"The website."

I sighed and sank into the couch. Ace's words rang in my ears. *You have the chance to turn all of this over to that FBI guy, but you're not going to.* What was it? Was I just being stubborn? Did I want to get myself deeper and deeper into trouble until I couldn't get myself out again? Maybe I was on some kind of self-destructive jag, acting out because of this low-grade depression that permeated my world. I decided to prove my brother wrong.

"At my parents' house," I said with a sigh. "I saw it on my father's computer." The admission felt like a failure on my part. It was like saying, "I can't handle this alone." It also felt like a betrayal of my father. I didn't know what the website was or who was using it. But it couldn't be good.

"But when I saw it there, it was just a red screen, no video," I added.

He pulled up a chair at the table, straddled it in that way he had, rested his arms on the back of it. He had an odd look on his face. I might have thought it was concern if I believed he was capable of it. Maybe I was being too hard on him. Then again, *Trust no one.* I should have had it tattooed on my arm.

"I tried to access it again from my computer here with the same results. Just the red screen," I said when he didn't say anything.

He nodded uncertainly, kept his eyes on

me. He looked at me like that a lot, as if he was trying to figure out if I was lying to him, as if he might be able to see it on my face. I turned away; there was something about that gray gaze that made me nervous. There was a lot more I could tell him. But I didn't. It was like flirting — give a little, keep a little. Maybe Ace was right about me after all.

"Do you have any idea what that site is?" I asked, my curiosity getting the better of me. I didn't want to have a conversation with Dylan Grace, and yet here we were again.

He shrugged. "The best I can figure at this point is that it's some kind of encrypted website. A place to leave and retrieve messages. There must be a way to log in, but I couldn't figure it out."

"And the video?"

He shrugged again. "We have some people working on it. We'll figure it out soon enough." His voice went low at the end of the sentence, as if he was issuing a warning.

I lifted my feet onto the couch, made myself comfortable. Fatigue was pulling at the lids of my eyes. Now that I knew Jake was okay, or at least that it wasn't his blood on the floor of the studio, everything else seemed less terrifying and urgent. But that was just one of the many things I'd be wrong about in the next twenty-four hours.

The next thing I was aware of was sunlight streaming in my east-facing windows. It took me a second to orient myself, then everything of the day before came back at me with sickening clarity. Had Agent Grace really been here? Did he really tell me it wasn't Jake's blood on the floor? I felt nauseated that I might have dreamed it all. Or that I had fallen asleep while he was sitting in my apartment. How weird was that? I noticed then that someone had taken the chenille throw from my bed and covered me with it. A dull pain throbbed behind my eyes as I sat up. There was a note on my coffee table. *We'll talk tomorrow,* it threatened, signed with the initials *DG.* It was the handwriting of an arrogant pain in the ass if ever I'd seen it — big looping letters, huge initials. I had to smile. I still hated him but he was starting to grow on me.

I tried Jake. Still no answer. I made some coffee so strong it tasted bitter in my throat. I walked into my office and looked over the notes I'd jotted down during my conversations with Jenna and Dennis. I checked the time; it was seven a.m. I had thirteen hours to find out as much as I could about Myra

Lyall and about that website before I went to the Cloisters that night.

I know what you're thinking: that I was at best reckless and foolish, at worst suicidal. What can I say? You might be right.

It was too early to call a hacker-wannabe like Jenna's ex-beau Grant, but ambitious people don't sleep in. A young assistant at the *New York Times,* especially one worried for her job, was likely to be at her desk before the sun came up. I called through the main number at the *Times* and was surprised and disappointed to get voice mail. I left a message.

"Sarah, this is Ridley Jones. Before her disappearance Myra Lyall was trying to reach me. Some pretty odd things have been happening to me since. I wonder if we can talk, get together for coffee?"

I left my number and hung up. I know, it was a pretty risky message to leave, considering how many ears and eyes might be on my communications — not to mention hers. But I needed the message to be interesting enough to warrant a callback. The phone rang before five minutes had passed.

"Is this Ridley?" Her voice was young; she was practically whispering.

"Sarah?"

"Yeah."

"You got my message?"

"Yes," she said. "Can we get together?"

We arranged to meet in a half hour at the Brooklyn Diner, a tourist trap in Midtown where no real New Yorker would ever eat. I wondered at her choice but figured she just didn't want to run into anyone from the *Times.*

"How will I recognize you?" I asked her.

"I know what you look like."

One of the advantages of infamy, I guess.

The diner was crowded; a cacophony of voices and clinking silverware rose up as soon as I opened the door. Strong aromas competed for attention: coffee, eggs and bacon, the sugary smell of pastries on a tray at the counter. My stomach rumbled. I stood by the door and scanned the room for a woman sitting alone. There was a petite blonde with her hair pulled back severely from her face, but she had her nose buried in a copy of the *Post,* sipping absently from a thick white coffee cup. A mix of people sat at the counter. A pink puffy family of three, all wearing I ♡ NY T-shirts, huddled over a guidebook with the Statue of Liberty on the cover. I said a silent prayer that they wouldn't get mugged. A businessman chatted loudly on his cell phone, oblivious to the annoyed stares of people around him. An elderly lady dropped her napkin; the young man sitting next to her bent down and picked it up, handing it to her with a smile.

I watched, losing myself as I'm prone to do in wondering about people. Who are they? Are they kind or cruel, happy or sad? What causes them to act rudely or to be polite? Where will they go when they leave this place? Who will die in the next week? Who will live to be a hundred? Who loves his wife and family? Who's secretly thinking about shedding his identity, hiding his assets, and running away for good? Questions like these move through my brain rapid-fire; I'm barely aware of them. I can exhaust myself with my own inner catalog of questions and possible answers. I think it's why I write, why I've always enjoyed profiles. At least I get the answers about one person — or the answers they want to give, anyway.

I felt a hand on my elbow and turned around to see a fresh-faced girl with hair as orange as copper wire, skin as pale and flawless as an eggshell. The smudges under her bluest of blue eyes told me that she was stressed and not sleeping. The urgency in her face told me that she was scared.

"I'm Sarah," she said quietly. I nodded

and shook her hand; it was cold and weak in mine.

The hostess showed us to a booth toward the back of the restaurant and we both slid in. I noticed that she didn't take off her jacket, so I left mine on as well.

"I can't stay long," she said. "I have to get back to the office."

"Okay," I said. I got right to the point. "Why was Myra trying to reach me before she disappeared? I thought originally that she wanted to talk to me about her article, but I know now that it went to bed before she started trying to reach me. What did she want?"

A waitress came. We ordered coffees and I asked for an apple turnover.

"I don't know what she wanted," she said, leaning into me. "I know that she was working on the Project Rescue story. It wasn't a news piece, just a series of profiles on these people who might have been some of the children removed from their homes. She wasn't that into it, did it more to make a new editor at the *Magazine* happy. But she learned something during her research that really got her jazzed."

"What?" I said. There was something skittish about her, as if she might get up and bolt at any second. I had the urge to reach out and hold on to her wrist to keep her from fleeing.

She shook her head. "I have no idea."

I looked at her, tried not to seem exasperated. "Okay," I said, releasing a breath and giving her a patient smile. "Let's start at the beginning. She was working on these profiles . . ." I began, letting my voice trail off. She picked up the sentence.

"And she was doing some background research about the investigation, about Maxwell Allen Smiley and about you. She talked to some people at the FBI. She got really annoyed one day. She'd just come back from an interview at FBI headquarters and said that she'd never had so much resistance on a 'fluff piece,' especially when the investigation was already closed. She said she was getting the feeling that there was much more to the story than had been revealed."

"So she set out to find out what that was?"

She looked at me with wide eyes. I was starting to think there might be something wrong with this girl. She was either a little on the slow side or scared and reticent because of it. I wondered why she had agreed to meet me.

"I'm not sure. I think so. Everything happened so fast."

She looked down at the table, and when she looked back up at me, she had tears in her eyes. I was quiet, waited for her to collect herself and go on.

"She was in her office. I heard her phone ring. She took the call, then got up and closed her door. I couldn't hear her conversation. About a half an hour later, she left her office, told me she was leaving for the day on a lead, and she was gone."

"You didn't ask her where she was going? What she was working on?"

She looked at me. "She wasn't like that. She didn't talk about her work. Not until the words were on the page. Anyway, I guess she was right about me."

"What do you mean?"

"During my last review with her, she told me she worried that I wasn't *curious* enough, that I didn't seem to have a 'fire in the belly,' as she put it. And that maybe I was more cut out for research than news investigation."

I could see that the comment had hurt her, but I could also see that it might have been dead on.

The waitress brought our coffee and my pastry. I wanted to shove the whole buttery, sweet turnover in my mouth all at once in an effort to comfort myself.

"When I went to shut down her computer and turn off her light for the night," she said, after a sip of her coffee, "I saw something strange on her computer."

I paused my own coffee cup between the table and my lips, looked at her.

"There was a website open. The screen was completely red."

She slipped a piece of paper across the table. I recognized the website address as the same one I'd seen at my father's and at Jake's. That humming I get in my right ear started up. I found myself looking around the restaurant, wondering if anyone was watching us. Just the mention of that website made me nervous. I didn't know why.

"Did you tell this to the people investigating her disappearance?" I asked.

"Yes," she answered, with a shrug. "They didn't seem to think much of it."

"Do you know anything about that site? What it means?"

She shook her head slowly. "I don't know much about computers," she said, casting her blue eyes down.

I put my coffee cup on the table and rubbed my forehead. I was getting the feeling that she didn't know any more than I did about any of this. I wondered again why she had wanted to meet with me. This time

I asked her as much.

"I want to help her. I feel like if I'd been more curious, the way she wanted me to be, then I might have been able to tell the police more. They might have been able to find her. I thought *you* might know something," she said plaintively. After a moment's pause: "Do you?"

I shook my head. "Not really."

"You said weird things have been happening to you. Like what?"

The warning in the text message came back to me. I'd already confided in Ace; for all I knew, that had been a mistake. I looked at this girl and wondered what could be accomplished by telling her anything, if there was more potential for gain than for risk. Finally I slid the matchbook across the table at her. She picked it up and held it close to her face, squinting and wrinkling up her nose. She took glasses from her pocket, placed them on her face, and gazed at it a while longer. She opened it and read the note inside. She handed it back to me with a shrug.

"I'm sorry," she said. There was something odd on her face.

"It doesn't mean anything to you?" I said.

She was rummaging through her bag then. She placed five dollars on the table and got

213

up quickly. "I have to go," she said. "I don't think we can help each other. You should —" I noticed she was looking over my head at something behind me. I turned to follow her eyes but I didn't see what she was seeing.

"You should," she repeated, "be careful."

"Careful of what?" I said, turning back to her.

She moved out of the booth and headed quickly for the door. I put another five on the table and followed. On the street, she had broken into a light jog.

"Sarah!" I called, picking up my pace. "Please wait."

She stopped abruptly then, almost as if something had startled her. She stood still for a second as I moved closer. Then she reached her hand behind her, as if she was trying to scratch an itch on her back she couldn't quite reach. She jerked again. By the time I caught up with her, she was on her knees and all the street noise around us seemed to go deathly silent. I dropped to my knees beside her. Her face was a mask of pain, her skin so pale it was nearly blue. She opened her mouth to say something and a rivulet of blood traveled down her chin and onto the pink collar of her shirt. People around us started to notice some-

thing was wrong and cleared a path; someone screamed.

"Help me. I need an ambulance," I said,
holding on to her as she sagged into me.
Soon I was supporting her full weight. A
young man stopped beside us and used his
cell phone to dial 911, dropping his brief-
case on the sidewalk.

"What's wrong with her?" he said.

I didn't answer him; I didn't know. He
lifted her off of me and laid her on the
ground, opened her coat, moved the strap
of the messenger bag she wore slung across
her body. Her hair fell around her like a
halo. Two bloodred blossoms marred the
front of her shirt. She looked like a broken
angel lying there on the concrete.

He looked at me, incredulous. "She's been
shot."

I stared at him, then past him. In the
crowd of people gathering around us, a man
in black moved slowly away. He wore a long
dark coat and a black felt hat. He seemed
to glide, to be swallowed by the crowd. I
heard the wail of sirens.

"Hey!" I yelled.

The young guy kneeling over Sarah turned
to look at me, his face flushed. "What is it?"

But I was already up and running, pushing my way through the throng.

"You can't leave!" I heard him call after me. "Don't you know her?"

My eyes locked on the man in black as he moved quickly up the crowded street. I kept losing and regaining sight of him as he got farther away. He was moving west, impossibly fast. By the time we'd crossed Eighth Avenue, I was breathless. At Ninth, I lost him completely. I stood on the corner and looked up and down the avenue.

A homeless guy lying on a cardboard mat gazed at me with interest. He looked as relaxed and comfortable as if he were lying on a couch in his own living room. He held a quivering Chihuahua in his right arm, a sign in his left hand. It read DON'T IGNORE ME. THIS COULD BE YOU ONE DAY. I ignored him.

"For five bucks, I'll tell you where he went," he said after a minute.

I regarded his dirty face and matted blond beard, his ripped Rangers team shirt, his mismatched shoes. He didn't look *that* bad for someone who was lying on the street on a piece of cardboard. I pulled a five from my pocket and handed it to him. He pointed south.

"He dropped something in those trash cans, hailed a cab."

"He hailed a cab?" I said, dismay and annoyance creeping into my voice.

He shrugged. The little dog yipped at me nastily.

I walked over to the trash cans he had pointed out; there were three gathered together at the curb. The smell was awful. "Which one?"

"That one," he said, pointing to the right. I hesitated.

"Pretty girl doesn't want to get her hands dirty," he said to his little dog, giving me an amused grin. "Welcome to my world."

I gave him a dirty look, grabbed the lid, and lifted it up. I was assailed by the odor and by what I saw inside. On top of the white trash bag lay a handgun with a silencer on its muzzle. I don't know if it was the smell or the gun, but I felt as if I might vomit. In spite of that, I reached in and picked it up, more to convince myself it was real than anything else. It was real. I stared at it in disbelief. I'd watched a girl get shot on the street, chased her assailant, and found his gun with a silencer. I felt a weight on my chest; my hands started to shake. I'm not sure how long I stood like that.

"Put the gun down. Put your hands in the air."

I froze and lifted my eyes from the object in my hand. I was surrounded by cops. Four uniformed officers stood around me. Two patrol cars pulled up next to us. The homeless guy was gone.

Depression is not dramatic, but it is total. It's sneaky — you almost don't notice it at first. Like a cat burglar, it comes in through an open window while you're sleeping. It takes little things at first: your appetite, your desire to return phone calls. Then it comes back for the big stuff, like your will to live.

The next thing you know, your legs are filled with sand. The thought of brushing your teeth fills you with dread, it seems like such an impossible task. Suddenly you're living your life in black and white — nothing is bright, nothing is pretty anymore. Music sounds tinny and distant. Things you found funny seem dull and off-key.

I was sinking into that hole as I was questioned by homicide detectives at the Midtown North Precinct. I told my half-truth to them, over and over in as many different ways as they wanted me to: I was returning a call from Myra Lyall and found out about her disappearance from Sarah. Sarah asked to meet me. There was a misunderstanding; she thought I could help her find out what happened to Myra. She left the diner when she realized I didn't know any more than she did. I went after her, feeling bad. I watched her fall to the street. By the time I got to her, she had two gunshot wounds in her chest and was dead. I saw the man who I thought might have shot her running away. I gave chase and found his gun.

If Sarah had saved my message, they'd know there was a bit more to my story than I'd mentioned. But I imagined she would have deleted it, as skittish as she'd seemed.

"So why was Myra Lyall trying to reach you?" said the third guy who'd come in to talk with me. He was older, looked pasty and tired. His belly strained the buttons on his shirt; his gray pants were too short. He'd introduced himself but I'd already forgotten his name. At this point, my depression felt more like apathy.

"I guess for a story she was working on, a profile on Project Rescue babies."

He looked at me for a second. "That's where I know your face."

"That's right," I said, yawning in spite of how rude and arrogant it seemed to do so, or maybe because of that. I was so sick of all these cops, playing their stupid games. They all thought they were so savvy, that they knew something about the human condition, that they knew something about me. But they didn't. They didn't know the first thing. I'd sat in too many rooms like this since the investigations into Project Rescue began. The process had lost its ability to scare and intimidate me.

The cop kept his eyes on me. They were rimmed red, flat and cold. He was a man who'd seen so much bad, he probably didn't even recognize good anymore.

"Are you tired, Ms. Jones?"

"You have no idea."

He gave a little sigh, looked down at his ruined cuticles. Then he looked at me again.

"A girl is dead. Do you care about that at all?"

His question startled me. Of course I cared about that. In fact, if I let myself think on it at all, on my responsibility for what had happened to her, how she was the second person to die in front of me in less than two years, I would crumble into a pile of broken pieces on the floor.

"Of course," I said softly. The admission brought a pain to my chest and a tightness in my throat. I hoped I wouldn't cry. I didn't want to cry. "But I don't know who killed her or why. I'd only known her for twenty minutes."

He nodded at me solemnly. He got up and left the room without another word. I folded my arms across the table and rested my forehead there. I tried not to see Sarah collapsing on the street in front of me, tried not to remember the night that Christian Luna had slumped over on the park bench, a perfect red circle in his forehead. I tried not to see the gun and silencer on the trash bag. But of course, all of these images flashed through my mind like some macabre slide show. Those black fingers were slowly tightening their grip around my neck.

The door opened and closed. I gave myself a few seconds before I looked up to see who was next to question me. I never thought I'd be happy to see Dylan Grace, but the sight of him caused every muscle in my body to relax. That's when I started to cry. Not sobbing, just tearing with a little nose running. He walked over to me and helped me up.

"Let's get you out of here," he said quietly.

"You're not going to cuff me, are you?" I said, wiping my eyes with the tissue he produced from his pocket. I figured that he was taking me into federal custody. I couldn't think of any other way for him to spring me from the NYPD.

"No. Not if you behave yourself."

His partner, whose name I still didn't know

and didn't really care to know, escorted me out to the sedan while Agent Grace filled out the necessary paperwork. They were calling me a federal witness, I'd overheard in the discussion between Agent Grace and one of the detectives who had questioned me. I wasn't sure what that meant.

His partner didn't talk to me, just opened the back door and closed it once I slid inside. He stood right outside. It was a bright, sunny day, cool and windy. He lit a cigarette with difficulty, then leaned against the trunk. I tried the door handle; it didn't open from the inside.

After agent grace got in the car, we drove uptown. I assumed we were heading to the FBI headquarters but eventually I realized we weren't. I didn't ask where we were going. I just used the drive to close my eyes and figure out how I was going to get away from these guys in time to get in touch with Grant, and get up to the Cloisters. Believe it or not, it wasn't even one o'clock in the afternoon yet. I still had time.

When the car came to a stop, I opened my eyes. Agent Grace handed his partner a manila envelope.

"This paperwork needs to be filed," he said.

"Why do I have to do it?"

"It's part of your training," Agent Grace said with a smile. "When *you're* training a rookie, then you can get him to go and do *your* paperwork."

"Where are you going with the witness?"

I watched their reflection in the rearview mirror, saw resentment on the partner's face and indifference on Agent Grace's. Agent Grace got out of the car without a word and then opened the door for me. We were at Ninety-fifth and Riverside. I wasn't sure what was happening. His partner gave him a dark look through the glass, then pulled out quickly into traffic, tires screeching.

"What are we doing?" I asked him.

"We're taking a walk," he said.

I felt my heart start to flutter. I didn't like Agent Grace's partner, but he did seem like the "good cop." He might be personally unpleasant, but he didn't seem dangerous. I guess I didn't trust Agent Grace very much. There weren't many people around us. It was a residential neighborhood, working class, bordering Morningside Heights. Riverside Park is a narrow strip of land nestled between Riverside Drive and the Hudson River. It rests atop a high divide and the highway runs alongside it, down a couple stories below. I could hear the traffic racing by, though a tree cover blocked my view of the road. A couple jogged by us as we walked the path into the park. Other than that, the park and the surrounding neighborhood seemed deserted.

"What are we doing here?" I asked him again, coming to a stop. I didn't want to walk any farther with him until I understood what he wanted. He stopped, too, put his hands in his pockets, and looked at me. Then he strolled over toward one of the park benches that lined the path and took a seat. Somewhere a car alarm blared briefly, then went silent. I hesitated a second, thought about sitting, then decided to stand.

"Let's cut the shit, shall we?" he said.

"What do you mean?"

"It's just you and me now, Ridley. No one can hear us. Just tell me what's going on."

"Why should I?"

"Because you and I have a common goal. We can help each other."

I looked up at the trees above us, the blue sky with its high white cirrus clouds. I smelled exhaust and wet grass. I heard a radio playing a salsa tune somewhere.

"I can't imagine what you think might be our 'common goal.' "

"Isn't it obvious?"

"No."

"We're both looking for your father."

I knew he meant Max, and I hated him for saying it like that. Maybe because it was true. I *was* looking for my father, literally and figuratively. Maybe I always had been. A denial bloomed in my chest, then lodged in my throat.

"We're all looking for him," he went on. "I am, you are, your boyfriend, too."

"Max is dead."

"You know what? You might be right. But you still need to find him, don't you? You still need to know who he was . . . or who he is."

I looked anywhere but into his face.

"Do you even know why?" he asked, leaning forward and resting his elbows on his thighs. I sensed another of those one-sided conversations coming on. "Because until you know, really *know,* you think you can't find out the answer to an even more important question. You can't know who *you* are. Who is Ridley Jones?"

"I know who I am," I said, raising my chin at him. But he'd opened a chasm of fear through my center, a fear that he might be right, that I wouldn't know who I was until I truly knew Max. Since last year, the only thing I knew for sure about myself was that I *wasn't* Ben and Grace's daughter. That I

225

wasn't the good child of good people. I didn't know whose daughter I was, not really. I had a better knowledge of my biology, but that was it.

You might be thinking that I am wrong. You might be thinking that if I was raised by Ben and Grace, taught and loved by them, then they are the people I come from — they are my true parents. And of course, in part that's right. But we're more than just our experiences, more than the lessons we have learned, aren't we? Isn't there some mystery to us? Any mother will tell you that her child was born with at least a part of his own unique personality, some likes and dislikes that had nothing to do with learning or experience. That was the piece of myself I was missing. I was missing my mystery, the part that existed before I was born, that lived in the strands of Max's DNA. If I didn't know him, how could I ever know myself? For some reason, I didn't have the same burning questions about Teresa Stone, my biological mother. She seemed distant and almost like a myth I didn't quite believe. Maybe those questions would come later. Max occupied this huge space in my life.

I'd been so hard on Jake for his obsession with Max. I guess I was really angry with myself for having one of my own.

"Do you?" Agent Grace asked. "Do you know who you are?"

"Yes," I said, defensively.

"So why are you chasing him?" he asked.

I gave a little laugh. "*I'm* not chasing him. Why are *you* chasing him?"

"It's my job."

"No," I said, sitting down beside him and looking at him hard. "It's more than that." Now it was his turn to look away. It wasn't until that moment that I realized why I didn't trust this man. He had an agenda, something that ran deeper than just a drive to do his job. He needed something from Max, too. I had sensed it in him, without being able to name what I was feeling.

"What is it, Dylan?" It was the first time I'd called him that. It felt right all of a sudden, made us equals. I'd noticed he'd started calling me Ridley a while back, though I'd denied him that privilege more than once. "What are you looking for?"

I expected him to snap at me or to tell me he didn't have to answer any of my questions. But he released a long breath instead, let his shoulders relax with it a little. I saw something I hadn't seen on his face before. It made him look older somehow, sharper and sadder around the eyes.

"Max Smiley —" he started, and then stopped, shut his mouth into a firm, tight line. The words seemed to stick in his throat. He looked at something off in the distance, something very far away. I didn't push him, cast my eyes to the concrete so it didn't seem as if I was staring at him. I shoved my hands in my pockets against the deepening cold.

After a while, maybe a minute, maybe five, he said, "Max Smiley killed my mother."

I let his words hang in the air, mingle with the sounds of traffic and distant salsa music. Somewhere I heard a basketball bouncing on concrete, slow and solitary. In the distance I caught sight of a painfully thin teenage boy alone on a court, shooting for the basket and missing.

I didn't know what to ask him first. How? When? Why? The information spread through my body. I tingled with it; a headache started a dull roar behind my eyes.

"I don't understand," I said.

"Forget it," he said. "It's irrelevant."

I put a hand on his arm but quickly withdrew it.

"Don't do that," I said. He still had his eyes on that faraway place. "Tell me what happened. If you didn't want to, you wouldn't have brought me here, you wouldn't have said anything at all."

I thought about Jake then, all the secrets in his past that I'd had to find out slowly, sifting through layers of lies and half-truths. The wondering of where he was and why he hadn't called was like having a sprained ankle — I was walking around but was always mindful of the pain. Since we met, there'd been only one other time that he'd disappeared like this, and that had occurred amid desperate circumstances. I'd wondered more than once if maybe he had killed Esme, if he was on the run. But I couldn't really see it. Or maybe I just didn't want to acknowledge the possibility that Jake's rage might have finally got the best of him.

"The details aren't important," he said.

"But you think he killed her."

"I know he did." He finally turned to look at me.

"How?" I asked him.

He remained stone-faced and silent.

"You can't just throw out an inflammatory statement like that and then clam up. Who was she? How did she know Max? How did she die?" I asked. "Why do you think Max killed her?"

He released a long breath. "Her body was found in an alley behind a Paris hotel.

She was beaten to death," he said. The information chilled me. I thought about the things Nick Smiley had told me. But Dylan's voice was flat, his face unreadable. He seemed to have checked out on an emotional level.

"I'm sorry," I said.

No response. I didn't understand this guy's communication style. One minute you couldn't shut him up, the next he was doing his best impression of a brick wall. I sighed, stood up, and walked a little back and forth to get my blood flowing through my freezing limbs. Something seemed off to me. I kept my eye on the time.

"Why do you think Max killed her?" I asked again. Without any details, the whole thing just seemed made up. It didn't ring true.

He opened his mouth, then closed it. Then: "Let's just say he had ample motive and opportunity."

I shook my head. I didn't want to disrespect him or his tragedy, but that wasn't exactly proof positive.

"You're going to have to do better than that," I said. "Anyway, I don't see what this has to do with me.

"I mean," I went on when he didn't answer, "if you've focused in on me because you think I know something about Max, you're talking to the wrong person."

"I don't think I am," he said. "I think you're exactly the person I need to be talking to. I've told you before that I don't think you're telling me everything you know. I'm giving you the opportunity to do that now, just you and me. Right now you're not a federal witness, I'm not an agent; we're just two people who can help each other find what we need to survive. You need to find your father. I need to find the person who killed my mother. They're the same person. We can help each other or we can hurt each other. It's up to you."

"I have a better idea. Why don't we just leave each other alone? I watched someone die today. I want to go home and forget that any of this ever happened. How about you go back to work and I go back to my life and we forget we ever met? You can get some therapy. Maybe I will, too."

At that, I started backing away from him.

Maybe we did have similar agendas: We both wanted Max Smiley to answer for things he might have done. But I didn't believe for one minute that we were on the same side. For all I knew, this was just some ruse to gain my trust so that I'd ally myself with him, share what I know, possibly lead him to the arrest of his life — a real career-maker.

I felt confused and scared, angry, too. I felt battered by the events of the last few days and by this man who wanted me to think he was my friend and my ally. I did the only thing I thought I could do in that moment. I ran.

10

I am a pathetically bad runner. I'm not built for it. No speed, no endurance. But I still managed to elude Dylan Grace, though only, I suspected, because he didn't get up and chase me with any real determination . . . and because I managed to hail a cab before he made it to the street.

"Ridley, don't be stupid!" he yelled.

I waved to him as the cab sped off.

"You shouldn't run away from your boyfriend," the cabdriver admonished. I looked at the ID plate: Obi Umbabwai. He had a heavy African accent. "There aren't that many good men around."

I gave him a dark look in the rearview mirror.

"Where are we going?" he asked after he'd driven south a block or two.

"I don't know yet," I answered. "Just drive around a minute."

"You must be rich," he said.

"Just drive please, sir," I said. I pulled my cell phone from my pocket and dialed the number I'd taken off of Grant's website. I prayed not to get voice mail as the phone rang. It was one-thirty.

"Go," he answered.

"I need to see you," I said.

There was a pause. "Do I know you?"

"Yeah, are you kidding? We met last night at Yaffa. You said you wanted to see me again."

He started to protest. Then he got it. Not too quick on the draw for a conspiracy theorist. He probably met his buddies on Thursday nights to play Dungeons & Dragons; that's probably as close as he'd come to any real intrigue.

"Oh, yeah," he said reverently. "Glad you called."

"Can you meet me right now?"

"Now?" he said, sounding surprised and a little uncertain.

"Now or never. I'm not a person with a lot of time."

Another pause. His breathing sounded heavy, excited. "Where?"

I told him where to meet me and hung up. I figured I was probably making his day or even his year. I repeated my destination to the cabdriver, who gave me a disapproving look in the mirror.

"Whatever you say, honey."

My cell phone rang and I saw Dylan's number on the screen. I pressed the button and put the phone to one ear but didn't say anything.

"Ridley, you are making a major mistake," he said. "Do you really want to be a fucking fugitive?"

I could tell by the pitch of his voice and by the fact that he'd resorted to cursing that he was *really* upset. I hung up and closed my eyes, leaned back against the faux leather interior of the spotlessly clean cab, and let it speed me toward Times Square.

You'd never know it by my adult life, but my adolescence was fairly free from drama. My brother caused enough chaos for both of us, so I always felt it was my responsibility to be the "good" kid, the one who never caused any trouble for anyone. I got caught with cigarettes once (they weren't even mine), broke curfew now and then. Nothing too terrible. I don't remember ever even being grounded for anything.

But there was a time after Ace left that I acted out a bit. I was just so *sad* and *angry.* I felt as if all this pain was living in my chest with no way of being released. I found I couldn't sleep well, couldn't concentrate at school. I lost interest in going to the mall or the movies with friends. I just wanted to stay in my room and sleep. I kept feigning illness so I could stay home. Not easy when your dad is a pediatrician. I'd just tell him I had cramps; he always seemed to accept this without question.

My parents didn't really seem to notice my distress, maybe because they were in their own states of depression. They'd tried to commit my brother to a drug treatment center against his will. Instead they'd driven him from the house. He was living somewhere in New York City, doing who knows what to himself. He'd dropped out of high school just months before graduation. And there was nothing my parents could do about it because he'd just turned eighteen. It was devastating for them. Sometimes at night when I couldn't sleep, I'd go down to the kitchen for a snack. Twice I'd heard my father weeping behind the closed doors to his study.

One morning my parents were screaming at each other as I ate my breakfast. I might as well have been invisible. I got my stuff and left the house without saying good-bye to them. Instead of waiting on the corner for the bus, I walked down the hill to the train station and hopped the 7:05 train. I got into Hoboken, took the PATH to Christopher Street, and walked around the West Village for a while. Eventually I worked my way to Fifty-seventh Street. Max had left for work by the time I reached his apartment. Dutch, the doorman, let me upstairs, and Clara, Max's maid, let me in the apartment. She made me a grilled cheese sandwich and gave me a glass of chocolate milk. After that, I went into the guest room, pulled down the shades, and went to sleep.

Clara didn't ask any questions, just looked in on me once and closed the door. I felt cocooned in the cool, dark place. I liked the silence, the soft sheets that smelled of lilac. I slept for I don't know how long.

Clara must have called Max because he came home in the early afternoon. He woke me with a light knock on the door.

"Let's get some lunch," he said, sitting on the edge of the bed.

He took me to American Grill at Rockefeller Plaza. We watched the ice skaters make their way around the rink as I wolfed down a huge cheeseburger, fries, and a milkshake. He didn't ask me any of the questions I was expecting. In fact, I don't remember saying much of anything. We just ate together in a comfortable silence until I was stuffed. Then he took me to the movies. I can't remember now what we saw — something funny and R-rated that my parents would have never allowed. Max laughed uproariously, drawing annoyed looks and angry hushes from the few other people in the matinee. All I remember is that the sound of his ridiculously loud laughter was contagious and soon I was giggling, too. I felt the heaviness in my chest lift, some of the sadness dissipated, and I could breathe again.

In the limo on the way back to his apartment, Max said, "Life sucks sometimes, Ridley. Some things go bad and they don't get better. But generally the bad stuff doesn't kill us. And the good things along the way are enough to keep us going. A lot of people have worked hard to make sure you see more good than bad. This thing with Ace . . . ?" He paused and shrugged his shoulders. "It's out of everyone's hands."

"I miss him," I told Max. It was a relief just to say it out loud. "I want him to come home."

"We all want that, Ridley. And it's okay to be sad about it. What I'm saying is, don't let it crush you. Don't fuck up your life because Ace fucked up his. Don't skip school and run out on your parents. Don't hide in the dark. You're a bright light. Don't let the Aces of the world snuff you out."

I nodded. It was good to talk about it with someone who wasn't in as much pain as I was.

"Your parents are wrecked right now. Take it easy on them."

My father was waiting for me at Max's apartment when we got back. As we crawled home to New Jersey in thick rush-hour traffic, my father and I talked about everything I was feeling. But he asked me not to talk about those things with my mother.

"When she's ready, we'll all sit down together. She's just too raw right now."

We never mentioned Ace's name in our house again.

I called Ace a couple of times from the cab. No answer. No voice mail. I quashed the fear that he might blow me off, that I might have to go to the Cloisters alone.

As we sped down the Hudson, I had to ask myself: Why were the men in my life so damaged? What was it about my karma that drew this kind of energy into my life? I thought of Max and wondered if it was really possible that he might be alive, if it was him I would find waiting for me at the Cloisters. Or maybe it would be Jake. I thought of the two of them out there circling my life like two dark moons. It felt to me as if they were on some kind of collision course, and if I didn't get to one or the other of them first, they'd both be destroyed in the impact — or I would. Add Dylan Grace to the mix and who knew how bad it could get.

Just off times square there's a virtual-reality arcade and Internet café called Strange Planet. It's three stories of all the latest video games, packed all day and late into the night with geeks and weirdos. Dark and crowded, with multiple exits, it was the perfect place for a clandestine meeting with a computer nerd. The windows were blacked out, so when I slipped inside, I felt as if I had entered some bizarre future world. Surfer dudes, skater chicks, punks, and hackers all shuffled about from game to game, drinking smoothies and trying to look cool. A crowd had gathered around an overweight kid jerking in front of a kung fu game. Techno music throbbed from big speakers but no one seemed to notice. An Asian chick dancing furiously on some odd disco game seemed to be moving to her own rhythm.

In a weird way, it reminded me of some of the drug dens I'd visited in desperate searches for my brother. They were dark, inhabited by zombies concerned only with the the next high. Where they were, the present moment, was lost to them; their eyes were glazed over, staring at things I could neither see nor understand. There, like here, I'd felt anonymous and invisible. Just the way I like it these days.

I jogged up a flight of stairs at the back of the building and entered the Internet café. I found a free kiosk toward the back, ordered myself a cappuccino, and checked my e-mail while I waited for Grant. I figured I'd know him when I saw him.

There was the usual crap in my in-box. I scrolled through the junk until I came across an e-mail from my father. The subject line gloated, *Having a wonderful time!* It was just a brief note from him, saying that they were in Spain and just loving the "spectacular architecture" and "glorious food and wine." I put my head in my hand against a wave of anger so intense that I thought I might puke up my cappuccino. I hit the delete button. As usual, my parents were off in their own little world while mine crumbled around me. I was starting to understand why Ace disliked them so much. Then I saw the e-mail from Ace, subject line blank. The message read, *I can't make it tonight, Ridley. I suggest you rethink this. Sorry.*

I wrote my reply: *Coward.* I hit send. Lately I'd deluded myself into thinking I would be able to count on my family in a pinch. But I was remembering what I'd learned last year. *You're on your own.*

I pulled the cell phone from my pocket and tried Jake again. His voice mail picked up before I even heard a ring. "Oh my God," I said softly into the phone. "Where are you?"

The café was crowded with all kinds of people — students with backpacks, businesspeople with soft laptop cases, even an elderly woman with a walker parked by her chair — their faces lit by the glow of the screens in front of them. But I'd never felt so alone. I looked at the time on my phone; Grant was already five minutes late. I had six hours until my appointment at the Cloisters — an appointment I would be keeping, as I'd feared, alone. I reached into the inside pocket of my coat and pulled out my wallet, which contained a clutter of receipts and business cards and very little cash. I sifted through the mess until I found what I was looking for: a business card given to me by the only FBI agent who treated me decently during my father's investigation. Her name was Claire Sorro; she was older than me by about ten years. Professional and courteous, she had been kind to me when other people were cold and officious. I dialed her number and leaned into the cover of the faux wood walls around me.

"Sorro," she answered.

"Agent Sorro, this is Ridley Jones."

"Ridley," she said. Her voice sounded cautious and I wondered if people already knew I'd gotten away from Agent Grace.

"I have to talk to someone about Special Agent Dylan Grace."

"Okay . . ." she said, her voice trailing off.

"He shouldn't be working on the case involving Myra Lyall. He has a history with Max Smiley — he believes that Max killed his mother. And he's using me to find out if Max might still be alive."

"Ridley," she started. But I interrupted her. If I'd been listening to myself, I would have realized that I wasn't making a whole lot of sense. I was assuming a lot of knowledge on her part.

"I know I shouldn't have run away from him, but I'd be willing to come into the FBI — if he was taken off the case. Sometime tomorrow. I didn't have anything to do with Sarah Duvall's murder." I took a breath.

"Ridley," she said quickly in the pause, "I

have no idea who you're talking about."

"Agent Dylan Grace," I repeated.

"I've never heard of him."

My heart started to thump.

"What I do know, Ridley, is that your face is all over the news. They're saying that you're a person of interest in the murder of Sarah Duvall and that an accomplice helped you to escape from NYPD custody."

"No, not an accomplice," I said, my mouth going dry. "Agent Grace took me. I'm a federal witness."

"Not anymore you're not. The Project Rescue case is long closed."

"I've been under surveillance for a year. Someone over there is still looking for Max Smiley. They thought he'd come for me, because he loved me."

In the silence that followed, I realized that I sounded like a crazy person. A sad, desperate crazy person searching for a dead man who loved her once.

"Ridley," Agent Sorro said carefully, her voice soothing, "Max Smiley is dead. You know that."

I tried to think back on all the things Dylan Grace had told me and suddenly it all seemed nebulous. How much had I filled in with my own imagination? How much had he really said? I told her how he'd showed me his ID on the street that day and took me in for questioning, about the photographs, how he was trailing me, how he'd had access to my phone records, how he'd taken me from the police precinct. I must have sounded hysterical, possibly delusional. I wondered if she was tracing this call, if she could triangulate the signal and figure out where I was.

Another heavy silence followed. "What did you say this man's name was again?"

"Dylan Grace," I said, feeling more and more foolish by the second. "Are you seriously telling me you've never heard of him?"

"I'm telling you I've never heard of him," she said. "And I'm looking on the database now." I could hear her fingers tapping on a keyboard. "There's no one listed in our files by that name. No one named Dylan Grace works for the FBI anywhere in the U.S."

I let the full impact of the information register. For a moment, I wondered if I'd imagined him altogether, if *all* of this was just a figment of my imagination. Maybe I should check myself into a hospital somewhere, get some meds.

"Listen, Ridley, it sounds to me like you're in more trouble out there than if you turned yourself in. The NYPD just wants to *talk*," she said with a slight singsong quality to her voice that told me she thought I'd gone over the edge. "I'll meet you somewhere and bring you in if you want. We'll get it all worked out. We need to find out who this guy is, why he's been impersonating an FBI agent, and what he really wants from you. We can help each other."

Just then I heard the lightest click on the line. It brought me back to myself. I weighed the pros and cons of just turning myself in. She was right; I'd probably be safer. But part of me had already decided that this meeting at the Cloisters was the only way to Max. Something inside me had seized on that, and even though I had no reason to think it was true, I just couldn't let it go. If eight o'clock came and went and I wasn't at the Cloisters, Max would elude me forever. I wasn't sure if I could live with that.

"Okay, Agent Sorro, thanks," I said.

"Where do you want to meet?"

"Um . . . I'll think about it and get back to you."

"Ridley —"

I ended the call then and sat there for a second, every nerve ending in my body tingling, my stomach in full rebellion. I had been lied to and tricked by Dylan Grace, my imaginary friend. I didn't even know how to react or what to think. Oddly, I didn't even feel that shocked or betrayed. In a way, I guess I had always expected him to be something other than what he appeared to be. It was almost a relief to know that I had been right about him.

I scanned the room around me. No one was looking in my direction, everyone hyper-focused on the screen in front of them. I wanted to scream for help, but of course I didn't. Then I saw a young guy huffing and puffing his way up the stairs. He was pasty and soft but had a pretty face framed by a mass of golden curls; he wore tiny round silver spectacles. I was sure it was Grant. I felt scared suddenly that I'd led the poor kid into danger, that I'd wind up kneeling over his dead body on the floor. I thought about bolting, but he saw me and made his way over.

"I knew it was you," he said as he sat down heavily. He took off his glasses and wiped them on the hem of his T-shirt. His shirt read THE ONLY THING NECESSARY FOR EVIL TO TRIUMPH IS FOR GOOD MEN TO DO NOTHING.

I didn't say anything just out of surprise that he'd recognized me.

"Man, you are in some serious shit." I heard admiration in his voice. "You must have done something pretty fucked up in another life to have this much trouble raining down on you again."

I thought it was a pretty insensitive thing to say and told him as much.

"Sorry," he said. "You're right. How'd you slip the NYPD?"

I was taken aback by his question. It really *was* all over the place. Part of me had been hoping that Agent Sorro was exaggerating or even making it all up, part of some elaborate ruse to cover up a secret investigation into Max's alive-or-dead status.

"I didn't *realize* I was slipping them," I said defensively. "I thought I was being taken into federal custody."

He cocked his head and looked at me. "What do you mean?"

I told him the whole story, starting from the day Dylan approached me on the street, ending with my leaving him in Riverside Park. I even told Grant about the text message and my meeting at the Cloisters.

"Man," he said, shaking his head. "This is bigger than I thought."

He was enjoying this a little too much. It was annoying me.

"Pretty brave of you to come, considering a number of people I have come in contact with during the last few days are dead or have disappeared," I said, paying him back for his earlier comment.

"No one's going to touch me. I'm too high profile," he said with a casual shrug and uncertainty in his eyes. I thought he might be kidding. Did he really consider himself high profile? I almost laughed but saw he was serious and gave him a knowing nod.

"Of course you are," I said. He didn't seem to hear the sarcasm in my voice.

"How did you hear about me? My website?"

"No," I said. "Jenna Rich told me about you."

"Oh," he said, looking embarrassed. I wondered if he'd heard through other sources the not-so-nice things she had to say about him. I felt bad for him suddenly.

"She said you were a computer genius and that you had some interesting theories about Myra Lyall. I looked on your site and thought you might be able to help me."

He seemed to brighten at this a bit. "Help you how?" he asked, leaning forward with alacrity.

I typed in the URL on my borrowed computer and up popped the red screen.

"I need to know what this website is," I said. I told him about the streaming video of Covent Garden that I'd seen on Jake's computer.

He slid in closer to me, pushed his little glasses up toward his eyes, and he smelled not unpleasantly like Krispy Kreme doughnuts. There was something teddy-bearish and appealing about him. He tapped away on the keyboard for a second and two small narrow windows opened. A curser blinked in one of the blank white spaces, waiting for a prompt.

"It's waiting for a log-in and password," he said, turning to look at me.

"How did you do that?" I said with grudging admiration.

He blew out arrogant disdain from his nostrils. "This is your basic cloak-and-dagger program. Wannabe spy shit one-oh-one."

I noticed a sheen of sweat on his forehead and wondered if he was nervous or just hot. He was pretty out of shape, the room was over-warm, and even I'd felt a little breathless after the flight of stairs.

I shook my head. "I don't understand."

"It's called steganography, deriving from the Greek, meaning 'covered writing.' It's a way to embed messages within other seemingly harmless messages. There's software, like Noise Storm or Snow, that allows you to replace useless or unused bits of data in regular computer files . . . like graphics or sound, even video. I just tabbed around until I hit the window where the prompts were hiding."

I looked at the prompts, my mind already working on what my father's log-in and password would be. Probably the same as his home computer; he's nothing if not predictable. I reached for the keyboard.

"Wait. Don't just make a quick guess. If you enter the wrong thing, you might alert the webmaster of an unauthorized attempt to enter the site. The prompts or the site itself might disappear altogether."

I just looked at him, withdrew my hand.

"This is not typical of steganographic sites, though," he said, as if thinking aloud. "I mean, usually it would be masquerading as something else, like a porn site, or even a mystery bookstore. Then messages would be hidden in elements of the site, like I said . . . images or sound files."

"Or streaming video," I said, thinking of Jake's computer. He nodded.

"Those messages might be encrypted on top of that. There's a program called Spam Mimic. Say there was a message waiting for you at a site like this. You'd get a message in your in-box that would look like ordinary spam that most people would delete. But you'd know it was an alert to check the site."

I thought about my father's computer, all the junk mail there. I wondered if one of those spam messages had been an alert that a message was waiting for him.

Grant went on. "When you click on the link, it leads you to the message site. You get your message and supposedly you have the means to decrypt it."

"Who would set up this kind of thing?"

He shrugged. "The government has been making a lot of noise that terrorists are using communications like this. They want stricter regulations on the software that makes it possible to create these encrypted messages. They're virtually untraceable. Unless someone stumbles on a site like this and knows what they're looking at, there's no way to even know it exists. More and more, this type of thing is preferred to phone communications. The government is nervous because it significantly cuts down on the 'chatter' they monitor through conventional counterterrorism measures."

I wasn't sure what he meant by chatter, though I'd heard the term before. I asked him about it.

"Yeah, the government can monitor terrorist activity by watching the frequency of communications between known terrorist groups. When they see an increase in communications — or even a falling off of communications — coupled with other things, say content intercepts or satellite observations, they know something is going on. But things like these websites, disposable cell phones, even Internet cafés like this one are making things a lot harder for them. Of course, organizations like the FBI and CIA probably use sites like this all the time to communicate with agents in the field, freelance contacts, God only knows who else. They just don't want anyone else using it."

"Sarah Duvall told me that Myra Lyall had a screen like this up on her computer when she ran out of the *Times* that afternoon."

"No shit?" he said. "Can I put that on my site?"

I gave him a look. "I wouldn't advise it."

He took his glasses off again and rubbed them on his T-shirt. He was sweating profusely now.

"Is there any way to know who set up this site or where it originates from?"

"I can take the URL and go back to my place, see what I come up with," he said, putting his spectacles back on. "There are ways to trace these things, and I know a

couple of guys who might be able to help."
I could tell he was trying to act cool, but it
wasn't working. A tiny bead of sweat
dripped down the side of his face.

"Can I get you some water or something?"

"Sorry," he said, rubbing his brow with
his hand and then wiping his hand on his
pants. "I sweat when I get really excited.
This is pretty exciting stuff. I mean, I can't
believe I'm sitting here with Ridley Jones."

The way he said my name, with such awe
and reverence, made me a little queasy.
"What are you talking about?"

"I've been writing about the whole Project
Rescue thing for months. If it weren't for
you, none of it ever would have been exposed. Now you're on the run from the
police. Max Smiley might be alive. It's too
rich."

I felt my face go hot with anger and annoyance. "This is my *life,* Grant, not some
movie of the week. People are *dead.* This is
serious."

"I know," he said. "That's what makes it
so cool."

"Look," I said, rubbing my eyes. I felt so
tired suddenly. "Can you help me or not?"

"What do you want me to do?"

"I want to know where this website originates from, how to log in, and what kind of

messages are contained inside."

He took his glasses off again and looked me dead in the eye. The teddy-bear sweetness was gone. "What's in it for me?"

I shrugged. "What do you want?"

"An exclusive interview with Ridley Jones for my website," he said without hesitation.

What a vulture, I thought. His eyes suddenly looked beady; he had an aura of smugness about him as he leaned back in his chair. I wanted to punch him in his big, soft belly.

"Okay," I said. "When this is over."

He raised his eyebrows. "No offense, but how do I know you're going to make it, you know? You said yourself everyone else in this mess has disappeared or is dead. What makes you think you'll be any different?"

I felt my stomach bottom out. People say the shittiest things, don't they?

I forced an aura of confidence and gave him a wan smile. "That's a chance you're going to have to take, Grant."

I wondered if he'd walk away. He didn't have to do this, would probably be better off if he didn't. But I was banking on his curiosity getting the better of him.

"How will I reach you?" he asked.

I slid him one of my business cards, which displayed my name, home phone, cell, and e-mail address. "I'll be in touch with you in a couple of hours."

"A couple of *hours*," he protested, lifting his hands. "Dude. Impossible."

"Grant, I don't have a lot of time. Just do your best."

He nodded, scribbled down the URL on the back of my card, and shoved it into the pocket of his jeans. "I better bolt." He handed me a card as well. "Here are my numbers. They're all secure. There's a secure e-mail address on there, too."

I slipped it into my pocket and watched him get up. "I'm serious, you know," he said, looking at me. "Your face is everywhere — on the television, the *Times* website . . . will probably make the evening editions. If you're not looking to get caught, be careful."

I remembered the last time my face had been all over the place, just after I'd saved Justin Wheeler. People had stopped me on the street to hug me, to give their well wishes. And even still, my life had gone to hell as a result of that exposure. I wondered what happens when your face is all over because you're wanted by the police. I realized it might not be so easy to get to the Cloisters.

"You, too," I answered. "Nothing on the

site, Grant. Not about the call or this meeting — you could get us both in a lot of trouble."

He nodded, started walking away.

"So, hey, first question," he said, turning back to me. "What's it like being the total Project Rescue baby?"

I looked at him.

"It sucks, dude," I said. "Totally."

I hung around in the dark safety of Strange Planet for a while, trying to figure out what to do. I had another cappuccino. I felt as if the second I stepped back out into the light, I'd be identified and taken into custody — which might not have been the worst thing in the world as far as my personal well-being was concerned. I spent a few minutes staring at the red screen, sipping coffee, and thinking about Agent Sorro's advice. But then I thought about Dylan Grace and the things he'd said in the park. It turned out he was a liar, and God knows who he worked for or what his agenda was, but he was right about one thing: Whether he was alive or dead, I *was* chasing Max.

Instead of finding clarity from knowing the truth about my past, I had felt my delicate self-concept becoming more and more nebulous. Every day, I felt less connected to the woman I was.

It was obvious that the only way to understand myself was to find Max, my father. I had to find him or I'd lose myself completely. I knew this with a stone-cold certainty. If I allowed myself to be taken in, I might never have the answers I needed. A door was closing, and if I didn't slip inside before it shut, it might be locked forever.

I remembered that day in the woods behind my house. Max had said, "There's a golden chain from my heart to yours. Trust me. I'll *always* find you." He was right. I knew it then, I knew it now. And I knew I was the only one who could bring Max home. That connection had always felt like a gift. Now it felt like a curse.

Then, of course, there were the other things I'd fallen into, or had been dragged into, depending on your perspective: Myra Lyall's disappearance, Esme Gray's and Sarah Duvall's murders, the question of Dylan Grace. (Not to mention, where the hell was Jake?) Myra Lyall had accused Sarah of lacking that belly of fire, that raging curiosity to just *know* the truth. She could never have accused me of the same. What was so awful that all these people were dead or missing or lying? What had they learned? Who wanted them to be quiet?

Who was the man in black who had killed Sarah Duvall so audaciously on the street and then disappeared? What did all of it have to do with me?

Ace had accused me of choosing trouble. Maybe he was right. But sometimes I had to think trouble chose me.

When I figured the light had gone low in the sky, I left Strange Planet, made a stop at a drugstore, and picked up a few things. I checked into an SRO near Forty-second Street, the kind of awful place nice girls from the suburbs never even know exist, populated by transients, the homeless, hookers, and people just clinging to the fringes of the world, barely able to make their rent day to day. Dark stairways, dirty hallways, hollowed-out people staggering through — it truly was a land of the lost.

The room was small and filthy in spite of smelling like antiseptic. I could hear yelling and the sound of multiple television sets blaring through the thin walls. I wasn't staying; I just needed the small private bathroom for a while. In my plastic bag was a bottle of hair dye, an electric shaver, a pair of sunglasses, and a black cap.

When I left that bathroom, my thick auburn tresses (one of the things I've been most vain about) were in the drugstore bag, tied tight and clasped in my hand, about to be stashed in the Dumpster outside. I'd turned my leather jacket inside out and cut out the tags, exposing the silk lining. I popped the dark lenses out of the sunglasses and wore only the frames (there's nothing more obvious than someone wearing sunglasses at night). I put the cap on over my new spiky platinum-blond hair.

The girl in the mirror? I didn't even know her.

11

I've always been attractive — not *hot,* not *gorgeous,* but pretty enough to get along, not so beautiful as to attract undue attention. Weirdly, I've always been grateful for this. I was never one to wish I looked like the girls in the Victoria's Secret catalog, with their jutting bones and vamping eyes, or the models on magazine covers, with their airbrushed beauty. I never primped or starved or strutted for male attention — attempts I've always found to be somewhat sad and desperate in other women. My mother always said, "You are the one to do the choosing, dear. Not the one who waits to be chosen." She knew something that most women don't seem to know anymore, that an awareness of your own worth is the most attractive quality in the world. That a woman centered and secure in her own power need never starve herself or subject herself to self-mutilating surgeries, may not even choose to hide her grays. She'll always have the kind of beauty that age and changing fads can't touch.

My mother also said, "If you do things to cheapen yourself, men will think they can have you cheaply and then discard you." These things included dyeing my hair, getting a henna tattoo, wearing midriff tops and fishnet stockings. Even when I resented these restrictions, even as I railed against them, I think I heard the truth in what she was saying. I was thinking about this because of the leering glances I drew on the street with my new platinum-blond hair peeking out of my cap. I wasn't used to being leered at on the street, really. I mean, this is New York, and there's always some lowlife catcalling or making a disgusting noise as you pass. But the most I might get from the average man is a quick glance or a smile. As I walked up Broadway toward the subway, men stared at me with odd looks and disrespectful grins. I walked faster and had to keep myself from running my hand through my hair. Was it the blond hair dye? Or was there something about me now that showed my fear and desperation?

I jogged down the stairs into the Times Square station and waited for the 1 or the 9. When a train came, I got on and walked through the cars to find the emptiest one, then sunk into a seat on the far end in the corner and closed my eyes.

I felt someone sit next to me and I scooched over toward the wall, kept my eyes shut.

"It's an interesting look for you. A little bit Madonna, the *Vogue* years."

I opened my eyes. Jake with an amused smile. I didn't know whether to slap him or hug him. I opted for the latter. He held me tight, as tight as I held him.

"I'm sorry," he said into my ear with a low whisper. "I'm sorry."

We got off the train at 191st Street and found a Cuban coffee shop in the bustle of the busy Inwood neighborhood. It's the tip of Manhattan, not quite the Bronx but close enough. The train is elevated here and the streets a grimy mix of mom-and-pop restaurants and Laundromats, bodegas and apartment buildings. It's a fairly safe working-class area but close enough to the bad stuff that liquor stores are gated, their clerks behind bulletproof glass. There's a heavily Latino influence in this area, which means the coffee is fantastic and the aromas of roast pork, rice and beans, and garlic are in the air.

We found a table toward the back, and I

took off my ridiculous glasses.

"They think you killed Esme," I said.

"And you're wanted for questioning in the murder of that *Times* assistant," he answered, "and escaping NYPD custody."

He seemed tired and pale but his eyes were bright. There was an edginess to him that was unfamiliar. The waitress came and we ordered café con leche and Cuban toast.

"I wasn't anywhere near Esme Gray yesterday," he said. "Last time I saw her was when I confronted her about Max."

"What about the blood in the studio?"

He shook his head. "I came back to the studio last night, hoping you'd meet me. The door was open. I knew I hadn't left it open, so I slipped into Tompkins Square Park. I thought I'd stop you before you went upstairs, but I looked away for a second, and when I saw you, you were moving so fast, I didn't get to you in time. I was about to follow you in when I saw the feds making their move. I hung back. Eventually I saw you leave with one of them. I bolted."

"You could have called," I said sullenly. "I've been sick about you. I left about a hundred messages."

He held up his cell phone. "Battery's dead. And I knew they've been watching you and your phone. I figured it was better if I just tried to tag you on the street some-where."

I nodded, looked down at the table. I noticed that he didn't seem surprised about the blood in the studio, that he didn't ask any questions about what else I had seen there or what the feds (if that's what they were) had found. I didn't ask him why he wasn't even curious.

"I almost didn't recognize you," he said, lifting his hand to my hair. "Why'd you do that to yourself? You should just turn your-self in. This is crazy."

"I can't," I answered, running one hand over my head, feeling the stiff, spiky pieces.

"Why not?"

"You know why."

"He's dead, Ridley."

"You don't believe that. And even if he is . . . I still —" I found I couldn't finish my sentence.

"You still what?"

"I still need to know who he was. You of all people should understand that."

He reached across the table and grabbed both of my hands. I looked into his beauti-ful face, those sea-glass green eyes, the soft lines at their corners, the dark stubble on his perfect jaw. His mouth was the most delicious shade of pink, like raspberry candy. I felt that physical pull to him.

He lowered his eyes for a minute, then raised them to me again.

"I was thinking about what Esme said. About changing our names and getting as far away from here as possible. Maybe we could do that. You and me. We could go anywhere in the world. Just start over. Start our own family. Just disappear. I want to let go. I want to move on. I feel like I've wasted so much of my life with this thing, with all the anger. It's possible, isn't it, just to walk away?"

Everything inside me wanted to tell him yes, yes, it is possible, and let's go. We could open some kind of tiki bar in the Caribbean or find an olive farm in Tuscany. I'll shift off my lousy family and the nightmare of Max and who he might have been. We'll have children and tell them we were both orphans, no family at all. They'd never be touched by the poison in each of our pasts. They'd have a clean slate. It sounded like a beautiful idea and for a split second I could almost believe it was possible. But we can't do that, can we? You can cut the ties that bind but not without losing a part of yourself. You can walk away and hide from the people who made you, but you'll always hear them calling your name. At least that's true for me.

I didn't say any of these things. But I know he saw my emotions play out on my face. He released my hands and leaned back in his chair. He started working his nail against a corner of laminate that was coming off the table. I saw him abandon his fantasy with a long exhale.

"So what now?" he asked. I didn't hear disappointment, only resignation, in his voice, as though he'd already known it wasn't possible for us. I hesitated only briefly before I told him about the text message, my meeting at the Cloisters. About Grant and the phone call I had to make.

"You saw it, too," I said. "The website. It was up on your computer. There was streaming video of a street in London. How did you log on?"

He shook his head. "I never saw it. I told you, I didn't go back to the studio that night." There was something oddly still about his face and I wasn't sure if I believed him. But I nodded. "And you didn't send that text message?"

He shook his head. "No, of course not." After a beat: "Who do you think sent you this message, Ridley? Who are you expecting to find up there?"

I didn't know the answer to that. Did I

expect to go and find Max waiting for me with answers to every question I had about him in my heart? That his answers would enable me to make peace with who he was and what he had done? Maybe part of me thought that might happen. But a larger part of me had no idea, wasn't even convinced that this was such a good idea. I know: *duh.*

We were there, Jake and I, in that place where silence is an answer, where you know each other so well that some questions don't require a response.

I took a sip of my coffee and kept my eyes on the door to the street, as I had done since arriving.

"I need you to promise me something," I said.

"What?"

"If he's alive, if we find him, I need to know you won't hurt him."

He gave me a flat look. "Is that what you think? That I want revenge on Max Smiley?"

"Isn't it?"

He didn't say anything for a second, just lifted his eyes to the ceiling. Then: "Why are you so interested in protecting him?"

"He's my father," I said.

"He's your *biological* father," he said, shifting forward in his seat.

"Yes. That counts for something. There are things I need from him even now, just like there are things you need from your biological parents. You get that, right?"

He nodded slowly. "I get that." Then: "The thing I'm most interested in is protecting you, Ridley. I don't want to see you get hurt. That's my only agenda."

"What do you need to protect me from?" I asked.

"Mostly from yourself. I'm trying to keep you from getting in over your head."

"Are you being purposely vague? What aren't you telling me?"

We had a staring contest then, which he lost. He cast his eyes to the table and didn't look up again. Jake seemed like a black box to me sometimes. I had the feeling that I wouldn't know everything there was to know about him until our lives were in a burning wreckage all around us.

"Call your Web guy," suggested Jake after a minute of silence. "We might at least have a better idea of what we're walking into."

He hadn't answered my questions. He hadn't given me the promise I'd asked for. I was starting to regret that I'd told him about the meeting at all.

I took the phone from my pocket and

noticed that the charge was dangerously low. I dialed each of the numbers Grant had given me and got voice mail. I was surprised; I imagined him waiting by the phone for my call. A dark sense of worry started to settle on me.

"No answer?" said Jake.

I shook my head and rubbed my eyes, then glanced at the clock over the counter. Just two hours to go. Jake seemed edgy suddenly, kept looking over his shoulder toward the door and around the restaurant.

"Let's get out of here. It's better to keep moving."

We walked along Broadway quickly, huddling close together, our arms interlaced. I'm sure that to anyone passing us, we looked like a normal young couple, maybe headed home for the evening. But we were so far from that, each running our own agenda, each with a head full of fears, a heart full of questions, and goals we barely understood ourselves. If I could have seen into the future a few hours, we would have hopped a cab to JFK, been in Tuscany by morning.

12

I awoke in a milky darkness that told me morning wasn't far off. My head pounded in a way that would seem natural only after a suicidal drinking binge or a minor car accident. The pain was so intense, I barely dared to move. Then I was aware of a bayonet of agony in my right side. I couldn't orient myself. I held back the urge to vomit. The room around me was one I didn't recognize. A hotel room — I could tell that much — posh and well-decorated with oatmeal walls and a rich bloodred carpet. The comforter on top of me was a bone-colored suede, the pillowcases fine cotton. Fear sat on my chest and pushed down on my lungs. I saw a dark wood bedside table where a small clock glowed 5:48 a.m. The room smelled of lavender.

I struggled to sit up but my head and my side wouldn't allow it. My throat was painfully sore and dry. I reached my arm out and pulled the phone to my ear with difficulty and pushed zero.

"Good morning, Ms. Jones. How can I help you?" A brisk male voice, British.

"Where am I?" I croaked. Was I dreaming?

He gave a light chuckle. "Quite a night, eh? You're at the Covent Garden Hotel. In London, ma'am."

Images danced in my mind then. High stone walls and strange men moving in from a glade of trees. I heard gunfire and the sound of my own screaming. I saw Jake falling. I saw blood, lots of blood. The man I'd seen on the street when Sarah Duvall was murdered moved closer, but I couldn't see his face. Over and over he asked me, "Where's the ghost? Where's the ghost?" I didn't have time to be horrified, to wonder whether these images were memories or dreams. I blacked out again.

Fort Tryon park was nearly silent except for the rush of traffic on the Henry Hudson whispering off in the distance. Jake and I had been here together before, the night Christian Luna died beside me. We'd sat in Jake's car in the parking lot so that he could comfort me while I wept hysterically in the passenger seat. That was a bad night; I hoped that tonight would be better. We cut across the lawn and made our way up toward the Cloisters. The air was moist and cool, but I felt a light sheen of perspiration on my brow as we moved through the trees.

I kept dialing for Grant as we walked, keeping my eye on the charge. There was no answer and my low-grade dread started to escalate as we moved from the relative safety of the tree cover onto the concrete of the drive. The stone shadow of the Cloisters loomed dark and Gothic ahead, rising against the starry night. I grabbed Jake's arm.

"Maybe this is a bad idea," I said as we approached the building.

He looked at me. "Um, *yeah,*" he said in a harsh whisper. "I'm only here because I figured you'd come without me. We can leave right now."

I was about to take him up on it when we saw the headlights of a car pulling slowly up the drive from Broadway. As we watched, the headlights went dark but the car kept moving toward us.

It was dark when I woke up again. The clock read 9:08. The pounding in my head had subsided some but not entirely. The sheets beneath me were damp. I reached to touch them, and when I drew my hand back, I could see that they were dark with my blood. I struggled up and turned on the light, fighting waves of nauseating pain. The blood had soaked through my shirt. I lifted the material and saw a bandage at my waist that was black with it.

I don't remember having any actual thoughts, just this weird calm — almost a blankness. I fought light-headedness to get to my feet. In the mirror over an ornate antique desk, I saw a girl I barely knew. She was pale, with dark smudges under her eyes, and looked shaky and unsure of her legs. Her blond spiky hair was matted and dirty. She had a nasty cut under her eye, bruising on her neck. I leaned over and puked bile into the wastepaper basket.

I managed to support myself with various pieces of furniture — an overstuffed chair, a dresser, a bookshelf — and made my way to the bathroom. I watched myself in the mirror and gingerly removed the bandage. A gaping red hole oozed blood. I had a slow leak. The sight of it made me swoon, but I fought not to pass out on the cold marble beneath my feet. I had to imagine that whoever had bandaged me had also removed the bullet that caused the wound. I pressed gently around the edges and didn't feel anything hard or foreign beneath my skin. But the pain caused me to puke more yellow bile into the sink.

I ran warm water over a washcloth, then sat down on the toilet. I put the washcloth to my side — I didn't really know what else to do. The idea of calling the police or an ambulance never even occurred to me. I must have been in shock. Anyway, the pain was too much. Everything went black again.

The car came to a stop and I stood rooted, feeling Jake behind me. I guess if I'd obeyed my instincts, we could have run at that point, but something kept me still, watching. My heart and stomach were in a weird chaos of excitement and fear, dread and hope. Was he there? Was he as close as that car? Had he seen me standing there? Jake started pulling on my arm. We moved back closer to the trees. I felt the phone vibrate in my pocket and withdrew it quickly; Grant's number glowed on the screen.

I answered it as Jake's tugging became more insistent. I started moving backward, away from the car. "This is not the time to be taking calls, Ridley," said Jake. He hated cell phones more than I did.

"Grant?" I said, ignoring Jake.

"Ridley," he said, his voice sounding funny

and tight. "Don't go there. Don't go to the Cloisters. You're fucked."

"What?" I struggled to remember if I'd told him about the Cloisters. I couldn't.

"They think you know where he is. They think you can lead them to him." His voice ended in a horrible strangle. I had no idea what he was talking about.

"Grant!" I yelled into the phone. I heard a terrible gurgle. "Grant," I said again. This time it felt more like a plea.

Before the line went dead he managed to say one more thing. He said, "Run, Ridley. Run."

I woke up back in the hotel room bed. I felt better. Or number, rather, as if someone had given me drugs. I had company. In the neat, comfortable sitting area beside my bed sat Dylan Grace on a sofa. His eyes were closed and he leaned his head against a closed fist, had his feet up on the coffee table. I couldn't tell if he was asleep. He looked pale and unwell. I didn't have enough energy to be afraid of him; I was too out of it. Definitely doped up, my whole being floaty and calm.

"Who *are* you?" I asked him. It was a philosophical question, really. He opened his eyes and sat up.

"You know who I am, don't you?" He frowned a little, as if he wasn't sure.

"I know who you've told me you are. I also know you're a liar," I said, my words thick and slurred.

"You're surrounded by liars," he answered. "I'm the least of your problems."

I thought this was a somewhat insensitive thing to say. I also wasn't sure what he meant.

"Where's Jake?" I asked him.

He rubbed his eyes, didn't answer.

"Where is he?" I asked again, louder. I struggled to sit up and he got up quickly off the couch, sat beside me.

"Easy, easy. You're going to fuck yourself up again," he said, putting a hand on my shoulder and pushing me back gently. "I don't know where Jake is. We'll find him. I promise."

"What happened to me? How did I get here?"

"There's time for all of that. Now you need to rest."

He reached for something on the bedside table. He came back with a syringe.

"No," I said, a sob rising in my chest. My voice sounded weak and insubstantial, like a child's; the hand I lifted to push him away had no strength. He didn't meet my eyes, tapped on the plastic tube.

"I'm sorry," he said, and jabbed the needle into my arm.

The pain was brief but intense, the darkness that followed total.

"What did he say?" Jake asked. He'd let go of my arm and was watching me with concern.

"He said to run," I answered, still looking at the phone in horror.

Jake took hold of my hand. "Sounds like good advice. Let's get out of here. This was a mistake."

But as he pulled me toward the trees, we could see the beams of flashlights cutting through the night. We stopped dead. There were five bouncing white points of light, maybe more, moving toward us, making their way through the woods we had come through just moments before. My heart started to thump. I saw Jake get that look he always got when we were in trouble, a dark intensity, a strategist's concentration.

Two men had exited the car, blocking our route back toward the street. The slamming of their doors sounded like gunfire in the quiet of the park. I stared at their forms, both of them tall and thin, moving with long gaits toward us. Neither of them were Max;

I could see that much even in the dark, even though I couldn't see their faces. Of course it wasn't Max. How foolish I had been to come, to bring Jake with me. I'd let myself be led here by some stupid fantasy. *They think you know where he is. They think you can lead them to him.* What did Grant mean? Who were these people? My feet felt rooted; something kept me staring, paralyzed. I barely felt Jake pulling at me.

"Ridley, snap out of it. Let's go," said Jake, moving me by placing both his hands on my shoulders and pushing me.

We turned and ran around the side of the museum, our footfalls echoing on the concrete. We had no choice; there was no way back to the street. On our way around the building, we tried a couple of the heavy wood and wrought-iron doors, the latched gabled windows. They were locked, of course. The museum was long closed. Inside were French medieval courtyards, labyrinthine hallways leading to high-ceiling rooms, a hundred places to hide. Outside we were exposed. The stone wall that edged the property was not far. I heard the sound of people running. I wasn't sure what our options were. It didn't seem as if we had many.

"Where do we go?" I asked Jake as we moved quickly toward the wall.

He took a gun I hadn't seen from beneath his jacket. "We get into the trees and just keep moving south along the wall, hope that they're not very motivated. Maybe they'll go away." I couldn't tell if he was trying to be funny. It was then that we heard the blades of a helicopter.

It rose as if it came from the highway below us. And soon we were deafened by the sound and the wind, blinded by the spotlight that shown from its nose. The men we had seen moving through the trees were suddenly approaching fast. We ran.

I woke up calling for Jake. In my mind's eye, I could see him falling. I woke up reaching for him but knowing he was far gone. I kept hearing that question: *Where's the ghost?* I hated my foggy head and my weak, strange body, which felt full of sand. Something awful had happened to me and to Jake, and I had no idea what it was.

The room was empty and I wondered if Dylan Grace had ever been here at all. Either way, I had to get moving. I couldn't be here anymore. I got up from the bed more easily than I had before. The bandage at my waist was dry and clean. I saw my jeans, shoes, and jacket on the floor by the door and, with a lot of pain, struggled into them. I looked around the room for any other belongings and saw nothing.

The hallway was deserted and the elevator came quickly. I didn't have anything — a bag, money, a passport, any identification at all. How did I get to London? Was I really in London? How would I get home? I was too confused and scattered to even be afraid.

In the posh lobby — dark wood floors covered with Oriental area rugs, dark red walls, plush velvet furniture — there was no one. I could hear the street noise outside; the restaurant and concierge desk were both closed. It must have been the small hours of the morning. I looked around for a clock and found one on the reception desk — 2:01 a.m. I rang the little bell. A man stepped out from a doorway off to the side of the counter. He was young and slight, with ash-blond hair and dark, dark eyes. He had an aquiline nose and thin lips. He was very pale and British-looking.

"Oh, Ms. Jones. You must want your things," he said. "Do you have your claim check?"

I reached into my pocket and (how about that?) retrieved a small ticket stub. I handed it to him without saying anything. I was afraid I might throw up on the gleaming wood. He nodded cordially and moved into the cloakroom, came back with the beat-up messenger bag I'd been carrying before all this (whatever it was) had happened. I took it from him and flipped it open. My wallet, notebook, passport, keys, makeup, cell phone were all inside. Somehow the sight of my stuff, benign and familiar, made me feel sicker and more afraid.

"I hope you don't mind," he said gently. I looked up at him. "But you don't look well."

I shook my head. The whole encounter was surreal; I couldn't be sure if it was actually happening. The ground beneath my feet felt soft and unstable. "I'm not. I'm . . . not sure how I got here. Do you know? How I got here, I mean? How do you know my name? How long have I been here?"

He walked from behind the counter and put an arm around my shoulders, a hand on my elbow. I let him lead me toward a couch and lower me onto its cushions.

"Do you think, Ms. Jones, that I might call you a doctor?"

I nodded. "I think that might be a good idea."

I caught him looking down. I followed his eyes and saw that the blood from my wound had soaked through its bandage again. A rose of blood bloomed in the snow white of my shirt. A shirt I didn't recognize as mine.

"Ms. Jones," I heard him say. He was looking at me with the most sincere concern; his voice sounded slightly panicked. He seemed like a very kind person.

"Ms. Jones, you sit right here and —" he was saying. But I never heard the end of his sentence.

■ ■ ■ ■

PART TWO:
THE GHOST

■ ■ ■ ■

13

Jung believed that one of the major reasons for violence against women was an unintegrated *anima,* or the archetypical feminine symbolism within a man's unconscious. He believed that all men have feminine characteristics and all women have masculine characteristics. Men, however, have been taught that the feminine parts of themselves are shameful and must be repressed. The result of this suppression has been a kind of global misogyny, soulless sexual encounters, and whole cultures where women are unsafe in their own homes. It's part of Jung's theories about the shadow side, the dark part of ourselves that we strive to hide and destroy, only to be confronted by it again and again, usually in the form of an "other." He believed that this aspect of the human psyche was the root of all racism, cultural bias, and gender hatred, that the us-against-them mentality was a thinking pattern exhibited by those who had not embraced their shadows, who projected the hated parts of their being onto a group of people they believed to be opposite to themselves.

I'm the girl with my homework done and my pajamas on, watching Max ride his bicycle up and down the street. It's late and cold but I'm darkly envious of his freedom. I wonder if he's darkly envious of my Howdy Doody pajamas and freshly washed face. Maybe we are the same. Maybe we are each other's shadows.

I awaken to sirens and these strange thoughts and this image of Max in my head. New York City sirens and London sirens are so different. London sirens with their waxing and waning seem so much more polite. *Coming through,* they seem to plead. *Stand aside.* New York City sirens are boldly insistent, downright rude. *What the hell are you waiting for?* they want to know. *Get out of the goddamn way. Can't you see this is an emergency?* When you live in New York, you live with the sound of sirens in the periphery of your consciousness. Ambulances, fire trucks, police cars — it seems like there's always someone in trouble in the city, always someone racing to the rescue. You stop hearing it; it becomes part of the city music.

London sirens seem mournful. They seem

to say *Something awful has happened and we'll respond the best we can, though it's probably too late.* New York sirens are brazenly sure that they can save the day.

It was a London siren I heard, waxing and waning, fading off into the distance. It took me a second to realize that I was in a hospital room, cool and quiet. It was dim, with some light coming in through a small glass window in the door and from between the drawn blinds and window frames — not from sunlight but from street lamps. I didn't know what time it was.

I lay still, scanning the room with my eyes. As they adjusted, I noticed the thin-framed woman sitting in a chair by the door. A rectangle of light fell across her. She had white-blond hair and a wide mouth that sloped dramatically at both corners in a caricature of a pout. In spite of the fact that she was slightly slumped to the side, leaning her head on her hand, she looked put-together and officious in a navy blue suit and sensible low-heeled pumps. She stared at the wall, a million miles away.

I cleared my throat and shifted myself up a bit. I was aware of a terrible dryness in my mouth and reached for the water pitcher I saw by my bed. The woman quickly got to her feet to stand beside me. She poured me a glass of water and handed it to me.

"Are you all right?" she asked.

Under the circumstances, it was a difficult question to answer.

"It depends," I said, my voice sounding hoarse and raw.

She looked at me quizzically.

"On where I am, on how I got here. On what's wrong with me."

I was trying for cool and smart-ass, but I felt hollow deep in my core.

She politely averted her eyes while I tried to drink from the cup in my shaking hand. Then she reached out to steady my wrist and things went better.

"I was hoping," she said, "that you'd be able to answer some of those questions for me." Her accent was thick, heavily Cockney though I could tell she struggled to keep that to a minimum.

"Who are you?" I asked.

"I'm Inspector Madeline Ellsinore. I'm investigating your case."

"My case?" I said, putting the water down on the table and leaning back.

"Well, yes," she said, crossing her arms over her chest and resting her eyes on my face. "An American woman shows up at a London hotel and checks herself in, hangs the 'Do Not Disturb' sign on her door for two days. The only time anyone hears from her is when she calls to find out where she is. She's then discovered to be suffering from a badly infected gunshot wound when she stumbles into the lobby at the end of the second day. She collapses and is rushed to the nearest hospital. Though she has sufficient ID, passport, cash, and credit, there is no record of her arriving in London on any commercial flight in the past six months. I'd say that warrants an open case, wouldn't you?"

I nodded slowly. She was official but not unkind. Her eyes were a pale blue. She was small, petite as she was thin; she looked like a runner, a fast and strong one.

"How did you get to England, Ms. Jones? And what are you doing here?"

I shook my head. "I have no idea."

It's a weird thing to admit. Have you ever woken up one morning after a night of drinking and found yourself in a strange apartment, a strange person sleeping beside you? It's like that but much, much worse. I felt as if I'd woken up in someone else's body.

She blinked at me twice. "That's hard to believe," she said finally.

"Sorry," I said. "It's true."

She gave me a blank, assessing look. There

was something cold and robotic about her in spite of her prettiness, in spite of her soft, smoky voice.

"Who shot you, then?" she asked matter-of-factly, as though she'd settle for that small bit of information as consolation.

I shook my head again. The ground had fallen away beneath my feet and I was floating in a life that didn't belong to me.

"Are you aware, Ms. Jones, that you're a 'person of interest' with the New York City Police Department, wanted for questioning in relation to the murder of a Sarah Duvall?"

That morning came rushing back to me, how Sarah fell and died in front of me, how I chased the man in black and was apprehended by the police. Dylan Grace came to get me and took me to Riverside Park, where I fled from him. It had all gone worse from there. I thought of Grant and his stupid website. Jake falling. I grasped for what had happened to us after the helicopter rose from nowhere, drowning us in light and sound. The harder I thought about it, the further it slipped away. I felt a terrible nausea, a pain behind my eyes.

"The FBI would like a go with you as well, in connection with a man named Dylan Grace."

I thought about the things he'd told me in the park. More lies? How could I be sure? Had he been in my hotel room or was that a dream? I remembered that he'd looked bad himself, that he'd jabbed me with a needle. I shook my head again.

"You really don't know what happened to you, do you?" she asked, incredulous, handing me a tissue from the box by my bed. I wiped my eyes, blew my nose. I entertained flashes of memory: running with Jake along the stone wall at the Cloisters, gunshots cracking the night air, falling hard to the ground as if I'd been shoved, the dark shadow of a man whose face I couldn't see asking, "Where's the ghost?" Most of all, I knew there was pain — white hot, total, nearly indescribable in its intensity, the kind of pain that mercifully kills memory.

"No," I said finally. "I really don't."

But between you and me, that wasn't the whole truth. Memories were filing back quickly. I remembered a knee on my back, a black hood being placed over my head. I just couldn't make sense of anything. It was a nightmarish jumble.

"Does the name Myra Lyall mean anything to you?"

I nodded my head slowly.

"An American crime reporter with the

New York Times," she said. "She had some connection to you, if I'm not mistaken. She wanted to talk to you regarding an article she was working on about Project Rescue. Then she disappeared."

"Yes," I admitted.

"Sarah Duvall was her assistant."

I nodded again.

"We found Myra Lyall's body yesterday in a canal about a mile from King's Cross, one of our red-light districts. She was in a trunk. In pieces."

I think she doled out the information like that for maximum impact. I tried to think about what she said in abstracts, not in logistics. Still the nausea and the shaking, which had been diminishing, returned with a vengeance.

"No record of her travel to London, either," she said.

I didn't say anything. I didn't know what to say. I felt some combination of grief for Myra Lyall's end and terror at how it had happened. I wondered how I had made it to a plush Covent Garden hotel and she had wound up in a trunk in a London canal. In pieces.

"Ms. Jones, if you have the first idea what's going on, I strongly recommend that you share what you know with me," she said. She walked over to the chair by the door and pulled it up beside my bed, sat down slowly as if she were settling in for a nice long chat. "I can't help you and I can't protect you if you don't. You seem like a nice girl, yeah? You seem frightened and I certainly don't blame you. But a lot of people are dead, and from the look of you, it's just luck that you're not one of them. Maybe we can help each other."

I didn't ask for this. Not for any of it, I'd said to Ace.

Are you sure about that? he'd wanted to know.

I decided finally that I was out of my league. I asked to see her identification, which she offered to me without hesitation. Fool me once, you know? When I'd determined that she was who she said she was, I told Inspector Ellsinore everything — everything I could remember, anyway. While we talked, various nurses and doctors made their appearances, poking and shining lights in my eyes, checking and then changing the bandage on the wound at my side.

Inspector Ellsinore took copious notes. When I had finished giving my statement, I asked her to help me contact the American embassy. She did and they promised to send a lawyer to the hospital.

When the call was finished, she put a hand on my arm and said, "You've done the right thing, Ridley. Everything is going to be fine."

I gave her an uncertain nod. "What happens now?"

She looked at her watch. "You get some rest. I'll contact the U.S. authorities and let them know that you're cooperating. And tomorrow we'll figure out when and how we can get you home. Is there anyone there you want me to call?"

My parents were cavorting around Europe, snapping pictures and sending postcards. They could probably be here in a matter of hours, but I didn't want them. Ace was clearly incapable of offering any help or support. I didn't even think he had a passport. I had no idea where Jake was or if he was okay. The thought of him brought tears to my eyes, and a now-familiar feeling of panic regarding his well-being and whereabouts.

"No. Just if you find out anything about Jake Jacobsen, I need to know. Please."

"I'll see what I can find out. Try not to worry."

She left her card on the table beside my bed, gathered up her things, and walked toward the door. With her hand on the knob, she turned back to me. "And I'm sorry, Ridley, but there are two officers outside this door. As much for your protection —"

"As for my detention," I finished her sentence.

She nodded. "Just until we're sure of what has happened to you, how you got here. You understand. So just stay put for tonight. Rest up. You have a busy couple of days ahead of you, I suspect."

The room was cool and sterile and I lay there wide awake for I don't know how long. I got up to pee once, but the journey and execution were so painful, I decided I'd hold it if I had to go again. There was a bedpan by my bed. But there was no way I was peeing in a bedpan. I just couldn't deal with that. I felt numb, depressed, and very, very lonely. The phone sat waiting by my bed, but I didn't feel that there was anyone in the world I could call. The truth was, I was on my own. I had been since the day Christian Luna sent me the photograph that changed my life. The only person I had been able to rely on consistently since then was Jake, and even that relationship was riven with lies and half-truths on his part. I tried to shut away the image of him bloodied and falling from some great height.

I tried to reflect on all that had happened, all that I knew: Dylan Grace and Myra Lyall, the things Grant had said, the streaming video from Covent Garden, the fact that I'd woken up in a hotel just blocks from that corner. I tried to apply my writer's mind to all these disparate events and to extrapolate possible connections, come up with theories, but I just wound up feeling sick and afraid. I thought of Myra Lyall's awful end, Sarah Duvall's death on the street, Esme Gray, Grant's last phone call to me. Even before recent events, Dylan had accused me of being the point at which everything connected. And I could see that he was right.

All this had started because I wanted to *know* Max, I wanted to see his true face in order to better know myself. But I was no closer to him. And I'd never been further from me — I barely even recognized my reflection in the mirror. All in all, the whole enterprise had been a deadly and unmitigated failure.

A nurse padded in and offered me some pills. "For sleeping, love," she said kindly. I took them from her and pretended to swallow, gave her a grateful smile. When she'd left, I took them from my mouth and dropped them in the cup beside my bed. I didn't want to be drugged into sleeping. I didn't feel safe enough for that.

I alternated between a kind of sleepy twilight and agitated restlessness until I heard something strange in the hallway that snapped me into total wakefulness, poked a finger of fear into my belly. It was a soft, sudden noise, a quick shuffle followed by a thud, that was over almost before it began. But something about it was not quite right . . . as if the energy of the air had changed. I sat wide-eyed and listened for a while.

I relaxed a little after a minute or two. Other than the ambient sounds — a television somewhere turned on low, the metronomic beeping of a machine, an odd ubiquitous humming that probably came from the fluorescent lights and a hundred medical machines — there was silence. I'd just started to drift off again when another noise came from just outside my door, the sudden jerking of a chair. I saw footsteps cross in the light that leaked in from the threshold. I got up from the bed with effort and looked around the room. The bathroom was a trap; no exit. I was in no condition to crouch between the bed and the window. I walked quietly and stood beside the door, looked around for something with which to defend myself. The effort it required to do this was staggering.

I must have been quite a sight, bare-assed in my hospital gown and stocking feet. I painfully bent over to pick up one of my boots, which stood beneath the chair upon which Inspector Ellsinore had sat with all her questions. It was the only thing that I had the strength to lift that looked substantial and heavy enough to do any damage.

My breathing became shallow and I could feel the adrenaline pumping in my veins. I noticed the phone with Inspector Ellsinore's card beside it, and also the call button, which I should have pressed while I was still lying in the bed. I thought about going back, but the distance of maybe five feet seemed insurmountable to walk or even crawl, considering how much effort it had taken to make it to the door. I leaned my weight against the wall, boot poised, and listened to the hallway. A minute passed, maybe two, and I started to wonder if I was suffering from paranoia (who would blame me?) or posttraumatic stress. I was about to put my boot down when the door started to open, so slowly I almost didn't notice until the dark form of a man slipped inside. He stood with his back to me, staring at my empty bed.

Before I could lose my nerve, I brought the boot around hard, hitting him solidly in the temple. The blow was so strong that it sent shock waves of pain through my own injured body, and I stumbled back, dropping the boot as he crumbled to the floor with a moan. My intention had been to strike the blow and then run screaming into the hallway, but I could barely catch my breath or move, the pain in my side was so intense. I'd been betrayed by my own body, and was outraged by my physical weakness. The anger and frustration got me to use the wall to move myself, however slowly, trying to get to the hallway.

"Ridley, stop."

I turned to look at him. Though it was dim, I could see his face as he sat with his hand against his temple, a rivulet of blood trailing down his cheek. It was Dylan Grace. There were a thousand things I wanted to ask him. All I could manage was, "Stay away from me . . . asshole."

I sunk to the floor against the wall. I thought I'd see if crawling was any less painful. It's a terrible and amazing thing to realize how totally you've taken your health and physical strength for granted. The door might as well have been a mile away.

Dylan grabbed my wrist. He was lucky I couldn't reach my other boot.

"They're coming for you, Ridley." His

voice was desperate. "Come with me. Or die here. Up to you."

I sagged against the wall, out of options, out of strength. Death — or at least unconsciousness — was starting to appeal to me. A slow fade to black, the cessation of fear and pain — how bad could it be? He started to move toward me and I was about to use my last ounce of will to scream my head off when I heard a sound out in the hallway. It was something I recognized, though at the moment I couldn't say how: the sound of metal spitting metal, a projectile slicing air without the concussion — a gun fired through a silencer. Maybe I'd heard it on the street without realizing what it was when Sarah Duvall was killed. It was followed by something — someone — falling heavily to the floor. These sounds froze the scream in my throat.

Dylan crawled over beside me, put his finger to his mouth. He drew a gun from somewhere inside his jacket. It was flat and black like the gun I'd seen Jake carry, like the one I'd fired badly myself in an abandoned warehouse in Alphabet City. I didn't know what kind it was, but I was glad to see it.

The silence that followed dragged on for hours or minutes. Where were the officers supposedly stationed outside my door? (Do they call them officers in England or is it bobbies? Either way they should give those poor guys some guns.) I guess I knew the answer. I tried to be brave. The fear and the pain and the fatigue were almost too much to handle. I could feel myself getting a weird giggly feeling I'd had before in times of grave stress and danger.

Then the door started to open. A tall, lanky form moved in like a wraith. A gun hung in a hand by his side. He stood still as stone with his back to us — I could smell his cologne, see that the hem on the back of his coat was ripped. I held my breath. Dylan rose and lifted his gun silent as a shadow. When the form turned quickly, sensing Dylan behind him, Dylan opened fire. The darkness exploded. I was deafened by the sound. The powder burned my nose and the back of my throat as the man fell heavily to the floor before he'd even had a chance to raise his gun. I stared at the crumpled pile of my would-be killer, listened to an awful gurgle that was coming from him.

Dylan held out his hand. "Can you walk?"

I hesitated, looked back and forth between Dylan and the man on the floor. Maybe he'd come to save me from Dylan Grace. Maybe they both wanted me for different nefarious reasons.

"You don't have any time to decide whether you can trust me or not," he said. I could hear a commotion out in the hallway. "These people can't protect you." I assumed he meant the police and the hospital staff. I couldn't argue with this. I gave him my hand and let him pull me up. He grabbed my bag from the closet, which I thought was awfully clear-headed of him since I would have forgotten all about it. I remembered with dismay that my passport had been confiscated by Inspector Ellsinore. I couldn't see my way out of any of this.

We moved out the door with me leaning on him heavily. In the hallway, the two officers charged with protecting and detaining me slumped in their chairs. A pool of blood was gathering beneath one of them. A nurse lay facedown on the linoleum, her neck bent unnaturally, one of her fingers twitching.

"How many more?" I asked. Even now I'm not sure if I was asking how many more people would die, or how many more would come for me.

"I don't know," he answered quietly.

As we passed through a doorway into a stairwell, I could hear shouting and running footfalls. Dylan put his warm wool coat on me and looked down at my socks.

"Well, there's nothing we can do about that, yeah?" I heard the accent on his words and didn't know what to make of it, didn't have the energy to ask.

We went down multiple flights; I could go into how slow and painful this was, but you're probably getting the picture. We exited into an alleyway and I heard banging on the stairs behind us. An old Peugeot waited in the cold, wet darkness. The upholstery was frigid against my skin, and my socks were wet as Dylan helped me into the backseat.

"Lie down," he said.

"Where are we going?" I asked as he closed my door.

"Just try to relax. We'll be okay," he said, getting into the driver's seat and shutting his door hard. For a minute I thought he was waiting for a driver, until I remembered the whole left-hand-side-of-the-road thing. He started the car. The engine sounded tinny and weak.

"Do you have some kind of plan?" I asked him as he backed the car out of the alley and drove slowly up a quiet street. A battalion of screaming police cars raced by us in the other direction. He didn't answer me. I was starting to get this about him. When he knew you wouldn't like the answer to your question, he just didn't answer it.

"Just try — not to worry," he said finally.

His accent was British. Definitely British. Or possibly Irish. Maybe Scottish. I wasn't good with accents.

"Who the fuck *are* you, man?" I asked him for the second time.

"Ridley," he said, resting his eyes on me in the rearview mirror. "I'm the only friend you've got."

He kept saying that. I was having a hard time believing him.

14

I felt frozen in the sound of the helicopter all around us. Jake pulled me and we kept running along the wall, staying close to the stone. The ground beside us spit and splintered with the shots fired from above. They were shooting at us; I couldn't believe it. I glanced behind us. The men I'd heard were nowhere in sight. Where were they? The fact that I couldn't see them made me more nervous than if they'd been at our heels. What if they were corralling us like sheep, if they turned up ahead of us somehow?

"It can't follow us into the trees!" Jake screamed back at me, pointing to where the wall ended and a thick wooded area began and ran all the way down to the highway. We could move through the sloping tree cover all the way down to the Henry Hudson. His voice sounded like a whisper in the deafening sound of the helicopter, but I heard him and nodded. We ran balls out toward what I prayed would be safety. When we reached the corner where the south wall hit the east wall, he climbed it quickly and then helped me up.

Not easy. I fell once and tried again, finally made it over the top. I think if it hadn't been for the sheer adrenaline of terror, I never would have made it over at all. I kind of climbed and then fell off the wall on the other side. Jake dropped down more gracefully beside me. We heard the copter retreat but stay close by. We listened. No voices, no footfalls.

"I'm sorry," I told him. "I'm sorry I brought us here."

"No, Ridley. I'm sorry."

"What are you sorry for? You were just trying to protect me," I said, looking up at him. He dropped his arm around my shoulder and pulled me close. I turned and wrapped my arms around him, rested my face against his neck.

"I've realized something in the last few days," he said. His voice sounded so grave and serious. "Ridley, I *can* walk away. It's nothing more than a single choice. We can both do it. We don't need all the answers to live our lives. It doesn't have to be like this."

He put his mouth to mine and he tasted so good. I could taste all the delicious possibilities of our life together. In that moment, I believed him. I believed he was right.

"If we get out of this," he whispered in my ear, "I promise you everything is going to be different. I swear to you, Ridley. I swear it."

We held each other like that until something started to slice the air around us like a razor through fabric. We stood to run but I watched as Jake's shoulder jerked and red seeped through his jacket, then through his pants leg. He reached out to me as he fell backward. I screamed his name and stretched for his hand. Then I felt a searing heat in my side, fell forward with as much force as if someone had shoved me hard from behind. I saw his face grow pale and still. I tasted blood and dirt in my mouth.

I awoke with a start and a sob in my throat. The car was moving fast; we were on a highway.

"Is he dead?" I asked.

"Who?" he asked, keeping his eyes on the road. The road was surrounded by blackness. We must have left the city far behind.

"Jake."

"I don't know, Ridley," he said softly.

"Don't lie."

"I'm not. I really don't know."

There are all kinds of death in this world. The death of the body is the least of them. The death of self, the death of hope — now, that's the hard stuff.

I've never been one to fear my own death. Not that I want to die, of course. I've just always seen death as a lights-out proposition. You're gone. Either it's the end of you . . . or it's a beginning. Either way, I don't imagine there's much looking back. I've never bought the whole fire-and-brimstone thing, the concept of reward or punishment at death. The idea that a tally has been kept of our good or evil or mediocre deeds, and that the soul is filed away accordingly for all eternity, just doesn't ring true. Humans judge that way. I tend to think that God probably doesn't. He or She just keeps doling out the lessons with endless patience until you finally "get it" in this life or the next.

I suspect that grief is worse than death. When someone you love has died, it's almost impossible to get your head around it. The totality of it, your utter helplessness against it, makes you feel as if you could burst into flames from sheer emotional agony. When Max died, I hurt so much that I couldn't believe I was still walking around, going through the motions of my life. I actually found myself wishing that a car would hit me or that I would fall from some medium height. It's not that I wanted to die. I just wanted to be in traction. I wanted my body to be as wrecked as my spirit so I could just lie down and heal.

I'm not afraid to die. I know there are far worse fates.

I was thinking this as Dylan drove on the dark highway and I lay in the backseat.

"Where are you taking me?"

"Someplace where we'll be safe for a while until we figure out what to do. I need to think."

"You're going to tell me what's going on. Right now," I said.

No answer. He turned off the highway and pulled onto a small road. There was nothing for miles but darkness, punctuated by the yellow lights of house windows, few and far between and off in the distance. I could smell grass and manure. He made a right onto a narrow dirt road and we drove slowly down a drive edged with tall trees. At the end, there was a dark stone structure. A house. It had the look of emptiness, of abandonment.

311

"This was my family's summer house."

"Was?"

"I don't have much family left. I guess it's mine."

"What about your murdered mother, Agent Grace? All that bullshit you told me in the park. Did Max kill the rest of your family, too?"

He flinched as if I'd slapped him.

"That was the truth," he said as he got out of the car. "Not the whole truth, but I didn't lie."

He opened the door for me and helped me out. I hated having to lean on him. I was dirty and wet and cold. My feet squished in the wet ground. When I lost the strength in my legs, he lifted me off the ground, which isn't as easy as it looks in the movies.

"Put me down, you asshole," I said, feeling annoyed and embarrassed.

"That's the second time you've called me that tonight," he observed, moving quickly toward the house.

He set me down on the stoop and unlocked a heavy wooden door with a key he took from above the doorjamb. Inside the air was musty and cold, like the breath of a grave. I hobbled over to a couch I saw. It was red and dusty, sat beside a matching chair and ottoman. It was stiff and uncomfortable but it was better than standing. There was a simple wood coffee table and a fireplace. A stack of wood sat ready for lighting. I curled up against the cold, stared at Dylan Grace with unabashed hatred as he started a fire, covered me with an ugly beige, stinky blanket. He left my sight and set about clanking around in what I assumed was the kitchen. I drifted off again.

When I woke, he was sitting in the chair with his feet up on the ottoman. The fire lit half his face. He was a handsome man in the rough way I mentioned. Even exhausted looking, pale with dark circles beneath his eyes, he had a hard sexuality to him. I could almost imagine being attracted to him if he wasn't a liar and a killer. Not that such things had stopped me before.

"No one is who you think they are," he said, somehow sensing that I was awake. "Not me, not Max Smiley, not even Jacobsen."

He didn't look at me, just kept his eyes on the flames. This seemed like such a pointless statement of the obvious that I didn't even bother to respond.

"Who's the ghost?" I asked. He turned to look at me sharply.

"Where'd you hear that?"

I shook my head. "I'm not sure. I just keep hearing it when I fall asleep. I hear a man asking me, 'Where's the ghost?' "

"A lot of people want the answer to that question," he said, keeping his eyes on me.

"Including you?"

He shrugged. "First you eat, then we talk." He got up and left the room quickly. I didn't bother to call after him to try to stop him. I was starting to get used to my own helplessness in all of this. I didn't have any clothes, any strength. I was in trouble with the police in two countries, not to mention the FBI. I was learning to be more patient. I just sat there for a while staring into the fire, trying to fit together all the million pieces I had, coming up with nothing except the usual headache.

He returned with tomato soup and some tea on a wooden tray. Based on the condition of the place, I didn't want to think about how long these things had been sitting in a cupboard. I was amazed at my own hunger, though, and couldn't remember the last time I ate. I tried to eat slowly, not wanting to make myself sick. But I couldn't keep myself from sucking down the soup in minutes. My stomach cramped but I didn't throw up, thankfully. When I was done, Dylan made me another bowl of soup, which I ate as well. Then he handed me some pills and a big glass of water.

I looked up at him.

"I'm not taking any pills from you."

He nodded toward the tray.

"You took the soup — and the tea. I could have drugged you that way, if that was my intention." The British accent again. It faded in and out. "They're antibiotics. Without them, you'll just get worse and worse."

They looked as if they *could* be antibiotics, little two-toned caplets. Against my better judgment, I took them. It seemed like a fair enough gamble.

"Where'd you get antibiotics?"

"I keep some around for emergencies."

I couldn't tell if he was making some kind of a joke, but I didn't ask.

He sat down across from me, rested his elbows on his knees. He didn't say anything as I sipped my water. I felt stronger, less light-headed. I was about to start prodding when he said, "Max Smiley picked a good time to die."

I looked at him, didn't say anything. He looked sad, exhausted on a level beyond physical. I almost felt bad for him.

"After a lifetime of evil, he made his exit just before some of the ugly came back at him. Death was too good for Max Smiley. People felt robbed."

"What kind of evil? You mean Project Rescue?"

"Project Rescue was the least of it."

I'd heard this before, from Jake. Almost those exact same words.

"I think you need to be more specific. I keep hearing what a monster Max was, how evil he was, but no one's told me a single thing to make me believe it. I know he wasn't the man I thought he was. I get that. But *evil* is kind of a strong word, you know. You need to back it up."

He stood up so quickly that he startled me. He walked past me and I turned to see him take a brown folder off a dining table that stood behind the couch. He sat back down with the file in his hand.

"This is as complete a dossier on Maxwell Allen Smiley as exists," he said.

"Compiled by whom?"

"Mostly by me, piecing together what I've found through various domestic and international law agencies."

The file was thick in his hand. It looked like something you'd see in the movies, ominous and top secret. I fought the urge to shrink from it, all my instincts for denial kicking in. I knew one thing: Nothing in a file like that could be good.

"How do I know this is not just more bullshit on your part?" I said, feeling suddenly angry and defensive. "You've done nothing but lie to me since the day we met. I know you're not an FBI agent. I don't even know if the name you gave me is real — I don't even know what to call you. One of my most recent memories is of you jabbing a needle into my arm. I'm sitting here in some cabin with you in the middle of fucking nowhere. Your accent keeps changing. For all I know, you're some psycho that's kidnapped me and is planning to eat my liver for dinner. For the last time, who the hell are you?"

That smile, that annoying smile he got, crept onto his face. If I weren't such a wreck, I would have leapt for his throat. Instead I had to settle for an angry glare, which we all know isn't nearly as effective.

"I *do* work for the FBI. Not many people know it, including your friend Agent Sorro. But I do."

"What is it, like some Black Ops thing?" I said with a little laugh. I wanted to sound sarcastic, as if I was making fun of him, but the way he sat there in the semidark, Dylan Grace was all mystery. I would have believed anything about him at that moment.

"Not exactly, no."

I waited for him to go on but, of course, he didn't.

"What, then?"

"It's not really important. The important thing is that I want to help you, not hurt you. You need to understand that."

I shook my head. "Why does everything have to be a riddle with you? Anyway, why should I believe a word you say about anything?"

"Because I just saved your ass," he said with predictable arrogance.

"Well, where's the backup, the cavalry? Are they coming to the rescue, coming to take us home? Why are we here, so you can 'figure out what to do next'?" I lifted my fingers obnoxiously as quotation marks. "If you don't mind me saying so, it seems to me like you're a little out of your league. And it doesn't seem like anyone's rushing to bail you out."

"You're right," he said, his smile fading just a little. "I'm unsupported at the moment."

I shook my head. I didn't know what to think about this man. "What does that even mean?"

He held my eyes but didn't say anything.

"It means we're on our own, right?"

He shrugged again and gave a single nod of his head.

"And your accent. You're British?"

"My father was American; my mother was British. My family lived in England from about a year after I was born until I was sixteen. Then I moved back to the States. The accent comes back when I'm stressed or drunk or exhausted."

I shook my head at him. "Why should I believe a word you say?"

"I haven't lied to you. Not once."

"You've just omitted significant details — is that more like it?"

More of that pregnant silence he'd mastered.

"God, you're really despicable," I said.

He held up the file. "It's all in here. Everything I know about Max — about your father."

He put the file on the couch beside me and left the room. I heard a door shut and I was alone with the fire. I was alone with Max. The Ghost.

15

We are not our parents. We're not. You've probably heard all your life that the traits you've found so annoying in your mother or your father will eventually manifest themselves in your own personality. Maybe you even believe it. Personally, I think it's bullshit. It's a cop-out, something people tell themselves to feel better about not taking responsibility for their lives. Maybe if you go through your life without examining yourself, without dealing with your issues, without consciously deciding what to bring forward and what to leave behind, or if you can't take responsibility for your own inner happiness, then perhaps it *is* likely that you become the drunk, the abuser, the cold and distant judge your mother or your father was. But I believe you have a choice. I believe we all choose our lives, that our existence is the sum of our choices — the little ones, the big ones. We don't always choose what happens to us, and we don't choose where we came from, but we do choose how we react to the events of our lives. We choose to be destroyed or to grow wiser. Nietzsche (whom I always thought was a bit of a psychopath) said, "What doesn't kill us makes us stronger." I cling to this philosophy; I need to believe it.

I have to believe now that I am not my father. That his DNA is not a contagion I carry in my body, a sleeper virus that might take hold of me one day and turn the blood in my veins to poison.

I think Dylan gave me an hour with the file and then returned to the room, sat back beside me. The file was open in my lap. There was more to read but I'd lost my nerve. I couldn't bring myself to turn the page. In my mind, I saw Max standing over his mother's beaten body, smiling ghoulishly. I saw him waiting outside Nick's window staring up with soulless eyes, his very presence a terrible threat. I saw him punching my brother in the face with his closed fist.

"I'm sorry," Dylan said.

I stared at the flames, which were flickering low. The air around me was growing colder. I could hardly believe the things I'd read, the photographs I'd seen. I tried to fit my brain around them, tried to make it work, but I felt like I do when I see images of grinding poverty or war on the television. You know it's real but part of you just can't accept what you're seeing, so removed are you from the actual experience.

"I don't know this man," I said.

He nodded; he understood what I meant.

"Why did you show this to me?" I asked him mildly. It seemed as if someone was always handing me a file filled with bad news. I was starting to resent it.

He was quiet for a moment, just stared at the floor between his feet.

"We've talked about this before. I think you're the only way to him."

I remembered then our conversation that first day.

Do you know the number one reason why people in the witness protection program get found by their enemies and wind up dead?

Why?

Love.

Love.

They can't stay away. They can't help but make that call or show up incognito at a wedding or a funeral. I've seen his apartment. It's practically a shrine to you. Max Smiley did some terrible things in his life, hurt a lot of people. But if he loved anyone, it was you.

I knew it was true. It had always been true. Max and I were connected. We would always find each other.

"You want to use me as bait," I said without emotion.

"The truth is, Ridley, you've been bait for a while. We just haven't had any bites until recently."

I didn't say anything.

"Jake Jacobsen has been using you since before he met you," he said softly.

"It might have started out that way," I admitted. "He wanted to get to Ben."

Dylan shook his head, lowered his eyes to the floor again. The conversation seemed to pain him.

"He saw my picture in the *Post*," I said, leaning forward. Something in my chest started to thump. "Same as Christian Luna did. It was a coincidence. He needed my help."

"You think that's how he found you?"

That day on the Brooklyn Bridge (it seemed like a lifetime ago) when Jake finally told me the truth (part of it, anyway), he admitted that he'd moved into my building to get close to me, to find a way to get closer to Ben. He needed to know more about Project Rescue and couldn't think of another way. I'd forgiven him for that — a long time ago. I told Dylan as much.

"Think about it, Ridley. *When* did Jake move into that building?"

I searched my memory for something that might orient the event in the time line of my recent life. I thought of the morning I'd saved Justin Wheeler. Two things had delayed me in getting out of the building. First there was my mailbox overstuffed with bills and magazines and an angry note from my mailman. I'd retrieved the mail from my box and run it back up to my apartment. But before that, it had been my elderly neighbor Victoria. She stopped me to talk about the noisy man moving in upstairs. I felt my stomach bottom out as I remembered the conversation. It was a week later that Jake and I met face-to-face. As it came back to me, the present disappeared and all the events of our meeting and what followed swirled around me.

Our meeting and the passion and the drama that had followed had been so intense, so all-consuming. Maybe that's why I never made the connection. Or maybe I just didn't want to. I realized now the point Dylan was trying to make: Jake moved into my building the night *before* the single event that forever altered my world.

Was it possible? What did it mean? I'm

not sure how long I sat there, analyzing the time line, trying to figure out a way that I might be wrong. A thick fog moved into my brain.

I had to force the words out. "Are you saying that he knew who I was . . . before *I* did?"

Dylan hung his head.

"How is that possible?" I felt so ashamed suddenly, like the kid who'd been the butt of a terrible joke at school, around whom everyone had gathered to laugh. I felt my face grow hot.

Acceptance was slow. Then, when I realized that it was true, I tried to think of something to make it all right that he'd lied to me about how he'd found me, a reason he would have to make up a false scenario as he did. Pathetic, I know. Anyway, I couldn't think of anything. Then I started to wonder: If he'd lied about how he found me, what else had he lied about? I thought about the things Jake had told me. How he'd tracked Max to a bar in Jersey and confronted him about Project Rescue. How just a few weeks later Max was dead.

I'd come to believe that it had been Max's realization of how much harm he'd done that led him to drink so much the night he died — that in a sense Max had killed himself by drinking and driving off that bridge. But the man in the dossier was not a man to die over the grief of others. The man in the dossier didn't have a conscience at all. Did that mean Jake had something more to do with his death than I'd believed? Or something more to do with Max than he'd revealed? The possibilities were chilling.

"A lot of what you know about Jake is true, I think," Dylan said kindly. "He didn't make up the stuff about his childhood, about his quest to find out who he really is and where he came from."

"How do you know?" I said angrily. "How do you know all this about Jake?"

"Because I've been watching him for years."

I looked at him sitting there.

"Why?" I asked him.

He smiled at me sadly. The answer was clear. I spoke for him.

"Because he's been watching me, waiting for Max to approach me. He never believed Max died that night, and he believed that one day Max would reach out for me, try to contact me. Is that what you're telling me?"

"And when Max did, Jake would be sleeping beside you," said Dylan. "He knew he'd be the first person you told."

I felt as if someone was stepping on my chest. I thought of all my nights with Jake and all the love I'd had for him. The idea that it had all been a part of some design, or something to do to pass the time as he waited for Max to make contact, sliced me open.

"And you'd be listening when I did."

He shrugged again. "Max Smiley is a man with the means, the resources, and the motives to drop off the face of the earth forever. As far as we know, he only has one weakness, one place in his heart that feels."

I didn't have to ask who or what that was. I thought about the patience it must have taken to wait day after day for Max to contact me, how badly Jake must have wanted it.

"I've never understood Jake's obsession. All this time, I thought it was just his needing to know what happened to him, his wanting to bring Max and the other people responsible for Project Rescue to justice. I thought he just wanted some closure. But there has to be more to it than that."

"That's probably how it started."

"Then?"

"My guess is that the more he learned about Max, the more obsessed he became with finding him. I think his obsession grew beyond his personal quest for answers. I think the search for Max became his whole reason for living. Eventually it started to define him."

I could see how that might happen; in fact, I could feel it happening to me. But at the same time, Dylan's answer didn't quite work for me. I realized then that Jake's obsession had seemed outsized for months; it had grown in a way that had felt incongruous. Early in our relationship, I'd believed that it would lessen over time, but the opposite had happened. It was one thing for me to be obsessed; the man was my father.

"I guess you know a thing or two about obsession," I said.

I thought about the crime-scene photos I'd seen in the dossier. I'd seen what Max did to Dylan's mother. I understood Dylan better now.

"I guess I do."

"You turned yours into a career."

He shrugged. "It's a living." He tried for a smile but it died on his face. I, for one, wondered if I'd ever smile again.

"How did Jake know I was Max's daughter?"

"Maybe he didn't. Maybe he just knew that Max had loved you."

"Then why would he lie about how he

328

found me?"

"I can't answer that."

There was so much more to ask, so many questions about the last couple of years and the last couple of weeks. We hadn't scratched the surface. But I sat there for a minute before launching into all that. I wanted to ask about the men at the Cloisters, how I'd wound up in London, and whom he had killed in the hospital. I was afraid that once I started, the answers would only lead to more questions.

"Myra Lyall is dead," I said. "They found her body floating in a trunk in a canal."

Dylan nodded. "I know."

"What did she find out? The people who took her — are they the same people who took me?"

"I'm not sure, Ridley. I don't know what happened to either one of you. I was hoping you could answer some of those questions."

I frowned at him. I guess I kind of had the idea that the only reason I didn't end up in a trunk floating is that Dylan Grace had saved my ass, as he so eloquently put it. Wrong again.

"Then how did you find me?"

Remember how easy it was for me to get away from Dylan in Riverside Park? It turns out he expected me to try to run from him. In fact, he wanted me to run.

"I thought you were hiding something. I figured I'd let you run and I'd follow, see where you led me. We were listening to your cell phone calls and were able to track your movements to the Internet café, the SRO on Forty-second Street. Then we lost you. Actually, you walked right by my partner. Nice job with your hair, by the way. You've got a whole Sex Pistols thing going there."

"Thanks," I said with a narrowing of my eyes. "You don't look that great, either."

"You made some calls from Inwood, so we headed up there. The last call we picked up was your conversation with Grant Webster. By the time we figured out where you were and got up there, you were gone. NYPD had already arrived — they'd been called about gunshots and a helicopter, but they didn't know what happened. They were searching the area, picked up some shell casings from automatic and semiautomatic fire. That was it."

"No sign of Jake."

He shook his head. "No, Ridley. I'd tell you if I knew something. I promise."

I nodded.

"We went to Grant Webster's apartment in the Village."

"Was he . . . ?" I couldn't stand to finish the question.

"Dead? Yes," answered Dylan softly. I felt that sick guilty feeling that was becoming so familiar to me. I held some culpability for the things that had happened to Sarah, to Grant, to Jake, even to myself. I wasn't sure how to deal with that. So I just blocked it out. Dylan went on.

"From his phone call, we knew you were in trouble, that he'd found something and tried to warn you. But Grant has some kind of kill button on his network. He managed to wipe all his data before he died. Anything he knew was gone."

I shook my head. "I really doubt that. There must be backup somewhere." I remembered his website, how he'd chastised people for not protecting and backing up sensitive data. He impressed me as a person who'd practiced what he preached.

"If there is, we haven't found it."

"He said I was walking into a trap, that 'they' thought I knew where Max was, that I could lead them to him."

"Is that true?"

I gave him a look. "Um, *no*. You know, why don't you believe me about this? You've been watching me for a long time now. If I was secretly communicating with Max, wouldn't you know?"

"I didn't know about the website. For all I know, you've been using the computer at your adopted parents' house to communicate with him."

I thought about what Grant had said about the government's dislike of encrypted websites and steganographic software. I started thinking about that streaming video and how maybe it was just a way to hide a message. Again, I wondered what my father's log-in might be. I was betting I could figure it out if I could get to a computer.

Dylan was watching me in that way that he had, as if he believed he could stare me into admitting all the many lies he'd thought I told. The sad part was I was just as clueless as he was. I sighed. What was obvious was that we didn't trust each other. We could go around and around like this for hours. I didn't bother repeating how I'd just found the website recently, that I had no way to log in.

"Anyway, the point is that we lost you," he said. "I didn't even know where to start looking. The fact that I'd taken you into custody when I really didn't have the right to and then allowed you to escape caused me a lot of trouble. I was reprimanded and might have been suspended, except that I'm so entrenched in this investigation, I would be impossible to replace at this point."

"So you do work for the FBI?"

He nodded slowly. "I work for the FBI Special Surveillance Group. We monitor foreign agents, spies, and others who are not specifically targets of criminal investigations."

"Like me?"

He nodded. "And like Jake Jacobsen. The point is that I'm not exactly a field agent. I gather data, conduct surveillance, monitor communications and movement. If I see something suspicious, I raise the alarm. Jacobsen has been interesting to us because of his skills as an investigator. We've been on him for nearly two years. As a result, we've also been watching you."

I thought about this for a second, the fact that I'd been under surveillance for I didn't know how long. I looked at Dylan Grace, a man who'd likely heard every private conversation, read every e-mail, seen every move I made since I met Jake. The thought embarrassed and intrigued me. How well could you know a person, watching her live her life from a bird's-eye view? You'd see all the faces she wore for the various people in her life. You'd hear the same stories and events repeated for different people, each version sounding a little bit different, tailored for the listener. You'd see her face when she thought no one was watching. You might hear her cry herself to sleep at night or make love to a man she cared for but couldn't trust. For all of this, would you know her better, more intimately, than if you'd been her lover or her friend? Or did you know her not at all, never having been allowed entry into her heart?

He went on. "I watched your cell phone records, credit cards, ATM records, passport control. I didn't find anything for two days. I feared the worst. I thought you'd disappeared like Myra Lyall."

"Then?"

"Then a charge from the Covent Garden Hotel popped up on your Visa bill. I was on the next plane to London. I bribed the desk clerk for your room number, found you in the state you were in. Through my London contacts, I was able to get you some antibiotics and painkillers — that's what I was jabbing into your arm. I went out to get some more bandages and antiseptic to take care of your wound. When I came back, you'd stumbled into the lobby. I watched as they took you away in an ambulance."

I thought about the time line of his story. It seemed credible enough under the circumstances. It was still hard for me to believe that this was my life now, that I'd wound up with him here at all. And while I didn't totally trust this man, I didn't fear him, either. And these days, that was something.

"Okay, so where's the rest of the FBI? If you really do work for them, why isn't there anyone to help us?"

"Because — don't you get it? I'm not supposed to *be* here. I'm supposed to be behind a desk listening to your phone calls. I'm not supposed to be out here *with* you."

"Unsupported?" I asked, using the word he'd used.

He nodded.

"Okay," I said. "What now?"

He pressed his mouth into a tight line, and glanced at the fire for a second, then back at me.

"I'm open to suggestions," he said.

"Great."

"If you really let life take you, if you release control and stop clinging to sameness, you can't imagine the places you'll end up. But most people don't do that. Most people get this death grip on what they know, and the only thing that loosens their grasp is some kind of tragedy. They live in the same town they grew up in, go to the same schools their parents went to, get a job that makes a decent living, find someone they think they love, marry and have children, take the same vacation every year. Maybe they get restless, someone has an affair, there's divorce. But it will just be the same boring life with the next person. Unless something awful happens — death, house fire, natural disaster. Then people start looking around, thinking, Is this all? Maybe there's another way to live."

Max always ranted like this when he was drinking. He was hung up on the concept of "normal" people and how sad they were. He felt that most people were just zombies, sleepwalking through their lives, and would just die without ever leaving even a footprint on the planet. Max was a titan, a shooting star. In his lifetime he was responsible for the erection of thousands of buildings, countless charitable works in countries all over the world. He put at least ten kids that I knew of through college with the scholarship he established in his mother's name in Detroit. He *had* to live a big life. That was his normal.

I think most people are just trying to be happy, and that most of their actions, however misguided, are in line with that goal. Most people just want to feel they belong somewhere, want to be loved, and want to feel they're important to someone. If you really examine all the wrongheaded and messed-up things they do, they can most often be traced back to that basic desire. The abusers, the addicted, the cruel and unpleasant, the manipulators — these are just people who started this quest for happiness in the basement of their lives. Someone communicated to them through word or deed that they were undeserving, so they think they have to claw their way there over the backs of others, leaving scars and creating damage. Of course, they only create more misery for themselves and others.

Even the psychopaths and sociopaths in this world who commit the most heinous possible acts against innocent victims are in this quest for happiness. But their ideas are twisted and black; these people were wired wrong. Many people believe that evil is the presence of something. I think it's the absence of something.

Was Max an evil man? I still didn't know. If I'd looked closer, I might have seen signs that told me yes, as Ace did. But I was in his thrall completely. If the series of events that shook the foundation of my life hadn't occurred, I may never have asked who he really was. I may have lived on in ignorance. A part of me — a big part of me — wishes I'd taken Nick Smiley's advice; I should have let the dead lie.

I looked down at the file in my lap, trying to reconcile the snapshots in front of me. They were of a man who looked different in every picture; they spanned decades. Max, maybe in his thirties at the time, slimmer than I'd known him, in a white shirt and khakis, exiting a black Mercedes near an abandoned stadium in Sierra Leone, flanked by two men armed with machine guns. Max sporting a full beard, sitting in a Paris café among a group of men, his hand resting on a fat manilla envelope, a wolfish grin on his face. Max shaking hands with a dark-skinned man wearing black robes and a turban. There were numerous shots like these, all vague, taken from a distance. Clandestine meetings around the world in empty fields and parking lots, boatyards and abandoned warehouses. Lots of guns and dangerous-looking men.

The Max Smiley I knew was an internationally renowned real-estate developer, whose business called for international travel. He built luxury condos in Rio, hotels in Hawaii, high-rises in Singapore. He golfed with senators and went deep-sea fishing with Saudi princes. There were always shades of gray in Max's business, yes, always whispers about whom exactly he conducted his business with. Then the Project Rescue scandal revealed that Max had dealings with organized crime, through his lawyer Alexander Harriman. The FBI starting digging deep into Max's banking history, though he was legally dead.

"We found hundreds of millions of dollars in offshore bank accounts." Dylan's voice interrupted my thoughts. "And that's just what we could trace. How much else is out there in accounts I couldn't link to him or his business or his various 'charities,' I couldn't even begin to guess."

I put the file on the table and lay down on the couch. I don't know how long we'd been talking. I should have been resting but sleep didn't seem like an option. My body was beyond fatigued but my mind was restless.

"And I take it that this money didn't come from real-estate development."

"No. Legitimately, Max Smiley was a rich man, making several million a year in pure personal profit. This money came from other dealings. We started watching some of the accounts. There was activity — withdrawals and deposits."

"That's what made you think he might still be alive?"

He nodded. "Then our investigation got blocked."

"By whom?"

"By the CIA."

"Why?"

"They told us our surveillance conflicted with an ongoing investigation. We were asked to stand down. Or told to."

"These men in the photographs, these meetings — what kind of business was he conducting?"

He came over and sat on the floor beside me, took the file from where I'd left it, and pulled a snapshot from the pile.

"These men are affiliated with the Albanian Mafia."

"How did he know them?" I said. My voice didn't sound like my own. It was thin and distant. Black thoughts were blooming in my mind. I thought of the Project Rescue babies. I had to wonder how much more there was to it all than I had even imagined. Dylan ran down the list of other men in the photographs. Known terrorists, men associated with the Russian, Italian, and Italian-American Mafia.

"So whatever his dealings were with these people, this is why the CIA is still looking for him."

"I think so."

I wondered if he was being vague on purpose, if he was stalling. I asked him as much.

"Like I told you, my investigation was blocked. I still don't know what Max was doing with these men. Here," he said, pulling out another snapshot that seemed more recent. "These men are CIA operatives. This meeting took place just a month before he died."

"CIA," I repeated.

"They could have been undercover. He most likely didn't know who he was really with. Their investigation started long before ours did."

"So Myra Lyall could have stumbled onto any of these dealings — whatever they were. Any one of these people could be responsible for her death. For Sarah Duvall, for Grant Webster. Any one of them could have taken me in the park, come after me in the hospital."

He nodded. "Any one of them. Including the CIA."

I let the information sink in. "Now you're just being paranoid."

He looked at me as if I was slow. I was about to ask him about his mother when he rose suddenly.

"I think that's enough for tonight. We can't stay here for long, and you need to rest before we start moving again."

I didn't argue. There was so much more to say and countless questions to ask, but I had too much to deal with already. I was in brain overload; if I took on any more information, I'd lose something crucial like my ability to add and subtract. I let him lead me to a small bedroom off the main room. There was a rocker and a queen-size bed with a wrought-iron headboard and a patch-work quilt. He helped me beneath the musty sheets, then started another fire. I lay there watching him, thinking that my father had killed his mother and that such a thing did not bode well for our relationship — whatever that was. I wondered if I'd ever meet a man whom Max had not totally destroyed on a deep emotional level. That was the last thought I had before I drifted into a light and troubled slumber.

Twice during the night, Dylan brought me pills, which I took without protest. The second time, I saw him linger in the doorway. I couldn't see his expression. I waited for him to say something, but after a minute or two, he left, closed the door softly behind him. I thought about calling him back and asking what he was thinking, but then I wondered if I really wanted to know.

The morning dawned to rain. It tapped at my window, and for a second before I opened my eyes, I could almost imagine that I was back in the East Village just an hour or so before I saved Justin Wheeler and set this nightmare in motion. I imagined the myriad choices that lay before me, beginning with sleep in or hop up and race to the dental appointment that I'd canceled instead. Anything I'd done differently that morning might have saved me from waking in this strange place, a stranger to myself.

My sinuses were swollen but my side hurt much less. I slipped out of bed, put my feet on the frigid wood floor and walked over to the six-pane window, and peered out into a thick glade of trees. There was a doe and her tiny foal nibbling on grass in the misting morning rain. I held my breath and watched them. They were perfect and peaceful, oblivious to me and my chaos. It soothed me to watch as they meandered back into the woods until I could no longer see them. I felt safe, as if nothing could hurt me here.

I saw some clothes neatly piled on the rocker by the door. A blue wool sweater, a pair of beat-up jeans, and some Nikes in halfway decent shape that looked like they might fit. No socks. No underwear. But what did I expect?

There was a small bathroom off the room to the side of the fireplace. The fire burned well, as if it had recently been stoked. I entered the bathroom and mopped myself off in cold water from the sink, spent a few minutes staring in dismay at my hair. I checked the bandage on my side and saw that it was clean and decided to leave well enough alone.

The sweater was huge; I rolled up the sleeves. The jeans were a tad tight in the rump and the sneakers pinched my little toe. But okay.

When I walked into the living room, I expected to see Dylan standing sentry by the door, but he was dozing on the couch.

"Some watchdog," I said.

"I'm not sleeping, just resting my eyes."

I saw the gun in his hand then and realized he probably hadn't slept at all. I should have felt bad for him but I didn't. Part of me blamed him for all of this, though I couldn't say why. I walked past him toward the door. He'd left my bag there and I bent down gingerly to pick it up and bring it over to the small dining table. I heard him sit up and felt his eyes on me as I rummaged through the contents, hoping I'd find what I was looking for. Near the bottom I did. I took the matchbook I'd found at Max's apartment a couple of lifetimes ago and handed it to Dylan.

I told him where I'd found it, how I'd sensed that someone else had been there that day. "Does it mean anything to you?"

He held it up to the light of the fire. After a second, he nodded slowly. "I think this is from an after-hours club in London called the Kiss. This symbol is part of Descartes's tangent-circle configuration. The Kiss is from a poem called 'The Kiss Precise,' which explains how each of the four circles touch the other three. Though Decartes's ideas were pretty much confined to circles, I think the club owner kind of sees it as a symbol of how all things are connected."

"Wow," I said after a beat. "I wouldn't have pegged you as a math geek."

He shrugged. "I guess I'm just full of surprises."

That's what I was afraid of.

"There's a note inside," I said. He opened the matchbook and read it, didn't say anything.

"Who do you think Angel might be?"

He shook his head. "No idea."

345

"We need to go there. And we need a computer to try our luck getting into that website. I'd like to check my e-mail, too, in case Grant sent me anything before he —" I couldn't bring myself to finish the sentence. These were the things I'd been thinking about as I'd washed and dressed. I wanted to somehow take back control of my trashed existence. I didn't like the broken person with the bleached blond hair, Max's daughter injured and in hiding from various threats. I wanted to be me again.

"Are you up to it?" he asked skeptically.

"Not really. But what are our choices, sit around here waiting for the cops or for one of Max's enemies to come after us? Better to be proactive, don't you think?"

"I was thinking we should turn ourselves in," he said, coming to stand beside me.

"No," I said quickly, certainly. "Not yet."

The thought of being trapped somewhere filled me with dread. A window was closing. If I didn't find Max soon, he'd be gone for good like the ghost that he was. There'd be time to pay for whatever mistakes I'd made. But later.

I turned to Dylan and was surprised to find him so close.

"I fucked up, Ridley. You were right — we're out of our league here." It was a

346

simple admission of error, nothing dramatic or even regretful about it. I liked the ease with which he could admit that he'd made mistakes. I think it's a good quality in a person.

He put a hand on my shoulder. I didn't like being so close to him, didn't like his scent, the warmth of his body. I wanted to move away but found that I couldn't, and moved in closer instead. He pulled me to him and then his lips were on mine. I felt heat travel through my body. It was in a desperate seeking of comfort that I let him kiss me, that I kissed him back. I felt his arms enfold me. He held me with conviction but also with care, with tenderness. Jake always kissed me with a kind of reverence, a painful gentleness. Dylan kissed me as if he owned me, as if he *knew* me. I pulled away from him, pushed him back, then slapped him hard. The sound my hand made against his face was a satisfying smack. It felt good. Almost as good as it had felt to kiss him.

"Asshole," I said, hating my pulse for racing and hating the mutinous heat on my face.

"That's three," he said with a big smile. He put his hand lovingly to his face as though I'd kissed him there.

"You think because you've read a few of

my e-mails, listened in on my conversations, that you know something about me."

He put his hands in his pockets and cast his eyes to the floor.

"Well, you don't. Okay?"

He nodded. I couldn't see if he'd stopped smiling but I didn't think so. I put my bag over my shoulder and walked toward the door.

"Are we going or what?"

I could tell you that it was cool, that the sky was a flat, dead concrete gray, and that the sun was trapped hopelessly behind thick cloud cover. But it was England and late autumn, so yeah. We drove in silence toward the city. I kept my eyes closed or turned out the window, so as not to invite any conversation from Dylan. I had a million questions but I wished I could get my answers from somewhere else.

For a while, I tried to retrieve some of the missing fragments of my memory: how I'd gotten to England, what had happened to me, how I'd come to check myself in to the Covent Garden Hotel, whose voice I heard in my head, asking the same question over and over. But I was overcome with a terrible foreboding that discouraged me from mentally exploring my recent past. Maybe some things were better off forgotten.

Eventually I got bored ignoring Dylan and turned to him.

"I was a shit to kiss you like that," he said as soon as I did. "You've got enough going on. I wasn't trying to take advantage of you. I just . . ."

He didn't finish and the sentence hung between us.

"Will you tell me about your mother?" I asked.

"You don't want to hear my sad story."

"I do," I said. I felt the urge to reach out to him, to touch him where I'd slapped him or to put my hand on his arm. But I didn't. "I really want to know."

There'd been crime-scene photographs in the file. Alice Grace was beaten to death and left to die in an alley behind the Hôtel Plaza Athénée in Paris in 1985.

He released a sigh. Then: "I always thought, growing up, that my parents were in the hotel business, that they traveled the world buying struggling hotels and turning them into five-star properties. That had been my mother's family business and I never questioned it. It wasn't until long after my mother was killed that I learned the truth. That my parents were both former intelligence officers with British Special

Forces and that upon their retirement from military service before I was born, they were recruited by Interpol."

He watched the road and didn't even glance at me. I could see that he had a white-knuckled grip on the wheel.

"Interpol's primary function is intelligence gathering and acting as a global police communication system. Agents are not law enforcement personnel; they have no rights of arrest or of search and seizure. My mother was really an analyst, specializing in the gathering and analyzing of intelligence in the form of clandestine communications and surveillance."

"Your mom was a *spy?*" I asked, staring at him. I wondered if he was a bit crazy. I was actually starting to feel a little sorry for him. I knew all about trying to find explanations for your family, trying to understand the things they'd done and coming up with a way to make it okay.

He nodded. "In a sense, I suppose that's what she was. My father was a surveillance photographer. Some of those older pictures you saw of Smiley, they were mostly taken by my father."

I waited for him to go on. I watched the trees race past us in a blur of green and black. He was driving fast.

"Most of their activities were classified. But I was able to find out through an old friend of my father's that they gathered data on Smiley for over seven years."

"Why? For whom?"

"It had come to the attention of the CIA that Max Smiley had some questionable relationships overseas and they were interested in knowing more about his activities. Interpol agreed to watch him when he was in Europe and Africa. My parents were two of the agents assigned to the task."

He released a long breath here. I kept my eyes on his profile, watching him as I'd felt him watching me for signs that he might be telling the truth. But what did I know about honesty? I probably wouldn't have recognized it if it kicked me in the teeth.

"There aren't many pictures of my mother, you know. I have one from when she was a girl. But mostly she avoided the camera. She couldn't afford to have her image floating around — it was so important for her to be invisible in her work. But she was stunning — jet-black hair and eyes so dark they were almost purple. Her skin was this nearly translucent white. She used to keep her hair back and wear these thick dark glasses, because when she didn't, everyone stared at her. My father used to call her the

Showstopper. When she walked into a room, everyone turned to look at her, men and women."

I could see some of this beauty in him. It resided in the gray of his eyes, in the fullness of his lips, in the strength of his jaw, in the blue-black shine to his hair. But there was something to him that kept him from being easy on the eyes, something about his aura maybe, that made me want to turn away.

"She went alone to Paris. My paternal grandmother was ill — near death. My father stayed behind to care for her.

"There should have been no risk to her. The maître d' was a supposed Interpol ally and had arranged for a microphone to be placed at the table where Smiley would be dining. Nobody knows how she was discovered. She wasn't a careless person; she was highly trained. Nobody knows how she wound up dying such a horrible death, her body discarded in the alley behind a grand hotel. She suffered, died slowly. We know that much. The maître d' was killed as well. Interpol suspected that he had betrayed her and then was killed for what he knew."

I let a moment pass in respect for his mother, for how she died and how much it must have pained him to discuss it. Then:

"How do you know Max killed her?"

I saw his grip tighten on the wheel. A small muscle started working in his jaw. "Because beating women to death with his bare hands was Max Smiley's signature. That's what he did to get his rocks off, or haven't you figured that out yet?"

His tone was so sharp and the words so harsh that I physically shifted away from him in my seat.

"Wake up, Ridley. Wake the *fuck* up. Your father, your beloved Max, *hated* women. He *murdered* them. Prostitutes, call girls, escorts, women he picked up in bars. Discarded them in hotel rooms and alleyways, in Dumpsters, in abandoned cars. In addition to Project Rescue and his involvement with the lowest scum on the planet there's a swath of brutally murdered women in his path. Women who he murdered with his own bare hands."

He pulled the car over so suddenly that I was jerked about unpleasantly, nearly knocking my head against the side window; my seat belt locked. He turned to me. His face had gone pale with anger. A blue vein throbbed in his temple.

"He liked to feel their bones collapse beneath his fists," he said, lifting and clenching his own hand. "He liked to hear them scream and then whimper and sob as he choked and beat the life out of them."

He was yelling now and I found myself covering my face and leaning against the cool glass until he went silent. I listened to him breathing hard, listened to the cars race by us, their wheels whispering on wet concrete, felt the Peugeot shake with the speed of their passing. When I lowered my hands, I could see that his eyes were wet and rimmed red. There was a grim intensity to the way he was watching me. I could already see regret in the line of his mouth. I stared back at him, mesmerized by what I saw. His was the face of the ugly truth; I recognized it in every pore. That's what had kept me turning away from him. I realized that I'd never seen it before, the face of someone who had no secrets to hide, no more lies to tell. I hated him for it.

I reached into the back of the car and grabbed my bag, flung the door open, got out, and started walking. The cold air, the now-driving rain, felt wonderful. I heard his door slam and the sound of his feet on the concrete.

"Ridley," he called after me. "Ridley, please."

There was so much sorrow in his voice that I almost stopped but kept going instead.

I thought I could hitch a ride, go to the police and get myself arrested or deported or murdered or whatever. It didn't matter.

When I felt his hand on my arm, I spun around and started pummeling him pathetically with my fists. I was so weak, so messed up, that instead of warding me off, he just pulled me into him, effectively pinning me against him. Eventually I stopped struggling. His body was shaking slightly, from cold or emotion, I didn't know. I could hear the beating of his heart fast and strong in his chest. I let myself sob, standing there on the highway in the pouring rain.

"I'm so sorry," he said into my ear. "I'm so sorry. You were right. I *am* an asshole. You didn't deserve that." He tightened his arms around me and I wrapped mine around his waist. "You didn't deserve any of this."

I looked up at him and saw all the pain in the world in the gray of his eyes.

"Neither did you," I said. There was a flash of something on his face. I think it was gratitude. And then his mouth was on mine. In his hunger and his passion, I tasted his honesty. I opened myself to it and took it all in — this man, his truth, and his kiss. In that moment, I knew one thing for sure. That Dylan Grace had been right all along.

He was the only friend I had.

I found that I had about two thousand pounds sterling in my bag, close to four thousand dollars. How it got there, I had no idea. We parked the Peugot in a public lot and then checked into a run-down hotel near Charing Cross Road. The room was ugly but clean and comfortable enough, and Dylan insisted we chill there for a while, wait for the sun to go down. He washed and rebandaged my wound with great tenderness. I let him, though I could have done it myself. Since our kiss on the road, there'd been a charged silence between us. We spoke to each other politely or not at all.

I was eager to get to an Internet café but saw the wisdom in waiting for dark. Plus, I was feeling worse and weaker by the minute. I lay down on the queen-size bed, which smelled vaguely of cigarettes. Dylan took the chair beside me and turned on the "telly." After an hour of watching the news, we still hadn't seen anything about ourselves. A check of the morning papers in the lobby on the way in showed that we hadn't made the print media, either.

"It's weird," said Dylan, looking at me from the chair. "I'd have thought our pictures would be all over the place after a mess like that."

"Maybe they want to keep it quiet."

"No way. Two cops and a nurse dead? Whoever I killed lying on the hospital room floor? You missing? No way to keep that quiet. They should be using every resource at their disposal to find us."

"But they did keep it quiet. Obviously."

He had his head in his hand and rubbed his temples.

"You can lie down if you want," I said. I thought he must be tired, every muscle in his body aching from driving and sitting up all night.

He looked up at me. "Yeah?"

I nodded. He rose from his chair and lay down beside me. The bed squealed beneath his weight. I moved into him and let him fold his arms around me. I heard him release a long, slow breath, felt the muscles in his chest and shoulders relax. I just wanted to feel safe for a minute. And I did. I drifted off like that. When I woke again, the sky outside our window was darkening.

He was sleeping soundly, his breathing deep and even. My head was on his shoulder and he had one arm curled around me, one flung over his head. I flashed on how his face had looked in the car when he talked about Max, about the things he'd said. How the pain of it had brought tears to his eyes. I hated what he had told me. I felt as if the knowledge was a cancer growing inside me, something black and deadly that would eventually take over and shut all my systems down. I would die from it; I was sure of that.

I remembered Max's parade of call girls, women I had always naively thought were his girlfriends. *A man like that, so damaged inside,* my mother had said once of him, *can't really love. At least he was smart enough to know it.* Did she know how much worse it really was? She couldn't have. She couldn't.

In the file there'd been a list — a kind of time line. I'd quickly passed it over because I didn't understand it. I realized now with horror what it was. I slipped myself away from Dylan and went over to the pile of our things on the chair. The file was there beneath my bag. I sat cross-legged on the floor and opened it in my lap, flipped through its leaves until I found what I was looking for. It was a time line, apparently compiled by the FBI's Serial Crimes Division in cooperation with Interpol, of a list of women found murdered, perpetrator unknown, organized by date and geographic location. It started in Michigan in the ghettos surrounding Michigan State, where Max went to college. Four women, streetwalkers, were found over the four-year period Max resided in that area. One: Emily Watson, seventeen, found in an alleyway beneath some bags of trash behind a Chinese restaurant. Two: Paris Cole, twenty-one, found beneath a bridge over the Detroit River. Three: Marcia Twinning, sixteen, found in a drug den in downtown Detroit. Four: Elsie Lowell, twenty-three, found in an empty lot, her body partially burned. The list went on. Women in New York, New Jersey, London, Paris, Cairo, Milan — around the country and around the world — with two things in common: the brutality of a beating death and the fact that Max was in the area around the time of their murders. Young women, lost women, walking the streets, fallen upon by a predator and left like trash. I noticed that the list ended the year Max died.

I felt my stomach churn, even as my mind clouded with a thousand questions. What did it mean precisely that these deaths corresponded with Max's passage through the world? Surely you could compile a list like this for almost anyone. People were murdered every day in a thousand different ways all over the globe. And if, in fact, there was any real evidence that he'd murdered these women or that he'd been involved in criminal enterprise with any of the people in the photographs, why wasn't he ever arrested? Why wasn't he ever charged? They didn't seem to have any difficulty finding and following him.

"You want to talk about some of that?" Dylan asked from the bed, startling me.

"No," I said. "I'm tired of talking." I felt as if we'd been talking for days.

There was so much I didn't know and didn't understand, so many things that didn't make sense with the information I had. And I always had Jake in the back of my mind. Where was he? What had happened to him? How much of our life together was a lie, a fabrication on his part to be close enough to me to know if Max was still alive? How much of what was in this file did Jake already know? I thought of his own file he'd shown me, the one that had disappeared after the last time we made love. I wished I had paid more attention to what was in there.

I heard Dylan sit up and crack his back. He issued a low groan and I turned to look at him; he was clearly in pain. Looking at him made me think of Jake again. They were such different men but driven by the same desire to find my father. It was weird, karmic in a way. I knew there was a lesson for me to learn here, but I was miles away from understanding. He rested his gaze on me and I felt an odd wash of attraction and guilt. I looked away.

"What do you want to do?" he said softly.

"I need some clothes. I can't go clubbing like this," I said, looking down at my pilled blue sweater and ugly, too-tight jeans. I'd unzipped them to spare my injury any additional discomfort, but I couldn't very well go running around London with my pants open.

16

We went to Knightsbridge for some new clothes for me, using the cash I'd discovered in my bag. Dylan trailed around after me, edgy and watchful, while I, in under an hour, got myself a pair of black jeans and a black suede jacket at Lucky (ripped and faded and beat to hell for a ridiculous sum, but oh so fab), a pair of pull-on Doc Martens boots (think skinhead chic), and a ribbed black lightweight sweater with a zip-up neck at Armani. I felt better after shopping, more normal. And more than that I looked cool, which almost made up for being in mortal danger, an international fugitive, and a partial amnesiac.

You're thinking it was an unlikely time for me to be shopping, that there were bigger fish to fry. And you're probably right. But sometimes you have to pull yourself together on the outside to pull yourself together on the inside.

My hair was growing on me, figuratively speaking, though I wondered if I should change it again. I opted for a ski hat and sunglasses instead. It's pretty traumatic to cut and dye your hair if you've never done anything like that, and I'd had enough trauma to last me a while.

Besides, since I hadn't seen myself on television or in the papers, I'd lulled myself into a false sense of security that we wouldn't be spotted by the police. Of course, I managed not to think about the fact that there were probably more dangerous people looking for me. Who knows, maybe I wanted to get caught. I was feeling pretty low, pretty disconnected from myself. I think *numb* is a good word for it. I was numb — except for the injury in my side, from which radiated a low-grade pain controlled somewhat with whatever pills Dylan was giving me.

The Internet café we found back near the hotel was also a pizza place, so we ordered a pie and found ourselves a quiet booth toward the back. A laptop hummed on each table and the room was filled with the weird blue glow of computer screens. It was pretty quiet, not too many other surfer diners. A young girl with a pile of textbooks and a sad face sat a few tables away from us, sipping from a mug and staring absently into space. A middle-aged man in a beige cardigan and thick glasses moved his mouth as he read something on the screen in front of him. He sat near the door. All the other tables were empty, and for that I was glad.

"I wonder if this is a good idea," said Dylan as I started to tap on the keyboard. "They're likely watching your account. They'll be able to tell where you accessed your e-mail."

"How long would that take them?"

He shrugged. "Could take a while."

"Then we'll be gone by the time they figure it out."

I assumed he was talking about the FBI, but maybe he meant the other people looking for Max, too. He'd said, *Max Smiley picked a good time to die. People felt robbed.* He hadn't really expounded on who else might be looking for Max and why. I asked him about it.

"A man like Max makes enemies," he said vaguely. "The people he dealt with would look for revenge. You're his daughter. It wouldn't take them long to come to the same conclusion that everyone else did, that you're the way to him."

"I get that," I said, thinking about the men

in the Bronx. "But who?"

He shook his head. "I don't know. . . . The Albanians, the Russians, the Italians. The families of women he might have murdered. There's a catalog to choose from."

I noticed Dylan kept scanning the room as he spoke, kept peering at the street outside the café window, glancing toward the door. He was edgy.

"What's wrong?"

"I don't know. It just seems strange that there doesn't appear to be any kind of search for us," he said, repeating his earlier concern. "It seems like a damn big news story, doesn't it?"

He was right, of course. An American woman appears in London, no record of her travel, a gunshot wound in her side. Someone removes her from police custody at a hospital, leaving a trail of bodies in their wake. Now she's missing, a victim or a fugitive, no one's certain. A rogue FBI agent, broken away from his agency, is also missing, and may be her suspected captor or rescuer or accomplice. Big news story. Irresistible, in fact.

Outside our window, two uniformed bobbies strolled by, their faces blank and bored. They didn't exactly seem to be on red alert, but Dylan tensed until they passed.

"Would you feel better if our faces were all over the place and we couldn't make a move?" I asked. "If we had no choice but to turn ourselves in?"

"In a way? Yeah. At least that would seem in line with the circumstances. I just have a weird feeling," he said, the British accent returning just slightly. It was funny that I knew him well enough now to know that he was stressed.

I logged into my e-mail account, then slid over to Dylan's side of the booth and turned the laptop around so that he could see. As I moved in close to him, he dropped an arm around my shoulder and I felt the hard metal of the gun at his waist. I'd forgotten he was carrying a weapon and it reminded me how screwed up everything was. I found myself wondering if he was right, if we should turn ourselves in. Jake's words at the Cloisters came back to me. I think he was trying to say that maybe we didn't need to understand the past in order to have a future. We didn't necessarily need to know where we'd come from in order to move ahead. Was he right?

I explained to Dylan what Grant had told me about the website with the red screen, how messages could be hidden in pieces of unused data. I described Spam Mimic, how messages that appeared to be spam could also be alerts to log into the website.

"You think your father was using this to communicate with Max?"

"It seems like a fair guess," I said. The thought made my chest constrict with anger, but I couldn't think about any of that now.

I scanned through the multiple spam messages on my account. I expected to see something from Ace but there was nothing. If he knew the trouble I was in, he didn't care. A message from my parents dated three days ago told me that they were in Corsica. They raved about the food. Unbelievable. I suspected that they might be on their way home by now. After sorting through the rest of my mail, I saw a message from Grant. I clicked on it immediately. It read:

You're in a world of trouble and I don't have much time. The site we discussed originates out of London. Where exactly and who set it up, I won't have time to find out. I'll tell you this, the code is very sophisticated. I wouldn't be surprised if it's a CIA communication hub. I attempted to log in and I might have set off some alarms. The site went dead. And my system alerted me that someone was trying to hack into my network. To be cautious, I'm going to have to get out of here. I've sent my backups someplace where they'll be secure. If anything happens to me, people are going to know why.

I'll contact you when I'm safe. In the meantime, don't attempt to log into that site unless you're in a public place . . . and even then I don't advise it. Be careful. And don't forget you still owe me that interview.

The e-mail was sent at 7:03 p.m. Dylan and I both knew that an hour later Grant was dead. It was my fault and I felt the full weight of that as I read and reread his note. Part of me hoped that there would be a message encrypted within his words, but even if there was, I'd have no way to decipher it. I fought off tears, ate a piece of the pizza that had been delivered to our table while I reread Grant's e-mail yet another time.

"Everybody who has attempted to log into that site is either dead or missing," said Dylan. "Myra Lyall, Sarah Duvall, Grant Webster, and Jake Jacobsen."

I nodded. "Everyone except for Ben," I said.

I remembered the address of the website and typed it into the browser. The red screen popped up seconds later.

"What are you doing?" asked Dylan, pulling my hand gently from the keyboard.

"I'm going to log in," I said, turning to look at him. "What choice do I have?"

"You have the choice *not* to log in."

"Don't you want to know? I mean, how long have you been pursing this obsession of yours?"

"Long enough to know it's going to kill me one day. I'm just not sure that I want it to be today." His answer startled me.

"For years after my mother died, I thought she'd been killed in a car accident. Like I told you, I didn't know they were agents with Interpol. After her death, my father turned into a ghost of a man. He went from this powerful, high-energy person to a walking corpse. He lost over twenty pounds, and he was quite slim already. All the color seemed to drain from him. He was never home. I felt like I'd lost them both.

"Nearly three years to the day that my mother died, my father was killed. I was sixteen. My uncle, my father's brother, brought me to the U.S. to live with his family. He told me the truth about my parents and how they had both died in the pursuit of Max Smiley."

"How did your father die?"

He took a sip from a tall glass of ice water that sat in front of him, and I could see that his hand was shaking slightly. "The official story was suicide, that he was unable to get over my mother's death. But according to classified files I've been able to access since I joined the FBI, I learned that he was executed, his body found in a whorehouse in Istanbul. They think he followed Smiley there and was killed before he could do what he'd clearly gone to do."

"Kill Max?"

He nodded. "I made a promise to myself that I would be the one to make Smiley pay for the things he'd done, that I'd be the one to bring him to justice. I've never wanted revenge. I've never wanted to hurt or to kill him. I just want him to answer for the deaths of my parents . . . and for the women he killed. But part of me has always believed that this would be my undoing and possibly my end. I feel like I'm not far from that day."

His words were grim and there was a terrible sadness on his face. I wanted to reach for him, to comfort him, but something stopped me. I was quiet for a second. Then: "How did you ever get a job with the FBI with such a history?"

He shrugged. "I passed a number of psych evaluations. And honestly, I don't think they considered my motivation a bad thing. But they did keep me out of the field. That's why I'm in surveillance and information gathering and not out on the streets bringing in the bad guys."

I didn't know what to say, so I just looked at the glowing red screen.

"This has been everything for me, you know — for a long time. Lately I've been wondering if I've made the right choices. I don't have much to show for my life except this quest, and I'm not getting any younger."

His voice had taken on a faraway quality, as if he was thinking aloud.

"What are you suggesting?"

He looked away. "Nothing. I don't know."

"Because I can't walk away now. If you want to, I understand. I really do. But I have to find him."

He regarded me for a second, then: "Why?"

"You know why. You said it yourself."

"But what if it's not true? What if knowing Max Smiley doesn't bring you any closer to yourself? What if the closer you get to him, the further you get from who you really are?"

I shook my head, then rested it in my hands.

"Look at Jacobsen, look at me. Look at what it's done to us."

I shifted away from him.

"But he's not your *father,*" I said, my voicing rising, even though I hadn't meant to yell. "You and Jake are looking for justice, maybe even revenge, though neither of you wants to admit it. They're artificial goals — that's why they're destroying you. Even if you get what you want, it's going to leave you cold."

He nodded, as if it was already something he'd considered. "And if you get what you want? Say you find him, literally or figuratively, or both. Then what, Ridley?"

"I don't know," I admitted.

We both turned to the red screen. I gazed back at him and he nodded. I tabbed like Grant had shown me until two small white rectangles opened in the red. I entered a log-in I knew Ben used often: *thegooddoctor.* And then I entered the password I knew he used for everything: *lullaby.*

I felt smugly confident. But I was wrong. After a few minutes of sitting there, waiting for something to happen, the red screen disappeared. An error page popped up in its place.

"Oh, shit," said Dylan quietly.

I quickly deleted the page and the page from which I'd accessed my e-mail from the computer's history file, then I took some money out of my bag and dropped it on the table and got to my feet. Dylan followed and took my hand. We moved slowly, careful not to seem panicked, toward an exit sign we saw at the rear of the long narrow space. We exited into a back alley through a green metal door. It let out onto the street behind the restaurant. Then we ran.

But of course running was pointless. If I'd been paying attention, I would have realized that. We weren't in hiding; we weren't on the run. We were already twisted in the sticky silken threads of an elaborate web. We just didn't know it yet. Or I didn't.

I should have been dead. Everyone else — Myra Lyall, Sarah Duvall, Grant Webster, and Esme Gray — had met their ends because of this mess, whatever it was. Why not me? Because no one wants the bait to die until the catch is on the line. But this hadn't occurred to me yet. I was running blind, scared, and was out of my league in every way.

A lack of good alternatives led us back to the hotel. I was ill and exhausted when we returned to the room, my side throbbing. I felt feverish and wondered if my infection was getting worse. There was nothing to do but wait. The after-hours club we were interested in, the Kiss, didn't even open until midnight. I sat on the bed and watched the room swim unpleasantly. Dylan sat beside me, put a hand to my forehead.

"You're sweating."

"I don't feel well."

He took some pills from a vial in his pocket and handed them to me. I dry-swallowed them and waited as they moved slowly down my throat. I lay down on my good side and looked up at Dylan.

"Who do you think killed Esme Gray?" I asked him.

He didn't say anything.

"The last time I saw her," I went on, "she told me to be careful or I'd end up like 'that *New York Times* reporter.' Don't you think that was a weird thing to say? Doesn't that imply that she knew something about Myra Lyall's death?"

"It could," he said.

"Do you think she had something to do with all of this?"

He shrugged. "She was intimately involved in Project Rescue. She identified Max's body."

"She was in love with him once, a long time ago."

"The way she died, beaten to death like that . . . That's how he kills."

His words chilled me; I shuddered. It wasn't only what he said but that he referred to Max in the present tense. It was something I still couldn't actually accept.

"If she was his ally, why would he kill her? Maybe someone was just trying to make it look like Max had killed her. Trying to make it seem like he might still be alive."

"My next best guess is your boyfriend, Jake Jacobsen."

I shook my head. "No way."

"Did you ask him about it? About the blood in his studio?"

It seemed like so long ago. "He said he hadn't been anywhere near Esme's and that he had no idea what had happened in his studio, that he hadn't been back there for hours."

"Then where was he all day?"

I shrugged. "I didn't ask."

"And he didn't say."

"No," I answered, closing my eyes, wondering what I'd really meant to Jake, wondering where he was now. I kept hearing the words he'd said to me, seeing him falling. He seemed so far away. I didn't know if we'd ever find each other again.

"Try to rest now. We're going to figure this all out. I promise."

"It's just that everyone else — Myra, Sarah, Grant — all these people stumbled into this mess. Maybe they found out things that someone didn't want them to know and they died for it. But Esme seemed like she might have been in on it. How did she wind up dead?"

I felt him put his hand on my forehead but he didn't answer me. After a while, I started to drift off. As I entered the twilight of sleep, I remembered.

I was aware that I wasn't alone as I came to on a hard, rough carpeted floor. I had the sense of movement, and the sounds and smells I quickly became aware of told me that I was on a plane. And there was pain, pain in my side from the fresh gunshot wound, pain in my jaw, in my leg. I slowly tried to move myself and cried out from the sheer agony of the effort.

He sat still in a leather seat nearby, watching me struggle. He didn't move to help me. The light was dim but I knew it was the man I had seen on the street, the one I had chased after Sarah Duvall was shot. I couldn't see his face, not really, but I could tell that at least part of it was badly scarred. He wore the same black felt hat and pair of dark glasses.

"Where am I?" I asked him. "Who are you?"

Somehow I managed to pull myself to my feet, using the armrest of the seat beside me. It was a small, obviously private plane. It had a bar and five wide leather seats. There was something run-down about it. A strange odor in the air made my stomach turn. I started to lose my legs again, so I sat.

"Where's the ghost?" he asked me, his accent heavy. I'd say Eastern European if I had to guess.

"Who?"

"The ghost," he said again. "Your father, Maxwell Smiley."

"He's dead," I said. I felt an odd calm wash over me. My circumstances were bizarre, almost incomprehensible. I think I was in shock. I'm sure I was.

"We've seen the photos," he said patiently. I kept my eyes off of him. I didn't want to see his face, somehow figuring that if I never looked at him, maybe I wouldn't die here with him. I stared at my lap and wondered whose blood was all over my legs. Probably mine, maybe Jake's.

"If you lead us to him," he said, "we can forget each other, you see what I mean?"

Yeah, right, I thought. Sure.

"He's dead. I scattered his ashes off the Brooklyn Bridge."

The man released a sigh, and almost on cue, two men entered the cabin. They spun my chair around, and when I looked up I saw they both wore black ski masks. It's an awful sight to see; I hope you never experience it. Whoever invented ski masks couldn't have been thinking about skiing. They're absolutely ghoulish, purposely designed to fill a person with terror. I tried to struggle, even though I knew it was pointless. One of them held me down easily with his two hands on my arms and his knee on my lap, while the other slowly applied pressure to my wound with his fist. I let out a terrible, inhuman sound that I almost didn't recognize as my own voice. Even now I don't really remember the pain. They say that your mind doesn't have the capacity to remember physical pain. I wish the same was true of fear.

"Where's the ghost?" the man in black asked patiently, over and over until I lost consciousness again.

The space between those events and my first waking in the Covent Garden Hotel is irretrievable to this day. It's not a memory that I'm interested in reclaiming. Sometimes the unconscious knows best. When it lets the sleeping dogs lie, better not to go kicking them.

I awoke with a start, causing Dylan, who'd been dozing in the chair beside me, to jump.

"What happened? What's wrong?"

"Why didn't they kill me?" I asked him, sitting up. "When they realized I didn't know where he was, why didn't they kill me?"

"They tried in the hospital," he said, rubbing his eyes.

"Okay, but why wait? They could have killed me much more easily while I was still in their control."

"You got away from them. You must have."

"How? I was trapped on a plane being tortured by men in ski masks."

He looked at me hard. There was something odd on his face: concern, anger, I wasn't sure what.

"What are you talking about?"

I told him about the memory I'd just had, or was it a dream? He came to sit beside me. He put his hands on my shoulders.

"Are you sure it happened like that?"

"Yes," I said. I thought about it. My

memory had a gauzy, nebulous quality to it. But I didn't think it was a dream. It didn't have that non-reality to it, that impressionism that dreams do. "No. I don't know."

"Do you remember anything else?" His gaze was intense. But then again, he was a pretty intense guy.

I shook my head. "Why didn't they kill me?" I asked again. I wanted to know. It seemed so important and it was. I just didn't know why.

"Just be glad they didn't," he said, looking away from me. He seemed angry and I didn't understand why. I looked at the clock. It was after midnight.

Even as I sat there, the memory was fading a little. I wondered who that man was. Was there something familiar about him? Had I seen him even before he shot Sarah? I scanned my memory of people I'd met in connection to Max. But I couldn't place him. Maybe it was just my mind playing tricks due to posttraumatic stress.

"Dylan?" I asked. He had risen and walked over to the window. He put his hand on the pane and stared outside.

"Yeah, Ridley?" The British accent again. Stress? Fatigue? Probably both.

"How much do you know about me?" I wasn't sure why I asked him that right then.

I'm still not.

"What?" he said, but didn't turn to look at me.

"I mean all this time watching me. How much do you know?"

He didn't answer me for a bit and I figured he wasn't going to. Then: "I know you still listen to Duran Duran. That you sing in the shower. That you snore."

I didn't say anything. I felt both surprised and violated. I was suddenly sorry I'd asked the question.

"I know you like to eat ice cream after you make love to Jake. I know you cry yourself to sleep sometimes. That you cry when you're stressed out or mad or just really tired. I know you're angrier with your parents than you'd ever admit. I know that you have an investigative mind, a terrible itch to know the truth about things and people, and that you're stubborn as hell."

I felt a powerful wash of anger then. "Shut up," I said.

He turned around to look at me, then walked over to stand near me. "I know that you miss the way your life used to be, that maybe you'd even turn the clock back if you could."

"Shut up," I said again, rising from my seat on the bed. Anger was constricting my airways. He put his hands on my forearms. I struggled against him but he held on hard.

"I know you hate everything about this. But most of all you hate what you know about Maxwell Smiley now. You hate that he's a part of you."

A sob escaped me and I fought his grip, but it only grew tighter. I wanted to put my hands to my ears and run away from him.

"But I also know that it doesn't matter, Ridley. That within you is a true, deep well of goodness. You're one of the few truly honest, kind, and loving people I have ever known. It doesn't matter who you came from. Nothing can ever change that." His voice had lowered almost to a whisper. He let go of my arms and used his thumbs to carefully wipe the tears from my face. Then he placed his hand at the base of my neck and pulled me to him. He pressed his whole body against mine as he kissed me. I found myself clinging to him, feeling the strength and power of his arms and chest, his thighs. Even if I'd wanted to, I wouldn't have been able to pull away from him. And I know he wouldn't have let me go easily, even if I'd asked, even if I'd struggled. I told you before that he held me as if he knew me. I guess maybe he did.

I felt how badly he wanted me, and it

surprised me. He was a man who held a lot back, who'd always seemed so distant even as he trampled all over my boundaries. What surprised me more was how badly I wanted him. Even with the specter of Jake over my shoulder — or maybe because of it — I wanted Dylan Grace. I still belonged to Jake in so many ways that the act of making love to Dylan was a betrayal to us all. In a weird way, I found that appealing. I was all about burning down the house these days.

He started working on my clothes; he held my eyes with his as one by one our garments fell to the floor. On the bed, his skin felt hot against mine, and for a while it was enough to just feel him, my legs wrapped around his, my arms around his shoulders, my lips on his neck. It was enough to mingle the lines of our bodies. I felt him sigh and hold me tighter.

"Ridley," he whispered. "God."

There was so much emotion in those two words that it kind of startled me and ratcheted up my desire. He was feeling something in that moment that I wasn't. But it didn't matter. I wanted to give him what he needed. He felt so good, so strong and solid, so safe, I wanted to live there for a minute, in the shelter of his knowledge of me.

When he took me, he said, "Look at me, Ridley."

We locked eyes. Even as he kissed me, he held my gaze. I suppose some people would find this bizarre. But I knew he needed to see my eyes and that he wanted me to see his. Because he had secretly watched me for so long, maybe he needed me to know that he was truly seeing me for the first time. I felt recognized. And I gave myself over to that, as my hands explored the tender landscape of his body, as I took in the scent of his skin, as I tasted the delicate flesh of his lips, his neck, the dip between his collarbone and throat.

He was careful to keep his weight off my wound, but being with him still caused as much pain as it did pleasure.

In the dark, we lay folded into each other, his arms wrapped around me. I held both of his hands in both of mine. I could hear in the silence that there was a lot he wanted to say, but he didn't say any of it. I listened to him breathing and thought I liked the sound of it, liked the feel of him beside me.

"I shouldn't have said those things to you," he said. "I shouldn't know those things about you yet. It's not fair."

He was right, of course. He should have

earned that knowledge of me. I should have had the chance to give it to him. But that was our reality. The cards had already been laid out before us. We either played or folded.

I told him as much. I felt him nod his understanding. We lay like that for a moment, both of us knowing that we didn't have much time. After a little while longer, we took turns in the small shower, got dressed in silence, and headed out the door. Before we crossed the threshold, he turned and kissed me gently. I held on to him tightly for a second.

"Thank you," he said into my ear. It would have sounded weird coming from anyone else, as though I had given him something and deserved his gratitude. But I knew what he meant and it touched me. I didn't know what to say, so I kissed him again. I felt the heat ignite between us, but there was no time. We pulled away from each other and headed out, hand in hand.

17

It occurred to me as we exited the fat black taxi that I had no idea what we were looking for exactly at this club. I'd found a name scrawled in a matchbook and here we were. That should tell you how lost and desperate we were. The industrial street in London's West End was nearly deserted. I paid the driver and shut the door, felt something like despair as the car pulled away and was gone.

"What is it?" asked Dylan, sensing my hesitation.

"Nothing. I'm good."

As we walked together I had the odd feeling that we were making some kind of mistake, as if it was just stubbornness and a lack of good alternatives that had led us here. I felt Dylan's energy go quiet and watchful as we moved up the street scanning numbers. There were no other clubgoers on the street; I didn't hear the pulse of music.

A glowing blue light over brushed metal doors was the only indication that we'd found the place. Two men — one black, one white, both big as refrigerators and clad in long black nero jackets and black sunglasses — stood sentry at the door.

"Name," asked the black guy curtly as we approached. He reached for a clipboard that hung beside him.

I handed him the matchbook in my pocket. "Am I in the right place?"

He pulled what looked to be a pen from his pocket, but it turned out to be a small black light. He shined the beam on the matchbook and another symbol appeared. I craned my neck to see what it was, but he flicked off the light before I could identify it. I was a little surprised when he handed it back to me, stood aside, and opened the door.

"Welcome to the Kiss. The elevator to your left will take you to the VIP room. Just swipe this card in the slot," he said, handing me a black key card. I took it from him and nodded my thanks. The doors closed behind us and we walked down a long dark corridor lit by more blue lights.

"You're a pretty cool customer, Ridley Jones," Dylan whispered as we reached the end of the corridor and swiped the card.

I gave him a weak smile. "We'll see."

The elevator took us down instead of up as I expected. When the doors opened, we entered a cavernous space where techno music pulsed and bodies heaved on a gigantic dance floor. There seemed to be no end to it, this sea of scantily clad bodies. I was overwhelmed with the same feeling I had at New York City clubs. My observer's mind almost couldn't handle all the input. The tattoos, the body piercing, one woman's purple contact lenses, another's raspberry-colored spiked hair. I felt instantly assaulted by the level of detail, started to get this weird zoned-out feeling I get under these circumstances. Dylan took my arm and pulled me close and we moved toward the bar.

"I don't want to get separated in here," he yelled in my ear, and even then I could barely make out what he was saying. I wondered if, under different conditions, he'd dance with me, if he'd move that body on the dance floor with as much grace and rhythm as he had in bed. I had a feeling he might. He looked pretty cool with his tousled black hair and dark glasses, the shadow on his jaw. He wore a leather jacket and an FCUK T-shirt I'd bought him in Knightsbridge, a pair of old Levi's. When we'd first met, I never would have pegged him as being particularly hip, but I guess he was.

"What?" he yelled.

I must have been staring at him. I shook my head.

The bartender's bottom lip was completely hidden beneath a row of silver hoop piercings. It was absolutely ghastly. I distrust people who pierce themselves in tender places. Isn't life painful enough? Doesn't it leave enough scars? He had a shaved head and the tattoo of a black four-leaf clover under his eye.

Dylan leaned over the bar and started yelling something at the bartender. I lost myself watching the crowd. The music was heavy; I could feel it beneath my skin. I remembered back in college when we'd take Ecstasy and go dancing, how the music seemed to pulse through my veins, take me over on some spiritual level. I didn't do too much experimenting with drugs after that. I found I never liked the feeling of being disconnected from reality. But dancing with Ecstasy altering the pathways in your brain was pretty intense, a memory that club music can always bring back for me. I felt the itch to get out there and mingle with all those bodies in the flashing strobes, to lose myself in the music.

I watched a black woman with razor-straight platinum-blond hair in a patent-leather dress and matching boots rub her fantastic body against an equally gorgeous blonde in a white tunic covered in some gauzy material that got picked up by the fans. The material swept around her like smoke. I watched a badly dressed man with thinning hair and insecurity in his eyes try to pick up a redheaded women who looked profoundly bored and slightly unstable on her feet. I watched a young girl in jeans and a tank top dancing alone, whirling around to no particular beat other than the one she was hearing in her own head. I could see in her glazed-over stare that she was as high as could be.

Dylan handed me a beer and pointed to a narrow staircase that led to a velvet curtain.

"Angel!" he yelled.

I nodded and we headed that way.

Life is like this weird puzzle, you know? You have some of the pieces before you even know where they belong. I thought about that as we ascended the staircase, how I'd found this matchbook in Max's apartment with a stranger's name scrawled inside, never imagining that it would lead me to a London club with a rogue FBI agent, both of us searching for the same but totally different things, both of our lives a tangled mess we kept tripping over. If I'd really been watching the signs, I'd have known that there was no good way out of this scenario, that only bad things could happen from here on out. But I was still naive enough to believe that somehow everything was going to be okay.

Behind the thick velvet curtain, it was quieter.

"This is the VIP room," said Dylan. "The bartender told me we'll find Angel here."

Beside another large brushed-chrome doorway waited a slot just like the one by the elevator. A red light turned green as I swiped the card, and a heavy click told us the door was open. We pushed inside.

It was as peaceful here as it had been loud downstairs. A light strain of jazz floated on the smoky air. A wide-open space, topped by a cavernous ceiling, was lined with long low tables and cushions on the floor. There were several tiny gathering areas, cozy booths with cocktail tables at their center. Some of them had sheer curtains drawn; forms moved and whispered behind them. The room was lit only by candles on the tables, on the walls, and in gigantic wrought-iron candelabras and chandeliers chained from the ceiling. It was at once Gothic and utterly modern. Behind one of the curtains, a woman laughed and it sounded like ice cubes in a glass. It would have been a cool place to hang out if my life didn't suck so much.

We slid into one of the curtained areas and sat close together on the plush velvet seat.

"Someone will come to us," he whispered. As I moved in closer to him, he dropped his arm easily around my shoulders. I tried to imagine us on a date. I tried to imagine us without all the awful things that had happened between us and around us. But I couldn't. I know, I was being pathetic, a total girl. I needed to focus, so I did.

After a time, a thin young man clad entirely in black, wearing black eyeliner and black lipstick, moved into our booth.

"We're here to see Angel," I told him when he asked for our drink order.

He raised his eyebrows at me. "Angel?" he said.

I nodded and he gave me a strange smile, looked back and forth between me and Dylan.

"As you like," he said, speaking with a

slight lisp. "Can I tell her who's asking for her?"

I hesitated, looked at Dylan.

"Tell her it's Max," he interjected quickly.

The man nodded and walked off. I stared at Dylan and he shrugged.

"You have a better idea?" he wanted to know.

I didn't answer him, just sipped on the Guinness he'd handed me downstairs. It was dark and savory, a little on the strong side. I wasn't much of a beer drinker in general, but it wasn't bad, actually, and the slight buzz it was already giving me felt good, helped me to relax.

After a while another man, this one more along the lines of the bouncers outside, came and escorted us down a corridor. He was stocky and stern looking, and his long black coat swept the ground as we walked past a row of doors, almost to the end of the hallway. I felt my mouth grow dry and adrenaline start to surge. I thought about the long hallways, the key-card doors, the elevator we'd have to pass through in order to get out of this place. I started to feel trapped. I wondered if we were making a terrible mistake. But it felt too late to say anything. This was our last lead. After this, I didn't know what would happen.

He opened the last door for us and we walked inside. Then he closed it behind us. It was pretty obvious what Angel did for a living. We stood in a dimly lit room dominated by a huge bed on the right. To the left there was a small sitting area. There was something cheap and seedy about the space. I guess I would have expected lots of velvet and candles, plush pillows and music, but that was just my writer's brain adding details, looking for atmosphere. Or the naive Ridley imaging assignations and adding romance where there was only a business transaction. This space was utilitarian. People who came here wanted one thing and they wanted it raw.

I looked at Dylan's face but it was blank. Behind his glasses, I couldn't see his eyes. I wanted to leave but I heard another door open and I knew it was too late.

She entered the room from behind a velvet curtain and then swept it open with an expansive sweep of her arms.

"Max," she said, soft and sultry. "I've been trying to reach you."

She wore a wide smile that faded almost immediately when she saw us. She would have been stunning, this Asian woman with long, thick tresses of dark black hair, the impossibly slim lines of her body. The memory of beauty resided in her fine features. But she looked used and tired. She looked broken. I thought of the women and girls abducted and sold into sexual slavery I'd read about in the articles in Jake's file. I wondered if she'd been one of those girls once, and if this was what you looked like ten, fifteen years later. The thought made me sad.

"Who are you?" she asked.

I saw her start to move backward toward the curtain, but Dylan was on her before she could get far. He grabbed her quickly and spun her around roughly, putting his hand around her mouth. She struggled against him, then she froze. It took me a second to realize that he had his gun to her back. I didn't even know he'd brought it with him. My stomach hollowed out.

"Keep your fucking mouth shut," he said to her, his voice low and menacing. He moved her over to the chair and sat her down heavily.

"Dylan," I said. I barely recognized him suddenly.

He ignored me. "How?" he asked her, wrapping his hand around her throat and pointing the gun to her temple. "How have you been trying to reach him?"

She released an awful gurgling noise and

clawed at the hand he had on her neck. I saw that she'd drawn blood from him but he didn't flinch.

"How?" I didn't even recognize his voice. It was more of a growl.

He released his grip on her just slightly and she drew a harsh, rasping breath. She looked at him with pleading eyes and I moved to put a hand on his shoulder.

"I can't tell you," she said. Tears welled in her eyes and ran down her face, horrible black rivers of mascara. "He'll kill me."

"Die now. Die later. Your choice."

Her eyes met mine and I felt a horrible clenching in my gut — guilt, fear, pain. *What* were we doing?

"Dylan, stop it," I said.

"Ridley," he said, turning to me, "stay out of this."

I backed away from him and stood by the door. I was useless, totally out of my league. I had no frame of reference for dealing with a situation like this. How had I imagined this encounter would go? I didn't know.

"I'm going to give you one more second and then I'm going to snap your neck, do you understand me?"

I froze. Would he really kill this woman if she didn't tell us what we wanted to know? I didn't think so, but he was convincing as

hell. Maybe that was part of being successful in a matter like this. I saw her nod and I
was flooded with relief. He released his grip
on her throat. She coughed and let out a
little sob.

"I can only leave messages for him on the
Internet," she said, her voice hoarse.
"There's a website."

"Give me the address, your log-in, and
password," he said. He looked at me and I
quickly produced a pen and paper from my
pocket and handed them to her. (Well, I *am*
a writer. We don't go very many places
without those things.) She scribbled on the
paper for a second and then handed it to
me. I wasn't surprised to see the address
that I had by now memorized. Her log-in
was *angellove,* her password *serendipity.*

"How do you know him?" I asked. "Who
is he to you?"

She looked at me as if I were a moron,
began massaging her neck where Dylan had
grabbed her.

I tried to imagine Max in a place like this.
I couldn't picture it, no matter how hard I
tried. So much about the things I'd learned
about Max just didn't compute with my
memories. I realized I was staring at her
and she turned away from my gaze. Dylan
took the paper from my hand, glanced at it

and then back at her.

"If you're lying, I swear to God, I'll find you," he said.

The way he looked, the way his voice sounded, I didn't even know him.

She shook her head, gave him a little laugh. "I'm already dead."

He moved into her quickly and hit her hard on the back of the head. She crumpled like a marionette with her strings cut, slumped into the chair. He turned and must have seen the horror on my face because it stopped him in his tracks.

"She's not dead, Ridley," he said. His accent was heavier than I'd ever heard it. "I just need her to be quiet for a few minutes so we can get out of here."

I went over to her and felt her throat. I was relieved to feel her pulse beneath my fingers. Dylan grabbed my arm and we walked out of the Kiss as if nothing had happened.

We hopped into a cab outside the club and asked the cabbie to take us to an Internet café. He talked the whole way about the subway bombings just a few months earlier and about the "fucking Arabs" and "fucking Americans" and how they were fucking up the whole world. I barely heard him as I stared out the window, watched the buildings race by. I kept stealing glances at Dylan, who'd taken his dark glasses off and kept stealing glances back at me.

"Did you think she was just going to *give* us the information?" he asked finally.

I shrugged and shook my head. "Would you have killed her if she hadn't?" I whispered.

"Of course not," he said, incredulous. "No."

"So you were just playing the tough guy?"

"Yes," he said, frowning at me.

"It was pretty convincing."

He shrugged. "It wouldn't have worked if it hadn't been."

We were silent for a second. Then he said, "I guess I keep forgetting."

"What?"

"That you don't know me as well as I know you."

I looked over at him and saw that the nail marks Angel had left looked raw and painful. I didn't know what to say. He was right, and it reminded me how inorganic this relationship was, how it had started under a veil of lies and existed in a crucible of danger and uncertainty. Our only social encounters consisted of a murder in a dark hospital room and the menacing of a prostitute in an after-hours club on the West End of London. I wondered if we had anything in common other than our shared obsession with my father. I wondered if we'd ever have a chance to find out.

Some of us are lost and some of us are found. I think that's really the difference Max had observed. Some people don't have that many questions and lack that belly of fire when it comes to their encounters with the world. They're content in their predictable lives, where everything that lies before them is like a rerun of *Jeopardy*. They already know the answers and how the game will end. They don't have the urge to travel or to ask the questions that boggle the mind: Who am I? Why am I here? Is this all there is? Instead there's a certainty about themselves and the world around them. They work. They go to church. They take care of their families. They know their beliefs are correct; they know that anything different is wrong or bad.

Others of us are lost. We're forever seeking. We torture ourselves with philosophies and ache to see the world. We question everything, even our own existence. We ask a lifetime of questions and are never satisfied with the answers because we don't recognize anyone as an authority to give them. We see life and the world as an enormous puzzle that we might one day solve, if only we collect enough pieces. The idea that we might never understand, that our questions might go unanswered until the day we die, almost never occurs to us. And when it does, it fills us with dread.

I was filled with this dread as we hovered over the computer screen in the back of the twenty-four-hour Internet café. It was nearly four a.m. and I felt as if we were the only two people in London. We entered the address into the browser and the red screen popped up. I tabbed for the windows and entered Angel's log-in and password. A small window opened in the center of the screen. I watched as the same streaming video piece I'd seen at Jake's place started. It was broad daylight in the video, so I knew that it wasn't a live feed. I found myself leaning in closer. Then, from the right of the screen, a man moved into the frame. He moved slowly, with the help of a cane. His motion was unsteady and the other people on the street seemed to race by him. He wore a long brown coat and a brimmed tweed cap. Then he stopped and turned.

He was thin and ghostly pale, as if something was eating him alive inside. He was not the man I knew. He was someone shelled out and broken. He lifted his eyes to the camera, which must have been somewhere across the street. He moved his mouth but I couldn't hear what he was saying, just like in my dreams. Even as changed as he was, there was no mistaking who I was looking at. It was Max. My father.

I felt this terrible ache inside that I suppose had always been there, that had been driving me all this time. This ache was the reason for everything I had done, every mistake I had made, every reckless and careless action since Dylan first approached me on the street. I had wrecked my whole life to fill the empty space inside me that was the dark shadow of my father. I needed something that I still believed only he could give me. And I'd almost destroyed myself to get it.

"What's he saying?" Dylan asked.

The video was on some kind of a loop. It came to an abrupt stop and then replayed Max walking slowly across the street, turning and saying something as he faced the camera. The whole thing lasted maybe ten seconds.

I watched it replay several times, zooming in on his mouth. After the fourth time, I knew. I leaned back in my chair.

"What?" Dylan asked me. "What is he saying?"

I looked up at Dylan. "He's saying, 'Ridley, go home.' "

They descended on us then, maybe realizing that it was the end of the road, that my pathetic little leads had led me as far as I could go. They entered from the front of the café and from the back. They shined their lights in the windows beside us. They entered with guns drawn, wearing body armor and making lots of noise. Overkill, if you ask me. But I just sat staring at the screen, watching Max, put my hands on my head, felt the spiky strands of my strange hair. Dylan, standing beside me, did the same. Two men patted him down and took his gun.

I wasn't surprised to see Inspector Madeline Ellsinore when she came through the door. She had her eyes on me; in them I imagined I saw empathy.

In fact, I wasn't even surprised to see Jake or the black bulletproof vest he wore over his clothes, the gun in his hand.

18

Up until recently, my life has been pretty uneventful. Not to say that I was just plodding along until a single event turned my world on its axis. But now that you mention it, that's not too far off. As I sat in a cold gray room, lit horribly with flickering fluorescent bulbs, I thought about that moment when I raced into the street to save Justin Wheeler. Dylan was right. Part of me would go back and change it all if I could. But I know now that all of this was set in motion long before that day. I had been laboring under the delusion that I had some control over my life. I was only beginning to understand that it wasn't true.

He walked into the room and closed the door. He didn't say anything as he sat across the table from me. I couldn't bring myself to raise my eyes. His betrayal was so profound, so incomprehensible, that in that moment I was afraid I'd burst into flames if

I looked at him.

"Ridley," he said finally.

"Was it all lies? Everything?"

He didn't answer for a second. Then: "I'm sorry."

"You're sorry?"

"I *have* cared for you, Ridley," he said in a voice I didn't recognize. There was something so cold and officious about him, especially in this place, in this setting. "I still do. You know that. But that wasn't part of the plan. It was a contingency I never planned for, a complication."

"A mistake," I said. Did he say "care for"? Like you *care for* the environment or *care for* an aging aunt? I thought of all the love I'd felt for this man, all the times I'd given him my body and my heart, my deepest trust; all the truths I'd revealed, all the painful confidences I'd shared. I'd sliced myself open and bared it all. I felt a deep sense of shame, a desire to cover my nakedness before him.

"Not a mistake," he said softly, more like the man I knew. I felt his hand on mine and I pulled it back quickly. I mustered my strength and looked up. He seemed tired and sad, with dark circles under his eyes, the line of his mouth straight and firm.

"Don't ever put your hands on me again," I said.

He hung his head. I couldn't have hated him more.

"I just need to be clear," I said. "Everything about you — your personal history as a Project Rescue baby, our relationship, your sculpture, everything I know about you as a person — all of it just lies? Just a cover story?"

He nodded slowly. "Yes."

I felt a wave of nausea so strong, I swear I thought I was going to puke right there. But I managed to hold it in. I tasted that dark beer I'd had a while ago. It tasted like the truth, bitter and acidic on the back of my throat.

"Why?" I asked, hearing the desperation in my own voice.

"You know why."

I shook my head. "No. You didn't need to deceive me so personally to find Max. You could have had me under surveillance, watched me from a distance. I never would have known."

He didn't answer me, let me think about it. And then I understood.

"You needed to be able to manipulate me. Keep the issues alive for me, plant little seeds here and there, show me that file. You got to know me well enough to push my buttons, to get me chasing when the time was right."

I was happy to see shame and regret on his face, but it didn't even come close to being enough. So many things that had never made sense to me were so obvious to me now: Jake's obsession with Max, how he always found me wherever I was, how he always seemed to know what I was thinking, how he managed to stoke the flames of my curiosity, always keeping the past alive. Nearly two years of this. Suddenly I didn't feel so bad about sleeping with Dylan.

I thought about our last moments together at the Cuban place in the Bronx and at the Cloisters over the wall.

"Those things you said to me the last time we were together. Those promises you made. Why would you say those things?"

He shook his head and I saw his eyes go damp. He got up and walked over to a narrow window that was laced with wire mesh. I understood. It wasn't all lies. There *was* something real between us. But it was irretrievable now. In those last moments, he must have known that the time was coming. In his way, he tried to save us. Somehow that just made it all worse.

"So it was the CIA that night. They sent

the text message. They chased us at the Cloisters. They brought me to London."

He shook his head. "No," he said.

"Then who?"

"We think Max sent the message. If you'd gone alone that night, you might have seen him."

I thought about the car that had slowly pulled up the drive, about the men in the trees. Had he been in the back of the sedan? Lurking in the woods?

"So those were your men that night? The CIA came to take Max in."

He shook his head again. I wasn't very good at this, I guess.

"There are a lot of people, a lot of very bad people, looking for Max. I don't know if they were following you or if they intercepted the text message, but they got there before my men did."

"Grant," I said quietly. "I told Grant Webster where I was going and when I'd be there. That's how they found out."

"Maybe," he said with a slow nod.

I hung my head, wondering if they had tortured him to find out. I remember how excited he'd been to be involved in all the intrigue.

"So who brought me to London?" I asked after a while. "How did my passport and all that cash get into my bag?"

"There are a number of suspects," he said vaguely.

"Like who?" I pressed.

He didn't say anything, just looked at me hard. I got mad.

"They *tortured* me!" I yelled, standing and lifting my shirt so that he could see my wound, the bruises on my body. "I didn't know anything about Max. I didn't even know they called him the Ghost. I didn't even know what they were asking me."

He said sharply, "I had *nothing* to do with that. I tried to protect you, Ridley. And I failed." He pulled at the neck of his sweater and exposed a thick bandage on his shoulder. I remembered watching him get shot. I remembered him falling. The memory made me dizzy. I looked into the green facets of his eyes for I don't know how long. To his credit, he didn't look away. I don't know what I was looking for there, but I'll tell you that I didn't find it. I didn't understand him or how he could have done what he did — or how I could have believed so totally the lie that he was. There we were, showing each other our wounds. I'm not sure what either one of us was trying to prove. I lowered my shirt and sat back down. He did the same.

"I never would have been a part of that," he said.

"Oh, but you were. You were the biggest part of it."

The silence that followed between us was a live wire.

"Why didn't they kill me?" I asked him finally. "When they figured out I didn't know where Max was, why would they let me live? How did I get to that hotel?"

He sighed. "Everyone wants the same thing from you, Ridley."

He put his hand on a file that lay between us on the table. I'd been so distracted I hadn't noticed it. He opened it and slid out a photograph, pushed it toward me. I recognized him right away. The man on the plane with the scars on his face. The same man who'd killed Sarah Duvall. He was ghoulishly ugly, with pale eyes that seemed lidless, a wide, thin mouth and oddly shaped nose. Those scars — burns, I think. He had the look of a man who'd suffered terrible agony, and it had made him evil. I shuddered. I didn't think I'd ever forget the sound of his voice.

"Who is he?"

"His name is Boris Hammacher."

I waited for him to go on but he didn't. Why did I feel as if I was always trying to pull information out of people? Couldn't anyone just ever tell me what I needed to know?

"And?" I said.

"And he's an assassin, for lack of a better word. He's the guy you call when you want someone found and killed."

"He's looking for Max?" I asked.

He nodded. "I think it's safe to operate under that assumption."

"He let me live because he thought Max would come for me."

"That would be my guess."

Notice how slippery he is, how he never confirms or denies anything? It's possible he just didn't know the answers to my questions, but more likely he just didn't want to answer them.

"He's the one I saw on the street," I said, taking the photograph in my hand. I remembered chasing him, how fast he'd been. "He killed Sarah Duvall. Why? She didn't know anything."

Jake got up and paced the room. "I don't know, Ridley. I don't know if he was following her or following you. Maybe he thought she knew something about Myra's disappearance, maybe he wasn't sure what kind of clues Myra had left behind. Maybe he thought she was a loose end. Or maybe he was trying to terrorize you."

"Did he kill Myra Lyall?" I asked.

"Myra Lyall got information she shouldn't have. As you know, she was researching an article on some Project Rescue babies, and someone leaked information to her about the CIA belief that Max Smiley was still alive. She started asking a lot of questions at the agency. She paid Esme Gray a visit. She was just fishing, though. As far as we know, she didn't have any real information. We believe Boris Hammacher thought she knew more than she did. When she didn't, he killed her."

"Who is he working for? Who's trying to find Max?"

"It could be any number of people. Max had a lot of enemies."

I thought about all of this for a second. I thought about how Myra, Sarah, and Grant were all dead because of Max and how the only reason I hadn't joined them was because everyone was banking on the likelihood that Max would be coming for me someday.

"Who killed Esme Gray?"

"Esme Gray is alive."

"But . . ."

He walked over to the table, sat back down.

"Didn't you ever wonder how she escaped prosecution? Didn't it seem strange to you that no one ever paid for Project Rescue? She came to us when Max tried to contact her. She brokered a deal for herself and for her son. She obtained immunity in exchange for her help in locating Max Smiley. Her son, Zack, will be out of prison within the next five years."

This information was unpleasant. But in comparison to everything else, it didn't seem like such a big deal that a man who'd tried to kill me and who still hated me might be out on the street fairly soon.

"So why fake her death?"

"She made mistakes in her dealings with you. She'd let you have too much information by mentioning Myra Lyall. Dylan Grace was harassing her. She'd been working with us since we realized she'd falsely identified Max Smiley's body, and so she knew a lot about the investigation. She was showing signs of stress at all the deception. She had a paranoia that Max would discover her betrayal and come for her. We were afraid she was a weak link, that she might snap if pulled too hard. So we removed her from the field."

"Was it on purpose that you chose a beating death for her? That's the way the FBI claims Max killed people."

He shrugged. "We just needed her face to be unrecognizable."

I didn't say anything. I just gave him a look that I hope communicated how much he disgusted me on so many levels.

"What about DNA and fingerprints, dental records? You can't just mash up someone's face and call it a day anymore."

"The CIA took over the investigation so that we could handle all of that. Happens for witness protection all the time."

We were both quiet for a while. There were so many questions. Some of them I wanted the answers to, some of them I didn't. I didn't even know where to go next. Finally: "Okay, so where is he?"

"We know now that he's not in London. He probably hasn't been in years. That image you saw had been superimposed on that street scene. Computer graphics. He could be anywhere in the world."

He could be anywhere in the world but he was alive. I was filled with dread and fury and, yes, the slightest glimmer of hope.

"Then why are we all here?"

"Like us, Boris Hammacher thought that Max was here. We suspect that's why he brought you here. And we followed Dylan Grace to you."

"Because everybody wants the same thing from me."

I thought of all these people circling like vultures the rotting carrion that was my life, all of them waiting for Max to make his move so that they could make theirs. But Max never came. I'd been shot, abducted, tortured, left to suffer alone in a foreign hotel room, brought to a hospital where another attempt was made on my life, abducted again, run all over London, and finally arrested. But Max never came. I guess the joke was on them. Or me.

I knew that even this conversation was probably fraught with lies and half-truths, but I also knew that it was the first nearly honest conversation I'd ever had with the man before me. It made me sad. I felt so tired suddenly, as if I could sleep for days. I was envious of Rip van Winkle. I wanted a hundred-year nap, where I woke and everything I hated and loved had turned to dust.

"So what is it? Why does everyone want Max Smiley so badly? Why is everyone looking for the Ghost?"

Jake's face was as still as stone.

"The murders he's suspected of committing?"

No answer.

"No," I said into the silence. "No one

cares about a few prostitutes. Though I imagine a couple of dead Interpol agents might cause some international difficulties. Still, it has to be more than that. It has to be more than just one man."

"Max Smiley is more than just a man," said Jake. "He's the linchpin in an international web of criminal activity. He has been for decades."

"What kind of criminal activity?"

"It's complicated, Ridley."

"We have time, don't we?"

He sighed, leaned back in his chair. "It started with Project Rescue. He and Esme Gray conceived of this way to get kids out of abusive homes and into the homes of the wealthy. Through Alexander Harriman, Max aligned himself with the Italian-American Mafia to get the dirty work done."

"I know all of this," I said impatiently.

He lifted a hand. "The enterprise became quite lucrative. It grew."

"But when things started to get ugly the night Teresa Stone was murdered, Max extracted himself, right?" I said. My heart started to race. I felt eager to cling to the story Alexander Harriman, Max's late lawyer, had told me.

Jake looked at me as though he pitied me. I must have seemed like a child to him, clinging to my fairy tales.

"If he had, Ridley, we wouldn't be here, would we?"

I didn't say anything. What could I say?

"Max Smiley was a businessman. There was money to be made and a lot of it. Project Rescue faded away, yes, but the connections Max had made led him into other arenas."

I remembered the articles about the sex slave trade from Albania I'd read in Jake's file. And I knew. I wanted to cover my ears to keep from hearing the rest.

"It's not such a big leap from stealing babies and selling them to the rich to luring women and girls from clubs and selling them into slavery," he said.

I put my head in my hands. "What are you saying?" I asked through my fingers. "How was he involved with that? What did he do?"

"We believe he financed the building of nightclubs in Europe that were run by Albanian gangs. In these clubs, mostly in places like the Balkans, the Ukraine, women were lured with the promise of good-paying jobs in the U.K. or the U.S., or they were simply drugged and abducted, then trafficked with false documents to other countries in Europe, the U.S., and Asia.

One of the clubs you visited yourself, the Kiss."

He glanced over at me quickly, then away again.

"He took a cut of the profits, both legal and illegal. Of course, there was the added benefit of having places to feed his appetites with no fear of discovery. These women are literally disappeared. False documents are created for them, they are injected with heroin to make them addicts, no one ever hears from them again. What particular monster they've fallen prey to matters not at all."

The room around me tilted unpleasantly.

"Isn't it possible that he didn't know what was going on in those clubs?" I asked.

I asked this though I already knew the answer. I was having a hard time understanding how a man who'd spent a great deal of his life raising money for abused women and children through his foundation could be involved with organizations that made their money selling young women and girls into sexual slavery. It didn't compute . . . like so many things. I remembered what Dylan had said, screamed at me, rather, in the car. *Wake up, Ridley. Wake the* fuck *up. Your father, your beloved Max,* hated *women. He* murdered *them.*

He didn't answer my question, just went on.

"In the commission of this business, Max Smiley dealt with some of the key players in the sex slave trade. If we manage to find and capture him, get him to talk, the CIA along with other international law enforcement agencies could cripple or severely damage some of their operations, save countless women, and possibly force principals to face charges in international courts. Do you understand, Ridley?"

I thought about the photos I'd seen. Max with these men, smiling with mobsters and terrorists in Paris cafés. I started to get that feeling I get when everything is closing in on me and panic starts to set in. My breathing suddenly felt labored and white spots danced before my eyes.

"Ridley," said Jake, who, in spite of everything, knew me quite well, "don't pass out."

He called out toward the door, "Get her some water, please."

He came and kneeled beside me. Another man entered with a small bottle of water and handed it to Jake. He cracked the lid and handed it to me. I sipped from it and focused on a spot on the wall. I had been humiliated enough for one lifetime to pass out when God knows how many people were staring at me on a closed-circuit screen. All I could think was, Do things like this happen to people?

"Ridley, just hold it together, okay? It's going to be okay."

I wasn't sure how he could say such a ridiculous thing.

"Why should I?" I wanted to know. "Why should I hold it together?"

"Because, Ridley, I need your help."

"*My* help? Don't be ridiculous."

He didn't say anything, just released a breath and looked at the floor, rested his hand on the back of my chair. I took a few more sips of the water he gave me, kept staring at the spot on the wall that was helping me hold on to consciousness.

"My help with what?" I asked finally, curiosity getting the better of me.

"I need you to help us bring Max Smiley in."

I almost laughed until I saw that he was deadly serious. I also saw that I had no choice. That, in fact, I never had.

Since the moment Max found me in my fort in the woods behind my parents' house, we'd been trekking toward this day. He'd said then, *There's a golden chain from my heart to yours. Trust me. I'll always find you.*

Years later, I finally understood what he meant. We were bound by experience, by blood, by a fierce love for each other that transcended our personalities, our identities, our good or bad deeds. When I was lost, Max had always found me and brought me home, no questions asked, no judgments, no recriminations. He respected my need to disappear and he accepted that he was the one charged with bringing me back. I hadn't realized until now that I was charged with the same. No matter what he'd done, no matter who he'd hurt or killed, no matter what kind of a monster Max Smiley was, he was my father. Whether he knew it or not, he was lost. It was my duty, and mine alone, to bring him home.

■ ■ ■ ■

PART THREE:
THE HOMECOMING

■ ■ ■ ■

19

About fifteen hours later, I watched my father, Ben (not Max), on a closed-circuit television screen. He was being questioned by two CIA agents: a man, tall with dark buzz-cut hair, and a woman, Latino and small, with burning coals for eyes, both wearing conservative blue suits. I noticed that he didn't look scared at all, that he leaned back in his chair and had his arms folded across his chest. That his face was stern, his eyes disdainful. He'd admitted to communicating with Max. But he didn't seem to think there was anything wrong with that.

"It's not a crime to disappear from your life, is it?" he asked.

"That's *not* his crime, Mr. Jones," said the female agent. She leaned against the wall.

"You have no proof, no evidence, that your other allegations against him are true," my father said with his signature huff. "If you had, you would have brought him in long ago."

I had to admit that I'd had the same thought. I'd brought it up with Jake, who'd told me that they'd never had enough solid evidence to scare him into giving up the men with whom he'd done business. They could have had him on hiding assets, possibly tax evasion, but they wanted him on charges that, if proven, might lead to the death penalty, which was the only way they figured they'd get him to bargain. Otherwise, a few years in a federal prison would be a cakewalk compared to what some of his associates might have done to him — or to the people he loved. They'd never get him to turn. So they watched and waited. But the longer it went on, the more ethereal he became, the less they saw of him, the more careful he was about his dealings. He turned to vapor before their eyes. And then he "died." That's why they started calling him the Ghost.

They'd been at my father for hours. But all they'd managed to get from him was an admission that he'd received a communication from Max about a year and a half after his death with instructions on how to decode messages in the red website. My father told them that he checked the website nearly daily and received communications maybe once every few months. The communications were vague — questions about me, about the rest of the family. Max never once said where he was, and Ben knew better than to ask.

"I didn't understand why he'd do such a thing, cause us all so much grief," my father said, "but I figured he had his reasons and I respected that."

The male agent shook his head, sat down across from my father, and leaned in. His face was a mask of disdain.

"You *respected* that? Do you mean to tell us that in all your years of knowing Max Smiley, you never suspected what he might be capable of, that he might be a murderer, that his business dealings contributed to the destruction of human lives? That he disappeared because it was all starting to catch up with him? He left you and Esme Gray to take the rap for Project Rescue. He nearly destroyed your adopted daughter's life — almost got her killed, in fact. And still you protected him."

My father turned away from the agent's hard gaze.

"I try to see the best in the people I love," he said. "I try to give them the benefit of the doubt."

He sounded defensive, nearly delusional. I was embarrassed for him. I felt ashamed and angry. My cheeks were hot and I sat down in the chair. Jake, who'd been standing behind me, put a hand on my shoulder. I shook him off.

"I told you not to touch me again," I snapped. I felt him shift back from me. I hated him. I hated my father. I hated everyone.

"What does he have on you, Mr. Jones?" the female agent asked with a shake of her head.

My father flinched. "I have nothing left to say. I want an attorney."

She gave a little laugh and looked at him with mock sympathy. "We're with the CIA, Mr. Jones. The usual rules don't apply."

"What is that supposed to mean?" he asked. He started to look afraid for the first time. I saw a sheen of sweat on his brow; he gripped the edge of the table and sat forward.

"It means that you don't have the right to an attorney. It means that we can hold you indefinitely if we believe you are a risk to national security. Max Smiley was a known associate of terrorist organizations. You have had contact with him. That makes you at best a witness, at worst an accomplice."

My father was silent. He rubbed his eyes with his thumb and forefinger. Was it loyalty or fear that kept him protecting Max? I didn't know.

I turned to Jake. I couldn't look at my father anymore. "What happens to me now?"

"Nothing," he said. "We let you go. You live your life, go about your business."

I looked at him. "In the meantime, you watch every move I make, every phone call, every e-mail. I live in a fishbowl."

He gave me a grave nod. "Then," he said, "after a few weeks, using the log-in you obtained from Angel, you try to reach Max. We'll go from there."

"And Dylan?"

Jake nodded again. "All charges and reprimands against him have been dropped," he said, handing me a document. "As per the terms of your agreement."

"He goes back to work?" I asked, scanning the page. I'd read it and signed it a few hours earlier.

Jake shook his head. "No. We weren't able to arrange that. He's been terminated from the Federal Bureau of Investigation. The guy is a loaded gun."

I couldn't help but stare at Jake. He didn't seem that different to me. Weird, after everything. He still seemed like Jake. Though he wore a suit and had a cool professionalism to him, I could still see the man I'd known for the last year. I felt as if something in my chest was splitting in half.

"And you?"

"You never have to see me again."

The thought gave me a little jolt. I saw that he could do just that. He could walk away from me as if he'd never made love to me, never held my hand, never listened to all my secrets. Maybe he didn't want to, maybe somewhere within him it would cause him pain, but he *could* do it. He *would* do it.

"But you'll be there, listening and watching," I said, thinking about how strange and sad that would be.

"Until we find Smiley. Then I disappear." He was frowning, looked stiff around the shoulders. I hoped it meant that he was in pain.

"Fine," I said, standing.

"Do you want to hear the rest of Ben's interview?"

"No," I said. "I've heard enough. From everyone. I want to go home."

We'd been back in the States since late the night before. After I agreed to help them, Jake and I got on a commercial flight with a couple of other agents and returned to New York. I'd been with the CIA ever since. I wasn't sure where in the city we were. I'd come to this location in the back of an unmarked white van with no windows. I hadn't seen Dylan since the Internet café in London.

I'd spent a few hours in a clinic where a doctor cleaned and dressed my wound and gave me some kind of antibiotic shot. He also gave me a course of antibiotics for the road. And some painkillers, which I hadn't taken yet. I wanted to be clearheaded.

Jake walked me down long white corridors lined with gray doors. We exited from the building into an underground garage and climbed into another van. Or the same van, who knows. There was a driver at the wheel, and as soon as Jake slammed the door, the van started moving. Sitting in the back beside me, he handed me a cell phone equipped with instant messaging and e-mail access. It was pretty cool looking, slick and flat. He told me how everything was pre-programmed for me to reach them.

"Keep this on you at all times. You'll have five minutes to return calls, e-mails, or instant messages from us. If you exceed that time, someone will come for you."

"To protect me or take me into custody?"

"Well, that depends upon the reason for your delay in responding."

I nodded my understanding.

"Remember, Ridley," he said after he'd finished with his various instructions — don't play my music too loud, don't expose the phone to moisture, don't loiter in cell phone dead zones, use stairs instead of elevators whenever possible (I didn't ask why) — "we may not be the only people watching you. You won't see us, you won't hear us, you won't know we're there. If you do suspect that someone might be following you, if you hear strange clicks or static on your phone, even if the screen on your computer monitor starts to act up, you need to let us know."

"Okay," I said. I was struck again with how bizarre this whole thing was. I thought that Grant would have gotten a kick out of it all. I personally had never been so depressed in all my life. I couldn't help but wonder if they'd listen to me going to the bathroom. This was a weird thing to wonder, I know.

I must have dozed off a little because the next thing I knew, we were coming to a stop. I sat there for a second, then looked at Jake. The look on his face communicated the gravity of my situation. He was worried —

whether it was because he thought I couldn't handle it, or he was afraid, even with all their surveillance, that he might not be able to keep any harm from coming to me, or he just grieved for all that was lost between us, I didn't know.

"Ridley," he said as he swung the door open for me. "Be careful."

I waited until I climbed over him and out of the van and came to stand on the sidewalk before I responded.

"This is never going to work, you know."

"We'll see," he said. We locked eyes for a second. I'm not sure what he saw there, but it caused him to shift closer to me.

"Ridley," he said, his voice a warning, "just follow the program, okay?"

"What choice do I have?" I said, and walked toward my building. He closed the door without another word and the van sped off. I moved quickly inside and was glad not to see anyone in the lobby or in the elevator. I'd barely made it into my apartment before I started sobbing. I knew they could hear me and I didn't care; I just let it all out, all the pain and fear and anxiety, into the cushions on my couch. When I felt better I ordered enough Chinese food for four people from Young Chow on Fourth Avenue and took the hottest shower

I could take without scalding myself.

When the food came, I ate it in front of the television set, flipping mindlessly through the channels. I didn't see a thing on the screen in front of me as I wolfed down egg rolls and wonton soup and sesame chicken. I was starving, absolutely ravenous. When I was totally stuffed, I took my antibiotics and three of the pain pills the doctor had given me. I ignored the message machine blinking beside the phone. I got into bed and slept for nearly twelve hours.

When I woke in the bright light of late morning, I expected to feel better. But I didn't. I felt utterly lost. Those black fingers of depression that had been pulling and tugging closed around me like a shroud. I spent the better part of the morning staring at a water stain on the ceiling over my couch.

They say that it's the first three years of a child's life that are the most critical, that if in those years a child is not cared for and loved, then the damage cannot be undone. If in those years, a child does not have the opportunity to see and learn, to develop empathy, compassion, and trust, he will never have the opportunity to learn those things again.

I don't know what happened to Max in

the early years of his life, but I can imagine now. Max was a damaged person. I know I've said this before, but I'm asking you now to really understand, to have true compassion. Imagine if you can an infant, fragile and pure, who instead of being the object of adoration was the object of anger, who instead of being stroked and cuddled was slapped and shaken. Imagine that instead of learning love, that child learned only fear. Imagine that all he knew was that fear and pain, and that somehow he would use these things to survive. What would such a person be capable of later in his life? I'm not making excuses. I'm just asking you to think about it.

Ben had asked to meet me at the fountain in Washington Square. I didn't answer his call when I saw his number blinking on my caller ID. I had halfway decided that I might never speak with him and Grace again. He left a message.

"You probably don't want to see me," he said. His voice was tired. He sounded old and afraid. "I don't blame you." A long pause followed where I could hear only his breathing. "But I am asking for you to meet me. I'll buy you a cappuccino and we can watch some chess — like we used to. A lifetime ago, I know. I'll be there around four. I'll wait."

I think he was trying to be sly by not naming the meeting place outright. He may have surmised that I was being watched or that he was. But it wouldn't have taken a genius to figure out where he was talking about. And I'd be followed there, anyway. I knew they had equipment in those vans that could make it so they could park blocks away and still pick up most of our conversation. I didn't plan on going, but then around three-thirty, I found myself bundling up and heading out.

The sky was that strange gray-blue tempered with black. The fountain in the center of the park was dry, and people hustled through the open space that sat at the bottom of Fifth Avenue, instead of lingering as they would in spring or summer. In those months, Washington Square would be full of people sitting on benches or along the edge of the fountains or on the grass, watching entertainers playing guitars or performing magic tricks for small crowds. The playground would be packed with kids playing on the swings and jungle gyms while parents and nannies looked on. In the warmer months, Washington Square was one of the most alive places in the city.

Today the trees were black with spindly branches reaching dark fingers into the sky.

I saw him sitting on the bench in a long black wool coat and cap. He had his hands in his pockets and he leaned back, looking up at the sky. I don't know what he was thinking about, but when I drew closer I could see that his eyes were rimmed red. I sat down beside him. He looked at me, then looked away. He looked back again and sat up.

"Ridley," he said, reaching for my hair. "I didn't even recognize you for a second."

I let him touch me, even though I wanted to slap his hand away. He touched my spiky hair, the side of my face.

I smiled without mirth. "It's my fugitive do," I said. "What do you think?"

He shook his head. "I don't like it."

"I don't like it, either," I snapped. "But it's just one of many things about my life I don't like. I can live it with, though, which is more than I can say for the rest of it."

The fog of my words hung in the cold air between us. I tried to hold his eyes but he looked away.

"I knew he couldn't be trusted," he said finally. "I never liked him."

"Who?"

"That Jake Jacobsen. He lied to you all

this time."

The nerve and the audacity of that statement, his absolute ignorance of its irony, stunned me. I looked at him and felt the most profound loss of faith, the deepest disappointment I think I've ever felt in anyone. Including Max. Anger was a stone in my chest, preventing me from answering. I tried to take a long breath, to compose myself. It took a while before I could speak again.

"Have you always known what he is?" I asked finally, surprised at how even and steady my voice sounded.

I wondered if he'd be coy, ask me who I was talking about, pretend I might be talking about Jake. Instead he surprised me.

"Of course," he said, turning his eyes on me. There was mettle in his expression. "Of course I knew. Why do you think we took you that night, no questions asked? Do you really think that we were that *ignorant,* that foolish to break the laws we broke, to risk Project Rescue? We took you out of fear, Ridley. We took you out of the terror of what a man like Max might do to a child."

I stared at him. He said it as if he thought I should understand, as if maybe I should have even surmised as much by now. I envied him his sense of righteousness. I

438

wondered what it was like to be so sure of the virtue of your actions and deeds, in spite of staggering evidence to the contrary.

"So you knew what Project Rescue was, too?"

He shook his head. "I've told you before that I only knew we were flying under the radar of the law. I didn't know about the dark side of the organization. I won't keep trying to convince you of that. Anyway, it's not important now what I knew then."

He had donned an air of huffiness that I found repulsive. I still loved him but I felt a growing chasm opening between us. I didn't know if I'd ever be able to cross it again. I grieved inside — because my dad had always been the love of my life.

"So tell me, Dad. What *do* you consider important now?"

"What have they asked you to do?"

"Who?"

He gave me a look. I shook my head.

"It's none of your business," I said.

He sat up quickly and grabbed my shoulders. "Don't *ever* say that to me. Everything about you is my business. You're my daughter. Not my blood, no, but my daughter in every way that counts. If anything ever happens to you . . . ." He let the words trail off and I didn't rush to fill the silence. I didn't squirm from his grasp, but I didn't sink into him like I wanted to, either. I looked at his face, his snow-white hair, the deep lines around his eyes, his full pink cheeks. No one could call my father handsome, I've told you before. But his face was strong, his gaze powerful.

"You can't understand," he said. "Not until you're a parent yourself. You'll never know the all-consuming love, the desire to protect that just eats you alive. You'd do anything to keep your child safe."

I wasn't sure if he was talking about himself or about Max. Then: "Stay away from him, Ridley."

"Why?"

"Just stay away."

"Why did you love him, Dad?"

He sighed. "I knew another side to him. The side that you loved. That was true, you know. That was Max, too. Understand, I didn't know anything about his business dealings. I didn't know about the —" He swallowed hard here, shied away from saying the word *murders*. "I didn't know about the other things of which he's accused. I didn't know."

Maybe he thought if he could just repeat the words *I didn't know* enough, he'd make them true. Or maybe he knew our conversation was likely being listened to and he was being careful to assert his ignorance of Max's dealings.

"But you knew he killed his mother," I said. "Or suspected it. Didn't you?"

He seemed startled, then hung his head. I was glad he didn't deny it.

"He loves you, Ridley. Truly, deeply, as any father loves his daughter. But I promise you, if he thinks you've turned on him, God help you."

His words ran like liquid nitrogen in my veins. I didn't say anything.

"I don't know what kind of deal they offered you. But stay away from Max. Let him die. They'll never find him. Never."

"How long have you known that he was alive?"

He shook his head. I knew he wouldn't say anything out loud. When he was being questioned, I'd heard him say that he'd received a communication from Max a year and a half after his alleged death, but I wondered if my father had helped Max to stage his death. I didn't ask, mainly because I didn't want to know.

"Where is he, Dad?"

He looked straight ahead, as if he was searching for a face in the crowd. "I'm begging you, lullaby, stay away from him."

He stood up and I stood with him. He took me into his arms then and held me with a terrible desperation. I put my arms around him and finally let myself sink into him. I clung to him, grieving for all that was lost between us, wondering what the future held.

"You will *always* be my daughter," he whispered fiercely. I wondered if it was true. I didn't know. I didn't know who he was. I didn't know who I was. I didn't know any longer who we were to each other.

"You do what you have to do, little girl," he said into my ear. "But protect yourself. Anything that happens to you happens to me. Remember that if you can. In spite of everything, it's as true today as it always has been."

He released me then, started to move away, but stopped to say, "There's something else you should know. About Ace."

I braced myself. On some level, I already knew. Since I'd heard him smoking on the phone that night, since he'd abandoned me when we were supposed to go to the Cloisters. Since I hadn't heard a word from him through everything.

"He's using again. I think we've lost him for good this time."

I nodded and looked up at the sky, shook

my head in grief and disappointment.

When I looked back down toward my father, he was walking away. I stood watching him for a long time as he grew smaller and smaller and then turned a corner. I sat back down on the bench and just sat there for a while, watched some kids playing hackey-sack badly. It wasn't until he was long gone that I realized he'd dropped something in my pocket. It was a smallish silver key with a flat round head. A key to what, I had no idea.

I decided to walk back to my apartment, wanting the space, the cold air on my face. By the time I got home, my hands were red and painful from the cold, my feet and thighs raw beneath my jeans and boots. All during the walk, my mind worked on what that silver key might unlock — a locker, a safety deposit box . . . I couldn't call my father and ask; I'd have to figure it out.

Jake had been serious when he'd said I'd never know they were there. In my imagination, I had anticipated seeing strange men in dark clothing lingering around, reading newspapers on benches, or whistling casually, leaning against lampposts as I passed. I imagined white vans trailing slowly behind me as I moved about my life. I thought they'd be calling all the time with instructions, but the phone I kept with me hadn't rung or beeped even once. I could almost convince myself that I'd imagined the whole thing. As I entered my building, I pretended for a second that I was just Ridley Jones, freelance writer, returning from a walk, that there was nothing more serious on my mind than what I'd have for dinner.

He was standing in the lobby by the mailboxes. It's not an exaggeration to say I ran to him, let him enfold me. I wrapped my arms around him and put my mouth to his. His body felt strong and wonderful through the thick suede of his jacket. He held on to me tight. I heard him sigh as I pulled my mouth from his and put my head to his chest.

"Are you okay?" he whispered into my ear, rubbing my back. It felt so good, the tension of the muscles there draining beneath his hands.

I nodded into him. I was afraid to speak.

"They can't hear us out here," he said.

"How do you know?" I said. I'd been wrong before when I said his face wasn't beautiful — the rock of his jaw, the warmth and depth of his eyes, the strength of his nose. I'd been afraid of all the ugly truths that had made a home in his features. That's what kept me looking away from him.

"Because when I was watching you, we always lost you between your building's front door and your apartment door. Must be lead in the walls."

We took the elevator up to my floor, making out the whole time. I couldn't get enough of him, the comfort of him. I felt a little of the blackness I'd been carrying lighten and lift. He waited in the hallway while I entered my apartment and made some noise, turned on the television. I ordered some Chinese food (yes, again) and went quietly back into the hallway, hoping whoever was listening would think I was just watching TV, waiting for my delivery. They told me there'd be only audio surveillance in my apartment so that I could have some privacy. I hoped they weren't lying. Either way, I wasn't sure it mattered. No one ever told me I couldn't see or talk to Dylan Grace.

We sat on the staircase, huddled together as if for warmth.

"They told me you made a deal so that the charges and reprimands against me would be dropped."

I nodded.

"Thank you, Ridley," he said, putting a hand to my face. "I wouldn't have asked

445

you to do that."

"I know. I'm sorry you lost your job."

He shrugged and gave me a weak smile. "It was probably killing me, anyway."

I just looked at the tiles beneath our feet.

"What do they want you to do?" he asked after some silence.

I told him everything about Jake and everything I'd learned from him. I told him what they wanted me to do.

He shook his head. "It's not going to work."

"I told them."

"I'm sorry about Jacobsen. I can imagine how that must hurt you. I didn't know. His cover was deep — I never realized he was CIA."

I shrugged, turned away from him so that he wouldn't see the pain on my face. It was a private pain; I didn't want to share.

He tightened his arm around me. "I'm sorry," he said again.

I told him about Esme Gray, about Ben, about meeting Ben in the park.

"Man," he said with a slow shake of his head. "They really played us."

"Yeah."

We sat there, thinking about it all. Then: "What are you going to do?"

"I'm not sure," I said.

He nodded. "Whatever it is, count me in."

I took his hand and squeezed it hard.

The buzzer in my apartment rang and I went inside quietly, asked who it was and let the delivery guy in. Dylan waited on the next level until it was clear, then came back downstairs. I took him by the hand and led him into the apartment and into the bedroom. There we made love in a silent intensity where I lost and found myself all at once.

Ridley, go home, Max's ghost had warned me from a computer screen. The image of him, thin and limping on a cane, was on a loop inside my brain. It came unbidden in my dreams and in idle moments. *Ridley, go home.* His face had been so pale, so devoid of the energy I'd always expected to see there. His message was grave and dark: an omen. He didn't look anything like the man I'd known, my dearest uncle, my failed father. But then, he wasn't either of those things. And yet he was both of them. And he was so much more.

In London, Dylan had asked me, *What if knowing Max Smiley doesn't bring you any closer to yourself? What if the closer you get to him, the further you get from who you really are?*

I didn't really understand what he meant by that. I was *from* Max, *of* him, and it was clear to me then that only in knowing him could I discover that part of my own mystery. I wasn't Ben's daughter, the good girl. I was Max's little girl, alone on the street after dark, no one to look after me. But as I lay in the dark beside Dylan, my naked body enfolded by his, I wondered something: Maybe it wasn't the sudden knowledge that I came from Max that had caused me to become unrecognizable to myself. Maybe it was my refusal to let him go. After all, it was only in the chase for him that my life started to come undone.

I had stepped out of my identity to follow Max. I had led people to their deaths; I had fled from federal custody (or so I thought); I'd cut off my long auburn hair and bleached it blond; I'd gone to the Cloisters in the middle of the night at the bidding of a mysterious text message, been abducted and tortured as a result; I'd fled from custody again in London with Dylan, a man I had no reason to trust, and looked on as he later tortured information from a prostitute in the blue room of an after-hours club in the West End, then been arrested in a gaudy show of international law enforcement agencies at an Internet café. With each outrageous action and awful consequence, I further convinced myself that I was less of Ben and more of Max. But really, the doing of it was all mine. It was neither Ben nor Max calling the plays of my life. It wasn't my adopted mother, Grace, or my biological mother, Teresa Stone. It was me.

The thought of it, as I listened to Dylan's steady breathing, hollowed me out inside. I think that's the moment when we all grow up, when we stop blaming our parents for the messes we've made out of our lives and start owning the consequences of our actions.

I lay beside Dylan, felt his breath in my hair, his arm curled over my hip and across my abdomen. My head rested on his other arm, his hand dangled off the bed. I watched the thick muscles of his forearm, the square of his hand as he shifted in his sleep. It was the kind of position that felt wonderful now but would wind up causing his muscles to stiffen and his arm to fall asleep. I shifted the weight of my head onto the pillow to spare him that.

I felt stronger suddenly. The thought that I might be more Ridley than Ben or Max was new and liberating. I felt some of my energy returning.

Ridley, go home.

I started to ponder a question that had been bothering me in the periphery of my consciousness: How could Max possibly have known that I'd log into that website using the log-in Dylan had forced out of Angel? And then it occurred to me what I should have realized all along. It was so obvious, I almost laughed. It wasn't me who'd been chasing Max. He'd been chasing me. When he said, "Ridley, go home," he didn't mean my home. He meant his.

20

I rolled over and looked at Dylan. He opened his eyes. I suspected he hadn't been sleeping any more than I had. Maybe his mind was churning with a million thoughts of his own. I turned on the radio beside the bed and hiked up the volume a little. Not loud enough to arouse suspicion, I hoped.

"I've been thinking," I whispered in his ear.

"What a surprise," he answered with a slow smile. I was starting to enjoy the shades of his accent.

We got dressed quietly and headed out into the hallway.

"How did he know we'd wind up logging into that website with Angel's password?" I said when we were outside. "How could he possibly have known?"

"I wondered the same thing. Maybe he knows you that well," he answered, leaning against the banister.

I shook my head. "Too many variables. There were too many factors involved in my getting to London." The tile floor was cold beneath my bare feet. I felt chilled and wrapped my arms around myself.

"But maybe you would have wound up there, anyway. Maybe you would have figured out where that club was without my help. Maybe you would have gone to London without the assistance of whoever it was that brought you there."

He was confirming what I already suspected, but I wanted to play devil's advocate, to see if I might be wrong.

"But I wouldn't have tortured the information out of that woman," I said.

"Maybe she would have given it to you, anyway."

"Why? How?"

He was silent for a second, kept his eyes on me.

"Because she was meant to tell me? Because he was leaving me clues, luring me there?" I said.

"It's possible, isn't it? Starting with the photos, then the phone calls, the incident in his apartment where you thought you could smell his cologne, that someone had used the shower. The matchbook you found. Then the text message."

"You think he sent that message?" I guess I thought so, too.

He shrugged. "Who else?"

No one else. Max had been reaching out to me from beyond the grave, drawing me closer to him. It must have killed him (no pun intended) to know I'd discovered he was my father, to wonder what else I might be discovering about him. He would have wanted his chance to talk to me, to make me understand.

"Love," Dylan said, echoing our first conversation. "He loves you."

I wondered if that was true. Could someone like Max really love in the truest sense of the word? If he really loved me, wouldn't he have let me be, rather than drag me into all of this? Love lets go; it doesn't hold on with a death grip. It doesn't drag you down into the grave with it.

I took the key from my pocket and showed it to him.

"I think I know what this key unlocks," I said.

"What?"

Lunchtime at Five Roses Pizza in the East Village is a bustle of students and cops and other East Village dwellers looking for the best slice of pizza in the city. Those of you who have been with me from the beginning know that this is where it all started, that it was out in front of this pizzeria, the ground floor of the building where I lived at the time, that I leapt into traffic to save a little boy.

I walked in the front door and barely heard the little bell that announced my arrival over the din of diners eating meatball Parmesan heros, calzones dripping with sauce and cheese, and Zelda's special Sicilian slices. The aromas of garlic and warm crust and tomatoes made my stomach growl.

Zelda, the cranky owner of the place, manned the counter, moving with grace and speed between the huge ovens and the old cash register. She'd helped me once before. In all the years I'd lived there, we'd never had a conversation that didn't involve my rent or my order of two slices and a soda. Then one day when I was in a desperate situation, she helped me escape the police. I wouldn't be surprised now if she threw me out of the place when she saw me. I wouldn't be surprised if she helped me again.

When it was my turn, she regarded me without interest, as if she still saw me every day.

"TwoslicesandaCoke?" she said, her heavily accented words all running together into one unintelligible mumble.

"No, Zelda."

She wiped her hands on her apron and placed them on her hips. She gave me a look that made me think of my mother. "You in trouble again?"

I'm not sure how she knew that. But she actually seemed as if she might care for half a second. I heard someone behind me sigh and start to grumble about the holdup.

"Because I don't want no trouble. You know that."

I leaned into her and lowered my voice. "I just want to use the bathroom."

She looked at me skeptically, then gave me a quick nod. We both knew I didn't have to use the bathroom, but she leaned over and lifted up the counter for me to go behind.

"Thanks, Zelda," I said as I moved past her, over the rubber-mesh grating on the floor and through the kitchen, where huge vats of sauce simmered on the stove tops and a legion of stromboli baked in an oven. I really wished I had time for lunch.

"You know where it is," she called to me, following me with her eyes.

I waved to tell her I did. She shook her

head as I exited into the hallway and went out into the courtyard. Zelda's three dogs greeted me noisily, jumping enthusiastically, and I smelled the aroma of pastry wafting out from the ventilation system of Veniero's on Eleventh Street. I moved toward the doors in the ground and pulled one of them open, walked down the stairs that led to the basement, and closed the door behind me, leaving the dogs baying mournfully in my wake. I was in the storage space where Zelda kept all of her supplies — olive oil, crates of garlic, flour — lining shelves that seemed to go on forever. It was dark and I didn't bother to flip on the light. I felt my way along the wall until I found what I was looking for. It was a doorway that led to a tunnel. This tunnel ran behind the buildings to the north of Five Roses and let out onto Eleventh Street. I unbolted the door and paused at the yawning darkness before me. I remembered it was a long tunnel, dark and cold. I felt along the wall for a light switch and instead found a flashlight on a hook. I took it and turned it on, shone it into the darkness. The beam was dim and weak, flickering in a threat to go dark just seconds after I turned it on. It was so quiet.

I took the cell phone Jake had given me and dropped it on the floor. Dylan suspected that it had some kind of tracking device they could use to follow my movements around the city. I was hoping they'd think I was just having a long, leisurely lunch at Five Roses, and that by the time they'd figured it out, it would be too late.

Why did I do this? I'd made a deal with the CIA and good sense would have dictated that I keep it. At the time, I probably couldn't have told you why I didn't. I have more insight into my actions now. But that afternoon, I was just overcome with the feeling that if I didn't get away from them, I'd never be able to find Max. He'd know they were watching me. He'd know to stay away. I knew him well enough to know that he wouldn't walk into an obvious trap. Alone, I might have a chance to find him. What would happen then, I didn't know.

I hesitated at the mouth of the tunnel. The looming blackness got the better of me for a second and the air felt electric with bad possibilities. I thought about turning around and going back the way I'd come in, rather than face that pitch black, but I finally steeled myself and ran, the low light of the flashlight illuminating only a foot or two in front and around me. I breathed easier when the beam fell on the metal door at the end of the tunnel. I reached for the bolt and found it stuck. My breathing started to become labored as I tried and failed to unlock it. I felt the blackness of the tunnel closing in on me, and for a second I thought of screaming, unable to face the tunnel again to return to the basement. Finally it gave way and I burst onto the street.

I was disoriented by the bright light of the outdoors. A woman looked at me strangely as she moved quickly past on Rollerblades. I let the door shut behind me and turned back to look at it. There was no knob or handle on the outside. I wouldn't have been able to open it again if I wanted to. I felt a twist of guilt and fear in my belly at what I'd just done, at what I was about to do.

I met Dylan at the Union Square subway station at the bottom of the Food Emporium entrance on Fourteenth Street. We took the train to Max's apartment building. Dutch let us up with his eternal cool and impartial gaze. What must he think of me? I wondered, not for the first time, as we stepped into the elevator and he gave me a nod. What did he think I did in Max's apartment? But his face, as always, was a mask. I would have more luck figuring out the gargoyles that loomed above the entryway to the building.

Inside Max's apartment, I turned and looked at Dylan, blocking his entry with a palm to his chest.

"Before we go any further, I have to know what your agenda is when it comes to this. Why are you helping me?"

He shrugged, gave a slow shake of his head. "I have no secrets from you, Ridley. I've always been honest about what I want from Max. I just want him to answer for the things he's done, same as you. I told you: I don't want revenge. And I want to protect you, make sure you don't get hurt. That's it. I promise you."

He reached for my hand and I remembered a time when I'd held Jake's hand like that. I felt my stomach clench at the memory. I nodded. I believed him. But we all know that doesn't mean anything.

We walked down the hallway, which was lined with framed photographs of my family and me. Jake was the one who pointed out to me that the whole apartment was more or less a shrine to me, that I was the center of all the photographs. I saw Dylan scanning the walls and remembered he'd said the same thing. I was embarrassed now by what seemed to me a gallery of lies — pretty pictures featuring the smiling faces of people whose foundation was rotten and on the verge of buckling. My mother and father were liars; my brother was a drug addict returned to the streets once again (I hadn't even had time to think about this yet); my uncle was really my father. And he was a murderer and a criminal so terrible that he was being pursued by law enforcement agencies around the world. And yet there we were, attractive people laughing, having birthday parties, dance recitals, trips to the zoo. There I was on Max's shoulders, in Ben's arms, being fed by my mother, trying to make myself invisible behind a tree while Ace looked for me in a game of hide-and-seek. All my beautiful lies.

I said as much to Dylan.

"No," he said as we moved into Max's bedroom. "Not all lies. There's as much truth there as there is deceit."

It made me think of what my father said about Max, that the man we knew was as true as his dark side. I wasn't sure I was buying it.

"I didn't know who my parents really were until after they were dead," he said in my silence. "It didn't make them any less of who they were to me."

"They lied about their jobs, probably because they had to, probably to protect you. It's different."

"I know it is. But it's the same, too. Lies are lies. Your parents probably thought they had to lie to protect you, too. They made a lot of mistakes, but they loved you."

I nodded. I wasn't sure I'd heard anyone defend my parents before. I was grateful to him for doing it, even though he was probably just trying to make me feel better. I flipped on the lights in Max's bedroom and walked over to the shelves. The little piece of pottery I'd made for him a lifetime ago sat where I'd left it. I lifted it, and for a split second I thought I'd hallucinated the keyhole I'd seen there. But there it was. I pulled the key from my pocket and slid it in, gave it a turn.

The whole shelf lifted slowly about six inches, revealing a drawer. I stood and looked at it. Inside there was a thick manila envelope. I took a second to observe the irony of it, since all of this began with a similar package. I reached for it, then hesitated, weighing my options. Every nerve ending in my body tingled; every instinct told me to walk away. But you know me better than that.

"What are you waiting for?"

I thought Dylan's voice sounded strange, so I turned to look at him. He wasn't looking at me. He was looking at something behind me and reaching for my arm. I spun around to see two dark forms standing in the bedroom doorway. I looked back at Dylan and expected to see him draw his weapon; instead he grabbed me and pulled me close, then stepped in front of me.

"They took my gun," he whispered. I deduced that the FBI had taken his weapon when they'd fired him. Bad news.

"Well, Miss Jones, what *are* you waiting for?"

When the first man stepped into the light, I took a step back in surprise. It was Dutch, the doorman. He'd lost his spiffy outfit and stood before me clad in black, a nasty-looking gun in his hand. I didn't recognize the man he was with, but he didn't look like a very nice person, with a thick, heavy brow, deep-set dark eyes, and a nasty scar that ran from his ear to his mouth. He also held a gun. It didn't seem fair. I was starting to wish I hadn't been so quick to dump the CIA. I was betting that they had *plenty* of guns.

"Dutch, I don't understand," I said lamely.

"Of course you don't," he answered, not unkindly.

It was hard to be afraid of him. I'd known him since I was a child. I remembered being down in the basement one day as a teenager looking through Max's storage space for an old skateboard of Ace's (I'd later break my wrist on the sidewalk in front of Max's building, getting both of us in big trouble with my parents). It was late-ish, maybe around ten or something, and I bumped into Dutch down there; there was a locker and changing room where the doormen could shower and change into their street clothes. He was all dressed up in a silver lamé shirt and black slacks, his hair slicked back. I think he was getting ready to go clubbing. I was shocked to see him as a person with a life outside the building, since I'd never seen him anywhere else. I remember that he looked a little embarrassed. It must have been the shiny disco shirt — but it was the eighties, after all.

"Good night, Miss Jones," he'd said with his usual light bow in my direction.

"Good night, Dutch," I'd answered, biting the inside of my cheek hard so that I wouldn't laugh. He left the basement quickly.

Back in the apartment, I told Max all about it, dissolving into childish giggles.

"There's more to everyone than meets the eye," he said with a small smile. "Remember that, kid."

Now his words seemed ominous, almost prophetic.

"Miss Jones, you and your friend will need to put your hands where I can see them."

He was so polite, even now. There was still that practiced kindness in his face, like a lace shroud over metal. My chest started to feel tight and my arms tingled with adrenaline. Dylan's face was as still as granite.

"And turn around please," he said as we complied.

"I have to say," he went on as he bound our hands with some type of thick plastic cinch, "you made this easier than it might have been by losing your entourage."

"Dutch," I said, hating the shake I heard in my voice. "What are you *doing?*"

"Never mind," he said softly. There was an explosion of white pain. And then there was nothing.

I woke up on my belly, my arms bound behind me, my cheekbone being knocked repeatedly against the corrugated metal floor of a moving vehicle. Dylan was beside me in a similar situation but he still seemed to be unconscious. A thin line of blood trailed from a nasty cut in his lip. It looked as if it would need several stitches — that is, if we didn't both die tonight.

I'm sure I don't have to tell you that my head felt as if it was on the business end of a jackhammer. I wondered how much abuse a body could endure before it just gave out. For someone who'd never been touched in anger, never even been spanked as a child, I'd certainly had a rude introduction to violence in recent years.

I could see the back of Dutch's head in the passenger seat. The other man was driving. I was scared, yes. Of course. But I was suddenly really, really angry, too. I started struggling against the binding on my hands and found out too late that it only made them tighter. Very painful.

"Dutch," I said loudly, "what are you doing?" I couldn't come up with a better question.

He didn't answer me, didn't even turn around. This made me even angrier.

"Help!" I started screaming when the van paused at a light. "Help us!"

It was pointless, I knew. No one was going to hear me. But I figured it was worth a try. I kept screaming.

"Miss Jones," said Dutch calmly, turning around after a few minutes of this and putting his gun to Dylan's head. "Please shut the fuck up. You're giving me a headache."

Seeing Dylan so helpless, I shut up immediately.

"I thought you worked for Max," I said weakly.

"Once upon a time, yes," he said. "Since his *demise,* the pay hasn't been as good. Others are offering more."

"You sold him out," I said, trying to sound indignant.

He gave me a pitying look. "Haven't we all?"

"I haven't sold out anyone," I said.

He just smiled at me and for a split second I saw him for what he was: a stone-cold killer. I wondered what this man had been for Max. Bodyguard? Hired gun? Maybe both. I asked him. The fact that he answered me didn't bode well for my future.

"I cleaned up his messes. It was ugly work, I'll tell you. Your father didn't like to get his hands dirty. Not that way."

I looked over at Dylan. His eyes were open now and he was watching me. He shook his head at me, the best he could.

"No more questions," he whispered. I saw the wisdom in his warning but we were far beyond that. Unless the CIA was able to figure out what had happened to me, I had a feeling things were going to end badly.

"That's good advice from your friend," said Dutch.

"I'm sorry," I said to Dylan.

"It's not your fault," he said.

But it was.

The van pulled into a large, cavernous space; a heavy metal door shut behind us. We were assisted from the back of the van and walked up a flight of metal stairs, through a thick door and into what appeared to be some kind of abandoned factory or warehouse floor. The space was dark around the edges, boxes piled high, graffiti on the walls. Some light filtered in through high windows so filthy they were nearly blacked out by grime. Our footfalls echoed, bouncing off the walls and high ceilings. There was a strong odor of mold and dust. I felt my sinuses start to swell.

I tried to think of where we could be. There were old sweatshops in the East Village, in Tribeca (though most of those had been converted into trendy lofts). The Meatpacking District was a possibility. I couldn't be sure; I was totally disoriented. I wasn't even sure how long we'd been driving. I figured we couldn't be farther than the outer boroughs or possibly Jersey. The space seemed so solid, so remote, it felt as if we might as well be on the moon. I listened for street noise and heard only silence. If we died here, I wondered, how long would it be before they found our bodies? The thought made me feel sick for Ben and the words he'd left me with. I imagined what it would be like for him if I disappeared and was never found. Or if my body turned up in the East River. I felt more guilty than I did afraid for my own life at that moment. And I realized that Dylan had been right. My parents made terrible mistakes but they did love me. That counted for something. It counted for more than I'd realized.

We were made uncomfortable in twin metal chairs against the far wall of the space. I hated that they hadn't bothered to conceal their identities in any way. It was really such a bad sign. Dylan and I locked eyes as they bound our legs to the chairs. I couldn't tell what he was thinking, but he didn't look scared. He looked . . . patient.

"What are you doing, Dutch? What do you want?" I asked as his associate finished lashing me to the chair with, I thought, unnecessary roughness.

He looked at me coolly. "I want what everyone wants, Miss Jones. I want Max Smiley."

I issued a sigh. "Well, I'll tell you what I tell everyone else. I don't know where he is."

He walked over closer to me and held up his slim mobile phone, not unlike the one issued to me by the CIA. He used the camera in his phone to take what I'm sure was a very unflattering picture of me. He handed the phone to the other man, who proceeded to set up a laptop on a makeshift table, a plank resting across two plastic crates. He used an old paint bucket to make a seat for himself.

"It was you," I said. "You put that matchbook there. You made the apartment smell like him. You ran the shower."

"As per my instructions," he said with a deferential nod.

"Your instructions from whom?"

"From Max," he said, as though he was stating the obvious.

"Then why don't you know where he is?"

I could see the red glow from the computer screen shining on the face of Dutch's partner.

"Are you sending him a picture so that he'll come for me? Because he won't," I said. I knew I should be keeping my mouth shut, but I just couldn't stop talking. Maybe it was nerves. "Who are you working for now? That freak Boris Hammacher?"

Turning to look at me, Dutch had the same expression he always had: cool, observing, disinterested.

"Miss Jones, I'm only going to ask you one more time to shut the fuck up."

"He's gone. No one's ever going to find him. Not me. Not the CIA. And certainly not a sorry fuck like you," I said. What was wrong with me?

His expression didn't change at all as he lifted his gun and shot Dylan in the leg. Dylan issued a sound, a cry of pain and surprise so terrible and primal, I'll never forget it. I felt as if I was going to crawl out of my skin with rage and sheer terror. I know I was screaming, too. But I can't remember what I said. I struggled pointlessly against my bindings.

"Please, Miss Jones, please be quiet," Dutch said, his tone measured and polite. He didn't have to tell me that he'd continue shooting until I was. I looked at Dylan, tried to shift my chair over toward him. His face was pale, his expression a grimace of pain. I looked at the wound in his leg and saw that it was bleeding heavily but not gushing. I prayed that the shot had missed a major artery.

"Dylan," I said, sobs wracking my whole body.

He didn't say anything. His eyes had a faraway look and I wondered if he was slipping into shock. I was pretty much hysterical at this point.

The man at the computer connected the phone with a USB cable and set to tapping away at the keyboard.

"Done," he said after a moment.

Dutch walked over to Dylan and took the belt from his pants. He wrapped the belt above Dylan's wound and tightened it hard. Dylan issued a low moan; his head lolled to the side.

"We'll keep your friend alive awhile to assure your continued cooperation," Dutch said as he moved away from us.

The two men left us alone with the glowing red computer screen. The door slammed heavily after their exit.

"Dylan," I said. "Dylan, answer me."

He only issued a low groan. I was able to shuffle my chair over until I was just inches from him. I could hear him breathing.

"I'm okay, Ridley," he said.

He didn't say anything else for a while. I was alone with my thoughts for hours as I worked and twisted my wrists and ankles in their bindings, as the light filtering in through the dirty windows faded to black.

21

When I look back on some of the mistakes I've made in all this, I think probably dropping that phone in the tunnel beneath Five Roses had the direst consequences. Like I said, at the time I probably couldn't have even said why I did it. I told myself it was the only way to Max, that he'd never fall into such an obvious trap as the one the CIA had set. But I wonder if that was really the reason. I wonder if, on some level, I was suicidal.

I don't mean that in the truest sense. I wasn't looking for a bottle of sleeping pills or a dive off the Brooklyn Bridge. But maybe I was looking for a death of self. Maybe I was looking to burn Ridley Jones to the ground, in order to see what might rise from the ashes. It never occurred to me that there might not be a resurrection. That dead was dead.

In the dark warehouse, with Dylan's

breathing the only sound in my ears, I could see how the next few hours would play out with sickening clarity. I knew in a while they'd come to get us. We'd be taken somewhere desolate in the back of that van. When we reached our destination, we'd be killed. There was simply no other way for things to go. Once they had Max, or if he didn't come for me, they'd have no use for us, and we'd make the awkward shift from assets to liabilities.

"They're going to kill us," I told Dylan, who'd been conscious and lucid for a while.

"Probably," he agreed. "You're bleeding. Stop struggling."

My hands were numb. But the bindings on my ankles felt looser. They'd used only rope to tie my ankles to the chair. But that plastic thing on my wrists would not come free. It just slowly ratcheted tighter and tighter and I didn't think I was getting any blood to my hands. It hurt terribly at first, then I stopped being able to feel my hands at all, except for a terrible burning around my wrists where I imagined the hard plastic was cutting into my skin. I felt the sticky warmth of my blood.

The door opened then, a rectangle of light at the far end of the space. Dutch and his associate approached us. The scarred man pointed a thick, flat gun at us as Dutch moved toward me with some kind of nasty-looking tool in his hand. He was behind me before I could even react. I saw Dylan crane his neck and, grimacing in pain, try to move his chair.

"I knew a man who very nearly severed both of his hands struggling against those bindings," said Dutch as he used whatever he had in his hand to release the plastic on my wrists. I felt the blood start flowing back to my hands and it was actually painful. I held them out in front of me; they were paper white and didn't even feel as if they belonged to me. Both wrists had nasty gashes.

"*Now* you tell me," I said. My pending death was making me bold and sarcastic.

Dutch chuckled softly. "I always did like you so much, Miss Jones."

I thought he'd go on to say how sorry he was that it had come to this, but he spared us the farce of that. Here was a man who didn't care about anything except hiring out his services to the highest bidder. He didn't seem inclined to pretend otherwise — which would have been refreshing if it wasn't so terrifying.

He handed me the tool, which looked like a pair of thick wire cutters. "Free your friend and help him to his feet."

I did this and Dylan leaned heavily on me, almost falling. I was able to support his weight but not easily. It took me a second to realize that the near-fall was a ruse to drop something in the pocket of my jacket. From the weight and feel of it, I determined it might be a pocketknife. I couldn't imagine that the small knife in my pocket was going to be much help. Dylan and I locked eyes. I didn't see fear in the expression on his face, not at all. It was something like defiance. His look asked me to be brave and to have hope, two things that had abandoned me a while back. I tried to dredge them back up from within. I had been an optimist once, a lifetime ago. I tried to remember what it felt like as we moved slowly through the heavy metal door and down the staircase toward the waiting van.

There is no more desolate or despairing a place on earth than Potter's Field. Located on Hart Island in the Bronx, it's a ferry ride across the Long Island Sound from the piers on City Island. It is home to the City Cemetery, where New York's destitute and anonymous are buried, one on top of the other in numbered graves dug by inmate labor. It is a barren, ugly island with only a few scattered trees and winding concrete paths. The grass grows high. In summer, blue asters bloom. On the island, there are several buildings — a hospital, a reformatory, a dilapidated old house — all once having had various functions for the city, now abandoned.

I've always had a fascination with the place and its million nameless dead; I'm not sure why. I'd read that unknowns were photographed and fingerprinted, then interred with all their clothes and belongings and death certificate, so that should anyone ever come to claim them, they could be identified. I'd found this piece of information unspeakably creepy and sad; it stayed with me.

For some reason, I'd always wanted to visit the cemetery, just to say I had. I even tried to get access in order to write about it back in college. But city morgue workers, inmates, and corrections officers are the only living people to ever set foot on Potter's Field, no exceptions.

"It's not a curiosity," said the public relations woman to whom I'd pleaded my case. "We *must* have respect for the unbefriended dead."

I remember being frustrated and annoyed at being denied. Her phrase, "the unbefriended dead," came back to me now. Be careful what you wish for, I thought as we stepped from the van onto the docks.

"Then Judas, which had betrayed Him, saw that he was condemned, repented himself, and brought again the thirty pieces of silver to the chief priests . . . and they took counsel, and bought with them the potter's field to bury strangers in," said Dutch with an unfriendly smile.

I'd heard this before, from the Gospel of Saint Matthew, as the probable origin of the term *potter's field.* I imagined that he was trying to be scary. It was working, but I didn't give him the satisfaction of a response.

I helped Dylan from the van. I suspected that he was acting more out of it than he was — at least that's what I was hoping. His eyes were lucid and he was carrying more of his weight than I think it appeared to the two other men. Still, one or the other of them kept a gun on us at all times.

"Are you a religious person, Miss Jones?" asked Dutch, slamming the van doors behind us. The air smelled of low tide and somewhere a halyard was clanging in the wind. I could see a white speedboat tied off at the end of the dock. I felt the cold air through my too-thin leather jacket. It seemed to leak into my jeans and boots as well.

I didn't answer him. I wasn't in the mood for small talk.

"No," he said. "I don't suppose you would be."

I wasn't sure what he meant.

We walked toward the end of the dock. The island sat black and ominous in the distance across the Sound. It seemed like a perfect place to dump a couple of bodies. I held on to Dylan even more tightly. He squeezed me hard, and that's when I knew for sure that he was with me. I felt a little better.

"Why here?" I asked Dutch as I handed off Dylan to the other man. Dutch gallantly helped me onto the boat, taking my hand and supporting my arm. It was all very polite, very civilized.

"Myriad reasons," he answered. "I like the poetry of it, first of all. There are other, more practical reasons, of course. It's easy to see if we're being followed, easy to see if your father comes alone."

"And it's a good place to dispose of bodies," I said.

"Your fate is in Max's hands, not mine," he said.

"So if all goes well, then you let us go

home tonight?" I said in a tone that I hoped conveyed my total disbelief.

He declined to answer as the other man took a seat behind the wheel and powered up the boat. The engine was unpleasantly loud, filling the night with a deep, watery rumble and gas fumes.

"So who are you working for?" I yelled above the din.

No answer.

"What was in the envelope?"

No answer.

You can see I hadn't learned my lesson. And I could tell I was truly starting to get on Dutch's nerves, like a precocious child who seems cute at first and then just gets *really* annoying. But I couldn't help myself. I was wired with nerves and fear, aggressive with anger at our situation, and just bold as hell because I figured we'd die one way or another on Potter's Field. It made me crazy that I might never know what was in that envelope. I thought about grabbing Dylan and throwing us both into the water. But it looked black and thick like tar, not to mention deadly frigid. Frankly, I just wasn't that brave.

After an unpleasantly rocky and freezing voyage, we came to the island. It was a sloppy landing and the boat knocked hard against the dock. Dutch almost dropped his gun, cursed at his associate. The man had no reaction except to tie the boat up quickly and to drag Dylan up onto the dock. Dutch assisted me with a gun in my back. I guess the time for niceties had passed. It was all business from here on out.

A haunting is a subtle thing. Nothing proves that like a cemetery island at night. No moaning specters, no hands reaching up from fresh graves. In the case of Hart Island it was the strange absences that made it so terrifying. The silence was the first thing that I noticed: the silence of acres of dead, nothing living. There's a heaviness to it, this lack of ambient noise. It causes every sound you make to seem a hundred times as loud; my own fearful breathing was a turbine engine.

Then there's the darkness. The moon hid behind thick cloud cover, only the slightest gray glow lighting the night. In the modern world, especially for urban dwellers, there's no such thing as a truly dark night. Streetlights, headlights, marquee lights, television screens, building lights, come together and create an eternal flame, forever banishing real darkness. The city is always lit; it shines its light into the sky so brightly, we can barely see the stars. Here on Hart Island, the only lights were far off in the distance. Darkness made a home here, settled deep into shadows, painted every strange shape pitch black.

We walked along a barren path. The abandoned buildings hulked menacingly in the distance. Our footfalls seemed to reverberate in the night as we turned a corner and took a steep slope uphill toward a large building — the abandoned reformatory I'd read about. It seemed to sag in its center. Dutch held up a hand suddenly and we all came to a stop.

"Something's not right," he said.

He turned in a circle, narrowed eyes scanning the night.

"What made you think he'd come for me?" I said. "What made you think he'd sacrifice himself to save me? You've made a mistake."

He didn't answer, but I could see from the look he gave me that he wouldn't have any problem killing me when the time came. The minutes slogged by in the dark and the cold. Dylan started to feel heavier and my back was aching with the effort of supporting him. I didn't like the look in his eyes, spacey and far away.

"You've overestimated his love for me."

"I don't think so," he said, a slow smile splitting his face. He nodded toward the building. Standing there was a dark, slender form, leaning on a cane. My heart started to pump hard, adrenaline making my throat dry and my hands shake.

"Max," Dutch said loudly, moving toward him. "Good to see you."

The other man grabbed me hard away from Dylan, who collapsed to the ground without me to help him. The man wrapped a thick arm around my throat and held his gun to my head. My hands instinctively flew to his arm. I clawed at him and began to struggle as my airways constricted.

"Hold still," he whispered fiercely. Then I remembered the knife in my pocket. I reached inside and flipped open the small blade, keeping it hidden there. In my memory of what happened next, time seemed to slow and yawn.

From the dark form on the hill: a muzzle flash and the sound of gunfire. I saw Dutch stagger back, teeter forward, and then fall heavily to his knees, where he stayed strangely for a moment before falling on his side. I took the knife from my pocket and jabbed it with all my strength into the throat of my captor, feeling nothing but fear and a terrible desire to draw air into my lungs. He released me with a girlish scream and moved back, blood gushing horribly through the fingers he raised to the wound. I felt sick as I watched him.

Dylan, who I'd thought was down for good, was immediately on him. He grabbed the gun from his hand and used it to put his lights out with a hard blow to the skull. The sound of it, metal on bone, was awful. I saw Dutch's gun lying on the concrete path and moved for it, took its cold heaviness into my hands. I stuck it in the waist of my jeans.

I looked up toward the dark form on the hill and yelled, "Max!"

He turned and moved away quickly. I started to follow.

"Ridley!" I heard Dylan call. I looked back and saw him limping after me. "Let him go. Just let him go."

I started to run.

22

"Ridley, don't do it. You'll never be able to live with it."

The voice comes from behind me and I spin around to see someone I didn't expect to see again. It's Jake.

"This is none of your business," I yell, and turn back to Max.

It's then that I realize why I've really been chasing him, what I really wanted to do once I'd found him. The thought makes me sick; I hold back vomit. He has continued to move closer. He moves through patches of light quickly, lowering his face. He either doesn't see or doesn't care that I have a gun aimed at him. Without wanting to, I start backing away just a bit.

"Ridley, don't be stupid. Put that gun down." Jake's voice behind me sounds desperate, cracks with emotion. "You know I can't let you kill him."

My heart rate responds to the fear in his

voice. *What am I doing?* Adrenaline is making my mouth dry, the back of my neck tingle. I can't fire but I can't lower the gun, either. I have the urge to scream in my fear and anger, my frustration and confusion, but it all lodges in my throat.

When Max is finally close enough to see, I gaze upon his face. And he's someone I don't recognize at all. I draw in a gasp as a wide, cruel smile spreads across his face. And then I get it. He is the man they say he is.

"Oh, God," I say, lowering my gun. "Oh, no."

Then for a second I see him. I look into his eyes and I see my uncle Max, the man who always found me and brought me home. He still resides in the eyes of this stranger. His face momentarily loses its cruelty and the little girl in me aches for him, wants nothing more than to run to him. Without thinking, I lower my gun and lift my hand to him. Our eyes lock briefly. Then night comes alive with sound and light, and he turns and runs.

Suddenly there are men all around me. Clad in body armor, guns drawn, they chase after Max's fleeing form. His cane has been discarded and he runs faster than I would have ever imagined he could. Jake grabs my arm hard. His face is pale and strained in anger.

"Stay here!" he yells at me. I can see that he's beyond furious. "Goddamn it, Ridley, don't fucking move."

He's gone then, too. They're all chasing Max. Dylan comes up behind me and I turn to him.

"I couldn't do it," I say. It's only as the words pass my lips that I realize the reason for all of this was not because I wanted to *find* my father, but because I wanted to kill him. I didn't want him alive in custody somewhere, helping the CIA end the sex slave trade. I wanted to cut him out of this world like a cancer, as if in doing so I could rid myself of every part of him that lived in me, good and bad. I guess I thought because I was his daughter, I had it in me to do that. Wrong again.

"Of course not," he answers. He takes my face in both his hands. "You're not him. You'll never be anything like him."

I hear the blades of a helicopter then and the sound of guns firing. We move quickly through the building toward the sound and come outside to find a black helicopter rising into the night. I see Max through the window and remember his wolfish smile. He lifts a hand and points to his heart, then

486

he points to me. I know then that I'll never see him again. As the helicopter grows smaller, I wonder what happened to the man I loved, if he ever existed at all.

Jake and the men with him continue to fire pointlessly at the helicopter long after it is out of range. Jake is screaming something into a cell phone as his eyes fall on me. He runs over to me.

"We're going to get him tonight, Ridley. He can't get far."

I can't tell if he thinks he's issuing a threat or making a promise to me. Either way, I find I don't care. I turn from him and into Dylan. I don't want to look at Jake's face ever again.

"The two of you are so fucked," says Jake, moving closer to us. He's in Dylan's face. "How could you do this?"

Dylan pushes him back. "Step off, man."

For a second, I think they'll come to blows. In both their voices I can hear anger and frustration. But the heat between them fizzles out. It hurts to be so close to the thing you've been chasing and then have it snatched away. There's nothing you can do about it. No one understands that better than me.

But as I look around me at the flat, dead island and into the sky at the fading lights of Max's helicopter, I don't feel their anger or their sadness. For the first time since I learned that I was Max's daughter, I feel free.

23

Who was Max Smiley? Even now, I don't know for sure. He was a shape shifter, he was whoever he had to be to control the situation. He was Nick Smiley's worst nightmare, Ben Jones's best friend, my beloved uncle. He was a murderer, a philanthropist, a real-estate magnate, a criminal directly and indirectly responsible for the enslavement and death of countless women. He was a man I loved and a man I hated. He was a man I feared and someone I'd never known at all. He was all these things equally and truly. He was my father.

The idea that we would sit and talk and he would answer for the things he'd done to me, to so many others, and that he'd show remorse, accept justice, do some kind of penance — it had been a child's dream. A child who's been injured by a parent waits her whole life for some acknowledgment of the wrong that's been done, some validation from him that her pain is real, that he's sorry and will make amends. The child will wait forever, unable to move forward, unable to forgive, without someone to acknowledge the past. In that powerlessness comes a terrible rage.

From that rage a darker, but equally childish, dream blossomed — one I didn't even acknowledge until the gun was in my hand. But of course, Dylan was right: I didn't have it in me. I didn't have enough of *Max* in me. I couldn't have lived with myself. I *was* the good girl with my homework done and my pajamas on. Besides, killing him wouldn't have made him any less my father; it wouldn't have killed the pieces of him that live inside me. What I needed was an exorcism.

I was thinking this as I sat alone in yet another interrogation room. They all seemed the same, these rooms with their harsh fluorescents and faux wood tables, hard metal and vinyl chairs. I was remarkably calm considering I had no idea what was going to happen to me now. I supposed it was possible that I'd be arrested — highly possible. I didn't even have a lawyer. I remembered what they'd told my father about being able to hold him indefinitely, how the usual rights didn't apply when it came to national security. I had a vivid fantasy of myself dressed in a gray jumpsuit and being moved through a network of secret CIA prisons around the world. Still, I felt an odd stillness. Probably just denial.

The door opened and Jake entered. He looked like hell, his face drawn. There were blue smudges of fatigue beneath his eyes. I felt my stomach twist at the sight of him. What did I feel? It's so complicated. Such anger; such a deep sense of betrayal; and, yes, still love, too.

He sat across from me. "He's gone. We lost him."

I nodded. I wasn't surprised.

"We weren't able to mobilize the satellite cameras in time. He put the chopper down somewhere and took off in another vehicle . . . we assume."

I didn't say anything. I wasn't sure how I felt about it. I realized that I had a white-knuckled grip on the table in front of me; I forced myself to relax. However complicated my feelings were for Jake, they were about a million times more complicated when it came to Max.

"How could you do this, Ridley? What were you trying to prove?"

"I wasn't trying to prove anything. I . . ." I said, letting the sentence trail off.

"You wanted to kill him," said Jake blandly.

"Yes. No. I don't know," I said. "I thought so."

He shook his head at me. He had such a look of disapproval on his face, I wanted to smack him.

"Don't you look at me like that," I said to him, all the heat of my anger rising to my face. "You're the king of liars. The things you've done are a hundred times worse than anything I've done. How do you live with yourself?"

"I was doing my job," he said weakly.

We sat there looking at each other in some kind of a sad standoff where he dropped his eyes first but we both lost. Then he reached under the table and I heard him flip two switches. The lights came on in the room behind the mirror and I saw that it was empty.

"It's just you and me in here, Ridley. I turned the audio surveillance off."

I wasn't sure what he was getting at.

"What? Are you going to beat me up? Try to torture information out of me?"

"No," he said, looking down at his hands. "I just need you to know that there was more between us than lies."

"I'm not sure it matters now, Jake."

"It does matter. It matters to me. I loved you, Ridley. That was the truth. I just need you to understand that. I still love you."

I looked into his face and saw that he needed me to believe him. I was reminded strangely of my encounter with Christian Luna, a man who believed he was my father. I remember how he pleaded his case to me, how desperate he was for me to understand the man he was and why he'd done the things he had. He wanted my forgiveness. But it was all about him — what *he* wanted, what *he* needed in order to find peace with himself.

"Is that why you started distancing yourself toward the end?"

He nodded.

"You knew things were coming to a head and you backed away so that when I finally understood what had happened, it would hurt less. You drifted far enough away to distance yourself but stayed close enough to keep manipulating me."

He hung his head here.

"Close enough to keep making love to me."

He looked up quickly. "Every time I touched you it was real. Every time, Ridley."

I heard a slight shake in his voice. And I believed that when we made love there was truth in it. But it just didn't matter. The terrible lie that ran beneath our life together was a dark river that washed everything else away. I could never forgive him . . . maybe especially because I believed he did love me in the way that he could. I told him as much.

He nodded, leaned back a little in his chair. His face was grim and I could see his pain in the tight line of his mouth, in the corners of his eyes. I was sorry for every lie that had passed between us. We could have been together for a long time, maybe forever. But that was another life, another universe of possibility that didn't even exist anymore.

"Look," I said, wanting to get down to business. "Whatever happens to me now, I need someone to know that Dylan Grace had nothing to do with this. He got dragged along because I was stubborn and he was trying to save my ass."

He looked at me and gave me a smile.

"Funny," he said. "He said just the opposite — that he'd dragged you into this, convinced you to dump the phone and to help him find Max."

"Well, he's just trying to protect me. It was my fault. I deserve to take all the fire for this."

He released a sigh and stood up. He

walked over to the window and stared into the empty room across from us. I could see his reflection in the dark glass. "The truth is that *I* deserve to take all the fire for this."

"You do? Why?"

"Because if I hadn't given you this defective piece of equipment," he said, pulling the cell phone I'd dumped in the tunnel beneath Five Roses from his pocket, "then we never would have lost you. And you wouldn't have been vulnerable to abduction by Dutch Warren."

"It wasn't . . . ," I said. The look on his face caused me to clamp my mouth shut. I got it.

"It was my job to protect you and I failed at that. I'm sorry you almost wound up a permanent resident of Potter's Field."

I cringed at the thought.

"You've held up your end of the deal," he said. "It's not your fault things played out like they did."

"And Dylan?"

"The terms of your agreement stand."

He still had his back to me but I could see him watching me in the glass.

"Who was he working for?" I asked.

"Dutch Warren? We think he was working for a man named Hans Carmichael. He's just one of the people looking for Max. The rumor is that Carmichael's daughter was a drug addict and a prostitute, that Max killed her in London about ten years ago. He's been seeking revenge ever since."

I nodded, wondering if there was any end to the havoc Max had wrought. "Was Boris Hammacher working for the same man?"

"We think so."

"And the man who tried to kill me in the hospital in London?"

"I'm not sure they would have killed you right away," he said. "But the man Dylan killed in London was another known associate of Carmichael's, so it's a safe bet that they tried to abduct you in London and failed, thanks to Dylan Grace." I thought I heard jealousy in his voice, but that might have just been wishful thinking on my part.

He came back to the table and sat down across from me. I found myself looking at his hands, thinking about all the places on my body they'd visited, how strong and tender they'd always been. That's the weirdest thing about the end of love: All the physical intimacy is immediately revoked. I'd never hold those hands again, they'd never have a right to roam my skin. He was a stranger physically and emotionally, though I'd loved him just a short time ago.

He put the cell phone on the table.

"These things cost a fortune and they never work when you need them to," he said with a smile that made my heart hurt.

"Well," he said, "I'll debrief you and then you're free to go."

"Why are you doing this?" I asked him. It was pretty surprising since I'd single-handedly destroyed everything he'd been working toward for years.

That smile again. "For old times' sake, Ridley. You know?"

I didn't answer him, just held his eyes a second longer, then gave a slow nod.

He flipped a switch under the table, to turn on the audio, I guessed. I told him everything that had happened in Max's apartment and on Potter's Field. He asked some questions here and there but it all went pretty quickly. When we were done, he stood up.

"I'm sorry, Ridley," he said. I could see that he was. I was, too.

"Jake," I said as he moved toward the door, "did you find the envelope?" I had told him I thought they left it on the boat.

He nodded, paused with his hand on the doorknob. I felt my heart flutter a little even as my stomach churned. As usual, I wanted to know as much as I didn't. Part of me hoped there was something in there for me.

497

I know. I'm screwed up.

"What was in it?" I asked finally.

"It's confidential, Ridley."

"I need to know, Jake."

"Files," he said. "Computer files."

"Containing?"

"He basically betrayed everyone with whom he's ever had illegal dealings. He gave up names, bank transactions, photographs. It would have taken a team of agents months, maybe a year, to compile so much data."

"Why would he do that?"

"It's genius, actually. Everything that we wanted him for is right at our fingertips now — names, dates, potential witnesses. We'll be able to make real cases against some very bad people."

"And the search for Max becomes less urgent."

"He's still one of our most-wanted fugitives. But, yes, likely some funding will be diverted to follow up these leads."

I was silent. I didn't know what to say.

"It was never just about him. I told you that," Jake said.

"Was there information about Project Rescue?"

He hesitated, then gave a quick nod. "I can't tell you anything about that, of course."

"Of course," I said. I wasn't even sure I needed to know anything else about Project Rescue. Did the logistics of who did the dirty work really mean anything to me? I wondered how many of those children had wound up in good homes and how many of them wound up in hell. It was too much for me to consider. I felt a familiar numbness wash over me, a familiar fog move into my brain. What could I do?

I thought about my father, Ben. Why had he given me that key? Hadn't he, in a sense, used me to help Max escape? Had it been intentional or was he trying to show me what Max really was? Or was he just following instructions from Max? I filed this away to be dealt with later.

"Was there anything for me?"

Jake shook his head. The expression on his face told me he couldn't believe, after all of this, that part of me still wanted to hear from Max.

"Go home, Ridley," said Jake, echoing Max's final message to me. I didn't know if it was intentional or not. But I took his advice.

24

The woods behind my parents' house were just as I remembered them. It was cold, and as usual I wasn't dressed for it. Another hour and the sun would be rising. Already I could see a silvery lightening of the horizon. As a child, I'd been frightened by these woods at night, my imagination turning slim black trees into witches, rocks into goblins, bushes into bogeymen. Tonight nothing scared me as I made my way through the thin tree cover. I could see the lights from the neighbor's porch as I stepped over the creek bed, which was always dry in winter.

It was still there, just as we left it a lifetime ago, when it was the center of all our imaginary play. The fort that Ace and I had built seemed so small as I came to stand beside it. I was surprised at how tiny it was; I always remembered it large, as big as a car. Instead it was more like the size of a refrigerator box, maybe a little bigger. But for its size, the unstable little structure seemed solid and righteous. It had a place in these woods and in my memory; it would always be there.

Ridley, go home.

I climbed inside and sat on the cool dirt of the ground. It was just barely big enough for me. I had to scrunch up a little to fit. Outside, I could almost hear the sounds of my childhood summers: crickets chirping, the sparrows waking with the rising sun, off in the distance the sound of the trains going to and from the city. But this winter night was silent. And I felt profoundly how far I was from my childhood, from the girl who hid herself so that she could be sought after, found, and brought home.

It glowed, the whiteness of the envelope stuck between the rotting slats of wood. The paper was still clean and fresh; it hadn't been there long. On its surface my name had been scrawled. I plucked it from its place, ripped the seal, and pulled out a single sheet of paper.

Hey, kid,

What a mess, huh? I wonder what you think of me as you read this . . . Do you hate me? Do you fear me? I guess I don't know. I like to think your memories of me are enough to keep you from despising me. But maybe not.

All I'm going to say is: Don't believe everything you hear.

I should have done better by you. I know that. Though I'm sure you agree that you would have been better off never knowing I was your father. Ben is the better man, by far. A better man and father than I could ever be. I stand by that decision. You come from ugly, kid. Ugly people, an ugly past. I tried to spare you the knowledge of that. And I was right . . . because you're a bright light, Ridley. I've told you that before. Don't let what you know about me and your grandparents change that about you. It doesn't have to.

I know you well enough to know that you're looking for answers. You always were a kid that wanted a beginning, a middle, and a happy ending. Remember how mad you got when we watched *Gone With the Wind?* You couldn't believe that Rhett would leave Scarlett after all of that. Or how you chased Ace for years. He was a junkie, using you, destroying himself, but still you met him, gave him money, tried to help. (You thought I didn't know? There's not much I don't know about you.) You always want to fix the broken things, make the wrong thing right. You always believed you could be the one to do that. That stubborn confidence is part of what makes you who you are, and I love you for it. But you can't do that here. I'm too far gone . . . have been since before you were born.

I'm not going to get into a catalog of the things I've done and haven't done. Some of the things they say about me are true, some of them aren't. I'll tell you that I have never been a good man, though I have done some good with my life. But I went bad, like unredeemable, early on. The only one who ever saw any good in me was Ben, and later you. I've always been grateful for that, even though now I suppose you think I was undeserving of your love. And probably it's true.

By the time you read this, if you ever do, I'll be gone. I'll ask you to remember only one thing about me: that whatever I've done, whoever I am, whatever you have come to think of me, I have always loved you more than my own life. I am your father and nothing can change that. Even if you killed me, I'd still be that.

A long time ago, we sat in this spot together and I told you: There's a golden chain from my heart to yours. I'll always find you. It's as true today as it ever was.

Anyway, kid, sorry for all of this. Pick up the pieces of your life and move forward. Don't lie around worrying about the past and where you come from. Just move on.

And be nice to your parents. They love you.

Yours always,
Max

I sat there holding the letter for a while, thinking how predictable I must be for him to know that one day I'd come back to this place. Or how connected we were that he knew he could leave a note for me here and I would find it. *Ridley, go home.* He'd meant for me to come here. Not my home. Not his. But the home of my childhood, where he had always been my beloved uncle Max. He meant for me to come home to the place where I had loved him. And a sad homecoming it was.

I heard some movement in the brush outside then, and I held my breath, tried to make myself small. The movements grew louder, moved closer. Then:

"Ridley, is that you?"

"Dad?"

I looked out the small window to see Ben standing there. He had on sneakers below his pajamas and robe.

"I was awake," he said, squatting down near me. "I heard your car and saw you walk across the back lawn. What in the world are you doing here?"

"I had a feeling I'd find something I was looking for here."

He reached a hand in and touched my face, looked at me strangely, as if he thought I might be losing my mind.

"Did you find it?"

"I found *something.*"

I handed him the letter and waited as he read it in the growing light of morning. I told him what had happened to me since Dylan Grace first stopped me on the street. I told him about Potter's Field and how I saw Max. I didn't tell him how a dark and secret part of myself had sought to kill him that night, and how I'd done reckless and stupid things to make that possible.

"Why did you give me that key?" I asked. "Did you know what was in that drawer?"

He shrugged. "He told me you needed it, that you'd know what to do with it. That everything had been lost, and you and I were in trouble for the things he'd done. He said it was our 'Get out of jail free' card."

I told him what was in that drawer, and what turning it over to the CIA had accomplished. He didn't seem upset or even surprised. "Max is always one step ahead," he said. "He's a street fighter, always has been. Me, I play by the rules. He's a berserker. Nobody beats Max Smiley."

There was unadulterated admiration in my father's voice. I was wondering if *he'd* lost *his* mind.

"Do you understand what I'm telling you, Dad? Do you understand who he was?"

"I understand what they think he is. But like the letter says, 'Don't believe everything you hear.' "

"He provided proof, Dad."

"He gave them what they wanted to keep them off his back. That's not the same thing."

When that cloak of denial wrapped around my father, there was no way through it. He had chosen to see only one sliver of Max, one thin shred of who he was, and he clung to that. He didn't care to see the whole man. Maybe he was afraid.

"What does he have on you, Dad? How has he held you in his thrall all these years?"

"He has the same thing on me that you

do, Ridley. That your mother does. Even Ace. Love."

I guess I had expected people to change. I had expected Max to own the things he'd done. I had expected Ben to acknowledge who Max truly was and the impact all their myriad lies had had on me. I had expected Ace to get clean, to live a decent life. Maybe *expect* is not the right word. *Hope* is better, however equally pointless. But you cannot hope for change in others, you can only work toward it in yourself. And that's hard work.

I left my father in the woods and crossed the back lawn. I felt the dew soak through my boots as the rising sun painted the windows of my parents' house golden. The air was frigid and the sky was pink. I saw my mother standing in the master bedroom window, looking down at me, just as she had a year ago. Since then, nothing had changed here — except for me. I guess that's what they mean when they say you can't go home again.

EPILOGUE

So, no, I didn't shack up with Dylan Grace. I had grown smart enough to realize that after everything I'd been through, all the shape shifting I'd done, I needed time to get to know Ridley Jones. I had learned the hard way that I wasn't Ben and Grace's daughter, and I wasn't Max and Teresa Stone's daughter, but I was both of those things. And more than that, I was my own person forging my own path in this life. Nature, nurture, free will — it all plays a role. Ultimately it's all about choices. The big ones, the little ones . . . Well, by now you know my shtick.

So Dylan and I are dating. I think it's funny that his last name is my mother's first name. It's such a feminine name and he's such a tough guy — there's something cool about the dichotomy of it. There are lots of cool things about Dylan Grace. Anyway, we go to the movies, go out to dinner, visit museums . . . but most of all we talk.

"All that time, watching you," he said during our first official date dinner. "That was the thing that drove me crazy, that we couldn't have a conversation."

He pretends he doesn't know everything about me, and we stay up all night trying to find out if we have anything in common, other than our obsession with Max, and a knack for getting into mortal danger and high drama. And I don't think I have to tell you, the sex is white hot.

I was thinking about how nice it all was between us, as we walked up Fifth Avenue after doing some gallery hopping in SoHo. I think he thought most of the art we saw was pretty awful, though he didn't say anything. We'd cut through Washington Square and were passing Eighth Street, sipping hot chocolate from Dean & Deluca cups. I caught my reflection in a storefront window. I'd been to the John Dellaria Salon earlier in the week and had my hair dyed back close to my natural color, but it was still short and spiky. I'd kind of started to like it like that, though I guessed I'd probably let it grow out eventually. As I was looking at myself, I caught another reflection: a thin man in a long overcoat, across the street, resting his weight upon a cane.

I turned to look at him. A stranger. Not Max.

This happens a lot and I suppose it will continue to, though I know he'll never come looking for me again. He's with me. He'll always be with me. In my darkest fantasy, I thought I could rid myself of him, but I know now that had I done that, he would have haunted me day and night as long as I lived.

As it is, there are things that still bother me; I'll never understand some of the things that have happened. I don't think I'll ever fully remember my voyage on the plane, or how I got from the Cloisters to that plane in the first place. The passport in my bag was a fake; mine was waiting undisturbed in its file when I got home. And all that cash in my bag? That wasn't mine, either. Looking on the bright side, at least I got some cool new clothes out of the deal.

"What are you thinking about?" Dylan asked as we waited at the light. I guess I'd been quiet for a while.

We usually avoided talking about Max. Neither of us brought up Potter's Field — how we didn't get what we were looking for that night, and we never would.

"I was wondering if you ever felt robbed. Like you didn't get the justice you were seeking for your parents, for the women Max murdered. He got away. Does it hurt you? Do you think about it?"

He shook his head. "He didn't get away."

I looked at him, wondered if he knew something I didn't. I couldn't see his eyes behind the thin sunglasses he wore. He tossed his empty cup in a wire trash basket.

"I have come to believe that we carry our deeds with us. The evil he's done must eat at him like a cancer. One day it will consume him."

I wasn't sure I agreed. I thought of my conversation with Nick Smiley.

He wasn't sorry, Nick had told me. *I could tell by the way he looked at me. He was so sad-faced for everyone else. But when we were alone, he turned those eyes on me and I knew. He killed his mother, accused and then testified against his father. Effectively, he killed them both. And I don't think he lost a night's sleep over it.*

"I'm not talking about remorse," said Dylan, reading the doubt on my face. "I'm saying that justice is more organic than a trial and punishment. Karma, you know?"

I nodded. I wasn't going to argue with him. If he'd found a way to make peace with the fact that the man who killed his parents was at large and probably living pretty well,

I wasn't going to try to talk him out of it. He was clearly a more evolved person than I.

I won't lie to you; I have lost some sleep over the fact that Max got away, that his appetites probably haven't diminished. If anything, I imagine exile has made him more ravenous. I'm sure you were hoping for a neater package — the villain is caught and brought to justice. I live happily ever after. Wouldn't it be great if we could change all the people and circumstances that pain us? But, of course, that's not always the way life works. Sometimes things are as they are, no matter how you struggle against them. The real challenge is making peace with that, making the best of it, and moving forward, even if that means, as it does in my case, that you'll always be looking over your shoulder.

I tossed my own cup into the trash and Dylan took my hand. We walked in heavy silence toward the Flatiron Building.

"What about you?" he asked, lifting up his sunglasses and resting them on top of his head. He turned those gray eyes on me. "Is that how you feel, Ridley? Do you feel robbed?"

I thought about it a second, remembered that last sight of Max as he lifted away in his helicopter, the note he'd left for me. I'd always have to wonder where he was, if he was watching me somehow.

"Not robbed," I said. "Haunted."

I saw that my answer made him feel sad. He put his arm around me and squeezed me close as we walked the rest of the way home.

I've spent a lot of time cataloging all the mistakes I've made. I'm sure you'll agree that the list is long and colorful. But I think my biggest folly was believing that I could bring Max home. I'll forgive myself for that one. Because there was something I didn't understand until the moment I saw him disappear: In death, the ghost is already home.

ACKNOWLEDGMENTS

It might be true that writers work in isolation. But the work I do would surely stay behind closed doors without the network of believers and supporters I am so blessed to have in my life. I'll list them here with a glowing catalog of their many qualities:

My husband, Jeffrey, has heard me give the same talks and answer the same questions for years — and not just at home. I have yet to appear at a bookstore, conference, or writers' or readers' group without my husband in the audience. And, frankly, that's the least of what he does. He's the best husband, friend, publicist, reader, event coordinator, and — most recently — the best father I have ever known. And he cooks! I thank my lucky stars every day for him.

My agent, Elaine Markson, and her assistant, Gary Johnson, are positively my lifeline in this business. From the time I was signed on at the Elaine Markson Literary Agency almost seven years ago, Elaine has been my first reader, my champion, and my friend. Gary keeps me organized, keeps me laughing, and keeps me up on all the industry gossip. Every year I try to think of something new to say, but the unchanging truth is this: I'd be lost without him.

If I could build a shrine to my editor, Sally Kim, and worship at it, I would. Seriously. The author-editor relationship is so delicate, so crucial. Authors are such quirky, fragile people; in the wrong hands they can be bruised and demoralized. In the right hands, they grow and get better at their craft. Sally has the loveliest way of guiding without pushing, suggesting without dictating, making me a better writer, and letting me think it was all my doing. She's a co-conspirator, therapist, champion, and friend.

A publisher like Crown/Shaye Areheart Books is every writer's dream. I can't imagine a more wonderful, supportive, and loving home. My heartfelt thanks to Jenny Frost, Shaye Areheart, Tina Constable, Philip Patrick, Jill Flaxman, Whitney Cookman, Jacqui LeBow, Kim Shannon, Kira Stevens, Roseann Warren, Tara Gilbride, Christine Aronson, Linda Kaplan, Karin

Schulze, and Kate Kennedy . . . to name just a few. Every one of these people has brought their unique skills and talents to bear on my work and I can't thank them enough.

Special Agent Paul Bouffard understands the way I think. We are of one mind. He is my source for all things legal and illegal. With his vast experience in federal law enforcement, he is a wealth of information, a wellspring of details and thrilling anecdotes that never cease to capture my imagination, a tireless sounding board, and along with his wife, Wendy, a great friend.

My family and friends cheer me through the great days and drag me through the bad ones. My mom and dad, Virginia and Joseph Miscione (aka Team Houston), are tireless promoters and cheerleaders. At every store I visited in Houston, a clerk or manager said to me, "Oh, yeah! Your mom was in here moving your books to the front table!" My brother, Joe Miscione, takes pictures with his cell phone whenever he sees my books in stores and e-mails them to me. My friend Heather Mikesell has read every word I have written since we met almost thirteen years ago. I count on her insights — and her eagle-eye editing. My oldest friends, Marion Chartoff and Tara

Popick, each offer their own special brand of wisdom, support, and humor. I am grateful to them for more reasons than I can count here.

ABOUT THE AUTHOR

Lisa Unger is the author of *Beautiful Lies,* a *New York Times* bestseller and International Book-of-the-Month Selection. She lives in Florida with her husband and daughter. Visit her at www.lisaunger.com